# SAGEBRUSH AND SPURS

# SAGEBRUSH AND SPURS

Classic Western Short Stories

*Edited & Introduced by*

Eric Tripp

BELLEW PUBLISHING
London

This collection first published in Great Britain
in 1992 by Bellew Publishing Company Limited
8 Balham Hill, London, SW12 9EA

ISBN 1 85725 056 7

Phototypeset by Intype, London

Printed and bound in Great Britain by
Hartnolls Ltd

# CONTENTS

# ACKNOWLEDGEMENTS

THE extract relevant to F. J. Turner is taken from *The Oxford Companion to American Literature*.

The information relevant to the Indian Wars is derived from *The Encyclopedia of Military History*, Dupuy & Dupuy, MacDonald & Co.

While all reasonable attempts have been made to contact the original copyright holders, the Publishers would be happy to hear from those they have been unable to trace, and due acknowledgements will be made in future editions.

# INTRODUCTION

I OWE my interest in the Western to the acumen of a stallholder in Soho's Berwick Market whose gaslit stall represented the summit of my Saturday excursions during the long afternoons of the 1920s. Unable to keep pace with my demands for back numbers of the Robin Hood Library, he suggested I try the Buffalo Bill companion series. Although the buckskinned hero did not replace my boyhood idol he remained a firm favourite, gently leading me to a new world of juvenile writers. Among many, I still remember with affection *The Prairie Chief* by R. M. Ballantyne and *Ishmael of the Prairies* by Harry Mortimer Batten, two long-running serials discovered in old copies of the *Boys Own Paper* and *Chums* annuals respectively. Once enjoyed, the habit is hard to break and through the years that followed I was glad to find a liking for Westerns was classless, breaking down artificial barriers both here and abroad.

Even in my early years it was soon apparent that the outlaw of the plains operated solely for selfish reasons and there was no one with any altruistic motive such as robbing the rich to help the poor. One could cite Zorro or The Lone Ranger in defence but the former is not really a Western hero in the truest sense and both characters move freely between differing social spheres, unlike our own Dick Turpin and Robin Hood. Even the more recent trend of 'whitewashing' the outlaw breed has done little to alter this basic, though human, failing.

With the exception of James Hall, a contemporary of Fenimore Cooper but lacking something of that writer's humanity, and the much filmed Jack Schaefer (e.g. *Shane*), who sadly died last year aged eighty-four, all the writers in this collection of stories were born well before 1900, many of them representing the high noon of Western writing with their emphasis on finely drawn characters, believable plots and close attention to detail. In their formative years the West was still riding towards maturity and most of the authors were aware not only of the legends that sprang up around the open prairie and advancing frontier but knew of situations and real-life characters that gave a flesh and blood realism to their books. The heart of the Western reflects its coming of age in the memorable years that gave it life prior to the official closing of the frontier in 1890, during which time the cowboy came to replace the frontiers-man as the typical American hero.

In the period 1850–65 there were at least thirty separate 'wars' or major disturbances involving conflict with the Indians, a figure that grew as a natural and national expansion westward brought almost incessant guerilla-type clashes between Indian and white man. Between 1865–98 the regular army fought 943 actions in twelve separate campaigns against a brave and resourceful enemy. It is interesting that whereas the Texas Ranger certainly achieved an equal (devotees of Oliver Strange might say greater) popularity with the Royal Canadian Mounted Police and the reading public, the army was less fortunate.

Even with the inception of the cinema the cavalryman, the cow-boy's martial counterpart, never quite enjoyed the esteem with which the British soldier was held in stories of the North-West Frontier of India as told by such contemporary practitioners as Kipling, Henty, Maud Diver and S. C. Grier. This may have been due in part to the public reaction to such events as the Sand Creek Massacre but that was perpetrated by militiamen, and disciplined regular troops were rarely guilty of such atrocities. The Pathan tribesman is an enemy to stand comparison with the Apache, Sioux or Cheyenne and such characters as Sergeant Houck and Lieutenant Ranson, in the stories by Jack Schaefer and Richard Harding Davis, would find their counterparts in the ranks of the Victorian army.

The most popular conception of the American frontier in Western lore is derived from F. J. Turner (1862–1932), teacher of history and posthumous recipient of a Pulitzer Prize. '. . . to the frontier the American intellect owes its striking characteristics. That coarseness and strength, combined with acuteness and acquisitiveness; that practical, inventive turn of mind, quick to find expedients; that masterful grasp of material things, lacking in the artistic but power-ful to effect great ends, that restless, nervous energy; that dominant individualism, working for good and evil, and withal that buoyancy and exuberance which comes with freedom – these are the traits of the frontier, or traits called out of elsewhere because of the existence of the frontier.'

It can be said that the frontier of 1865 to 1890 provided a needed colonnade to the hall of history where a young nation could hang a rich tapestry of fact and legend as a monument to its courage, and where the passions of its forbears posed no threat to the creation of the American dream by a more civilised society. The cowboy, with his horse and Colt revolver, became the modern Galahad, carrying a Winchester rifle for a lance and incorporating strength, moral values and a personal honour that could sustain a series of quests and challenges, while providing welcome vindication for his deeds in overcoming primal hostility. These riders and the myths that surrounded them came into being through the demands of a public who enjoyed a new literacy and greater leisure. They embodied a continuing tension in their confrontation with the differing forces ranged against them, whether these were Indians, outlaws or the very elements themselves.

It is, perhaps, understandable therefore that it was a city-dweller and an Easterner who fulfilled the public need and put his brand on a new generation of Western writers. Since its publication in 1902, Owen Wister's *The Virginian* has spawned a thousand imitators on films and television and in outpourings that range from dime novels to popular contemporary authors who love, respect and mine the rich vein of legend and reality offered by the old West. The heroic age was further enhanced and perpetuated by such artists as Frederick S. Remington (1865–1909) the well-loved painter and magazine illus-trator who chose for his various media such subjects as cowboys, Indians and soldiers, usually portrayed in scenes of exciting action and frequently with an historical background.

Within my literary corral you will find writers who are among the earliest protagonists of what was later called the 'formula' Western. Because of this all have a freshness and true vitality, with their characters personifying the code of the West in its best tradition; not for them raw violence, explicit sex or brutality for its own sake. To some the values may seem a little old-fashioned, without economic overtones, or the problems posed by ecology or the place of women, or even race relations. In justification I would plead that these stories are a personal selection chosen for their entertainment value and as an affectionate tribute to some classic storytellers.

Because this book is confined to the short story it has meant a number of popular and important writers being excluded from representation. Among these I regret Eugene M. Rhodes, Andy Adams and Emerson Hough. The vast canvas of the Civil War has been excluded with the exception of the one story by Jack London, timeless in its appeal and its tragedy. Neither will you find stories of the Klondike, wagon trains or the building of the great railways which really came into their own with the advent of the motion picture.

Among the contributors are the always readable O. Henry with his love of the surprise ending; the precise images of Stephen Crane, drawn from his experiences as a correspondent in Mexico and the South-West, contrasting with the delicate shading of Bret Harte, and the only short story by Conan Doyle set in the West. An early Frank Harris gives a reminder of the style that made his literary reputation; Owen Wister leaves his more chivalrous heroes for a welcome dash of humour, and Zane Grey, who wrote all too few short stories, makes his Indian hero driven by the demands of personal as well as tribal honour, colourful and believable. Alfred Henry Lewis and Stewart Edward White have both left an indelible mark on the development of the Western and there is no apology needed for the originator of the Bar–20, although here Clarence Mulford is in a very different mood.

Such is the popularity of the Western that authors have been quick to follow a lucrative trail, many whose knowledge of the subject derives solely from the lending library. However I remain confident that the universal appeal of these classic tales and their authors with their individual evocation of the real West will long outlast the regrettable trend towards the pornographic and the supernatural fostered by modern publishers intent on transmuting true riches into fools gold.

# SAGEBRUSH AND SPURS

# THE LOS AMIGOS FIASCO

## *Sir Arthur Conan Doyle*

I USED to be the leading practitioner of Los Amigos. Of course, every one has heard of the great electrical generating gear there. The town is widespread, and there are dozens of little townlets and villages all around, which receive their supply from the same centre, so that the works are on a very large scale. The Los Amigos folk say that they are the largest upon earth, but then we claim that for everything in Los Amigos except the gaol and the death-rate. Those are said to be the smallest.

Now, with so fine an electrical supply, it seemed to be a sinful waste of hemp that the Los Amigos criminals should perish in the old-fashioned manner. And then came the news of the electrocutions in the East, and how the results had not after all been so instantaneous as had been hoped. The Western engineers raised their eyebrows when they read of the puny shocks by which these men had perished, and they vowed in Los Amigos that when an irreclaimable came their way he should be dealt handsomely by, and have the run of all the big dynamos. There should be no reserve, said the engineers, but he should have all that they had got. And what the result of that would be none could predict, save that it must be absolutely blasting and deadly. Never before had a man been so charged with electricity as they would charge him. He was to be smitten by the essence of ten thunderbolts. Some prophesied combustion, and some disintegration and disappearance. They were waiting eagerly to settle the question by actual demonstration, and it was just at that moment that Duncan Warner came that way.

Warner had been wanted by the law, and by nobody else, for many years. Desperado, murderer, train robber and road agent, he was a man beyond the pale of human pity. He had deserved a dozen deaths, and the Los Amigos folk grudged him so gaudy a one as that. He seemed to feel himself to be unworthy of it, for he made two frenzied attempts at escape. He was a powerful, muscular man, with a lion head, tangled black locks, and a sweeping beard which covered his broad chest. When he was tried, there was no finer head in all the crowded court. It's no new thing to find the best face looking from the dock. But his good looks could not balance his bad deeds. His advocate did all he knew, but the cards lay against him, and Duncan Warner was handed over to the mercy of the big Los Amigos dynamos.

I was there at the committee meeting when the matter was discussed. The town council had chosen four experts to look after the arrangements. Three of them were admirable. There was Joseph M'Connor, the very man who had designed the dynamos, and there was Joshua Westmacott, the chairman of the Los Amigos Electrical Supply Company, Limited. Then there was myself as the chief medical man, and lastly an old German of the name of Peter Stulpnagel. The Germans were a strong body at Los Amigos, and they all voted for their man. That was how he got on the committee. It was said that he had been a wonderful electrician at home, and he was eternally working with wires and insulators and Leyden jars; but, as he never seemed to get any further, or to have any results worth publishing, he came at last to be regarded as a harmless crank, who had made science his hobby. We three practical men smiled when we heard that he had been elected as our colleague, and at the meeting we fixed it all up very nicely among ourselves without much thought of the old fellow who sat with his ears scooped forward in his hands, for he was a trifle hard of hearing, taking no more part in the proceedings than the gentlemen of the press who scribbled their notes on the back benches.

We did not take long to settle it all. In New York a strength of some two thousand volts had been used, and death had not been instantaneous. Evidently their shock had been too weak. Los Amigos should not fall into that error. The charge should be six times greater, and therefore, of course, it would be six times more effective. Nothing could possibly be more logical. The whole concentrated force of the great dynamos should be employed on Duncan Warner.

So we three settled it, and had already risen to break up the meeting, when our silent companion opened his mouth for the first time.

'Gentlemen,' said he, 'you appear to me to show an extraordinary ignorance upon the subject of electricity. You have not mastered the first principles of its actions upon a human being.'

The committee was about to break into an angry reply to this brusque comment, but the chairman of the Electrical Company tapped his forehead to claim its indulgence for the crankiness of the speaker.

'Pray tell us, sir,' said he, with an ironical smile, 'what is there in our conclusions with which you find fault?'

'With your assumption that a large dose of electricity will merely increase the effect of a small dose. Do you not think it possible that it might have an entirely different result? Do you know anything, by actual experiment, of the effect of such powerful shocks?'

'We know it by analogy,' said the chairman pompously. 'All drugs increase their effect when they increase their dose; for example – for example –'

'Whisky,' said Joseph M'Connor.

'Quite so. Whisky. You see it there.'

Peter Stulpnagel smiled and shook his head.

'Your argument is not very good,' said he. 'When I used to take whisky, I used to find that one glass would excite me, but that six would send me to sleep, which is just the opposite. Now, suppose that electricity were to act in just the opposite way also, what then?'

We three practical men burst out laughing. We had known that our colleague was queer, but we never had thought that he would be as queer as this.

'What then?' repeated Peter Stulpnagel.

'We'll take our chances,' said the chairman.

'Pray consider,' said Peter, 'that workmen who have touched the wires, and who have received shocks of only a few hundred volts, have died instantly. The fact is well known. And yet when a much greater force was used upon a criminal at New York, the man struggled for some little time. Do you not clearly see that the smaller dose is the more deadly?'

'I think, gentlemen, that this discussion has been carried on quite long enough,' said the chairman, rising again. 'The point, I take it, has already been decided by the majority of the committee, and

Duncan Warner shall be electrocuted on Tuesday by the full strength of the Los Amigos dynamos. Is it not so?'

'I agree,' said Joseph M'Connor.

'I agree,' said I.

'And I protest,' said Peter Stulpnagel.

'Then the motion is carried, and your protest will be duly entered in the minutes,' said the chairman, and so the sitting was dissolved.

The attendance at the electrocution was a very small one. We four members of the committee were, of course, present with the executioner, who was to act under their orders. The others were the United States Marshal, the governor of the gaol, the chaplain, and three members of the press. The room was a small, brick chamber, forming an out-house to the Central Electrical station. It had been used as a laundry, and had an oven and copper at one side, but no other furniture save a single chair for the condemned man. A metal plate for his feet was placed in front of it, to which ran a thick, insulated wire. Above, another wire depended from the ceiling, which could be connected with a small, metallic rod projecting from a cap which was to be placed upon his head. When this connection was established Duncan Warner's hour was come.

There was a solemn hush as we waited for the coming of the prisoner. The practical engineers looked a little pale, and fidgeted nervously with the wires. Even the hardened Marshal was ill at ease, for a mere hanging was one thing, and this blasting of flesh and blood a very different one. As to the pressmen, their faces were whiter than the sheets which lay before them. The only man who appeared to feel none of the influence of these preparations was the little German crank, who strolled from one to the other with a smile on his lips and mischief in his eyes. More than once he even went so far as to burst into a shout of laughter, until the chaplain sternly rebuked him for his ill-timed levity.

'How can you so far forget yourself, Mr. Stulpnagel,' said he, 'as to jest in the presence of death?'

But the German was quite unabashed.

'If I were in the presence of death I should not jest,' said he, 'but since I am not I may do what I choose.'

This flippant reply was about to draw another and a sterner reproof from the chaplain, when the door was swung open and two warders entered leading Duncan Warner between them. He glanced round him with a set face, stepped resolutely forward, and seated himself upon the chair.

'Touch her off!' said he.

It was barbarous to keep him in suspense. The chaplain murmured a few words in his ear, the attendant placed the cap upon his head, and then, while we all held our breath, the wire and the metal were brought in contact.

'Great Scott!' shouted Duncan Warner.

He had bounded in his chair as the frightful shock crashed through his system. But he was not dead. On the contrary, his eyes gleamed far more brightly than they had done before. There was only one change, but it was a singular one. The black had passed from his hair and beard as the shadow passes from a landscape. They were both as white as snow. And yet there was no other sign of decay. His skin was smooth and plump and lustrous as a child's.

The Marshal looked at the committee with a reproachful eye.

'There seems to be some hitch here, gentlemen,' said he.

We three practical men looked at each other.

Peter Stulpnagel smiled pensively.

'I think that another one should do it,' said I.

Again the connection was made, and again Duncan Warner sprang in his chair and shouted, but, indeed, were it not that he still remained in the chair none of us would have recognised him. His hair and his beard had shredded off in an instant, and the room looked like a barber's shop on a Saturday night. There he sat, his eyes still shining, his skin radiant with the glow of perfect health, but with a scalp as bald as a Dutch cheese, and a chin without so much as a trace of down. He began to revolve one of his arms, slowly and doubtfully at first, but with more confidence as he went on.

'That jint,' said he, 'has puzzled half the doctors on the Pacific Slope. It's as good as new, and as limber as a hickory twig.'

'You are feeling pretty well?' asked the old German.

'Never better in my life,' said Duncan Warner cheerily.

The situation was a painful one. The Marshal glared at the committee. Peter Stulpnagel grinned and rubbed his hands. The engineers scratched their heads. The bald-headed prisoner revolved his arm and looked pleased.

'I think that one more shock—' began the chairman.

'No, sir,' said the Marshal; 'we've had foolery enough for one morning. We are here for an execution, and an execution we'll have.'

'What do you propose?'

'There's a hook handy upon the ceiling. Fetch a rope, and we'll soon set this matter straight.'

There was another awkward delay while the warders departed for the cord. Peter Stulpnagel bent over Duncan Warner, and whispered something in his ear. The desperado stared in surprise.

'You don't say?' he asked.

The German nodded.

'What! No ways?'

Peter shook his head, and the two began to laugh as though they shared some huge joke between them.

The rope was brought, and the Marshal himself slipped the noose over the criminal's neck. Then the two warders, the assistant and he swung their victim into the air. For half an hour he hung – a dreadful sight – from the ceiling. Then in solemn silence they lowered him down, and one of the warders went out to order the shell to be brought round. But as he touched ground again what was our amazement when Duncan Warner put his hands up to his neck, loosened the noose, and took a long, deep breath.

'Paul Jefferson's sale is goin' well,' he remarked. 'I could see the crowd from up yonder,' and he nodded at the hook in the ceiling.

'Up with him again!' shouted the Marshal, 'we'll get the life out of him somehow.'

In an instant the victim was up at the hook once more.

They kept him there for an hour, but when he came down he was perfectly garrulous.

'Old man Plunket goes too much to the Arcady Saloon,' said he. 'Three times he's been there in an hour; and him with a family. Old man Plunket would do well to swear off.'

It was monstrous and incredible, but there it was. There was no getting round it. The man was there talking when he ought to have been dead. We all sat staring in amazement, but United States Marshal Carpenter was not a man to be euchred so easily. He motioned the others to one side, so that the prisoner was left standing alone.

'Duncan Warner,' said he slowly, 'you are here to play your part, and I am here to play mine. Your game is to live if you can, and my game is to carry out the sentence of the law. You've beat us on electricity. I'll give you one there. And you've beat us on hanging, for you seem to thrive on it. But it's my turn to beat you now, for my duty has to be done.'

He pulled a six-shooter from his coat as he spoke, and fired all the shots through the body of the prisoner. The room was so filled with smoke that we could see nothing, but when it cleared the prisoner was still standing there, looking down in disgust at the front of his coat.

'Coats must be cheap where you come from,' said he. 'Thirty dollars it cost me, and look at it now. The six holes in front are bad enough, but four of the balls have passed out, and a pretty fine state the back must be in.'

The Marshal's revolver fell from his hand, and he dropped his arms to his sides, a beaten man.

'Maybe some of you gentlemen can tell me what this means,' said he, looking helplessly at the committee.

'Peter Stulpnagel took a step forward.

'I'll tell you all about it,' said he.

'You seem to be the only person who knows anything.'

'I *am* the only person who knows anything. I should have warned these gentlemen; but, as they would not listen to me, I have allowed them to learn by experience. What you have done with your electricity is that you have increased the man's vitality until he can defy death for centuries.'

'Centuries!'

'Yes, it will take the wear of hundreds of years to exhaust the enormous nervous energy with which you have drenched him. Electricity is life, and you have charged him with it to the utmost. Perhaps in fifty years you might execute him, but I am not sanguine about it.'

'Great Scott! What shall I do with him?' cried the unhappy Marshal.

Peter Stulpnagel shrugged his shoulders.

'It seems to me that it does not much matter what you do with him now,' said he.

'Maybe we could drain the electricity out of him again. Suppose we hang him up by the heels?'

'No, no, it's out of the question.'

'Well, well, he shall do no more mischief in Los Amigos, anyhow,' said the Marshal, with decision. 'He shall go into the new gaol. The prison will wear him out.'

'On the contrary,' said Peter Stulpnagel, 'I think that it is much more probable that he will wear out the prison.'

It was rather a fiasco, and for years we didn't talk more about it than we could help, but it's no secret now, and I thought you might like to jot down the facts in your case-book.

# HORSES

## *Stephen Crane*

RICHARDSON pulled up his horse, and looked back over the trail where the crimson serape of his servant flamed amid the dusk of the mesquit. The hills in the west were carved into peaks, and were painted the most profound blue. Above them the sky was of that marvellous tone of green – like still, sun-shot water – which people denounce in pictures.

José was muffled deep in his blanket, and his great toppling sombrero was drawn low over his brow. He shadowed his master along the dimming trail in the fashion of an assassin. A cold wind of the impending night swept over the wilderness of mesquit.

'Man,' said Richardson in lame Mexican as the servant drew near, 'I want eat! I want sleep! Understand – no? Quickly! Understand?'

'Si, señor,' said José, nodding. He stretched one arm out of his blanket and pointed a yellow finger into the gloom. 'Over there, small village. Si, señor.'

They rode forward again. Once the American's horse shied and breathed quiveringly at something which he saw or imagined in the darkness, and the rider drew a steady, patient rein, and leaned over to speak tenderly as if he were addressing a frightened woman. The sky had faded to white over the mountains, and the plain was a vast, pointless ocean of black.

Suddenly some low houses appeared squatting amid the bushes. The horsemen rode into a hollow until the houses rose against the sombre sundown sky, and then up a small hillock, causing these habitations to sink like boats in the sea of shadow.

A beam of red firelight fell across the trail. Richardson sat sleepily on his horse while his servant quarrelled with somebody – a mere voice in the gloom – over the price of bed and board. The houses

about him were for the most part like tombs in their whiteness and
silence, but there were scudding black figures that seemed interested
in his arrival.

José came at last to the horses' heads, and the American slid stiffly
from his seat. He muttered a greeting, as with his spurred feet he
clicked into the adobe house that confronted him. The brown stolid
face of a woman shone in the light of the fire. He seated himself on
the earthen floor and blinked drowsily at the blaze. He was aware
that the woman was clinking earthenware, and hieing here and
everywhere in the manœuvres of the housewife. From a dark corner
there came the sound of two or three snores twining together.

The woman handed him a bowl of tortillas. She was a submissive
creature, timid and large-eyed. She gazed at his enormous silver
spurs, his large and impressive revolver, with the interest and admiration of the highly-privileged cat of the adage. When he ate, she
seemed transfixed off there in the gloom, her white teeth shining.

José entered, staggering under two Mexican saddles, large enough
for building-sites. Richardson decided to smoke a cigarette, and then
changed his mind. It would be much finer to go to sleep. His
blanket hung over his left shoulder, furled into a long pipe of
cloth, according to the Mexican fashion. By doffing his sombrero,
unfastening his spurs and his revolver belt, he made himself ready
for the slow, blissful twist into the blanket. Like a cautious man he
lay close to the wall, and all his property was very near his hand.

The mesquit brush burned long. José threw two gigantic wings
of shadow as he flapped his blanket about him – first across his chest
under his arms, and then around his neck and across his chest again
– this time over his arms, with the end tossed on his right shoulder.
A Mexican thus snugly enveloped can nevertheless free his fighting
arm in a beautifully brisk way, merely shrugging his shoulder as he
grabs for the weapon at his belt. (They always wear their serapes
in this manner.)

The firelight smothered the rays which, streaming from a moon
as large as a drum-head, were struggling at the open door. Richardson heard from the plain the fine, rhythmical trample of the hoofs
of hurried horses. He went to sleep wondering who rode so fast
and so late. And in the deep silence the pale rays of the moon must
have prevailed against the red spears of the fire until the room was
slowly flooded to its middle with a rectangle of silver light.

Richardson was awakened by the sound of a guitar. It was badly played – in this land of Mexico, from which the romance of the instrument ascends to us like a perfume. The guitar was groaning and whining like a badgered soul. A noise of scuffling feet accompanied the music. Sometimes laughter arose, and often the voices of men saying bitter things to each other, but always the guitar cried on, the treble sounding as if some one were beating iron, and the bass humming like bees. 'Damn it – they're having a dance,' he muttered, fretfully. He heard two men quarrelling in short, sharp words, like pistol shots; they were calling each other worse names than common people know in other countries. He wondered why the noise was so loud. Raising his head from his saddle pillow, he saw, with the help of the valiant moonbeams, a blanket hanging flat against the wall at the further end of the room. Being of opinion that it concealed a door, and remembering that Mexican drink made men very drunk, he pulled his revolver closer to him and prepared for sudden disaster.

Richardson was dreaming of his far and beloved north.

'Well, I would kill him, then!'

'No, you must not!'

'Yes, I will kill him! Listen! I will ask this American beast for his beautiful pistol and spurs and money and saddle, and if he will not give them – you will see!'

'But these Americans – they are strange people. Look out, señor.'

Then twenty voices took part in the discussion. They rose in quavering shrillness, as from men badly drunk. Richardson felt the skin draw tight around his mouth, and his knee-joints turned to bread. He slowly came to a sitting posture, glaring at the motionless blanket at the far end of the room. This stiff and mechanical movement, accomplished entirely by the muscles of the waist, must have looked like the rising of a corpse in the wan moonlight, which gave everything a hue of the grave.

My friend, take my advice and never be executed by a hangman who doesn't talk the English language. It, or anything that resembles it, is the most difficult of deaths. The tumultuous emotions of Richardson's terror destroyed that slow and careful process of thought by means of which he understood Mexican. Then he used his instinctive comprehension of the first and universal language, which is tone. Still, it is disheartening not to be able to understand the detail of threats against the blood of your body.

Suddenly, the clamour of voices ceased. There was a silence – a silence of decision. The blanket was flung aside, and the red light of a torch flared into the room. It was held high by a fat, round-faced Mexican, whose little snake-like moustache was as black as his eyes, and whose eyes were black as jet. He was insane with the wild rage of a man whose liquor is dully burning at his brain. Five or six of his fellows crowded after him. The guitar, which had been thrummed doggedly during the time of the high words, now suddenly stopped. They contemplated each other. Richardson sat very straight and still, his right hand lost in his blanket. The Mexicans jostled in the light of the torch, their eyes blinking and glittering.

The fat one posed in the manner of a grandee. Presently his hand dropped to his belt, and from his lips there spun an epithet – a hideous word which often foreshadows knife-blows, a word peculiarly of Mexico, where people have to dig deep to find an insult that has not lost its savour. The American did not move. He was staring at the fat Mexican with a strange fixedness of gaze, not fearful, not dauntless, not anything that could be interpreted. He simply stared.

The fat Mexican must have been disconcerted, for he continued to pose as a grandee, with more and more sublimity, until it would have been easy for him to have fallen over backward. His companions were swaying very drunkenly. They still blinked their little beady eyes at Richardson. Ah, well, sirs, here was a mystery! At the approach of their menacing company, why did not this American cry out and turn pale, or run, or pray them mercy? The animal merely sat still, and stared, and waited for them to begin. Well, evidently he was a great fighter! Or perhaps he was an idiot? Indeed, this was an embarrassing situation, for who was going forward to discover whether he was a great fighter or an idiot?

To Richardson, whose nerves were tingling and twitching like live wires, and whose heart jolted inside him, this pause was a long horror; and for these men, who could so frighten him, there began to swell in him a fierce hatred – a hatred that made him long to be capable of fighting all of them, a hatred that made him capable of fighting all of them. A 44-calibre revolver can make a hole large enough for little boys to shoot marbles through; and there was a certain fat Mexican with a moustache like a snake who came extremely near to have eaten his last tomale merely because he frightened a man too much.

José had slept the first part of the night in his fashion, his body hunched into a heap, his legs crooked, his head touching his knees. Shadows had obscured him from the sight of the invaders. At this point, he arose, and began to prowl quakingly over toward Richardson, as if he meant to hide behind him.

Of a sudden the fat Mexican gave a howl of glee. José had come within the torch's circle of light. With roars of ferocity the whole group of Mexicans pounced on the American's servant. He shrank shuddering away from them, beseeching by every device of word and gesture. They pushed him this way and that. They beat him with their fists. They stung him with their curses. As he grovelled on his knees, the fat Mexican took him by the throat and said – 'I am going to kill you!' And continually they turned their eyes to see if they were to succeed in causing the initial demonstration by the American. But he looked on impassively. Under the blanket his fingers were clenched, as iron, upon the handle of his revolver.

Here suddenly two brilliant clashing chords from the guitar were heard, and a woman's voice, full of laughter and confidence, cried from without – 'Hello! hello! Where are you?' The lurching company of Mexicans instantly paused and looked at the ground. One said, as he stood with his legs wide apart in order to balance himself – 'It is the girls. They have come!' He screamed in answer to the question of the woman – 'Here!' And without waiting he started on a pilgrimage toward the blanket-covered door. One could now hear a number of female voices giggling and chattering.

Two other Mexicans said – 'Yes, it is the girls! Yes!' They also started quietly away. Even the fat Mexican's ferocity seemed to be affected. He looked uncertainly at the still immovable American. Two of his friends grasped him gaily – 'Come, the girls are here! Come!' He cast another glower at Richardson. 'But this—,' he began. Laughing, his comrades hustled him toward the door. On its threshold, and holding back the blanket, with one hand, he turned his yellow face with a last challenging glare toward the American. José, bewailing his state in little sobs of utter despair and woe, crept to Richardson and huddled near his knee. Then the cries of the Mexicans meeting the girls were heard, and the guitar burst out in joyous humming.

The moon clouded, and but a faint square of light fell through the open main door of the house. The coals of the fire were silent, save for occasional sputters. Richardson did not change his position. He remained staring at the blanket which hid the strategic door in the far end. At his knees José was arguing, in a low, aggrieved tone, with the saints. Without, the Mexicans laughed and danced, and – it would appear from the sound – drank more.

In the stillness and the night Richardson sat wondering if some serpent-like Mexican were sliding towards him in the darkness, and if the first thing he knew of it would be the deadly sting of a knife. 'Sssh,' he whispered, to José. He drew his revolver from under the blanket, and held it on his leg. The blanket over the door fascinated him. It was a vague form, black and unmoving. Through the opening it shielded were to come, probably, threats, death. Sometimes he thought he saw it move. As grim white sheets, the black and silver of coffins, all the panoply of death, affect us, because of that which they hide, so this blanket, dangling before a hole in an adobe wall, was to Richardson a horrible emblem, and a horrible thing in itself. In his present mood he could not have been brought to touch it with his finger.

The celebrating Mexicans occasionally howled in song. The guitarist played with speed and enthusiasm. Richardson longed to run. But in this vibrating and threatening gloom his terror convinced him that a move on his part would be a signal for the pounce of death. José, crouching abjectly, mumbled now and again. Slowly, and ponderous as stars, the minutes went.

Suddenly Richardson thrilled and started. His breath for a moment left him. In sleep his nerveless fingers had allowed his revolver to fall and clang upon the hard floor. He grabbed it up hastily, and his glance swept apprehensively over the room. A chill blue light of dawn was in the place. Every outline was slowly growing; detail was following detail. The dread blanket did not move. The riotous company had gone or fallen silent. He felt the effect of this cold dawn in his blood. The candour of breaking day brought his nerve. He touched José. 'Come,' he said. His servant lifted his lined yellow face, and comprehended. Richardson buckled on his spurs and strode up; José obediently lifted the two great saddles. Richardson held two bridles and a blanket on his left arm; in his right hand he had his revolver. They sneaked toward the door.

The man who said that spurs jingled was insane. Spurs have a mellow clash – clash – clash. Walking in spurs – notably Mexican spurs – you remind yourself vaguely of a telegraphic linesman. Richardson was inexpressibly shocked when he came to walk. He sounded to himself like a pair of cymbals. He would have known of this if he had reflected; but then, he was escaping, not reflecting. He made a gesture of despair, and from under the two saddles José tried to make one of hopeless horror. Richardson stooped, and with shaking fingers unfastened the spurs. Taking them in his left hand, he picked up his revolver, and they slunk on toward the door. On the threshold he looked back. In a corner he saw, watching him with large eyes, the Indian man and woman who had been his hosts. Throughout the night they had made no sign, and now they neither spoke nor moved. Yet Richardson thought he detected meek satisfaction at his departure.

The street was still and deserted. In the eastern sky there was a lemon-coloured patch. José had picketed the horses at the side of the house. As the two men came round the corner Richardson's beast set up a whinny of welcome. The little horse had heard them coming. He stood facing them, his ears cocked forward, his eyes bright with welcome.

Richardson made a frantic gesture, but the horse, in his happiness at the appearance of his friends, whinnied with enthusiasm. The American felt that he could have strangled his well-beloved steed. Upon the threshold of safety, he was being betrayed by his horse, his friend! He felt the same hate that he would have felt for a dragon. And yet, as he glanced wildly about him, he could see nothing stirring in the street, nothing at the doors of the tomb-like houses.

José had his own saddle-girth and both bridles buckled in a moment. He curled the picket-ropes with a few sweeps of his arm. The American's fingers, however, were shaking so that he could hardly buckle the girth. His hands were in invisible mittens. He was wondering, calculating, hoping about his horse. He knew the little animal's willingness and courage under all circumstances up to this time; but then – here it was different. Who could tell if some wretched instance of equine perversity was not about to develop? Maybe the little fellow would not feel like smoking over the plain at express speed this morning, and so he would rebel, and kick; and be wicked. Maybe he would be without feeling of interest, and run listlessly. All riders who have had to hurry in the saddle know what it is to be on a horse who does not understand the dramatic situation. Riding a lame sheep is bliss to it. Richardson, fumbling furiously at the girth, thought of these things.

Presently he had it fastened. He swung into the saddle, and as he did so his horse made a mad jump forward. The spurs of José scratched and tore the flanks of his great black beast, and side by side the two horses raced down the village street. The American heard his horse breathe a quivering sigh of excitement. Those four feet skimmed. They were as light as fairy puff balls. The houses glided past in a moment, and the great, clear, silent plain appeared like a pale blue sea of mist and wet bushes. Above the mountains the colours of the sunlight were like the first tones, the opening chords of the mighty hymn of the morning.

The American looked down at his horse. He felt in his heart the first thrill of confidence. The little animal, unurged and quite tranquil, moving his ears this way and that way with an air of interest in the scenery, was nevertheless bounding into the eye of the breaking day with the speed of a frightened antelope. Richardson, looking down, saw a long, fine reach of forelimb as steady as steel machinery. As the ground reeled past, the long, dried grasses hissed, and cactus plants were dull blurs. A wind whirled the horse's mane over his rider's bridle hand.

José's profile was lined against the pale sky. It was as that of a man who swims alone in an ocean. His eyes glinted like metal, fastened on some unknown point ahead of him, some fabulous place of safety. Occasionally his mouth puckered in a little unheard cry; and his legs, bended back, worked spasmodically as his spurred heels sliced his charger's sides.

Richardson consulted the gloom in the west for signs of a hard-riding, yelling cavalcade. He knew that, whereas his friends the enemy had not attacked him when he had sat still and with apparent calmness confronted them, they would take furiously after him now that he had run from them – now that he had confessed himself the weaker. Their valour would grow like weeds in the spring, and upon discovering his escape they would ride forth dauntless warriors. Sometimes he was sure he saw them. Sometimes he was sure he heard them. Continually looking backward over his shoulder, he studied the purple expanses where the night was marching away.

José rolled and shuddered in his saddle, persistently disturbing the stride of the black horse, fretting and worrying him until the white foam flew, and the great shoulders shone like satin from the sweat.

At last, Richardson drew his horse carefully down to a walk. José wished to rush insanely on, but the American spoke to him sternly. As the two paced forward side by side, Richardson's little horse thrust over his soft nose and inquired into the black's condition.

Riding with José was like riding with a corpse. His face resembled a cast in lead. Sometimes he swung forward and almost pitched from his seat, Richardson was too frightened himself to do anything but hate this man for his fear. Finally, he issued a mandate which nearly caused José's eyes to slide out of his head and fall to the ground, like two coins: – 'Ride behind me – about fifty paces.'

'Señor—' stuttered the servant. 'Go,' cried the American furiously. He glared at the other and laid his hand on his revolver. José looked at his master wildly. He made a piteous gesture. Then slowly he fell back, watching the hard face of the American for a sign of mercy. But Richardson had resolved in his rage that at any rate he was going to use the eyes and ears of extreme fear to detect the approach of danger; so he established his panic-stricken servant as a sort of outpost.

As they proceeded, he was obliged to watch sharply to see that the servant did not slink forward and join him. When José made beseeching circles in the air with his arm, he replied by menacingly gripping his revolver. José had a revolver too; nevertheless it was very clear in his mind that the revolver was distinctly an American weapon. He had been educated in the Rio Grande country.

Richardson lost the trail once. He was recalled to it by the loud sobs of his servant.

Then at last José came clattering forward, gesticulating and wailing. The little horse sprang to the shoulder of the black. They were off.

Richardson, again looking backward, could see a slanting flare of dust on the whitening plain. He thought that he could detect small moving figures in it.

José's moans and cries amounted to a university course in theology. They broke continually from his quivering lips. His spurs were as motors. They forced the black horse over the plain in great headlong leaps. But under Richardson there was a little insignificant rat-coloured beast who was running apparently with almost as much effort as it takes a bronze statue to stand still. The ground seemed merely something to be touched from time to time with hoofs that were as light as blown leaves. Occasionally Richardson lay back and pulled stoutly at the bridle to keep from abandoning his servant. José harried at his horse's mouth, flopped about in the saddle, and made his two heels beat like flails. The black ran like a horse in despair.

Crimson serapes in the distance resemble drops of blood on the great cloth of plain. Richardson began to dream of all possible chances. Although quite a humane man, he did not once think of his servant. José being a Mexican, it was natural that he should be killed in Mexico; but for himself, a New Yorker—! He remembered all the tales of such races for life, and he thought them badly written.

The great black horse was growing indifferent. The jabs of José's spurs no longer caused him to bound forward in wild leaps of pain. José had at last succeeded in teaching him that spurring was to be expected, speed or no speed, and now he took the pain of it dully and stolidly, as an animal who finds that doing his best gains him no respite. José was turned into a raving maniac. He bellowed and screamed, working his arms and his heels like one in a fit. He resembled a man on a sinking ship, who appeals to the ship. Richardson, too, cried madly to the black horse. The spirit of the horse responded to these calls, and quivering and breathing heavily he made a great effort, a sort of a final rush, not for himself apparently, but because he understood that his life's sacrifice, perhaps, had been invoked by these two men who cried to him in the universal tongue. Richardson had no sense of appreciation at this time – he was too frightened; but often now he remembers a certain black horse.

From the rear could be heard a yelling, and once a shot was fired – in the air, evidently. Richardson moaned as he looked back. He kept his hand on his revolver. He tried to imagine the brief tumult of his capture – the flurry of dust from the hoofs of horses pulled suddenly to their haunches, the shrill, biting curses of the men, the ring of the shots, his own last contortion. He wondered, too, if he could not somehow manage to pelt that fat Mexican, just to cure his abominable egotism.

It was José, the terror-stricken, who at last discovered safety. Suddenly he gave a howl of delight and astonished his horse into a new burst of speed. They were on a little ridge at the time, and the American at the top of it saw his servant gallop down the slope and into the arms, so to speak, of a small column of horsemen in grey and silver clothes. In the dim light of the early morning they were as vague as shadows, but Richardson knew them at once for a detachment of Rurales, that crack cavalry corps of the Mexican army which polices the plain so zealously, being of themselves the law and the arm of it – a fierce and swift-moving body that knows little of prevention but much of vengeance. They drew up suddenly, and the rows of great silver-trimmed sombreros bobbed in surprise.

Richardson saw José throw himself from his horse and begin to jabber at the leader. When he arrived he found that his servant had already outlined the entire situation, and was then engaged in describing him, Richardson, as an American señor of vast wealth, who was the friend of almost every governmental potentate within two hundred miles. This seemed profoundly to impress the officer. He bowed gravely to Richardson and smiled significantly at his men, who unslung their carbines.

The little ridge hid the pursuers from view, but the rapid thud of their horses' feet could be heard. Occasionally they yelled and called to each other. Then at last they swept over the brow of the hill, a wild mob of almost fifty drunken horsemen. When they discerned the pale-uniformed Rurales, they were sailing down the slope at top speed.

If toboggans half-way down a hill should suddenly make up their minds to turn round and go back, there would be an effect something like that produced by the drunken horsemen. Richardson saw the Rurales serenely swing their carbines forward, and, peculiar-minded person that he was, felt his heart leap into his throat at the prospective volley. But the officer rode forward alone.

It appeared that the man who owned the best horse in this astonished company was the fat Mexican with the snaky moustache, and, in consequence, this gentleman was quite a distance in the van. He tried to pull up, wheel his horse, and scuttle back over the hill as some of his companions had done, but the officer called to him in a voice harsh with rage. '—!' howled the officer. 'This señor is my friend, the friend of my friends. Do you dare pursue him, —? —! — ! —! —!' These dashes represent terrible names, all different, used by the officer.

The fat Mexican simply grovelled on his horse's neck. His face was green: it could be seen that he expected death. The officer stormed with magnificent intensity: '—! —! —!' Finally he sprang from his saddle, and, running to the fat Mexican's side, yelled – 'Go!' and kicked the horse in the belly with all his might. The animal gave a mighty leap into the air, and the fat Mexican, with one wretched glance at the contemplative Rurales, aimed his steed for the top of the ridge. Richardson gulped again in expectation of a volley, for – it is said – this is a favourite method for disposing of objectionable people. The fat, green Mexican also thought that he was to be killed on the run, from the miserable look he cast at the troops. Nevertheless, he was allowed to vanish in a cloud of yellow dust at the ridge-top.

José was exultant, defiant, and, oh! bristling with courage. The black horse was drooping sadly, his nose to the ground. Richardson's little animal, with his ears bent forward, was staring at the horses of the Rurales as if in an intense study. Richardson longed for speech, but he could only bend forward and pat the shining, silken shoulders. The little horse turned his head and looked back gravely.

# RIDING WITH THE MAIL

## *Clarence E. Mulford*

REED threw down the cards and pushed back from the rickety table. He was unsteady from the liquor he had drunk and enraged by his losses. The night had not been well spent, aside from any question of gaming, because before him lay his eighty-mile Pony Express ride, to be covered in the usual seven hours. The combination of liquor and rage was not a good one.

The two men at the table exchanged looks with each other and with the bar-tender, whose face was as villainous as their own.

'You can't be lucky all the time,' said one of the seated pair. 'Bound to run ag'in ye once in a while. Come back an' set down.'

Reed opened the door and looked out. Dawn was still a few hours off, and the cold of that early morning hour nipped him and was emphasized by the chill brightness of the gleaming stars.

Reed stepped back into the room and closed the door. This was his day to ride, but he had plenty of time. Frisco was not due until nine o'clock. The stove felt good and one drink seemed to call for another. He returned to his chair and relaxed. Between then and dawn he heard a great deal against the old man who kept the station, and learned from sympathetic friends how he himself was abused.

By the time that the pale streamers of dawn levelled swiftly across the eastern prairie, Reed believed himself to be a martyr. He now was flat broke, for the game, renewed, had not changed the course of its current. Again he arose from the table and made his way toward the door, staggering now. The cold morning air still had its nip, but it was somewhat tempered.

He glanced up at the little valley at his left, where the stage buildings were: mere huts of distorted cedar, with dirt roofs, squat and ugly, with every imperfection revealed by the slanting rays of the sun. In the stables behind them were the horses for the Concord relay; and one magnificent animal of thoroughbred strain munched his oats in contentment, in a stall of his own, ignorant of the fact that those same oats had been hauled by ox-trains some hundreds of miles to provide him with a worth-while breakfast, to give him speed and endurance over his measured run beyond that of the grass-fed mongrel ponies indigenous to the country.

Reed's face softened a little as he thought of this splendid animal. Involuntary he moved toward the stable to go through the regular morning ritual of rubbing down a glossy coat that had been rubbed already; to pass inquiring and affectionate hands gently over fetlock and knees, to rub the silky nose, and to feel the cool muzzle against his face.

Reed's face softened more, and then hardened like flint: the station-keeper was stepping through the stable door, carefully closing it behind him.

Old man Gibson turned and saw the scowling watcher, and a shadow passed over the old man's face. He liked Reed. There was something in that boy that had held out rare promise of a fine manhood. Then the groggery had come and had gone up in a night, an affair of posts and canvas.

The station-keeper's glance passed from the flushed and scowling rider to the groggery over the knoll behind him. Reed was drunk again, despite the pledge he had signed; despite the arguments and entreaties of the station-keeper. Drunk again, for the third time. It was Gibson's duty to report this youth, or to discharge him then and there, knowing full well that in this he would be upheld by the division superintendent.

'There's the stable. See that you keep out of it. Its door has no lock,' said the station-keeper, 'save this,' and his right hand touched his thigh, a terse and graphic warning. 'Yore ridin' days are over, Reed, so far as Russell, Majors an' Waddell are concerned. By rights you have lost yore pay: you know how the employment pledge reads, an' you've broke it three times; but I've no mind to go that far. What's comin' to you you've earned fairly, an' you'll get it. I'll give you an order on the super, an' you can join up with the next freight outfit an' travel home with it. Now, then, get off this property, an' stay off it.'

Reed shuffled his feet, shame beating in through the stupor of the liquor and tinging his anger; and, somehow, the anger died. Pride remained, however, and prompted him to shrug his shoulders, turn abruptly and stalk back the way he had come, straight for the canvas groggery, as though persistence could justify an evil course of action. But when he reached the saloon he did not enter it. He passed around it and staggered down the easy slope toward the whispering river. An old buffalo wallow, choked with softer weeds, lay before him, and he stumbled into it, finding it soft and warm in the rays of the sun. The wind did not reach him here, and gratefully he flung himself down to rest and to sleep; but somehow he could not sleep at first. Thoughts pounded reverberatingly within his aching head.

He had been a cog in that great, smoothly running machine of the horseback mail; he had been proud of himself, of his horse and of his calling; in his soul was the spirit of that mail, the spirit so typical of many things on those wide and rolling prairies, of that barely stirring West. It had become a part of him. Danger he had welcomed, exultantly; fatigue and the fierce punishments of sun and rain and snow and frost had been proudly endured. Never once had he hesitated, no matter what might lie before. Whether the saddle-cover contained one letter, or one hundred letters, or no letter at all, made no difference; it, itself, was the heart of the whole pony system; a sweat-stained, foam-flecked, grease and dust-covered piece of leather, with its four pockets in its four corners.

Back in the little hollow the station-keeper had stood without moving until the head of the discharged rider had lowered beyond the top of the sloping ridge. The old frontiersman, scout and cavalry-man readily shifted his gaze to the ridge-pole of the saloon, already throwing its shadow down the sloping roof.

He had no authority to order that groggery to leave, or to make war on it; but, then, neither did the groggery have authority to ruin one of the best riders on the line and to interfere with the regular and clock-work operation of mile-clipping. This matter of right, somehow, seemed to be about even; and the subject mechanically resolved itself into one of might. With might Gibson was better acquainted, more certain of his footing, having served a crowded apprenticeship through several of its higher degrees.

He looked at his watch. Charley, the absent stableman, should be back in time to welcome Frisco and to take his part in the changing of mounts.

You could never tell about these stablemen of the Overland, working for their miserable stipend, and smelling of their labours. They had been known to perform prodigious feats of valour, for the honour of the service and to boost their own overweening self-esteem. Charley had shown indications of being just that sort of man, and so it was better that he was in the hills, trying to coax antelope with his old red muffler.

The old man arose, looked around his comfortable quarters with kindly eyes, and from his pocket he removed his beloved corncob.

Then he walked slowly but steadily across the bottom, over the rill of water which accounted for the location of this particular station, and breasted the farther slope, taking the hill at a slant and in a straight line for the canvas groggery.

His entrance made a stir, a stir of disbelief and strong curiosity. The men at the table leaned forward a trifle, one of them pushing aside the bottle at his wrist, as if clearing a deck for action.

'I seen yore mules nigh the river bank jest now,' said the old man in a pleasantly conversational voice. 'Most likely the spokes an' felloes of yore waggin have shrunk a mite, like they all do up here in this country. Chances are they'll rattle a little; but you can wedge 'em an' wrap 'em so's they'll hold together till you can soak 'em at yore camp tonight. Hadn't oughta take you long to hitch up, load this here stuff, an' pull out. If you waits till Frisco gits here there'll be two of us instid of one. He's plumb short on temper, Frisco is – an' a right good friend of young Reed.'

Three amazed faces regarded him, their owners doubting their ears. They looked from one to the other, and then all three looked at him at the same time. They saw a placid and friendly face, with little crinkles of humour puckered about the eyes and lips. They saw a lamb bleating in a lion's den. Simultaneously the three broke into loud and jeering laughter.

'What was that you was sayin' to us about packin' up an' gittin' out?' asked the bar-tender.

'Did sound sorta 'brupt, didn't it?' commented the station-keeper, mildly apologetic. 'Reckon, howsomever, you heard it right plain. You've plumb ruined one of my riders, a likely sort of boy; I had to fire him jest now. An' right now he's blamin' me, instead of you; an' when he gets sober his heart'll mebbe near break from shame

an' sorrer. Strikes me I'm right easy-goin' to give you the chance
to git away.'

'Takin' it that yo're in earnest,' said the bar-tender, very slowly,
'I'm tellin' you to clear outa here. Clear out, right now, an' damn'
quick. Don't you ever come back no more, neither!'

'I'm goin',' said the old man, resignedly. 'Only dropped in to tell
you that I'm figgerin 'on givin' you jest ten minutes to make a start
for them mules an' that waggin,' he explained, beaming upon them.
'After the time is up I figger to lock myself up in the station yonder,
an' start to turnin' bullets through this here hell-hole as fast as I can
pull trigger.'

Their wildest hopes did not dare to suggest that he would turn
and walk out, but they were quick to act upon the unexpected. He
started to turn and walk out, and then whirled as he ducked, their
bullets going through the canvas to scream across the plain outside.
The room was instantly filled with swirling, choking powder
smoke, through which hazy figures crept and crawled, leaped,
darted and dodged; and red flashes winked their stabbing ways here
and there in a roar of sound. The bar upended as its moaning tender
convulsively arose on stiffening legs, the plank across a shoulder.

Plank and man crashed simultaneously against the flimsy table.
Two smoke-shrouded figures met and locked on the floor near the
sheet iron stove. The falling gun-butt of the gambler landed about
the same instant that a muffled roar came from his side. The gambler
bridged grotesquely in one last agony of contracting muscles, and
his dying kick drove the stove into a pile of odds and ends against
the rear of the canvas shack, where it spilled its blazing embers
generously. The station-keeper, blinded by the blood from the gun-
butt wound, crawled toward the third man, who was taking deliberate aim with a newly filled derringer.

The old man writhed swiftly sidewise and got the bullet through
his cheek instead of through his forehead; and then his arm rose and
fell, and the weight of his empty Colt hammered again and again
on its mark. He knew that he was losing consciousness, and he
barely had sense enough to read the threat of the leaping flames and
the smoke of burning wood and canvas. Inch by inch, driven by a
blind instinct, he wriggled and clawed to the flapping door, and
through it into the clear air outside.

Down in the buffalo wallow the shadow of the sagebrush had moved across and beyond the sleeper's face.

He stirred, opened his reddened eyes and blinked. Ah, yes; nearly time to go. Moving his head, he noticed that the customary building was not to be seen, and for a moment he stared incredulously at the sagebrush. Rubbing his eyes, he leaped to his feet in a mild panic, and looked anxiously around. A finger of smoke, high up on the slope, made him blink again.

A moment's mad and chaotic clashing of thoughts, and it all began to come back to him. He no longer was a rider of the Pony Express; the canvas groggery had burned down; it lacked but a brief time for the arrival of the incoming letter mail. Stumblingly he made his way at his best speed up the interminable slope, tripping over sagebrush, and smashing through it.

The sight he looked upon would have sobered him even had he not been nearly sobered already. Old man Gibson, a gory mess, lay curled at the edge of his beloved road, his chest spasmodically rising and falling.

Reed growled in his throat like an animal, drew his gun while he rapidly glanced over the smouldering ruins; but there was no need for bullets there. He ran an arm under the sagging shoulders and raised the old man's head from the ground. Looking around with one swift glance, he saw the figure of a mounted man top the far distant skyline and pause to look down into the valley below him. Charley was coming back again, proud of the antelope swung behind his saddle cantle.

And then, over the ridge in the road not one hundred yards away, pushed up the proud head of a racing horse, its silky mane flying like a battle flag, its wide-spread nostrils greedily gulping the now heated air. The saddle was empty, and a swift chill enfolded the heart of the waiting youth. The saddle was empty; aye, but the precious saddle-cover shone greasily, and the sunlight flicked on the jolting padlocks.

Reed lowered the old man to the ground again, leaped to his feet and held out his arms to stop the racing roan; but the roan knew that its journey was not ended until it stopped at the cedar stable. It swerved, but not enough; Reed's desperate grip fastened to the bridle and hung on like a vice, while low words in a voice the roan well knew pleaded to the cavorting animal. An arrow, bouncing and jiggling from a blood-soaked rump, told its grim story. A bleeding furrow across a wither gave further proof.

Somewhere in that fourteen miles between the stations Frisco lay dead or dying on the trail; no other explanation could be held for one minute. But there was the saddle-cover, with its precious mail; safe, brought by a horse too proud, too game, to fail.

Charley was tearing down the slope and could take care of the old station-keeper. This, however, would never do: Reed owed the old man a debt he felt he never could repay. He got the inert bulk across the saddle and led the proud and snorting roan, a little restless from all this blood that tainted the air, toward the ugly buildings, which, somehow, now looked strangely beautiful. Quickly the youth carried the old man inside the station and placed him in a bunk, glancing at the loudly ticking clock in instinctive apprehension. Four minutes had elapsed beyond the two allowed for changing mounts. Four minutes! This was scandalous.

Into the stable and out again at top speed, Reed worked frantically, a little handicapped by the black's impatient eagerness. Saddle and cover in place and made secure, Reed vaulted astride. Somewhere out on that heated plain his friend lay dead or dying; here, near him in a tumbled bunk, another friend might have breathed his last. Behind him, somewhere on that arid plain, were scurrying Sioux warriors.

'Damn the Sioux!' snapped Reed, leaning quickly forward in the saddle, and thrilled at the swift rush of air against his face. 'Go on, boy! To hell with the Sioux; we're *ridin' with the mail!*'

# THE INDIAN HATER

## James Hall

S OME years ago, I had occasion to travel over the beautiful prairies of Illinois, then a frontier state, containing but few inhabitants, and those chiefly of the class called backwoodsmen. In the course of my journey, I stopped one day at a village to rest; and while my horse was eating his corn, and mine hostess was picking the chicken that was to be broiled for my dinner, I stepped into a neighbouring store to purchase some small article of which I stood in need. I found a number of persons there, engaged, some in buying merchandise, some in talking politics, and others in reading the manuscript advertisements of stray horses and constable's sales, that were pasted on the walls. There were a bottle of whiskey and a pitcher of water on the counter, free for all comers, as was the hospitable fashion of those days, before temperance had got to be a tip-top virtue, or Father Mathew the greatest of modern reformers. Being not unwilling to observe a scene which might afford amusement, and to while away a few minutes in conversation, I leaned my back against the counter, and addressed myself to a person having the appearance of a substantial farmer, who answered my inquiries respecting the country with intelligence and civility.

While thus engaged, my attention was drawn to a person who stood near. He was a man who might have been about fifty years of age. His height did not exceed the ordinary stature, and his person was rather slender than otherwise; but there was something in his air and features which distinguished him from common men. The expression of his countenance was keen and daring. His forehead was elevated, his cheek bones high, his lips thin and compressed. Long exposure to the climate had tanned his complexion to a deep brown, and had hardened his skin and muscles, so as to give him the appearance of a living petrifaction. He seemed to have lived in the open air, exposed to the elements, and to every extreme of temperature.

There was nothing in the dress of this individual to attract attention; he was accosted occasionally by others, and seemed familiar with all who were present. Yet there was an air of abstraction, and standing aloof about him, so different from the noisy mirth and thoughtless deportment of those around him, that I could not help observing him. In his eye there was something peculiar, yet I could not tell in what that peculiarity consisted. It was a small grey orb, whose calm, bold, direct glances, seemed to vouch that it had not cowered with shame, or quailed in danger. There was blended in that eye a searching keenness, with a quiet vigilance – a watchful, sagacious self-possession – so often observable in the physiognomy of those who are in the habit of expecting, meeting, and overcoming peril. His heavy eyebrows had been black, but time had touched them with his pencil. He was dressed in a coarse grey hunting shirt, of homespun cotton, girded round the waist with a broad leather belt, tightly drawn, in which rested the long knife, with which the western hunter despatches his game, cuts his food, picks his flint and his teeth, and whittles sticks for amusement.

Upon the whole, there was about this man an expression of quiet determination, of grim and gloomy sternness, of intense but smothered passion, which stamped him as something out of the ordinary view of character; yet there were indications of openness and honesty, that forbade distrust. He was rough, but not a ruffian. His was not the unblushing front of hardy guilt, nor the lurking glance of underhanded villany. A stranger would not have hesitated to confide in his faith or courage, but would have been extremely reluctant to provoke his hostility.

I had barely time to make these observations, when several Indians, who had strolled into the village, entered the store. The effect of their presence upon the backwoodsman, whom I have described, was instantaneous and remarkable. His eyes rolled wildly, as if he had been suddenly stung to madness, gleaming with a strange fierceness – an intense lustre, like that which flashes from the eyeballs of the panther, when crouched in a dark covert, ready to dart upon his prey. His sallow cheek was flushed; the muscles, that but a moment before seemed so rigid, became flexible, and twitched convulsively. His hand sliding quietly to the hilt of his large knife, as if by an involuntary impulse, grasped it firmly; and it was easy to perceive that a smothered fire had been disturbed, and that a single breath would be sufficient to light up a blaze. But, except these indications, he remained motionless as a statue, gazing with a look of intense ferocity at the intruders. The Indians halted when their eyes met his, and exchanged glances of intelligence with each other. Whether it was from instinct, or that they knew the man, or whether the natural sagacity of their race enabled them to read the signs of danger in his scowling visage, they seemed willing to avoid him, and retired. The backwoodsman made a motion, as if to follow; but several of the company, who had watched this silent, though momentary scene, with interest, gently withheld him, and after conversing with him a few moments in an earnest, but under tone, led him off in one direction, while the Indians rode away in another.

Having understood from the farmer, with whom I had been talking, that he was about to return home, and that my route led through his neighbourhood, I accepted the offer of his company and guidance, and we set out together. It was a pleasant afternoon in the fall, and as our horses trotted quietly over the smooth prairie road, the discourse naturally fell upon the scene we had just witnessed, and I expressed a curiosity to learn something of the history and character of the man, whose image had impressed itself so forcibly on my mind. I was young and romantic then, and singular as this being certainly was, his peculiarities were probably magnified to my excited fancy.

'He is a strange, mysterious-looking being,' said I, 'and I should think he must be better, or worse, than other men.'

'Samuel Monson is a very good neighbour,' replied the farmer, cautiously.

'You say that in a tone,' rejoined I, 'which seems to imply, that in some other respects he may not be so good.'

'Well – as to that, I cannot say, of my own knowledge, that I know any harm of the man.'

'And what do other people say of him?'

The farmer hesitated, and then, with a caution very common among people of this description, replied:

'People often say more than they can prove. It's not good, no how, to be talking of one's neighbours; and Monson, as I said before, is a good neighbour.'

'But a bad man, as I understand.'

'No – far from it – the man's well enough—'

My companion hesitated here, as gossips of both sexes are apt to do, when conscious of a strong inclination to tell all they know on a delicate subject; but my laudable thirst for useful knowledge had, I suppose, awakened a benevolent desire to gratify it, and the worthy man added, in a low tone, and looking cautiously around:

'—Except – The folks do say he are rather too keen with his rifle.'

'How so? does he shoot his neighbour's cattle?'

'No, sir – Samuel Monson is as much above a mean action as any other man.'

'What then, is he quarrelsome?'

'Oh, bless you, no! There's not a peaceabler man in the settlement; but he used to be a great Indian fighter in the last war, and he got sort o' haunted to the woods; and folks do say that he's still rather too keen on the track of a moccasin.'

'I do not exactly understand you, my dear sir. – The Indians are now quiet, I believe, and at peace with us?'

'Why yes, they are very peaceable. They never come near us, except now and then a little party comes in to trade. There's not many of them in these parts, and they live a good piece off.'

'They are civil and harmless, are they not?'

'Yes, sir, quite agreeable – bating the killing of a hog once in a while – but that we don't vally – it is but just nateral to the poor savage to shoot anything that runs in the woods. They have a honing in that way, and you can't stop them, no way you can fix it.'

'In what way, then, does this Monson interfere with them?'

'I did not say, stranger, that Monson done it. No, no; I wouldn't hurt no man's character; but the fact and the truth are about this: now and then an Indian are missing; and now and then one are found dead in the range; – and folks will have their notions, and their talk, and their suspicions about it – and some talk hard of Monson.'

'But why charge it upon him?'

'Well, if you must have it out, stranger, – in this country we all know the bore of every man's rifle. Monson's gun carries just fifty to the pound. Now the bullet holes in all these Indians that have been shot are the same, and we know whose rifle they suit. Besides this, horse tracks have been seen on the trail of the moccasin. They were very particular tracks, and just suited the hoof of a certain horse. Then a certain man was known to be lying out in the range, about that same time; and when all these things are put together, it don't take a Philadelphia lawyer to tell who done the deed. No mistake in Sam Monson. He likes a skrimmage with them. He goes off sometimes, and is gone for weeks, and people reckon that he goes to their own hunting grounds to lie in wait for them. They do say, he can scent a red-skin like a hound, and never lets a chance slip – no how.'

'But is it possible, that in a civilized country, within the reach of our laws, a wretch is permitted to hunt down his fellow-creatures like wild beasts; to murder a defenceless Indian, who comes into our territory in good faith, believing us to be what we profess, as a Christian people!'

'Well, stranger, – as to the matter of that – it is not exactly permitted; we don't know for certain who does it, and it's not any particular man's business to inquire into it, more than another. There's no love for the Indians among us, no how. Many of the people have had their kin murdered by the savages in early times; and all who have been raised in the back woods, have been learned to dislike them, and fear them. Then Monson is an honest fellow, works hard, pays his debts, and is always willing to do a good turn, and it would seem hard to break neighbourhood with him for the matter of a few Indians. People don't think the Indians of much account, no how!'

'But the wickedness of such unprovoked murder – the shame – the breach of law, the violation of hospitality!'

'Well, so it is. It are a sin; and sorry would I be to have it on my conscience. But, then, some think an Indian or so will never be missed; others, again, hate to create an interruption in the settlement; others, who pretend to know the law, say that the general government has the care of the business of the Indians, and that our state laws won't kiver the case – so they allow it's none of our business. Some folks, you know, go in heavy for state rights, and don't believe in meddling with any thing that belongs to Uncle Sam; and withal Monson keeps his own counsel, and so among hands he goes his own road, and no questions asked.'

All this seemed very strange to me. Border wars, we all know, are productive of feuds, which are implacable and lasting. Predatory incursions, which hardly attract the notice of the government, bring carnage and devastation, ruin and sorrow, to the fireside. Private property is wasted, and the war is against individuals, rather than the public. The actors in each scene are identified; men and families feel the sense of personal injury, and hatred and revenge are the consequence. But I was not aware that such a state of feeling existed on our own frontier. While these thoughts passed through my mind, we rode forward in silence, which was broken by my inquiring what injury this individual had suffered from the Indians, which could justify him in thus destroying them with impunity.

'Injury enough!' replied my companion: 'to tell the plain sentimental truth, he has cause enough to hate them; and many a man that would not dip his own hand in the blood of an Indian, would as soon die as betray him; for few of us could lay our hands upon our hearts and say we would not do the same in his situation.'

At this point of the conversation we were joined by several horsemen, who were pursuing the same road with ourselves, and joined us, in accordance with the gregarious habits of the country, which induce men to prefer a larger company to a smaller, on all occasions; and my companion being unwilling to pursue the subject in their hearing, I was unable to learn from him what injury the Indian hater had received, to provoke his sanguinary career of vengeance. Nor did another opportunity occur; for we soon came to a point where the roads diverging, obliged us to separate, and although my friendly fellow-traveller, with the usual hospitality of the country, invited me to take up my lodgings at his house for the night, I was obliged to decline the invitation, and we parted.

I continued my journey into the northwestern part of Illinois, which was then just beginning to attract the attention of settlers, and contained but few inhabitants. Delighted with this beautiful wilderness, unspoiled by art, and retaining all its native loveliness, and wishing to explore the lands lying between this tract and the Wabash, I determined, on my return, to strike directly across, through a district of country in which there were as yet no settlements, of about one hundred and fifty miles in extent. I hired an Indian guide, who was highly recommended to me, and set out under his protection.

It is not easy to describe the sensations of a traveller, unaccus-
tomed to such scenery, on first beholding the vast prairies, which I
was about to explore. Those I had heretofore seen were comparatively small; both are unique, and highly attractive, but as they differ
in their features and scenic effect, I shall endeavour to describe them
separately.

The smaller prairies, or those in which the plain and woodland
alternate frequently, are the most beautiful. The points of woodland
which make into them like so many capes or promontories, and the
groves which are interspersed like islands, are in these lesser prairies
always sufficiently near to be clearly defined to the eye, and to give
the scene an interesting variety. We see plains, varying from a few
hundred acres to several miles in extent, not perfectly level, but
gently rolling or undulating, like the swelling of the ocean when
nearly calm. The graceful curve of the surface is seldom broken,
except when, here and there, the eye rests upon one of those huge
mounds, which are so pleasing to the poet, and so perplexing to
the antiquarian. The whole is overspread with grass and flowers,
constituting a rich and varied carpet, in which a ground of lively
green is ornamented with a profusion of the gaudiest hues, and
fringed with a rich border of forest and thicket. Deep recesses in
the edge of the timber resemble the bays and inlets of a lake; while
occasionally a long vista, opening far back into the forest, invites
the eye to roam off and refresh itself, with the calm beauty of a
distant perspective.

The traveller, as he rides along over these smaller prairies, finds
his eye continually attracted to the edges of the forest, and his
imagination employed in tracing the beautiful outline, and in finding
out resemblances between these wild scenes and the most tastefully
embellished productions of art. The fairest pleasuregrounds, the
noblest parks of European noblemen and princes, where millions
have been expended to captivate the senses with Elysian scenes, are
but mimic representations, on a reduced scale, of the beauties which
are here spread by nature; for here are clumps and lawns, groves
and avenues, the tangled thicket, and the solitary tree, the lengthened
vista, and the secluded nook, and all the varieties of scenic attraction,
but on a plan so extensive, as to offer a wide scope, and an endless
succession of changes, to the eye.

There is an air of refinement here, that wins the heart – even here, where no human residence is seen, where no foot of man intrudes, and where not an axe has ever trespassed on the beautiful domain. It is a wilderness shorn of every savage association, a desert that 'blossoms as the rose'. So different is the feeling awakened from anything inspired by mountain or woodland scenery, that the instant the traveller emerges from the forest into the prairie, he feels no longer solitary. The consciousness that he is travelling alone, and in a wilderness, escapes him; and he indulges in the same pleasing sensations which are enjoyed by one who, having lost his way, and wandered bewildered among the labyrinths of a savage mountain, suddenly descends into rich and highly cultivated plains, and sees around him the delightful indications of taste and comfort. The gay landscape charms him. He is encompassed by the refreshing sweetness and graceful beauty of the rural scene; and recognises at every step some well-remembered spot, or some ideal paradise in which the fancy had loved to wander, enlarged and beautified, and, as it were, retouched by nature's hand. The clusters of trees so fancifully arranged, the forest outline so gracefully curved, seem to have been disposed by the hand of taste, for the enjoyment of intelligent beings; and so complete is the illusion, that it is difficult to dispel the belief that each avenue leads to a village, and each grove conceals a splendid mansion.

Widely different was the prospect exhibited by the more northern and central districts of the State. Vast in extent, the distant forest was either beyond the reach of the eye, or was barely discernible in the shapeless outline of blue, faintly impressed on the horizon. As the smaller prairies resembled a series of larger and lesser lakes, so these boundless plains remind one of the ocean waste. Here and there a solitary tree, torn by the wind, stood alone like a dismantled mast in the ocean. As I followed my guide through this lonely region, my sensations were similar to those of the voyager, when his bark is launched upon the sea. Alone, in a wide waste, with my faithful pilot only, I was dependent on him for support, guidance, and protection. With little to diversify the path, and nothing to please the eye but the carpet of verdure, which began to pall upon the sense, a feeling of dreariness crept over me – a desolation of the spirit, such as one feels when crossed in love, or when very drowsy on a hot afternoon, after a full dinner. But these are feelings which, like the sea-sickness of the young mariner, are soon dispelled. I

began to find a pleasure in gazing over this immense, unbroken
waste, in watching the horizon under the vague hope of meeting a
traveller, and in following the deer with my eyes as they galloped
off – their agile forms growing smaller and smaller as they receded,
until they shrunk into nothing. Sometimes I described a dark spot
at an immense distance, and pointed it out to my companion with
a joy like that of the seaman who discovers a sail in the distant speck
which floats on the ocean. When such an object happened to be in
the direction of our path, I watched it with interest as it rose and
enlarged upon the vision – supposing it at one moment to be a
solitary horseman, and wondering what manner of man he would
turn out to be – at another supposing it might be a wild animal, or
a wagon, or a pedestrian; until, after it had seemed to approach for
hours, I found it to be a tree.

Nor was I entirely destitute of company; for my Pottowottomie
guide proved to be both intelligent and good-humoured; and
although his stock of English was but slender, and his habit of
taciturnity somewhat confirmed, his conversational powers, when
exerted, were quite respectable. His knowledge of the country was
extensive and accurate, so that he was able, not only to choose the
best route, but to point out all the localities. When we halted he
kindled a fire, spread my pallet, and formed a shelter to protect me
from the weather. When we came to a stream which was too deep
to ford, he framed a raft to cross me over, with my baggage, while
he mounted my horse and plunged into the water. Throughout the
journey, his assiduities were as kind and unremitting as all his
arrangements were sagacious and considerate. A higher motive than
the mere pecuniary reward which he expected for his services gover-
ned his actions. He considered himself my companion; not only
responsible for my safety, as a matter of contract, but kindly
interested for my comfort. A genuine integrity of purpose, a native
politeness and manliness of deportment, raised him above the
ordinary savage, and rendered him not only a respectable, but an
interesting man.

After travelling nearly five days without beholding a human habi-
tation, we arrived at the verge of a settlement on the Wabash. We
passed along a rich bottom, covered with huge trees, whose limbs
were hung with immense grape vines, and whose thick shade
afforded a strong contrast to the scenes we had left behind us, and

then ascending a gentle rise, stood on a high bluff bank of the Wabash. A more secluded and beautiful spot has seldom been seen. A small river, with a clear stream, rippling over a rocky bed, meandered round the point on which we stood, and then turning abruptly to the left, was lost among the trees. The opposite shore was low, thickly wooded, and beautifully rich in the variety of mellow hues painted by the autumn sun.

The spot we occupied was a slip of table land, a little higher than the surrounding country. It had once been cleared for cultivation, but was now overgrown with hazel bushes, vines, and briars, while a few tall, leafless trunks, once the proudest oaks of the forest, weather-beaten and blackened by fire, still adhered tenaciously to the soil. A heap of rubbish, intermingled with logs half burnt and nearly rotten, showed the remains of what had once been a chimney, and indicated the spot where a cabin had stood, the residence of human beings – but all else had been destroyed by time or fire. We gazed on the ruins of a desolated homestead, but many years seemed to have rolled away since it had been inhabited. The clearing had been of small extent; it was now covered with a rank vegetation, which was fast restoring it to the dominion of the wilderness. One spot only, which had probably been the yard in front of the little dwelling, and had been beaten hard, was covered with a smooth green sward, unmixed with weeds or brush; and here we stood gazing at this desolate spot, and that beautiful river. It was but a moment, and neither of us had broken silence, when the crack of a rifle was heard, and my guide, uttering a dismal yell, fell at my feet.

Recovering his senses for an instant, he grasped his gun, partly raised his body, and cast upon me a look of reproach, which I shall never forget; and then, as if satisfied by the concern and alarm of my countenance, and my prompt movement to assist him, he gave me one hand, and pointing with the other towards the woods, exclaimed – 'Bad – bad, white man! – take care' – and expired. The aim had been unerring – the bullet had penetrated deep in a vital spot, and life was extinguished in a moment.

I was so much surprised and shocked at this fatal catastrophe, that I stood immoveable, thoughtless of my own safety, mourning over the stout Indian, my kind and worthy guide, who lay sweltering in his gore, when I was startled by a slight rustling in the bushes close behind me, and as I turned with an involuntary shudder, a backwoodsman, rifle in hand, issued from the covert. Advancing hastily, without the least appearance of shame or fear, until he came to the corpse, and paying not the slightest attention to me, he stood and gazed sternly at the fallen warrior. It was Monson! The fierce and gloomy picture, which had been impressed so indelibly upon my memory, stood before me in living presentation, his hand imbrued in blood, and his soul freshly steeped in murder.

'There's another of the cursed crew gone to his last account!' he exclaimed. 'He is not the first, and he shall not be the last. – It's an old debt, but it shall be paid to the last drop!'

As he spoke, he gnashed his teeth, and his eyes gleamed with the malignity of gratified revenge. Then turning to me, and observing the deep abhorrence with which I shrunk back, he said gruffly,

'May be, stranger, you don't like this sort of business.'

'Wretch – miscreant – murderer! begone! Approach me not,' I exclaimed, shrinking back in disgust and terror, and drawing a large pistol from my belt; but, before I was aware, the backwoodsman, with a sudden spring, caught my arm, and wrested the weapon from me; and then remaining perfectly calm, while I was ready to burst with rage, he proceeded:

'This is a poor shooting-iron for a man to have about him – it might do for young men to tote in a settlement, but it's of no use in the woods – no more than a shot-gun.'

'Scoundrel!' said I, 'you shall repent your violence—'

'Young man!' interrupted he, very coolly, 'I am no scoundrel, no more than yourself; you mistake, you do not know me.'

'Murderer!' repeated I, 'for such I know you to be. My life is in your power, but I dread not your vengeance! If I live, this bloody deed shall not go unpunished!'

While I was thus exhausting myself, in the expression of my rage and horror, the more politic Monson, having possessed himself of the Indian's gun, dropped it, together with my unlucky pistol, on the ground, and placing one foot on them, proceeded deliberately to load his rifle.

'Don't be alarmed, young man,' said he, in reply to my last remark, 'I shall not hurt a hair of your head. You cannot provoke me to it. I never harmed a Christian man, to my knowledge!'

But although his habitual command of his temper enabled him to treat the matter thus coolly, he was evidently under high excitement, and as he finished loading his piece, he exclaimed, 'See here!' Then pointing to the ruins of the cabin, he proceeded in a hurried tone.

'This was my home. Here I built a house with my own labour. With the sweat of my brow I opened this clearing. Here I lived with my wife, my children, and my mother. We worked hard – lived well – and were happy.'

His voice became choked; he paused, as if overcome by the recollections of the past; but after a moment's hesitation, he proceeded with the simple and vehement eloquence of passion:

'I am a rough man, stranger, but I have feelings like other men. My blood is up now, and I will tell you a tale that will explain this deed. One night – it was in the fall – just at this season – I had gathered my corn, ready for shucking, the labour of the year was done, and I was sitting by the fire with my family, with the prospect of plenty and comfort around me – when I heard the Indian yell! I never was a coward, but I knew that sound too well; and when I looked round upon the women and helpless babes, that depended on me for protection, a cold chill ran over me, and my heart seemed to die. I ran to the door, and beheld my stacks in a blaze. I caught up my gun – but in a moment a gang of yelling savages came pouring in at my door, like so many howling wolves. I fired, and one of them fell – I caught up an axe and rushed at them with such fury that I cleared the cabin. The vile varments then set fire to the roof, and we saw the flames spreading around us. What could I do?

'Stranger, you never were in such a fix, and you don't know how a man feels. Here was my poor old mother, and my wife, and my little children, unable to fight, or to escape. I burst open the door, and rushed madly out; but they pushed me back. The yelling wretches were determined to burn us in our house. The blazing timbers came falling among us – my wife hung on my neck, and called on me to save our children – our pious old mother prayed – the savage butchers roared, and laughed, and mocked us. They caught my dog, that we loved as one of the family, hung him, and then threw his carcass among us.

'I grasped my axe, and rushed out again – hoping to beat them back, until the neighbours could be alarmed, and come to our assistance. I killed several of them; but they overpowered me, bound me, and led me up to witness the ruin of all that was dear to me.

Wife – children – mother – all, all perished here in the flames before my eyes. They perished in lingering torments – screaming with terror – racked with pain. I saw their agonies – heard their cries – they called on my name. Tied hand and foot, what could I do? Oh Heaven, can I ever forget it!'

The man of sorrows paused in his tragical narrative, overcome by the tender and terrible recollections that it called forth. He looked wildly around. Tears came to his relief – that hard, ferocious misanthrope, the fountains of whose tenderness seemed to have been long since broken and dried up, melted at the recital of his own griefs. Nature had resumed her sway over him. The pause was but brief; when, brushing the tears from his rough visage, he continued:

'They carried me off a prisoner. I was badly wounded, and so heart-broken, that for three days I was helpless as a child. Then a desire of revenge grew up in my heart, and I got strong. I gnawed the strings they had bound me with, and escaped from them in the night. I thought that God had spared me to be a scourge to the savage. The war with the Indians broke out soon afterwards, and I joined every expedition – I was foremost in every fight; but I could not quench my thirst for the blood of the miscreants. I swore never to forgive them, and when peace came, I continued to make war. I have made it a rule to kill every red-skin that came in my way; my revenge is not yet satisfied, and so long as I have strength to whet my knife on a stone, or ram a ball into my rifle, I shall continue to slay the savage!

'As for this fellow,' he continued, 'I would not have troubled him, anywhere else, if I had seen him in your company. I would not harm nor trouble any Christian man, especially a stranger. But when he came *here*, setting his cursed feet on *this soil* – stepping over the ruins of my homestead, and the ashes of my family – when he intruded upon me as I sat here alone, thinking over the fate of my poor wife and children, it was not my nater to spare him – I couldn't do it.

'Let us part friends, young man, I have done you no harm; if I have hurt your feelings, I ask your pardon. Pursue your own way, and leave me to mine. If you have a grey-headed mother that prays for you, a wife and children that love you – they will welcome you, and you will be happy. I am alone; – there is none to mourn with me, no one to rejoice at my coming. When all that you cherish is torn from you in one moment, by hellish ruffians, condemn me if you can: but not till then. – That path will lead you to a house.'

# THE BEST MAN IN GAROTTE

## *Frank Harris*

LAWYER Rablay had come from nobody knew where. He was a small man, almost as round as a billiard ball. His body was round, his head was round; his blue eyes and even his mouth and chin were round; his nose was a perky snub; he was florid and prematurely bald – a picture of good-humour. And yet he was a power in Garotte. When he came to the camp, a row was the only form of recreation known to the miners. A 'fuss' took men out of themselves, and was accordingly hailed as an amusement; besides, it afforded a subject of conversation. But after Lawyer Rablay's arrival fights became comparatively infrequent. Would-be students of human nature declared at first that his flow of spirits was merely animal, and that his wit was thin; but even these envious ones had to admit later that his wit told, and that his good-humour was catching.

Crocker and Harrison had nearly got to loggerheads one night for no reason apparently, save that each had a high reputation for courage, and neither could find a worthier antagonist. In the nick of time Rablay appeared; he seemed to understand the situation at a glance, and broke in:

'See here, boys. I'll settle this. They're disputin' – I know they are. Want to decide with bullets whether 'Frisco or Denver's the finest city. 'Frisco's bigger and older, says Crocker; Harrison maintains Denver's better laid out. Crocker replies in his quiet way that 'Frisco ain't dead yet.' Good temper being now re-established, Rablay went on: 'I'll decide this matter right off. Crocker and Harrison shall set up drinks for the crowd till we're all laid out.

And I'll tell a story,' and he began a tale which cannot be retold here, but which delighted the boys as much by its salaciousness as by its vivacity.

Lawyer Rablay was to Garotte what novels, theatres, churches, concerts are to more favoured cities; in fact, for some six months, he and his stories constituted the chief humanizing influence in the camp. Deputations were often despatched from Doolan's to bring Rablay to the bar. The miners got up 'cases' in order to give him work. More than once both parties in a dispute, real or imaginary, engaged him, despite his protestations, as attorney, and afterwards the boys insisted that, being advocate for both sides, he was well fitted to decide the issue as judge. He had not been a month in Garotte before he was christened Judge, and every question, whether of claim-boundaries, the suitability of a nickname, or the value of 'dust,' was submitted for his decision. It cannot be asserted that his enviable position was due either to perfect impartiality or to infallible wisdom. But everyone knew that his judgments would be informed by shrewd sense and good-humour, and would be followed by a story, and woe betide the disputant whose perversity deferred that pleasure. So Garotte became a sort of theocracy, with Judge Rablay as ruler. And yet he was, perhaps, the only man in the community whose courage had never been tested or even considered.

One afternoon a man came to Garotte, who had a widespread reputation. His name was Bill Hitchcock. A marvellous shot, a first-rate poker-player, a good rider – these virtues were outweighed by his desperate temper. Though not more than five-and-twenty years of age his courage and ferocity had made him a marked man. He was said to have killed half-a-dozen men; and it was known that he had generally provoked his victims. No one could imagine why he had come to Garotte, but he had not been half an hour in the place before he was recognized. It was difficult to forget him, once seen. He was tall and broad-shouldered; his face long, with well-cut features; a brown moustache drooped negligently over his mouth; his heavy eyelids were usually half-closed, but when in moments of excitement they were suddenly updrawn, one was startled by a naked hardness of grey-green eyes.

Hitchcock spent the whole afternoon in Doolan's, scarcely speaking a word. As night drew down, the throng of miners increased. Luck had been bad for weeks; the camp was in a state of savage ill-humour. Not a few came to the saloon that night intending to show, if an opportunity offered, that neither Hitchcock nor anyone else on earth could scare them. As minute after minute passed the tension increased. Yet Hitchcock stood in the midst of them, drinking and smoking in silence, seemingly unconcerned.

Presently the Judge came in with a smile on his round face and shot off a merry remark. But the quip didn't take as it should have done. He was received with quiet nods and not with smiles and loud greetings as usual. Nothing daunted, he made his way to the bar, and, standing next to Hitchcock, called for a drink.

'Come, Doolan, a Bourbon; our only monarch!'

Beyond a smile from Doolan the remark elicited no applause. Astonished, the Judge looked about him; never in his experience had the camp been in that temper. But still he had conquered too often to doubt his powers now. Again and again he tried to break the spell – in vain. As a last resort he resolved to use his infallible recipe against ill-temper.

'Boys! I've just come in to tell you one little story; then I'll have to go.'

From force of habit the crowd drew towards him, and faces relaxed. Cheered by this he picked up his glass from the bar and turned towards his audience. Unluckily, as he moved, his right arm brushed against Hitchcock, who was looking at him with half-opened eyes. The next moment Hitchcock had picked up his glass and dashed it in the Judge's face. Startled, confounded by the unexpected suddenness of the attack, Rablay backed two or three paces, and, blinded by the rush of blood from his forehead, drew out his handkerchief. No one stirred. It was part of the unwritten law in Garotte to let every man in such circumstances play his game as he pleased. For a moment or two the Judge mopped his face, and then he started towards his assailant with his round face puckered up and out-thrust hands. He had scarcely moved, however, when Hitchcock levelled a long Navy Colt against his breast:

'Git back, you – – – – .'

The Judge stopped. He was unarmed but not cowed. All of a sudden those wary, long eyes of Hitchcock took in the fact that a score of revolvers covered him.

With lazy deliberation Dave Crocker moved out of the throng towards the combatants, and standing between them, with his revolver pointing to the ground, said sympathetically:

'Jedge, we're sorry you've been jumped, here in Garotte. Now, what would you like?'

'A fair fight,' replied Rablay, beginning again to use his handkerchief.

'Wall,' Crocker went on, after a pause for thought. 'A square fight's good but hard to get. This man,' and his head made a motion towards Hitchcock as he spoke, 'is one of the best shots there is, and I reckon you're not as good at shootin' as at – other things.' Again he paused to think, and then continued with the same deliberate air of careful reflection, 'We all cotton to you, Jedge; you know that. Suppose you pick a man who kin shoot, and leave it to him. That'd be fair, an' you kin jes' choose any of us, or one after the other. We're all willin'.'

'No,' replied the Judge, taking away the handkerchief, and showing a jagged, red line on his forehead. 'No! he struck *me*. I don't want anyone to help me, or take my place.'

'That's right,' said Crocker, approvingly; 'that's right, Jedge, we all like that, but 'tain't square, and this camp means to hev it square. You bet!' And, in the difficult circumstances, he looked round for the approval which was manifest on every one of the serious faces. Again he began: 'I guess, Jedge, you'd better take my plan, 'twould be surer. No! Wall, suppose I take two six-shooters, one loaded, the other empty, and put them under a *capote* on the table in the next room. You could both go in and draw for weapons; that's be square, I reckon?' and he waited for the Judge's reply.

'Yes,' replied Rablay, 'that'd be fair. I agree to that.'

'Hell!' exclaimed Hitchcock, 'I don't. If he wants to fight, I'm here; but I ain't goin' to take a hand in no sich derned game – with the cards stocked agen me.'

'Ain't you?' retorted Crocker, facing him, and beginning slowly. 'I reckon *you'll* play any game we say. *See!* any damned game *we* like. D'ye understand?'

As no response was forthcoming to this defiance, he went into the other room to arrange the preliminaries of the duel. A few moments passed in silence, and then he came back through the lane of men to the two combatants.

'Jedge,' he began, 'the six-shooters are there, all ready. Would you like to hev first draw, or throw for it with him?' contemptuously indicating Hitchcock with a movement of his head as he concluded.

'Let us throw,' replied Rablay, quietly.

In silence the three dice and the box were placed by Doolan on the bar. In response to Crocker's gesture the Judge took up the box and rolled out two fives and a three – thirteen. Everyone felt that he had lost the draw, but his face did not change any more than that of his adversary. In silence Hitchcock replaced the dice in the box and threw a three, a four, and a two – nine; he put down the box emphatically.

'Wall,' Crocker decided impassively, 'I guess that gives you the draw, Jedge; we throw fer high in Garotte – sometimes,' he went on, turning as if to explain to Hitchcock, but with insult in his voice, and then, 'After you, Jedge!'

Rablay passed through the crowd into the next room. There, on a table, was a small heap covered with a cloak. Silently the men pressed round, leaving Crocker between the two adversaries in the full light of the swinging lamp.

'Now, Jedge,' said Crocker, with a motion towards the table.

'No!' returned the Judge, with white, fixed face, 'he won; let him draw first. I only want a square deal.'

A low hum of surprise went round the room. Garotte was more than satisfied with its champion. Crocker looked at Hitchcock, and said:

'It's your draw, then.' The words were careless, but the tone and face spoke clearly enough.

A quick glance round the room and Hitchcock saw that he was trapped. These men would show him no mercy. At once the wild beast in him appeared. He stepped to the table, put his hand under the cloak, drew out a revolver, dropped it, pointing towards Rablay's face, and pulled the trigger. A sharp click. That revolver, at any rate, was unloaded. Quick as thought Crocker stepped between Hitchcock and the table. Then he said:

'It's your turn now, Jedge!'

As he spoke a sound, half of relief and half of content came from the throats of the onlookers. The Judge did not move. He had not quivered when the revolver was levelled within a foot of his head; he did not appear to have seen it. With set eyes and pale face, and the jagged wound on his forehead whence the blood still trickled, he had waited, and now he did not seem to hear. Again Crocker spoke:

'Come, Jedge, it's your turn.'

The sharp, loud words seemed to break the spell which had paralyzed the man. He moved to the table, and slowly drew the revolver from under the cloak. His hesitation was too much for the crowd.

'Throw it through him, Jedge! Now's your chance. Wade in, Jedge!'

The desperate ferocity of the curt phrases seemed to move him. He raised the revolver. Then came in tones of triumph:

'I'll bet high on the Jedge!'

He dropped the revolver on the floor, and fled from the room.

The first feeling of the crowd of men was utter astonishment, but in a moment or two this gave place to half-contemptuous sympathy. What expression this sentiment would have found it is impossible to say, for just then Bill Hitchcock observed with a sneer:

'As he's run, I may as well walk'; and he stepped towards the bar-room.

Instantly Crocker threw himself in front of him with his face on fire.

'Walk – will ye?' he burst out, the long-repressed rage flaming up – 'walk! when you've jumped the best man in Garotte – walk! No, by God, you'll crawl, d'ye hear? crawl – right out of this camp, right now!' and he dropped his revolver on Hitchcock's breast.

Then came a wild chorus of shouts.

'That's right! That's the talk! Crawl, will ye! Down on yer hands and knees. Crawl, damn ye! Crawl!' and a score of revolvers covered the stranger.

For a moment he stood defiant, looking his assailants in the eyes. His face seemed to have grown thinner, and his moustache twitched with the snarling movement of a brute at bay. Then he was tripped up and thrown forwards amid a storm of, 'Crawl, damn ye – crawl!' And so Hitchcock crawled, on hands and knees, out of Doolan's.

Lawyer Rablay, too, was never afterwards seen in Garotte. Men said his nerves had 'give out'.

JULY, 1892.

# DICK BOYLE'S
# BUSINESS CARD

*Bret Harte*

THE Sage Wood and Dead Flat Stage-Coach was waiting before the station. The Pine Barrens mailwagon that connected with it was long overdue with its transfer passengers, and the station had relapsed into listless expectation. Even the humours of Dick Boyle, the Chicago 'Drummer'[1] – and the, so far, solitary passenger – which had diverted the waiting loungers, began to fail in effect, though the cheerfulness of the humorist was unabated. The ostlers had slunk back into the stables, the station-keeper and stage-driver had reduced their conversation to impatient monosyllables, as if each thought the other responsible for the delay. A solitary Indian, wrapped in a commissary blanket and covered by a cast-off tall hat, crouched against the wall of the station looking stolidly at nothing. The station itself, a long rambling building containing its entire accommodation for man and beast under one monotonous shed-like roof, offered nothing to attract the eye. Still less the prospect; on the one side two miles of arid waste to the stunted far-spaced pines in the distance, known as the 'Barrens'; on the other an apparently limitless level with darker patches of sage brush, like the scars of burnt-out fires.

Dick Boyle approached the motionless Indian as a possible relief. '*You* don't seem to care much if school keeps or not, do you, Lo?'

The Indian, who had been half crouching on his upturned soles, here straightened himself with a lithe, animal-like movement, and

---

[1] 'Drummer,' *i.e.* commercial traveller or 'bagman.'

stood up. Boyle took hold of a corner of his blanket and examined it critically.

'Gov'ment ain't pampering you with A1 goods, Lo! I reckon the agent charged 'em four dollars for that. Our firm could have delivered them to you for 2 dols. 37 cents, and thrown in a box of beads in the bargain. Suthin' like this!' He took from his pocket a small box containing a gaudy bead necklace and held it up before the Indian.

The savage, who had regarded him – or rather looked beyond him – with the tolerating indifference of one interrupted by a frisking inferior animal – here suddenly changed his expression. A look of childish eagerness came into his gloomy face; he reached out his hand for the trinket.

'Hol' on!' said Boyle, hesitating for a moment; then he suddenly ejaculated, 'Well! take it, and o' these,' and drew a business card from his pocket, which he stuck in the band of the battered tall hat of the aborigine. 'There! show that to your friends, and when you're wantin' anythin' in our line—'

The interrupting roar of laughter, which came from the box-seat of the coach, was probably what Boyle was expecting, for he turned away demurely and walked towards the coach. 'All right, boys! I've squared the noble red man, and the star of Empire is taking its westward way. And I reckon our firm will do the "Great Father" business for him at about half the price that it is done in Washington.'

But at this point the ostlers came hurrying out of the stables. 'She's comin',' said one. 'That's her dust just behind the lone Pine – and by the way she's racin' I reckon she's comin' in mighty light.'

'That's so,' said the mail-agent, standing up on the box-seat for a better view, 'but darned ef I kin see any outside passengers. I reckon we haven't waited for much.'

Indeed, as the galloping horses of the incoming vehicle pulled out of the hanging dust in the distance, the solitary driver could be seen urging on his team. In a few moments more they had halted at the lower end of the station. 'Wonder what's up?' said the mail-agent.

'Nothin'! Only a big Injin scare at Pine Barrens,' said one of the ostlers. 'Injins doin' ghost dancin' – or suthin' like that – and the passengers just skunked out and went on by the other line. Thar's only one ez dar come – and she's a lady.'

'A lady?' echoed Boyle.

'Yes,' answered the driver, taking a deliberate survey of a tall, graceful girl who, waiving the gallant assistance of the station-keeper, had leaped unaided from the vehicle. 'A lady – and the Fort Commandant's darter at that! She's clar grit, you bet – a chip o' the old block. And all this means, Sonny, that you're to give up that box-seat to *her*. Miss Julia Cantire don't take anythin' less when I'm around.'

The young lady was already walking, directly and composedly, towards the waiting coach – erect, self-contained, well gloved and booted, and clothed, even in her dust cloak and cape of plain ashen merino, with the unmistakable panoply of taste and superiority. A good-sized aquiline nose, which made her handsome mouth look smaller; grey eyes, with an occasional humid yellow sparkle in their depths; brown pencilled eyebrows, and brown tendrils of hair, all seemed to Boyle to be charmingly framed in by the silver-grey veil twisted around her neck and under her oval chin. In her sober tints she appeared to him to have evoked a harmony even out of the dreadful dust around them. What *he* appeared to her was not so plain; she looked him over – he was rather short; through him – he was easily penetrable; and then her eyes rested with a frank recognition on the driver.

'Good-morning, Mr Foster,' she said, with a smile.

'Mornin', miss. I hear they're havin' an Injin scare over at the Barrens. I reckon them men must feel mighty mean at bein' stumped by a lady!'

'I don't think they believed I would go, and some of them had their wives with them,' returned the young lady indifferently; 'besides, they are Eastern people, who don't know Indians as well as *we* do, Mr Foster.'

The driver blushed with pleasure at the association. 'Yes, ma'am,' he laughed, 'I reckon the sight of even old "Fleas in the Blanket" over there,' pointing to the Indian who was walking stolidly away from the station, 'would frighten 'em out o' their boots. And yet he's got inside his hat the business card o' this gentleman – Mr Dick Boyle, travelling for the big firm o' Fletcher and Co. of Chicago' – he interpolated, rising suddenly to the formal heights of polite introduction, 'so it sorter looks ez ef any *skelpin'* was to be done it might be the other way round, ha! ha!'

Miss Cantire accepted the introduction and the joke with polite but cool abstraction, and climbed lightly into the box-seat as the mail-bags and a quantity of luggage – evidently belonging to the evading passengers – was quickly transferred to the coach. But for his fair companion, the driver would probably have given profane voice to his conviction that his vehicle was used as a 'd——d baggage truck,' but he only smiled grimly, gathered up his reins, and flicked his whip. The coach plunged forward into the dust, which instantly rose around it, and made it thereafter a mere cloud in the distance. Some of that dust for a moment overtook and hid the Indian, walking stolidly in its track, but he emerged from it at an angle, with a quickened pace and a peculiar halting trot. Yet that trot was so well sustained that in an hour he had reached a fringe of rocks and low bushes hitherto invisible through the irregularities of the apparently level plain, into which he plunged and disappeared. The dust cloud which indicated the coach – probably owning to these same irregularities – had long since been lost on the visible horizon.

The fringe which received him was really the rim of a depression quite concealed from the surface of the plain – which it followed for some miles through a tangled trough-like bottom of low trees and underbrush – and was a natural cover for wolves, coyotes, and occasionally bears, whose half-human footprint might have deceived a stranger. This did not, however, divert the Indian, who, trotting still doggedly on paused only to examine another footprint – much more frequent – the smooth, inward-toed track of moccasins. The thicket grew more dense and difficult as he went on, yet he seemed to glide through its density and darkness – an obscurity that now seemed to be stirred by other moving objects, dimly seen, and as uncertain and intangible as sunlit leaves thrilled by the wind, yet bearing a strange resemblance to human figures! Pressing a few yards further, he himself presently became a part of this shadowy procession, which on closer scrutiny revealed itself as a single file of Indians, following each other in the same tireless trot. The woods and underbrush were full of them; all moving on, as he had moved, in a line parallel with the vanishing coach. Sometimes through the openings a bared blanket was visible, but nothing more. And yet only a few hundred yards away, stretched the dusky, silent plain – vacant of sound or motion!

Meanwhile the Sage Wood and Pine Barren Stage-Coach, pro-

foundly oblivious – after the manner of all human invention – of
everything but its regular function, toiled dustily out of the higher
plain and began the grateful descent of a wooden cañon, which was,
in fact, the culminating point of the depression just described, along
which the shadowy procession was slowly advancing, hardly a mile
in the rear and flank of the vehicle. Miss Julia Cantire, who had
faced the dust volleys of the plain unflinchingly, as became a soldier's
daughter, here stood upright and shook herself – her pretty head
and figure emerging like a goddess from the enveloping silver cloud.
At least Mr Boyle, relegated to the back seat, thought so – although
her conversation and attentions had been chiefly directed to the
driver and mail-agent. Once, when he had light-heartedly addressed
a remark to her, it had been received with a distinct but unpromising
politeness that had made him desist from further attempts, yet,
without abatement of his cheerfulness, or resentment of the evident
amusement his two male companions got out of his 'snub.' Indeed,
it is to be feared that Miss Julia had certain prejudices of position,
and may have thought that a 'drummer' – or commercial traveller
– was no more fitting company for the daughter of a Major than
an ordinary pedlar. But it was more probable that Mr Boyle's
reputation as a humorist – a teller of funny stories and a boon
companion of men – was inconsistent with the feminine ideal of
high and exalted manhood. The man who 'sets the table in a roar'
is apt to be secretly detested by the sex, to say nothing of the other
obvious reasons why Juliets do not like Mercutios!

For some such cause as this Dick Boyle was obliged to silently
amuse himself alone on the back seat with those liberal powers of
observation which nature had given him. On entering the cañon he
had noticed the devious route the coach had taken to reach it, and
had already invented an improved route which should enter the
depression at the point where the Indians had already (unknown to
him) plunged into it, and had conceived a road through the tangled
brush that would shorten the distance by some miles. He had figured
it out, and believed that it 'would pay.' But by this time they were
beginning the somewhat steep and difficult ascent of the cañon on
the other side. The vehicle had not crawled many yards before it
stopped. Dick Boyle glanced around. Miss Cantire was getting
down. She had expressed a wish to walk the rest of the ascent, and
the coach was to wait for her at the top. Foster has effusively begged

her to take her own time – 'there was no hurry!' Boyle glanced a little longingly after her graceful figure, released from her cramped position on the box, as it flitted youthfully in and out of the wayside trees; he would like to have joined her in the woodland ramble, but even his good nature was not proof against her indifference. At a turn in the road they lost sight of her, and, as the driver and mail-agent were deep in a discussion about the indistinct track, Boyle lapsed into his silent study of the country. Suddenly he uttered a slight exclamation, and quietly slipped from the back of the toiling coach to the ground. The action was, however, quickly noted by the driver, who promptly put his foot on the brake and pulled up. 'Wot's up now?' he growled.

Boyle did not reply, but ran back a few steps and began searching eagerly on the ground.

'Lost suthin'?' asked Foster.

'Found something,' said Boyle, picking up a small object. 'Look at that! D——d if it isn't the card I gave that Indian four hours ago at the station!' He held up the card.

'Look yer, sonny,' retorted Foster gravely, 'ef yer wantin' to get out and hang round Miss Cantire, why don't yer say so at onct. That story won't wash!'

'Fact!' continued Boyle eagerly. 'It's the same card I stuck in his hat – there's the greasy mark in the corner. How the devil did it – how did *he* get here?'

'Better ax him,' said Foster grimly, 'ef he's anywhere round.'

'But I say, Foster, I don't like the look of this at all! Miss Cantire is alone, and—'

But a burst of laughter from Foster and the mail-agent interrupted him. 'That's so,' said Foster. 'That's your best holt! Keep it up! You jest tell her that! Say thar's another Injin skeer on; that that thar blood-thirsty ole "Fleas in His Blanket" ez on the warpath, and you're goin' to shed the last drop o' your blood defendin' her! That'll fetch her, and she ain't bin treatin' you well! G'lang!'

The horses started forward under Foster's whip, leaving Boyle standing there, half inclined to join in the laugh against himself, and yet impelled by some strange instinct to take a more serious view of his discovery. There was no doubt it was the same card he had given to the Indian. True, that Indian might have given it to another – yet, by what agency had it been brought there faster than the coach travelled on the same road, and yet invisibly to them? For an instant the humorous idea of literally accepting Foster's challenge, and communicating his discovery to Miss Cantire occurred to him; he could have made a funny story out of it, and could have amused any other girl with it, but he would not force himself upon her, and again doubted if the discovery were a matter of amusement. If it were really serious, why should he alarm her? He resolved, however, to remain on the road, and within convenient distance of her, until she returned to the coach; she could not be far away. With this purpose he walked slowly on, halting occasionally to look behind.

Meantime the coach continued its difficult ascent, a difficulty made greater by the singular nervousness of the horses, that, only with great trouble and some objurgation from the driver, could be prevented from shying from the regular track.

'Now, wot's gone o' them critters?' said the irate Foster, straining at the reins until he seemed to lift the leader back into the track again.

'Looks as ef they smelt suthin' – bar or Injin ponies,' suggested the mail-agent.

'Injin ponies?' repeated Foster scornfully.

'Fack! Injin ponies set a hoss crazy – jest as wild hosses would!'

'Whar's yer Injin ponies?' demanded Foster incredulously.

'Dunno,' said the mail-agent simply.

But here the horses again swerved so madly from some point of the thicket beside them that the coach completely left the track on the right. Luckily it was a disused trail and the ground fairly good, and Foster gave them their heads, satisfied of his ability to regain the regular road when necessary. It took some moments for him to recover complete control of the frightened animals, and then their nervousness having abated with their distance from the thicket, and the trail being less steep though more winding than the regular road, he concluded to keep it until he got to the summit, when he would regain the highway once more and await his passengers. Having done this the two men stood up on the box, and, with an anxiety they tried to conceal from each other, looked down the cañon for the lagging pedestrians.

'I hope Miss Cantire hasn't been stampeded from the track by any skeer like that,' said the mail-agent dubiously.

'Not she! She's got too much grit and *sabe* for that, unless that drummer hez caught up with her and unloaded his yarn about that kyard.'

They were the last words the men spoke. For two rifle-shots cracked from the thicket beside the road; two shots aimed with such deliberateness and precision, that the two men, mortally stricken, collapsed where they stood, hanging for a moment over the dashboard before they rolled over on the horses' backs. Nor did they remain there for long, for the next moment they were seized by half a dozen shadowy figures and with the horses and their cut traces dragged into the thicket. A half dozen, and then a dozen other shadows flitted and swarmed over, in and through the coach, reinforced by still more, until the whole vehicle seemed to be possessed, covered, and hidden by them, swaying and moving with their weight, like helpless carrion beneath a pack of ravenous wolves. Yet, even while this seething congregation was at its greatest, at some unknown signal it as suddenly dispersed, vanished, and disappeared, leaving the coach empty – vacant and void of all that had given it life, weight, animation, and purpose – a mere skeleton on the roadside. The afternoon wind blew through its open doors and ravaged rack and box as if it had been the wreck of weeks instead of minutes, and the level rays of the setting sun flashed and blazed in its windows as though fire had been added to the ruin. But even this presently faded, leaving the abandoned coach a rigid, lifeless spectre on the twilit plain.

An hour later there was the sound of hurrying hoofs and jingling accoutrements, and out of the plain swept a squad of cavalrymen bearing down upon the deserted vehicle. For a few moments they, too, seemed to surround and possess even as the other shadows had done, penetrating the woods and thicket beside it. And then as suddenly at some signal they swept forward furiously in the track of the destroying shadows.

Miss Cantire took full advantage of the suggestion 'not to hurry' in her walk with certain feminine ideas of its latitude. She gathered a few wild flowers and some berries in the underwood, inspected some birds' nests with a healthy youthful curiosity, and even took the opportunity of arranging some moist tendrils of her silky hair with something she took from the small reticule that hung coquettishly from her girdle. It was, indeed, some twenty minutes before she emerged into the road again; the vehicle had evidently disappeared in a turn of the long, winding ascent, but just ahead of her was that dreadful man, the 'Chicago drummer'. She was not vain, but she made no doubt that he was waiting there for her. There was no avoiding him, but his companionship could be made a brief one. She began to walk with ostentatious swiftness.

Boyle, whose concern for her safety was secretly relieved at this, began to walk forward briskly too without looking around. Miss Cantire was not prepared for this; it looked so ridiculously as if she were chasing him! She hesitated slightly, but now as she was nearly abreast of him she was obliged to keep on.

'I think you do well to hurry, Miss Cantire,' he said as she passed. 'I've lost sight of the coach for some time, and I dare say they're already waiting for us at the summit.'

Miss Cantire did not like this any better. To go on beside this dreadful man, scrambling breathlessly after the stage – for all the world like an absorbed and sentimentally belated pair of picknickers – was really *too* much. 'Perhaps if *you* ran on and told them I was coming as fast as I could,' she suggested tentatively.

'It would be as much as my life is worth to appear before Foster without you,' he said laughingly. 'You've only got to hurry on a little faster.'

But the young lady resented this being driven by a 'drummer'. She began to lag, depressing her pretty brows ominously.

'Let me carry your flowers,' said Boyle. He had noticed that she was finding some difficulty in holding up her skirt and the nosegay at the same time.

'No! no!' she said in hurried horror at this new suggestion of their companionship. 'Thank you very much – but they're really not worth keeping – I am going to throw them away. There!' she added, tossing them impatiently in the dust.

But she had not reckoned on Boyle's perfect good-humour. That gentle idiot stooped down, actually gathered them up again, and was following! She hurried on; if she could only get to the coach first, ignoring him! But a vulgar man like that would be sure to hand them to her with some joke! Then she lagged again – she was getting tired, and she could see no sign of the coach. The drummer, too, was also lagging behind – at a respectful distance, like a groom or one of her father's troopers. Nevertheless, this did not put her in a much better humour, and, halting until he came abreast of her, said impatiently: 'I don't see why Mr Foster should think it necessary to send any one to look after me.'

'He didn't,' returned Boyle simply. '*I* got down to pick up something.'

'To pick up something?' she returned incredulously.

'Yes. *That.*' He held out the card. 'It's the card of our firm.'

Miss Cantire smiled ironically. 'You are certainly devoted to your business.'

'Well, yes,' returned Boyle good-humouredly. 'You see, I reckon it don't pay to do anything half-way. And whatever I do, I mean to keep my eyes about me.' In spite of her prejudice, Miss Cantire could see that these necessary organs, if rather flippant, were honest. 'Yes, I suppose there isn't much on that I don't take in. Why now, Miss Cantire, there's that fancy dust-cloak you're wearing – it isn't in our line of goods – nor in anybody's line west of Chicago; it came from Boston or New York, and was made for home consumption! But your hat – and mighty pretty it is too, as *you've* fixed it up – is only regular Dunstable stock, which we could put down at Pine Barren for four and a half cents a piece, net. Yet I suppose you paid nearly twenty-five cents for it at the Agency!'

Oddly enough this cool appraisement of her costume did not incense the young lady as it ought to have done. On the contrary, for some occult feminine reason, it amused and interested her. It would be such a good story to tell her friends of a 'drummer's' idea of gallantry; and to tease the flirtatious young West Pointer who had just joined. And the appraisement was truthful – Major Cantire had only his pay – and Miss Cantire had been obliged to select that hat from the Government stores.

'Are you in the habit of giving this information to ladies you meet in travelling?' she asked.

'Well, no!' answered Boyle – 'for that's just where you have to keep your eyes open. Most of 'em wouldn't like it, and it's no use aggravating a possible customer. But you are not that kind.'

Miss Cantire was silent. She knew she was not of that kind, but she did not require his vulgar endorsement. She pushed on for some moments alone, when suddenly he hailed her. She turned impatiently. He was carefully examining the road on both sides.

'We have either lost our way,' he said, rejoining her, 'or the coach has turned off somewhere. These tracks are not fresh, and as they are all going the same way they were made by the up coach last night. They're not *our* tracks; I thought it strange we hadn't sighted the coach by this time.'

'And then—' said Miss Cantire impatiently.

'We must turn back until we find them again.'

The young lady frowned. 'Why not keep on until we get to the top?' she said pettishly. 'I'm sure *I* shall—' She stopped suddenly as she caught sight of his grave face and keen, observant eyes. 'Why can't we go on as we are?'

'Because we are expected to come back to the *coach* – and not to the summit merely. These are the "orders", and you know you are a soldier's daughter!' He laughed as he spoke, but there was a certain quiet deliberation in his manner that impressed her. When he added, after a pause, 'we must get back and find where the tracks turned off,' she obeyed without a word.

They walked for some time eagerly searching for signs of the missing vehicle. A curious interest, and a new reliance in Boyle's judgment obliterated her previous annoyance, and made her more natural. She ran ahead of him with youthful eagerness, examining the ground, following a false clue with great animation, and confessing her defeat with a charming laugh. And it was she who, after retracing their steps for ten minutes, found the diverging track with a girlish cry of triumph. Boyle, who had followed her movements quite as interestedly as her discovery, looked a little grave as he noticed the deep indentations made by the struggling horses. Miss Cantire detected the change in his face; ten minutes before she would never have observed it. 'I suppose we had better follow the new track,' she said inquiringly, as he seemed to hesitate.

'Certainly,' he said quickly, as if coming to a prompt decision. 'That is safest.'

'What do you think has happened? The ground looks very much cut up,' she said in a confidential tone, as new to her as her previous observation of him.

'A horse has probably stumbled and they've taken the old trail as less difficult,' said Boyle promptly. In his heart he did not believe it, yet he knew that if anything serious had threatened them the coach would have waited in the road. 'It's an easier trail for us, though I suppose it's a little longer,' he added presently.

'You take everything so good-humouredly, Mr Boyle,' she said after a pause.

'It's the way to do business, Miss Cantire,' he said. 'A man in my line has to cultivate it.'

She wished he hadn't said that, but, nevertheless, she returned a little archly: 'But you haven't any business with the stage company nor with *me*, although I admit I intend to get my Dunstable hereafter from your firm at the wholesale prices.'

Before he could reply, the detonation of two gunshots, softened by distance, floated down from the ridge above them. 'There!' said Miss Cantire eagerly. 'Do you hear that?'

His face was turned towards the distant ridge, but really that she might not question his eyes. She continued with animation: 'That's from the coach – to guide us – don't you see?'

'Yes,' he returned, with a quick laugh, 'and it says hurry up – mighty quick – we're tired waiting – so we'd better push on.'

'Why don't you answer back with your revolver?' she asked.

'Haven't got one,' he said.

'Haven't got one?' she repeated in genuine surprise. 'I thought you gentlemen who are travelling always carried one. Perhaps it's inconsistent with your gospel of good-humour.'

'That's just it, Miss Cantire,' he said, with a laugh; 'you've hit it.'

'Why,' she said hesitatingly, 'even *I* have a derringer – a very little one, you know, which I carry in my reticule. Captain Richards gave it to me.' She opened her reticule and showed a pretty ivory-handled pistol. The look of joyful surprise which came into his face changed quickly as she cocked it and lifted it into the air. He seized her arm quickly.

'No, please don't, you might want it – I mean the report won't carry far enough. It's a very useful little thing, for all that, but it's only effective at close quarters.' He kept the pistol in his hand as they walked on. But Miss Cantire noticed this, also his evident satisfaction when she had at first produced it, and his concern when she was about to discharge it uselessly. She was a clever girl, and a frank one to those she was inclined to trust. And she began to trust this stranger. A smile stole along her oval cheek.

'I really believe you're afraid of something, Mr Boyle,' she said, without looking up. 'What is it? You haven't got that Indian scare, too?'

Boyle had no false shame. 'I think I have,' he returned, with equal frankness. 'You see, I don't understand Indians as well as you – and Foster.'

'Well, you take my word and Foster's that there is not the least danger from them. About here they are merely grown-up children, cruel and destructive as most children are; but they know their masters by this time, and the old days of promiscuous scalping are over. The only other childish propensity they keep is thieving. Even then they only steal what they actually want – horses, guns, and powder. A coach can go where an ammunition or an emigrant wagon can't. So your trunk of samples is quite safe with Foster.'

Boyle did not think it necessary to protest. Perhaps he was thinking of something else.

'I've a mind,' she went on slyly, 'to tell you something more. Confidence for confidence: as you've told me *your* trade secrets, I'll tell you one of *ours*. Before we left Pine Barrens, my father ordered a small escort of cavalrymen to be in readiness to join that coach if the scouts, who were watching, thought it necessary. So, you see, I'm something of a fraud as regards my reputation for courage.'

'That doesn't follow,' said Boyle admiringly, 'for your father must have thought there was some danger, or he wouldn't have taken that precaution.'

'Oh, it wasn't for me,' said the young girl quickly.

'Not for you?' repeated Boyle.

Miss Cantire stopped short, with a pretty flush of colour and an adorable laugh. 'There! I've done it; so I might as well tell the whole story. But I can trust you, Mr Boyle.' (She faced him with clear, penetrating eyes.) 'Well,' she laughed again, 'you might have noticed that we had a quantity of baggage of passengers who didn't go! Well, those passengers never intended to go, and hadn't any baggage! Do you understand? Those innocent-looking heavy trunks contained carbines and cartridges from our Post for Fort Taylor' – she made him a mischievous curtsy – 'under *my* charge! And,' she added, enjoying his astonishment, 'as you saw, I brought them through safe to the station, and had them transferred to this coach with less fuss and trouble than a commissary transport and escort would have made.'

'And they were in *this* coach?' repeated Boyle abstractedly.

'Were? They *are!*' said Miss Cantire.

'Then the sooner I get you back to your treasure again the better,' said Boyle, with a laugh. 'Does Foster know it?'

'Of course not! Do you suppose I'd tell it to anybody but a stranger to the place? Perhaps, like you, I know when and to whom to impart information,' she said mischievously.

Whatever was in Boyle's mind he had space for profound and admiring astonishment of the young lady before him. The girlish simplicity and trustfulness of her revelation seemed as inconsistent with his previous impression of her reserve and independence, as her girlish reasoning and manner were now delightfully at variance with her tallness, her aquiline nose and her erect figure. Mr Boyle, like most short men, was apt to overestimate the qualities of size.

They walked on for some moments in silence. The ascent was comparatively easy but devious, and Boyle could see that this new *détour* would take them still some time to reach the summit. Miss Cantire at least voiced the thought in his own mind. 'I wonder what induced them to turn off here? and if you hadn't been so clever as to discover their tracks, how could we have found them. But,' she added, with feminine logic, 'that, of course, is why they fired those shots.'

Boyle remembered, however, that the shots came from another direction, but did not correct her conclusion. Nevertheless, he said lightly: 'Perhaps even Foster might have had an Indian scare.'

'He ought to know "friendlies" or "Government reservation men" better by this time,' said Miss Cantire; 'however, there is something in that. Do you know,' she added, with a laugh, 'though I haven't your keen eyes I'm gifted with a keen scent, and once or twice I've thought I *smelt* Indians! That peculiar odour of their camps, which is unlike anything else, and which one detects even in their ponies. I used to notice it when I rode one; no amount of grooming could take it away.'

'I don't suppose that the intensity or degree of this odour would give you any idea of the hostile or friendly feelings of the Indians towards you?' asked Boyle grimly.

Although the remark was consistent with Boyle's objectionable reputation as a humorist, Miss Cantire deigned to receive it with a smile, at which Boyle, who was a little relieved by their security so far, and their nearness to their journey's end, developed further ingenious trifling until, at the end of an hour, they stood upon the plain again.

There was no sign of the coach, but its fresh track was visible leading along the bank of the ravine towards the intersection of the road they should have come by, and to which the coach had indubitably returned. Mr Boyle drew a long breath. They were comparatively safe from any visible attack now. At the end of ten minutes Miss Cantire, from her superior height, detected the top of the missing vehicle appearing above the stunted bushes at the junction of the highway.

'Would you mind throwing those old flowers away now,' she said, glancing at the spoils which Boyle still carried.

'Why?' he asked.

'Oh, they're too ridiculous. Please do.'

'May I keep one?' he asked, with the first intonation of masculine weakness in his voice.

'If you like,' she said, a little coldly.

Boyle selected a small spray of myrtle and cast the other flowers obediently aside.

'Dear me, how ridiculous!' she said.

'What is ridiculous?' he asked, lifting his eyes to hers with a slight colour. But he saw that she was straining her eyes in the distance.

'Why, there doesn't seem to be any horses to the coach!'

He looked. Through a gap in the furze he could see the vehicle now quite distinctly, standing empty, horseless and alone. He glanced hurriedly around them; on the one side a few rocks protected them from the tangled rim of the ridge; on the other stretched the plain. 'Sit down, don't move until I return,' he said quickly. 'Take that.' He handed back her pistol, and ran quickly to the coach. It was no illusion – there it stood vacant, abandoned – its dropped pole, and cut traces, showing too plainly the fearful haste of its desertion! A light step behind him made him turn. It was Miss Cantire, pink and breathless, carrying the cocked derringer in her hand. 'How foolish of you – without a weapon,' she gasped in explanation.

Then they both stared at the coach, the empty plain, and at each other! After their tedious ascent, their long *détour*, their protracted expectancy and their eager curiosity, there was such a suggestion of hideous mockery in this vacant, useless vehicle – apparently left to them in what seemed their utter abandonment – that it instinctively affected them alike. And as I am writing of human nature I am compelled to say that they both burst into a fit of laughter that for the moment stopped all other expression!

'It was so kind of them to leave the coach,' said Miss Cantire faintly, as she took her handkerchief from her wet and mirthful eyes. 'But what made them run away?'

Boyle did not reply, he was eagerly examining the coach. In that brief hour and a half the dust of the plain had blown thick upon it, and covered any foul stain or blot that might have suggested the awful truth. Even the soft imprint of the Indians' moccasined feet had been trampled out by the later horse-hoofs of the cavalrymen. It was these that first attracted Boyle's attention; but he thought them the marks made by the plunging of the released coach horses.

Not so his companion! She was examining them more closely, and suddenly lifted her bright, animated face. 'Look!' she said, 'our men have been here, and have had a hand in this – whatever it is.'

'Our men?' repeated Boyle blankly.

'Yes! – troopers from the Post – the escort I told you of. These are the prints of the regulation cavalry horseshoe – not of Foster's team, nor of Indian ponies, who never have any! Don't you see?' she went on eagerly, 'our men have got wind of something and have galloped down here – along the ridge – see!' she went on, pointing to the hoof-prints coming from the plain. 'They've anticipated some Indian attack and secured everything.'

'But if they were the same escort you spoke of they must have known you were here, and have—' he was about to say 'abandoned you,' but checked himself, remembering they were her father's soldiers.

'They knew I could take care of myself, and wouldn't stand in the way of their duty,' said the young girl, anticipating him with quick professional pride that seemed to fit her aquiline nose and tall figure. 'And if they knew that,' she added, softening with a mischievous smile, 'they also knew, of course, that I was protected by a gallant stranger vouched for by Mr Foster! No!' she added, with a certain blind, devoted confidence, which Boyle noticed with a slight wince that she had never shown before, 'it's all right! and

"by orders", Mr Boyle, and when they've done their work they'll
be back.'

But Boyle's masculine common-sense was, perhaps, safer than
Miss Cantire's feminine faith and inherited discipline, for in an
instant he suddenly comprehended the actual truth! The Indians had
been there *first*; *they* had despoiled the coach and got off safely with
their booty and prisoners on the approach of the escort – who were
now naturally pursuing them with a fury aroused by the belief
that their commander's daughter was one of their prisoners. This
conviction was a dreadful one, yet a relief as far as the young girl
was concerned. But should he tell her? No! Better that she should
keep her calm faith in the triumphant promptness of the soldiers –
and their speedy return.

'I dare say you are right,' he said cheerfully, 'and let us be thankful
that in the empty coach you'll have at least a half-civilised shelter
until they return. Meantime I'll go and reconnoitre a little.'

'I will go with you,' she said.

But Boyle pointed out to her so strongly the necessity of her
remaining to wait for the return of the soldiers that, being also
fagged out by her long climb, she obediently consented, while he,
even with his inspiration of the truth, did not believe in the return
of the despoilers, and knew she would be safe.

He made his way to the nearest thicket, where he rightly believed
the ambush had been prepared, and to which undoubtedly they first
retreated with their booty. He expected to find some signs or traces
of their spoil which in their haste they had to abandon. He was
more successful than he anticipated. A few steps into the thicket
brought him full upon a realisation of more than his worst convic-
tions – the dead body of Foster! Near it lay the body of the mail-
agent. Both had been evidently dragged into the thicket from where
they fell, scalped, and half stripped. There was no evidence of any
later struggle; they must have been dead when they were brought
there.

Boyle was neither a hard-hearted nor an unduly sensitive man.
His vocation had brought him peril enough by land and water; he
had often rendered valuable assistance to others, his sympathy never
confusing his directness and common-sense. He was sorry for these
two men, and would have fought to have saved them. But he had
no imaginative ideas of death. And his keen perception of the truth

was consequently sensitively alive only to that grotesqueness of aspect which too often the hapless victims of violence are apt to assume. He saw no agony in the vacant eyes of the two men lying on their backs in apparently the complacent abandonment of drunkenness, which was further simulated by their tumbled and disordered hair matted by coagulated blood which, however, had lost its sanguine colour. He thought only of the unsuspecting girl sitting in the lonely coach, and hurriedly dragged them further into the bushes. In doing this he discovered a loaded revolver and flask of spirit which had been lying under them, and promptly secured them. A few paces away lay the coveted trunks of arms and ammunitions, their lids wrenched off and their contents gone. He noticed with a grim smile that his own trunks of samples had shared a like fate, but was delighted to find that while the brighter trifles had attracted the Indians' childish cupidity they had overlooked a heavy, black merino shawl of a cheap but serviceable quality. It would help to protect Miss Cantire from the evening wind which was already rising over the chill and stark plain. It also occurred to him that she would need water after her parched journey, and he resolved to look for a spring, being rewarded at last by a trickling rill near the ambushed camp. But he had no utensil except the spirit flask, which he finally emptied of its contents and replaced with the pure water – a heroic sacrifice to a traveller who knew the comfort of a stimulant. He retraced his steps, and was just emerging from the thicket when his quick eye caught sight of a moving shadow before him close to the ground, which set the hot blood coursing through his veins.

It was the figure of an Indian crawling on his hands and knees towards the coach, scarcely forty yards away. For the first time that afternoon Boyle's calm good-humour was overswept by a blind and furious rage. Yet, even then he was sane enough to remember that a pistol-shot would alarm the girl, and to keep that weapon as a last resource. For an instant he crept forward as silently and stealthily as the savage, and then, with a sudden bound, leaped upon him, driving his head and shoulders down against the rocks before he could utter a cry, and sending the scalping-knife he was carrying between his teeth flying with the shock from his battered jaw. Boyle seized it – his knee still in the man's back – but the prostrate body never moved beyond a slight contraction of the lower limbs. The shock had broken the Indian's neck. He turned the inert man on his back – the head hung loosely on the side. But in that brief instant Boyle had recognised the 'friendly' Indian of the station to whom he had given the card.

He rose dizzily to his feet. The whole action had passed in a few seconds of time, and had not even been noticed by the sole occupant of the coach. He mechanically cocked his revolver, but the man beneath him never moved again. Neither was there any sign of flight or reinforcement from the thicket around him. Again the whole truth flashed upon him. This spy and traitor had been left behind by the marauders to return to the station and avert suspicion; he had been lurking around but, being without firearms, had not dared to attack the pair together.

It was a moment or two before Boyle regained his usual elastic good-humour. Then he coolly returned to the spring, 'washed himself of the Indian,' as he grimly expressed it to himself, brushed his clothes, picked up the shawl and flask, and returned to the coach. It was getting dark now, but the glow of the western sky shone unimpeded through the windows, and the silence gave him a great fear. He was relieved, however, on opening the door, to find Miss Cantire sitting stiffly in a corner. 'I am sorry I was so long,' he said apologetically to her attitude, 'but—'

'I suppose you took your own time,' she interrupted in a voice of injured tolerance. 'I don't blame you; anything's better than being cooped up in this tiresome stage for goodness knows how long!'

'I was hunting for water,' he said humbly, 'and have brought you some.' He handed her the flask.

'And I see you have had a wash,' she said, a little enviously. 'How spick and span you look! But what's the matter with your necktie?'

He put his hand to his neck hurriedly. His necktie was loose, and had twisted to one side in the struggle. He coloured quite as much from the sensitiveness of a studiously neat man as from the fear of discovery. 'And what's that?' she added, pointing to the shawl.

'One of my samples that I suppose was turned out of the coach and forgotten in the transfer,' he said glibly. 'I thought it might keep you warm.'

She looked at it dubiously and laid it gingerly aside. 'You don't mean to say you go about with such things *openly*?' she said querulously.

'Yes, one mustn't lose a chance of trade, you know,' he resumed, with a smile.

'And you haven't found this journey very profitable,' she said dryly. 'You certainly are devoted to your business!' After a pause, discontentedly: 'It's quite night already – we can't sit here in the dark.'

'We can take one of the coach lamps inside; they're still there. I've been thinking the matter over, and I reckon if we leave one lighted outside the coach it may guide your friends back.' He *had* considered it, and believed that the audacity of the act, coupled with the knowledge the Indians must have of the presence of the soldiers in the vicinity, would deter rather than invite their approach.

She brightened considerably with the coach lamp which he lit and brought inside. By its light she watched him curiously. His face was slightly flushed and his eyes very bright and keen looking. Man-killing, except with old professional hands, has the disadvantage of affecting the circulation.

But Miss Cantire had noticed that the flask smelt of whisky. The poor man had probably fortified himself from the fatigues of the day.

'I suppose you are getting bored by this delay,' she said tentatively.

'Not at all,' he replied. 'Would you like to play cards? I've got a pack in my pocket. We can use the middle seat as a table, and hang the lantern by the window strap.'

She assented languidly from the back seat; he on the front seat, with the middle seat for a table between them. First, Mr Boyle showed her some tricks with the cards and kindled her momentary and flashing interest in a mysteriously evoked but evanescent knave. Then they played euchre, at which Miss Cantire cheated adorably, and Mr Boyle lost game after game shamelessly. Then once or twice Miss Cantire was fain to put her cards to her mouth to conceal an apologetic yawn, and her blue-veined eyelids grew heavy. Where-upon Mr Boyle suggested that she should make herself comfortable in the corner of the coach with as many cushions as she liked and the despised shawl, while he took the night air in a prowl around the coach and a look-out for the returning party. Doing so, he was delighted, after a turn or two, to find her asleep and so returned contentedly to his sentry round.

He was some distance from the coach when a low moaning sound in the thicket presently increased until it rose and fell in a prolonged howl that was repeated from the darkened plains beyond. He recognised the voice of wolves; he instinctively felt the sickening cause of it. They had scented the dead bodies, and he now regretted that he had left his own victim so near the coach. He was hastening thither when a cry, this time human and more terrifying, came from the coach. He turned towards it as its door flew open and Miss Cantire came rushing towards him. Her face was colourless, her eyes wild with fear and her tall, slim figure trembled convulsively as she frantically caught at the lapels of his coat, as if to hide herself within its folds, and gasped breathlessly:

'What is it? O Mr Boyle, save me!'

'They are wolves,' he said hurriedly. 'But there is no danger; they would never attack you; you were safe where you were; let me lead you back.'

But she remained rooted to the spot, still clinging desperately to his coat. 'No, no!' she said, 'I dare not! I heard that awful cry in my sleep. I looked out and saw it – a dreadful creature with yellow eyes and tongue, and a sickening breath as it passed between the wheels just below me. Ah! what's that?' and she again lapsed in nervous terror against him.

Boyle passed his arm around her promptly, firmly, masterfully. She seemed to feel the implied protection, and yielded to it gratefully, with the further breakdown of a sob. 'There is no danger,' he repeated cheerfully. 'Wolves are not good to look at, I know, but they wouldn't have attacked you. The beast only scents some carrion on the plain, and you probably frightened him more than he did you. Lean on me,' he continued as her step tottered, 'you will be better in the coach.'

'And you won't leave me alone again?' she said, in hesitating terror.

'No!'

He supported her to the coach gravely, gently – her master and still more his own – for all that her beautiful loosened hair was against his cheek and shoulder, its perfume in his nostrils, and the contour of her lithe and perfect figure against his own. He helped her back into the coach – with the aid of the cushions and shawl arranged a reclining couch for her on the back seat, and then resumed his old place patiently. By degrees the colour came back to her face – as much of it as was not hidden by her handkerchief.

Then a tremulous voice behind it began a half-smothered apology. 'I am *so* ashamed, Mr Boyle – I really could not help it! But it was so sudden – and so horrible! I shouldn't have been afraid of it had it been really an Indian with a scalping-knife – instead of that beast! I don't know why I did it – but I was alone – and seemed to be dead – and you were dead too – and they were coming to eat me! They do, you know – you said so just now! Perhaps I was dreaming. I don't know what you must think of me – I had no idea I was such a coward!'

But Boyle protested indignantly. He was sure if *he* had been asleep and had not known what wolves were before, he would have been equally frightened. She must try to go to sleep again – he was sure she could – and he would not stir from the coach until she waked, or her friends came.

She grew quieter presently, and took away the handkerchief from a mouth that smiled though it still quivered; then reaction began, and her tired nerves brought her languor and finally repose. Boyle watched the shadows thicken around her long lashes until they lay softly on the faint flush that sleep was bringing to her cheek; her delicate lips parted, and her quick breath at last came with the regularity of slumber.

So she slept, and he, sitting silently opposite her, dreamed – the old dream that comes to most good men and true once in their lives. He scarcely moved until the dawn lightened with opal the dreary plain, bringing back the horizon and day, when he woke from his dream with a sigh, and then a laugh. Then he listened for the sound of distant hoofs, and hearing them, crept noiselessly from the coach. A compact body of horsemen were bearing down upon it. He rose quickly to meet them, and throwing up his hand, brought them to a halt at some distance from the coach. They spread out, resolving themselves into a dozen troopers and a smart young cadet-like officer.

'If you are seeking Miss Cantire,' he said in a quiet, businesslike tone, 'she is quite safe in the coach and asleep. She knows nothing yet of what has happened, and believes it is you who have taken everything away for security against an Indian attack. She has had a pretty rough night – what with her fatigue and her alarm at the wolves – and I thought it best to keep the truth from her as long as possible, and I would advise you to break it to her gently.' He then briefly told the story of their experiences, omitting only his own personal encounter with the Indian. A new pride, which was perhaps the result of his vigil, prevented him.

The young officer glanced at him with as much courtesy as might be afforded to a civilian intruding upon active military operations. 'I am sure Major Cantire will be greatly obliged to you when he knows it,' he said politely, 'and as we intend to harness up and take the coach back to Sage Brush station immediately you will have an opportunity of telling him.'

'I am not going back by the coach to Sage Brush,' said Boyle quietly. 'I have already lost twelve hours of my time – as well as my trunk – on this picnic, and I reckon the least Major Cantire can do is to let me take one of your horses to the next station in time to catch the down coach. I can do it, if I set out at once.'

Boyle heard his name, with the familiar prefix of 'Dicky,' given to the officer by a commissary servant, whom he recognised as having met at the Agency, and the words 'Chicago drummer' added, while a perceptible smile went throughout the group. 'Very well, sir,' said the officer, with a familiarity a shade less respectful than his previous formal manner. 'You can take the horse, as I believe the Indians have already made free with your samples. Give him a mount, sergeant.'

The two men walked towards the coach. Boyle lingered a moment at the window to show him the figure of Miss Cantire still peacefully slumbering among her pile of cushions, and then turned quietly away. A moment later he was galloping on one of the trooper's horses across the empty plain.

Miss Cantire awoke presently to the sound of a familiar voice and the sight of figures that she knew. But the young officer's first words of explanation – a guarded account of the pursuit of the Indians and the recapture of the arms, suppressing the killing of Foster and the mail-agent – brought a change to her brightened face and a wrinkle to her pretty brow. 'But Mr Boyle said nothing of this to me,' she asked, sitting up. 'Where is he?'

'Already on his way to the next station on one of our horses! Wanted to catch the down stage and get a new box of samples, I fancy, as the braves had rigged themselves out with his laces and ribbons. Said he'd lost time enough on this picnic,' returned the young officer, with a laugh. 'Smart business chap; but I hope he didn't bore you?'

Miss Cantire felt her cheek flush, and bit her lip. 'I found him most kind and considerate, Mr Ashford,' she said coldly. 'He may have thought the escort could have joined the coach a little earlier, and saved all this; but he was too much of a gentleman to say anything about it to *me*,' she added dryly, with a slight elevation of her aquiline nose.

Nevertheless, Boyle's last words stung her deeply. To hurry off, too, without saying 'good-bye', or even asking how she slept! No doubt he *had* lost time, and was tired of her company, and thought more of his precious samples than of her! After all, it was like him, to rush off for an order!

She was half inclined to call the young officer back and tell him how Boyle had criticised her costume on the road. But Mr Ashford was at that time entirely preoccupied with his men around the ledge of rock and brushes some yards from the coach, yet not so far away but that she could hear what they said. 'I'll swear there was no dead Injin here when we came yesterday! We searched the whole place – by daylight, too – for any sign. The Injin was killed in his tracks by some one last night. It's like Dick Boyle, lieutenant, to have done it, and like him to have said nothin' to frighten the young lady. He knows when to keep his mouth shut – and when to open it.'

Miss Cantire sank back in her corner as the officer turned and approached the coach. The incident of the past night flashed back upon her – Mr Boyle's long absence, his flushed face, twisted neck-tie, and enforced cheerfulness. She was shocked, amazed, dis-comfited – and admiring! And this hero had been sitting opposite to her, silent all the rest of the night!

'Did Mr Boyle say anything of an Indian attack last night?' asked Ashford. 'Did you hear anything?'

'Only the wolves howling,' said Miss Cantire. 'Mr Boyle was away twice.' She was strangely reticent – in complimentary imi-tation of her missing hero.

'There's a dead Indian here who has been killed,' began Ashford.

'Oh, please don't say anything more, Mr Ashford,' interrupted the young lady, 'but let us get away from this horrid place at once. Do get the horses in. I can't stand it.'

But the horses were already harnessed and mounted, postillion-wise, by the troopers. The vehicle was ready to start when Miss Cantire called 'Stop!'

When Ashford presented himself at the door, the young lady was upon her hands and knees, searching the bottom of the coach. 'Oh dear! I've lost something. I must have dropped it on the road,' she said breathlessly, with pink cheeks. 'You must positively wait and let me go back and find it. I won't be long. You know there's "no hurry."'

Mr Ashford stared as Miss Cantire skipped like a schoolgirl from the coach and ran down the trail by which she and Boyle had approached the coach the night before. She had not gone far before she came upon the withered flowers he had thrown away at her command. 'It must be about here,' she murmured. Suddenly she uttered a cry of delight, and picked up the business card that Boyle had shown her. Then she looked furtively around her, and selecting a sprig of myrtle among the cast-off flowers, concealed it in her mantle and ran back, glowing, to the coach. 'Thank you! All right, I've found it,' she called to Ashford, with a dazzling smile, and leaped inside.

The coach drove on, and Miss Cantire alone in its recesses drew the myrtle from her mantle and folding it carefully in her handker-chief, placed it in her reticule. Then she drew out the card, read its dryly practical information over and over again, examined the soiled edges, brushed them daintily, and held it for a moment, with eyes that saw not, motionless in her hand. Then she raised it slowly to her lips, rolled it into a spiral, and, loosening a hook and eye, thrust it gently into her bosom.

And Dick Boyle, galloping away to the distant station, did not know that the first step towards a realisation of his foolish dream had been taken!

# WAR

## *Jack London*

HE was a young man, not more than twenty-four or five, and he might have sat his horse with the careless grace of his youth had he not been so catlike and tense. His black eyes roved everywhere, catching the movements of twigs and branches where small birds hopped, questing ever onward through the changing vistas of trees and brush, and returning always to the clumps of undergrowth on either side. And as he watched, so did he listen, though he rode on in silence, save for the boom of heavy guns from far to the west. This had been sounding monotonously in his ears for hours, and only its cessation would have aroused his notice. For he had business closer to hand. Across his saddle-bow was balanced a carbine.

So tensely was he strung, that a bunch of quail, exploding into flight from under his horse's nose, startled him to such an extent that automatically, instantly, he had reined in and fetched the carbine halfway to his shoulder. He grinned sheepishly, recovered himself, and rode on. So tense was he, so bent upon the work he had to do, that the sweat stung his eyes unwiped, and unheeded rolled down his nose and spattered his saddle pommel. The band of his cavalry-man's hat was fresh-stained with sweat. The roan horse under him was likewise wet. It was high noon of a breathless day of heat. Even the birds and squirrels did not dare the sun, but sheltered in shady hiding places among the trees.

Man and horse were littered with leaves and dusted with yellow pollen, for the open was ventured no more than was compulsory. They kept to the brush and trees, and invariably the man halted and peered out before crossing a dry glade or naked stretch of upland pasturage. He worked always to the north, though his way was devious, and it was from the north that he seemed most to apprehend that for which he was looking. He was no coward, but his courage was only that of the average civilized man, and he was looking to live, not die.

Up a small hillside he followed a cowpath through such dense scrub that he was forced to dismount and lead his horse. But when the path swung around to the west, he abandoned it and headed to the north again along the oak-covered top of the ridge.

The ridge ended in a steep descent – so steep that he zig-zagged back and forth across the face of the slope, sliding and stumbling among the dead leaves and matted vines and keeping a watchful eye on the horse above that threatened to fall down upon him. The sweat ran from him, and the pollen-dust, settling pungently in mouth and nostrils, increased his thirst. Try as he would, nevertheless the descent was noisy, and frequently he stopped, panting in the dry heat and listening for any warning from beneath.

At the bottom he came out on a flat, so densely forested that he could not make out its extent. Here the character of the woods changed, and he was able to remount. Instead of the twisted hillside oaks, tall straight trees, big-trunked and prosperous, rose from the damp fat soil. Only here and there were thickets, easily avoided, while he encountered winding, park-like glades where the cattle had pastured in the days before war had run them off.

His progress was more rapid now, as he came down into the valley, and at the end of half an hour he halted at an ancient rail fence on the edge of a clearing. He did not like the openness of it, yet his path lay across to the fringe of trees that marked the banks of the stream. It was a mere quarter of a mile across that open, but the thought of venturing out in it was repugnant. A rifle, a score of them, a thousand, might lurk in that fringe by the stream.

Twice he essayed to start, and twice he paused. He was appalled by his own loneliness. The pulse of war that beat from the west suggested the companionship of battling thousands; here was naught but silence, and himself, and possible death-dealing bullets from a myriad ambushes. And yet his task was to find what he feared to find. He must go on, and on, till somewhere, some time, he encountered another man, or other men, from the other side, scouting, as he was scouting, to make report, as he must make report, of having come in touch.

Changing his mind, he skirted inside the woods for a distance, and again peeped forth. This time, in the middle of the clearing, he saw a small farmhouse. There were no signs of life. No smoke curled from the chimney, not a barnyard fowl clucked and strutted. The kitchen door stood open, and he gazed so long and hard into the black aperture that it seemed almost that a farmer's wife must emerge at any moment.

He licked the pollen and dust from his dry lips, stiffened himself, mind and body, and rode out into the blazing sunshine. Nothing stirred. He went on past the house, and approached the wall of trees and bushes by the river's bank. One thought persisted maddeningly. It was of the crash into his body of a high-velocity bullet. It made him feel very fragile and defenseless, and he crouched lower in the saddle.

Tethering his horse in the edge of the wood, he continued a hundred yards on foot till he came to the stream. Twenty feet wide it was, without perceptible current, cool and inviting, and he was very thirsty. But he waited inside his screen of leafage, his eyes fixed on the screen on the opposite side. To make the wait endurable, he sat down, his carbine resting on his knees. The minutes passed, and slowly his tenseness relaxed. At last he decided there was no danger; but just as he prepared to part the bushes and bend down to the water, a movement among the opposite bushes caught his eye.

It might be a bird. But he waited. Again there was an agitation of the bushes, and then, so suddenly that it almost startled a cry from him, the bushes parted and a face peered out. It was a face covered with several weeks' growth of ginger-colored beard. The eyes were blue and wide apart, with laughter-wrinkles in the corners that showed despite the tired and anxious expression of the whole face.

All this he could see with microscopic clearness, for the distance was no more than twenty feet. And all this he saw in such brief time, that he saw it as he lifted his carbine to his shoulder. He glanced along the sights, and knew that he was gazing upon a man who was as good as dead. It was impossible to miss at such point blank range.

But he did not shoot. Slowly he lowered the carbine and watched. A hand, clutching a water-bottle, became visible and the ginger beard bent downward to fill the bottle. He could hear the gurgle of the water. Then arm and bottle and ginger beard disappeared behind the closing bushes. A long time he waited, when, with thirst unslaked, he crept back to his horse, rode slowly across the sun-washed clearing, and passed into the shelter of the woods beyond.

## II

Another day, hot and breathless. A deserted farmhouse, large, with many outbuildings and an orchard, standing in a clearing. From the woods, on a roan horse, carbine across pommel, rode the young man with the quick black eyes. He breathed with relief as he gained the house. That a fight had taken place here earlier in the season was evident. Clips and empty cartridges, tarnished with verdigris, lay on the ground, which, while wet, had been torn up by the hoofs of horses. Hard by the kitchen garden were graves, tagged and numbered. From the oak tree by the kitchen door, in tattered, weather-beaten garments, hung the bodies of two men. The faces, shriveled and defaced, bore no likeness to the faces of men. The roan horse snorted beneath them, and the rider caressed and soothed it and tied it farther away.

Entering the house, he found the interior a wreck. He trod on empty cartridges as he walked from room to room to reconnoiter from the windows. Men had camped and slept everywhere, and on the floor of one room he came upon stains unmistakable where the wounded had been laid down.

Again outside, he led the horse around behind the barn and invaded the orchard. A dozen trees were burdened with ripe apples. He filled his pockets, eating while he picked. Then a thought came to him, and he glanced at the sun, calculating the time of his return to camp. He pulled off his shirt, tying the sleeves and making a bag. This he proceeded to fill with apples.

As he was about to mount his horse, the animal suddenly pricked up its ears. The man, too, listened, and heard, faintly, the thud of hoofs on soft earth. He crept to the corner of the barn and peered out. A dozen mounted men, strung out loosely, approaching from the opposite side of the clearing, were only a matter of a hundred yards or so away. They rode on to the house. Some dismounted, while others remained in the saddle as an earnest that their stay would be short. They seemed to be holding a council, for he could hear them talking excitedly in the detested tongue of the alien invader. The time passed, but they seemed unable to reach a decision. He put the carbine away in its boot, mounted, and waited impatiently, balancing the shirt of apples on the pommel.

He heard footsteps approaching, and drove his spurs so fiercely into the roan as to force a surprised groan from the animal as it leaped forward. At the corner of the barn he saw the intruder, a mere boy of nineteen or twenty for all of his uniform, jump back to escape being run down. At the same moment the roan swerved, and its rider caught a glimpse of the aroused men by the house. Some were springing from their horses, and he could see the rifles going to their shoulders. He passed the kitchen door and the dried corpses swinging in the shade, compelling his foes to run around the front of the house. A rifle cracked, and a second, but he was going fast, leaning forward, low in the saddle, one hand clutching the shirt of apples, the other guiding the horse.

The top bar of the fence was four feet high, but he knew his roan and leaped it at full career to the accompaniment of several scattered shots. Eight hundred yards straight away were the woods, and the roan was covering the distance with mighty strides. Every man was now firing. They were pumping their guns so rapidly that he no longer heard individual shots. A bullet went through his hat, but he was unaware, though he did know when another tore through the apples on the pommel. And he winced and ducked even lower when a third bullet, fired low, struck a stone between his horse's legs and ricochetted off through the air, buzzing and humming like some incredible insect.

The shots died down as the magazines were emptied, until, quickly, there was no more shooting. The young man was elated. Through that astonishing fusillade he had come unscathed. He glanced back. Yes, they had emptied their magazines. He could see several reloading. Others were running back behind the house for their horses. As he looked, two already mounted, came back into view around the corner, riding hard. And at the same moment, he saw the man with the unmistakable ginger beard kneel down on the ground, level his gun, and coolly take his time for the long shot.

The young man threw his spurs into the horse, crouched very

low, and swerved in his flight in order to distract the other's aim.
And still the shot did not come. With each jump of the horse, the
woods sprang nearer. They were only two hundred yards away,
and still the shot was delayed.

And then he heard it, the last thing he was to hear, for he was
dead ere he hit the ground in the long crashing fall from the saddle.
And they, watching at the house, saw him fall, saw his body bounce
when it struck the earth, and saw the burst of red-cheeked apples
that rolled about him. They laughed at the unexpected eruption of
apples, and clapped their hands in applause of the long shot by the
man with the ginger beard.

# THE TREACHERY OF CURLY BEN

## Alfred Henry Lewis

'Yere! you black boy Tom!' and the Old Cattleman's voice rose loudly as he commanded the approach of that buoyant servitor, who supervised his master's destinies, and performed in the triangular role of valet, guardian and friend. 'Yere, you; go to the barkeep of this tavern an' tell him to frame me up a pitcher of that peach brandy an' honey the way I shows him how. An' when he's got her organized, bring it out to us with two glasses by the fire. You-all ain't filin' no objections to a drink, be you?' This last was to me. 'As for me, personal,' he continued, 'you can put down a bet I'm as dry as a covered bridge.'

I readily assented to peach and honey; I would agree to raw whiskey if it were needed to appease him and permit me to remain in his graces.

'Thar's one thing, one redeemin' thing I might say, about the East,' he went on, when the peach and honey appeared, 'an' the same claims my respects entire; that's its nose-paint. Which we shorely suffers in the Southwest from beverages of the most ornery kind.'

'There's a word I've wanted to ask you about more than once,' I said. 'What do you mean by "ornery", and where do you get it?'

'Where do I get it?' he responded, with a tinge of scorn. 'Where do I rope onto any word? I jest nacherally reaches out an' acquires it a whole lot, like I do the rest of the language I employs. As for what it means, I would have allowed that any gent who escapes bein' as weak-minded as Thompson's colt – an' that cayouse is that imbecile he used to swim a river to get a drink – would hesitate with shame to ask sech questions.

' "Ornery" is a word the meanin' whereof is goin' to depend a heap on what you brands with it.' This was said like an oracle. 'Also, the same means more or less, accordin' to who-all puts the word in play. I remembers a mighty decent sort of sport, old Cape Willingham it is; an' yet Dan Boggs is forever referrin' to old Cape as "ornery". An' I reckon Dan thinks he is. Which the trouble with this Cape, from Dan's standp'int, is this: Cape is one of these yere precise parties, acc'rate as to all he does, an' plenty partic'lar about his looks. An Osage buck, paintin' for a dance, wouldn't worry more over his feachers, an' the way the ocher should be streaked on.

'Now this yere Cape is shy an eye, where an Apache pokes it out with a lance, back in Cochise's time; an', as he regyards his countenance as seemin' over rocky, bein' redooced to one eye as I relates, he sends East an' gets a glass eye. This ain't where Cape's technical't- ies about his looks trails in, however; an' if he had paused thar in his reehabilitations, Boggs allers put it up he'd a-found no fault. But Cape notices that about tenth drink time his shore-enough eye begins for to show up bloodshot, an' is a bad mate for the glass eye, the same bein' onaffected by drink. So what does Cape do but have a bloodshot eye made, an' takes to packin' the same on his person constant. As Cape drinks his forty drops all commodious, he sort o' keeps tab on himse'f in the lookin' glass back of the bar; an' when the good eye commences to turn red with them libations he's countin' into the corral, he ups an' shifts his bresh; digs out the white eye an' plants the drunken eye in the place.

'Shore! none of us cares except Dan Boggs; but Dan feels it to that extent, it's all Colonel Sterett an' Doc Peets an' Old Man Enright can do, added to Dan's bein' by nacher a born gent that a- way, to keep Dan from mentionin' it to old Cape.

' "A gent who comes from a good fam'ly, like you-all," says Old Man Enright to Dan, sort o' soothin' of him, "oughter be removed above makin' comments on pore old Cape shiftin' his optics. Troo! it's a weakness, but where is the sport who hasn't weaknesses like- wise. Which you-all is a mighty sight to one side of bein' perfect yourse'f, Dan, an' yet we don't go 'round breakin' the information off on you every time you makes a queer play. An' you must b'ar with Cape, an' them caprices of his.'

' "I ain't denyin' nothin'," declar's Dan. "I'm the last longhorn in Wolfville to be revilin' old Cape, an' refoosin' him his plain American right to go pirootin' 'round among his eyes as suits his taste. But I'm a mighty nervous man that a-way, an' Cape knows, or oughter know, how, as I states, I'm nacherally all onstrung, an' that his carryin's on with them eyes gives me the fantods. Onder all the circumstances, I claims his conduct is ornery, an' not what a invalid like me has a right to expect.'

'No; Dan never says nothin' to Cape; or does anythin' 'cept talk to Enright an' the rest of us about how he can't stand Cape shiftin' them eyes. An' it ain't affectation on the part of Dan; he shorely feels them shifts. Many a time, when it's got to be red-eye time with Cape, an' as the latter is scroop'lously makin' said transfers, have I beheld Dan arise in silent agony, an' go to bite hunks outen a pine shelf that is built on the Red Light wall.

' "Which that ornery Cape," says Dan, as he picks the splinters from his mouth after sech exercises, "would drive me as locoed as a coyote if I don't take refooge in some sech play like that.'

'But, as I su'gests about this term "ornery"; it depends a lot on who uses it, an' what for. Now Dan never refers to old Cape except as "ornery"; while Enright an' the rest of us sees nothin' from soda to hock in Cape, doorin' them few months he mingles with us, which merits sech obloquys.

'No; ornery is a word that means what it says an' is shore descriptif. Coyotes is ornery, sheep is ornery; an' them low-flung hoomans who herds sheep is ornery, speshul. Of course, the term has misapplications; as an extreme case, I've even heard ign'rant tenderfeet who alloodes to the whole West as "ornery." But them folks is too debased an' too darkened to demand comments.'

'You are very loyal to the West,' I remarked.

'Which I shorely oughter be,' retorted the old gentleman. 'The West has been some loyal to me. Troo! it stands to reason that a party fresh from the East, where the horns has been knocked offen everythin' for two or three hundred years, an' conditions gen'ral is as soft as a gooseha'r pillow, is goin' to notice some turgid changes when he lands in Arizona. But a shorthorn that a-way should reserve his jedgment till he gets acquainted, or gets lynched, or otherwise

experiences the West in its troo colours. While Arizona, for speci-
ment, don't go up an' put her arms about the neck of every towerist
that comes chargin' into camp, her failure to perform said rites arises
rather from dignity than hauteur. Arizona don't put on dog; but she
has her se'f-respectin' ways, an' stands a pat hand on towerists.

'If I was called on to lay out a system to guide a tenderfoot who
is considerin' on makin' Arizona his home-camp, I'd advise him to
make his deboo in that territory in a sperit of ca'm an' silent se'f-
reliance. Sech a gent might reside in Wolfville, say three months.
He might meet her citizens, buck her faro-banks, drink her nose-
paint, shake a hilarious hoof in her hurdy gurdies, ask for his letters,
or change in whatever sums seems meet to him at the New York
Store for shirts. Also, he might come buttin' along into the O. K.
Restauraw three times a day with the balance of the band, an' Missis
Rucker would shorely turn her grub-game for him, for the limit if
he so pleased. But still, most likely every gent in camp would
maintain doorin' his novitiate a decent distance with this yere
stranger; they wouldn't onbuckle an' be drunk with him free an'
social like, an' with the bridle off, like pards who has crossed the
plains together an' seen extremes. All this, with a chill onto it, a
tenderfoot would find himse'f ag'inst for the first few months in
Wolfville.

'An' yet, my advice to him would be not to get discouraged. The
camp's sizin' him up; that's all. If he perseveres, ca'm an' c'llected
like I states, along the trail of his destiny, he'll shore come winner
on the deal. At the end of three months, or mebby in onusual cases
four months, jest as this yere maverick is goin' into the dance hall,
or mebby the Red Light, some gent will chunk him one in the back
with his shet fist an' say, "How be you? You double-dealin', cattle-
stealin', foogitive son of a murdererin' hoss-thief, how be you?'

'Now, right thar is whar this yere shorthorn wants to maintain
his presence of mind. He don't want to go makin' no vain plays for
his six-shooter, or indulge in no sour ranikaboo retorts. That gent
likes him. With Wolfville social conditions, this yere greetin' is what
you sports who comes from the far No'th calls "the beginnin' of
the thaw." The ice is breakin' up; an' if our candidate sets in his
saddle steady an' with wisdom at this back-thumpin', name-callin'
epock, an' don't take to millin' 'round for trouble, in two minutes
him an' that gregar'ous gent who's accosted him is drinkin' an'

fraternizin' together like two stage hold-ups in a strange camp. The West ain't ornery; she's simply reserved a whole lot.

'Mighty likely now,' continued my friend, following a profound pause which was comfortably filled with peach and honey; 'it's mighty likely now, comin' down to folks, that the most ornery party I ever knows is Curly Ben. This yere Ben is killed, final; downed by old Captain Moon. Thar's a strange circumstance attendin', as the papers say, the obliteration of this Curly Ben, an' it makes a heap of an impression on me at the time. It shows how the instinct to do things that a gent is allers carryin' 'round in his mind, gets sort o' located in his nerves mebby, an' he'll do 'em without his intellects ridin' herd on the play – do 'em like Curly Ben does, after his light is out complete.

'This yere is what I'm trailin' up to: When Captain Moon fetches Curly Ben that time, Curly is playin' kyards. He's jest dealin', when, onbeknown to him, Moon comes Injunin' up from the r'ar surreptitious, and drills Curly Ben through the head; an' the bullet bein' a .45 Colt's – for Moon ain't toyin' with Curly an' means business – goes plumb through an' emerges from onder Curly Ben's off eye. For that matter, it breaks the arm of a party who's playing opp'site to Curly, an' who is skinnin' his pasteboards at the time, thinkin' nothin' of war. Which the queer part is this: Curly, as I states – an' he never knows what hits him, an' is as dead as Santa Anna in a moment – is dealin' the kyards. He's got the deck in his hands. An' yet, when the public picks Curly off the floor, he's pulled his two guns, an' has got one cocked. Now what do you-all deem of that for the workin' of a left-over impulse when a gent is dead?

'But, as I remarks yeretofore, Curly Ben is the most ornery person I ever overtakes, an' the feelin's of the camp is in nowise laid waste when Moon adds him to the list that time in the Red Light bar. It's this a-way:

'It's about a month before, when Captain Moon an' his nephy, with two 8-mule teams and four big three-an'-a-half Bain wagons, two lead an' two trail they be, comes freightin' out of Silver City with their eyes on Wolfville. It's the fourth night out, an' they're camped near a Injun agency. About midnight a half dozen of the bucks comes scoutin' 'round their camp allowin' to a moral certainty they'll see what's loose an little enough for 'em to pull. The aborigines makes the error of goin' up the wind from Moon's mules, which is grazin' about with hobbles on, an' them sagacious anamiles actooally has fits. It's a fact, if you want to see a mule go plumb into the air an' remain, jest let him get a good, ample, onmistakable smell of a Injun! It simply onhinges his reason; he ain't no more responsible than a cimmaron sheep. No, it ain't that the savage is out to do anything oncommon to the mule; its merely one of the mule's illoosions, as I've told you once before. Jest the same, if them Injuns is comin' to braid his tail, an' braid it tight, that mule couldn't feel more frantic.

'When these yere faithful mules takes to surgin' about the scene on two feet, Moon's nephy grabs a Winchester an' pumps a load or so into the darkness for gen'ral results. An' he has a heap of luck. He shorely stops one of them Apaches in his lopin' up an' down the land for good an' all.

'In less than no time the whole tribe is down on Captain Moon an' his nephy, demandin' blood. Thar's plenty of some sorts of wisdom about a savage, an' these yere Apaches ain't runnin' right in on Moon an' his relatif neither. They was perfeckly familiar with the accoomulation of cartridges in a Winchester, an' tharfore goes about the stirrin' up of Moon an' that nephy plumb wary.

'Moon an' the boy goes in between the wagons, blazin' an' bangin' away at whatever moves or makes a noise; an' as they've been all through such festivals before, they regyards their final chances to be as good as an even break, or better.

'While them Apaches is dodgin' about among the rocks, an' howlin' contempt, an' passin' resolootions of revenge touchin' the two Moons, the Injun agent comes troopin' along. He seeks to round-up his savages an' herd 'em back to the agency. The Apaches, on their side, is demandin' the capture of the nephy Moon for sp'ilin' one of their young men.

'The agent is a prairie dog just out from the East, an' don't know half as much about what's going on inside of a Apache as a horned toad. He comes down to the aige of hostil'ties, as you-all might call it, an' makes Moon an' his Winchester workin' nephy a speech. He addresses 'em a whole lot on the enormity of downin' Apaches who goes prowlin' about an' scarin' up your mules at midnight, in what this yere witless agent calls a "motif of childish cur'osity"; an' he winds up the pow-wow with demandin' the surrender of the "hom'cide".

' "Surrender nothin'!" says Captain Moon, "You tell your Injuns to line out for their camp; an' don't you yourse'f get too zealous neither an' come too clost, or as shore as I casts my first vote for Matty Van Buren, I'll plug you plumb centre.'

'But the nephy, he thinks different. In spite of Captain Moon's protests, he gives hims'f up to the agent on the promise of protection.

' "You're gone, lad," says Moon, when the nephy insists on yieldin'; "you won't last long as a pint of whiskey in a five-hand poker game."

'But this yere young Moon is obdurate, an' goes over an' gives himse'f to the agent, who puts it up he'll send him to Prescott to be tried in co't for beefin' the mule-thief Apache that a-way.

'Shore! it turns out jest as Captain Moon says. Before they'd gone a half mile, them wards of the gov'ment, as I once hears a big chief from Washin'ton call 'em, takes the nephy from this yere fallacious agent, an' by fourth drink time that mornin', or when it's been sun-up three hours, that nephy is nothing but a mem'ry.

'How do they kill him? In a fashion which from the coigne your Apache views things, does 'em proud,. That nephy is immolated as follows: They ropes him out wrist an' ankle, with four lariats; pegs him out like he's a hide they're goin' to dry. Thar's a big ant hill close at hand; it's with reference to this yere ant colony that the nephy is staked out. In three hours from the time them ants gets the word from the Apaches, they've done eat the nephy up, an' the last vestitch of him plumb disappears with the last ant, as the latter resoomes his labours onder the earth.

'Why, shore! these yere ants'll eat folks. They regyards sech reepasts as festivals, an' seasons of reelaxation from the sterner dooties of a ant. I recalls once how we loses Locoed Charlie, which demented party I b'lieve I mentions to you prior. This yere Charlie takes a day off from where he's workin' – at least he calls it labour – at the stage corrals, an' goes curvin' over to Red Dog. Charlie tanks up on the whiskey of that hamlet, compared to which the worst nose-paint ever sold in Wolfville is nectar. They palms off mebby it's a quart of this jooce on Charlie, an' then he p'ints out for Wolfville.

'That's the last of the pore drunkard. His pony is nickerin' about the corral gates, pleadin' with the mules inside to open 'em, in the mornin', but not sign or smoke of Locoed Charlie. An' he never does show up no more.

'If it's Enright or Cherokee Hall, or any valyooed citizen, thar would have issooed forth a war party, an' Red Dog would have been sacked an' burned but what the missin' gent would have been turned out.

'But it's different about Locoed Charlie. He hadn't that hold on the pop'lar heart; didn't feel sech a place in the gen'ral eye; an' so barrin' a word or two of wonder, over their drinks at the Red Light, I don't reckon now the Wolfville folks disturbs themse'fs partic'lar about the camp bein' shy Charlie.

'It's the second day when a teamster, trackin' over from the Red Dog, develops what's left of Locoed Charlie. He falls off his hoss, with that load of Red Dog whiskey, an' every notion or idee or sensation absolootely effaced. An' where Charlie loses is, he falls by a ant hill. Yes; they shorely takes Charlie in. Thar's nothin' left of him when the teamster locates the remainder, but his clothes, his spurs an' his 'natomy. The r'ar gyard of them ants has long since retired with the final fragments of Locoed Charlie.

'You-all might o' seen the story. Colonel Sterrett writes it up in the *Coyote*, an' heads it, "Hunger is a Terrible Thing." This sot Charlie comin' to his death that a-way puts a awful scare over Huggins an' Old Monte. It reforms 'em for more'n two hours. Huggins, who is allers frontin' up as one who possesses public sperit, tries to look plumb dignified about it, an' remarks to Dave Tutt in the New York Store as how he thinks we oughter throw in around an' build a monument to Locoed Charlie. Dave allows that, while he's with Huggins in them projecks, he wants to add a monument to the ants.

The founders of the scheme sort o' splittin' at the go-in that a-way, it don't get no further, an' the monument to Locoed Charlie, as a enterprise, bogs down. But to continyoo on the trail of Captain Moon.

'Moon comes rumblin' into Wolfville, over-doo mebby it's two weeks, bringin' both teams. Tharupon he relates them outrages.

Thar's but one thought; that agent has lived too long.

' "If he was the usual common form of felon," says Enright, "ondoubted – for it would be their dooty – the vig'lance committee local to them parts would string him up. But that ain't possible; this yere miscreant is a gov'ment official an' wears the gov'ment brand, an' even the Stranglers, of whatever commoonity, ain't strong enough, an' wouldn't be jestified in stackin' in ag'in the gov'ment. Captain Moon's only show is a feud. He oughter caper over an', as private as possible, arrogate to himse'f the skelp of this yere agent who abandons his relatif to them hostiles."

'Wolfville listens to Captain Moon's hist'ry of his wrongs; but aside from them eloocidations of Enright, no gent says much. Thar's some games where troo p'liteness consists in sayin' nothin' an' knowin' less. But the most careless hand in camp can see that Moon's aimin' at reprisals.

'This Curly Ben is trackin' about Wolfville at the time. Curly ain't what you-all would call a elevated character. He's a rustler of cattle, an' a smuggler of Mexican goods, an' Curly an' the Yoonited States marshals has had more turn-ups than one. But Curly is dead game; an' so far, he manages to either out-luck or out-shoot them magistrates; an', as I says, when Moon comes wanderin' in that time, mournin' for his nephy, Curly has been projectin' about camp for like it's a week.

'Moon sort o' roominates on the play, up an' down, for a day or so, makin' out a plan. He don't want to go back himse'f; the agent knows him, an' them Injuns knows him, an' it's even money, if he comes pokin' into their bailiwick, they'll tumble to his errant. In sech events, they're shore doo to corral him an' give them ants another holiday. It's the ant part that gives pore Captain Moon a chill.

' "I'll take a chance on a bowie knife," says Moon to Dan Boggs, – Dan, bein' a sympathetic gent an' takin' nacherally to folks in trouble, has Moon's confidence from the jump; "I'll take a chance on a bowie knife; an' as for a gun, I simply courts the resk. But them ants dazzles me – I lay down to ants, an' I looks on it as no disgrace to a gent to say so."

' "Ants shorely do sound poignant," admits Dan; " 'speshully them big black an' red ants that has stingers like hornets an' pinchers like bugs. Sech insecks, armed to the teeth as they be, an' laid out to fight both ways from the middle, is likewise too many for me. I would refoose battle with 'em myse'f."

'It aint long before Captain Moon an Curly Ben is seen confidin' an' conferrin with one another, and drinkin' by themse'fs; an' no one has to be told that Moon's makin' negotiations with Curly to ride over an' down the agent. The idee is pecooliarly grateful to Wolfville. It stands to win no matter how the kyards lay in the box. If Curly fetches the agent flutterin' from his limb, thar's one miscreant less in Arizona; if the agent gets the drop an' puts out Curly Ben, it comes forth jest the same. It's the camp's theery that, in all that entitles 'em to death, the case stands hoss an' hoss between the agent an' Curly Ben.

' "An' if they both gets downed, it's a whip-saw; we win both ways," says Cherokee Hall, an' the rest of us files away our nose-paint in silent assent tharwith.

'It comes out later that Moon agrees to give Curly Ben fifteen hundred dollars an' a pony, if he'll go over an' kill off the agent. Curly Ben says the prop'sition is the pleasantest thing he hears since he leaves the Panhandle ten years before; an' so he accepts five hundred dollars an' the pony – the same bein' in the nacher of payments in advance – an' goes clatterin' off up the canyon one evenin' on his mission of jestice. An' then we hears no more of Curly Ben for about a month. No one marvels none at this, however, as downin' any given gent is a prop'sition which in workin' out is likely to involve delays.

'One day, with onruffled brow an' an air all careless an' free, Curly Ben rides into Wolfville and begins orderin' whiskey at the Red Light before he's hardly cl'ar of the saddle. Thar ain't nobody in camp, from Doc Peets to Missis Rucker, but what's eager to know the finish of Curly's expedition, but of course everybody hobbles his feelin's in them behalfs. It's Captain Moon's fooneral, an' he oughter have a first, oninterrupted say. Moon comes up to Curly Ben where Curly is cuttin' the alkali dust outen his throat at the Red Light bar.

' "Did you get him?" Moon asks after a few p'lite preeliminaries. "Did you bring back his ha'r an' y'ears like we agrees?"

' "Have you-all got the other thousand ready," says Curly Ben, "in the event I do?"

' "Right yere in my war-bags," says Moon, "awaitin' to make

good for your time an' talent an' trouble in revengin' my pore
nephy's deemise by way of them insecks." An Moon slaps his
pocket as locatin' the *dinero*.

' "Well, I don't get him," says Curly Ben ca'mly, settin' his glass
on the bar.

'Thar's a pause of mebby two minutes, doorin' which Moon
looks cloudy, as though he don't like the way the kyards is comin';
Curly Ben, on his part, is smilin' like what Huggins calls "one of
his songstresses" over in the Bird Cage Op'ry House. After a bit,
Moon resoomes them investigations.

' "Don't I give you four stacks of reds an' a pony," he says, "to
reepair to that murderer an' floor-manage his obsequies? An' don't
I promise you eight stacks more when you reports with that outcast's
y'ears an' ha'r, as showin' good faith?"

' "C'rrect; every word," says Curly Ben, lightin' a seegyar an'
then leanin' his elbows on the bar, a heap onmoved.

' "Which I would admire to know, then," says Moon, an' his
eyes is gettin' little an' hard, "why you-all don't make good them
compacts."

' "Well, I'll onfold the reasons, an' make it as plain an' cl'ar an'
convincin' as a spade flush," says Curly Ben. "When I gets to this
yere victim of ours, I finds him to be a mighty profoose an' lavish
form of sport. The moment I'm finished explainin' to him my
mission, an' jest as I onlimbers my six-shooter to get him where he
lives, he offers me five thousand dollars to come back yere an' kill
you. Nacherally, after that, me an' this yere subject of our plot takes
a few drinks, talks it over, an' yere I be."

' "But what be you aimin' to do?" asks Moon.

' "What be you aimin' to do?" responds Curly Ben. As I states,
he's shore the most ornery coyote!

' "I don't understand," says Moon.

' "Why it's as obv'ous," retorts Curly Ben, "as the Fence Rail
brand, an' that takes up the whole side of a cow. The question now
is, do you raise this yere gent? He raises you as I explains; now do
you quit, or tilt him, say, a thousand better?"

' "An' suppose I don't?" says Moon, sort o' figerin' for a moment
or so. "What do you reckon now would be your next move?"

' "Thar would be but one thing to do," says Curly Ben mighty
placid; "I'd shorely take him. I would proceed with your destruction

at once, an' return to this agent gent an' accept that five thousand dollar honorarium he offers.' '

'Curly Ben is "bad" plumb through, an' the sights, as they says in the picturesque language of the Southwest, has been filed from his guns for many years. Which this last is runnin' in Moon's head while he talks with his disgustin' emmissary. Moon ain't out to take chances on gettin' the worst of it. An' tharfore, Moon at once waxes cunnin' a whole lot.

' "I'm a pore man," he says, "but if it takes them teams of mine, to the last tire an' the last hoof, I've got to have this agent's ha'r an' y'ears. You camp around the Red Light awhile, Curly, till I go over to the New York Store an' see about more money. I'll be back while your layin' out another drink."

'Now it's not to the credit of Curly, as a crim'nal who puts thought into his labours, that he lets Captain Moon turn his flank the easy way he does. It displays Curly as lackin' a heap in mil'tary genius. I don't presoome to explain it; an' it's all so dead onnacheral at this juncture that the only s'lootion I'm cap'ble of givin' it is that it's preedestinated that a-way. Curly not only lets Moon walk off, which after he hangs up that bluff about takin' them terms of the agent's is mighty irreg'lar, but he's that obtoose he sits down to play kyards, while he's waitin', with his back to the door. Why! it's like sooicide!

'Moon goes out to his wagons an' gets, an' buckles on, his guns. Quick, crafty, brisk as a cat an' with no more noise, Moon comes walkin' into the Red Light door. He sees Curly where he sits at seven-up, with his back turned towards him.

' "One for Jack!" says Curly turnin' that fav'rite kyard. Moon sort o' drifts to his r'ar.

' "Bang!" says Moon's pistol, an' Curly falls for'ards onto the table, an' then onto the floor, the bullet plumb through his head, as I informs you.

"Curly Ben never has the shadow of a tip; he's out of the Red Light an' into the regions beyond, like snappin' your thumb an' finger. It's as sharp as the buck of a pony; he's Moon's meat in a minute.

'No; thar's nothin' for Wolfville to do. Moon's jestified. Which his play is the one trail out; for up to that p'nt where Moon onhooks his guns, Curly ain't done nothin' to put him in reach of the Stranglers. Committees of vig'lance, that a-way, like shore-enough co'ts, can't prevent crime; they only punish it, an' up to where Moon gets decisive action, thar's no openin' by which the Stranglers could cut in on the deal. Yes, Enright convenes his committee an' goes through the motions of tryin' Moon. They does this to preserve appearances, but of course they throws Moon loose. An' as thar's reasons, as any gent can see, why no one cares to have the story as it is be made a subject of invidious gossip in Red Dog, an' other outfits envious of Wolfville, at Enright's su'gestion, the Stranglers bases the acquittal of Moon on the fact that Curly Ben deloodes Moon's sister, back in the States, an' then deserts her. Moon cuts the trail of the base sedoocer in Wolfville, an' gathers him in accordin', an' as a brother preyed on by his sister's wrongs is shorely expected to do.'

'But Curly Ben never did mislead Moon's sister, did he?' I asked, for the confident fashion wherewith my old friend reeled off the finding of Wolfville's vigilance committee, and the reasons, almost imposed on me.

'Which you can bet the limit,' he observed fiercely, as he prepared to go into the hotel; 'which you can go the limit open, son, Curly ain't none too good.'

# THE PASSING OF BLACK EAGLE

## O. Henry

FOR some months of a certain year a grim bandit infested the Texas border along the Rio Grande. Peculiarly striking to the optic nerve was this notorious marauder. His personality secured him the title of 'Black Eagle, the Terror of the Border'. Many fearsome tales are on record concerning the doings of him and his followers. Suddenly, in the space of a single minute, Black Eagle vanished from earth. He was never heard of again. His own band never even guessed the mystery of his disappearance. The border ranches and settlements feared he would come again to ride and ravage the mesquite flats. He never will. It is to disclose the fate of Black Eagle that this narrative is written.

The initial movement of the story is furnished by the foot of a bartender in St. Louis. His discerning eye fell upon the form of Chicken Ruggles as he pecked with avidity at the free lunch. Chicken was a 'hobo'. He had a long nose like the bill of a fowl, an inordinate appetite for poultry, and a habit of gratifying it without expense, which accounts for the name given him by his fellow-vagrants.

Physicians agree that the partaking of liquids at meal times is not a healthy practice. The hygiene of the saloon promulgates the opposite. Chicken had neglected to purchase a drink to accompany his meal. The bartender rounded the counter, caught the injudicious diner by the ear with a lemon squeezer, led him to the door and kicked him into the street.

Thus the mind of Chicken was brought to realize the signs of coming winter. The night was cold; the stars shone with unkindly brilliance; people were hurrying along the streets in two egotistic, jostling streams. Men had donned their overcoats, and Chicken knew to an exact percentage the increased difficulty of coaxing dimes from those buttoned-in vest pockets. The time had come for his annual exodus to the south.

A little boy, five or six years old, stood looking with covetous eyes in a confectioner's window. In one small hand he held an empty two-ounce vial; in the other he grasped tightly something flat and round, with a shining milled edge. The scene presented a field of operations commensurate to Chicken's talents and daring. After sweeping the horizon to make sure that no official tug was cruising near, he insidiously accosted his prey. The boy, having been early taught by his household to regard altruistic advances with extreme suspicion, received the overtures coldly.

Then Chicken knew that he must make one of those desperate, nerve-shattering plunges into speculation that fortune sometimes requires of those who would win her favour. Five cents was his capital, and this he must risk against the chance of winning what lay within the close grasp of the youngster's chubby hand. It was a fearful lottery, Chicken knew. But he must accomplish his end by strategy, since he had a wholesome terror of plundering infants by force. Once, in a park, driven by hunger, he had committed an onslaught upon a bottle of peptonized infant's food in the possession of an occupant of a baby carriage. The outraged infant had so promptly opened its mouth and pressed the button that communicated with the welkin that help arrived, and Chicken did his thirty days in a snug coop. Wherefore he was, as he said, 'leary of kids.'

Beginning artfully to question the boy concerning his choice of sweets, he gradually drew out the information he wanted. Mamma said he was to ask the drug store man for ten cents worth of paregoric in the bottle; he was to keep his hand shut tight over the dollar; he must not stop to talk to anyone in the street; he must ask the drug store man to wrap up the change and put it in the pocket of his trousers. Indeed, they had pockets – two of them! And he liked chocolate creams best.

Chicken went into the store and turned plunger. He invested his entire capital in C.A.N.D.Y. stocks, simply to pave the way to the greater risk following.

He gave the sweets to the youngster, and had the satisfaction of perceiving that confidence was established. After that it was easy to obtain leadership of the expedition; to take the investment by the hand and lead it to a nice drug store he knew of in the same block. There Chicken, with a parental air, passed over the dollar and called for the medicine, while the boy crunched his candy, glad to be relieved of the responsibility of the purchase. And then the successful investor, searching his pockets, found an overcoat button – the extent of his winter trousseau – and, wrapping it carefully, placed the ostensible change in the pocket of confiding juvenility. Setting the youngster's face homeward and patting him benevolently on the back – for Chicken's heart was as soft as those of his feathered namesakes – the speculator quit the market with a profit of 1,700 per cent. on his invested capital.

Two hours later an Iron Mountain freight engine pulled out of the railroad yards, Texas bound, with a string of empties. In one of the cattle cars, half buried in excelsior, Chicken lay at ease. Beside him in his nest was a quart bottle of very poor whisky and a paper bag of bread and cheese. Mr. Ruggles, in his private car, was on his trip south for the winter season.

For a week that car was trundled southward, shifted, laid over, and manipulated after the manner of rolling stock, but Chicken stuck to it, leaving it only at necessary times to satisfy his hunger and thirst. He knew it must go down to the cattle country, and San Antonio, in the heart of it, was his goal. There the air was salubrious and mild; the people indulgent and long-suffering. The bartenders there would not kick him. If he should eat too long or too often at one place they would swear at him as if by rote and without heat. They swore so drawlingly, and they rarely paused short of their full vocabulary, which was copious, so that Chicken had often gulped a good meal during the process of the vituperative prohibition. The season there was always spring-like; the plazas were pleasant at night, with music and gaiety; except during the slight and infrequent cold snaps one could sleep comfortably out of doors in case the interiors should develop inhospitality.

At Texarkana his car was switched to the I. and G.N. Then still southward it trailed until, at length, it crawled across the Colorado bridge at Austin, and lined out, straight as an arrow, for the run to San Antonio.

When the freight halted at that town Chicken was fast asleep. In ten minutes the train was off again for Laredo, the end of the road.

Those empty cattle cars were for distribution along the line at points from which the ranches shipped their stock.

When Chicken awoke his car was stationary. Looking out between the slats he saw it was a bright, moonlit night. Scrambling out, he saw his car with three others abandoned on a little siding in a wild and lonesome country. A cattle pen and chute stood on one side of the track. The railroad bisected a vast, dim ocean of prairie, in the midst of which Chicken, with his futile rolling stock, was as completely stranded as was Robinson with his land-locked boat.

A white post stood near the rails. Going up to it, Chicken read the letters at the top, S. A. 90. Laredo was nearly as far to the south. He was almost a hundred miles from any town. Coyotes began to yelp in the mysterious sea around him. Chicken felt lonesome. He had lived in Boston without an education, in Chicago without nerve, in Philadelphia without a sleeping-place, in New York without a pull, and in Pittsburg sober, and yet he had never felt so lonely as now.

Suddenly through the intense silence he heard the whicker of a horse. The sound came from the side of the track toward the east, and Chicken began to explore timorously in that direction. He stepped high along the mat of curly mesquit grass, for he was afraid of everything there might be in this wilderness – snakes, rats, brigands, centipedes, mirages, cowboys, fandangoes, tarantulas, tamales – he had read of them in the storypapers. Rounding a clump of prickly pear that reared high its fantastic and menacing array of rounded heads, he was struck to shivering terror by a snort and a thunderous plunge, as the horse, himself startled, bounded away some fifty yards, and then resumed his grazing. But here was the one thing in the desert that Chicken did not fear. He had been reared on a farm; he had handled horses, understood them, and could ride.

Approaching slowly and speaking soothingly, he followed the animal, which, after its first flight, seemed gentle enough, and secured the end of the twenty-foot lariat that dragged after him in the grass. It required him but a few moments to contrive the rope into an ingenious nose-bridle, after the style of the Mexican *borsal*. In another he was upon the horse's back and off at a splendid lope, giving the animal free choice of direction. 'He will take me somewhere,' said Chicken to himself.

It would have been a thing of joy, that untrammelled gallop over the moonlit prairie, even to Chicken, who loathed exertion, but that his mood was not for it. His head ached; a growing thirst was upon him; the 'somewhere' whither his lucky mount might convey him was full of dismal peradventure.

And now he noted that the horse moved to a definite goal. Where the prairie lay smooth he kept his course straight as an arrow's toward the east. Deflected by hill or arroyo or impracticable spinous brakes, he quickly flowed again into the current, charted by his unerring instinct. At last, upon the side of a gentle rise, he suddenly subsided to a complacent walk. A stone's cast away stood a little mott of coma trees; beneath it a *jacal* such as the Mexicans erect – a one-room house of upright poles daubed with clay and roofed with grass or tule reeds. An experienced eye would have estimated the spot as the headquarters of a small sheep ranch. In the moonlight the ground in the near-by corral showed pulverized to a level smoothness by the hoofs of the sheep. Everywhere was carelessly distributed the paraphernalia of the place – ropes, bridles, saddles, sheep pelts, wool sacks, feed troughs, and camp litter. The barrel of drinking water stood in the end of the two-horse wagon near the door. The harness was piled, promiscuous, upon the wagon tongue, soaking up the dew.

Chicken slipped to earth, and tied the horse to a tree. He halloed again and again, but the house remained quiet. The door stood open, and he entered cautiously. The light was sufficient for him to see that no one was at home. He struck a match and lighted a lamp that stood on a table. The room was that of a bachelor ranchman who was content with the necessaries of life. Chicken rummaged intelligently until he found what he had hardly dared hope for – a small, brown jug that still contained something near a quart of his desire.

Half an hour later, Chicken – now a gamecock of hostile aspect – emerged from the house with unsteady steps. He had drawn upon the absent ranchman's equipment to replace his own ragged attire. He wore a suit of coarse brown ducking, the coat being a sort of rakish bolero, jaunty to a degree. Boots he had donned, and spurs that whirred with every lurching step. Buckled around him was a belt full of cartridges with a big sixshooter in each of its two holsters.

Prowling about, he found blankets, a saddle and bridle with which he caparisoned his steed. Again mounting, he rode swiftly away, singing a loud and tuneless song.

Bud King's band of desperadoes, outlaws and horse and cattle thieves, were in camp at a secluded spot on the bank of the Frio. Their depredations in the Rio Grande country, while no bolder than usual, had been advertised more extensively, and Captain Kinney's company of rangers had been ordered down to look after them. Consequently, Bud King, who was a wise general, instead of cutting out a hot trail for the upholders of the law, as his men wished to do, retired for the time to the prickly fastnesses of the Frio valley.

Though the move was a prudent one, and not incompatible with Bud's well-known courage, it raised dissension among the members of the band. In fact, while they thus lay ingloriously *perdu* in the brush, the question of Bud King's fitness for the leadership was argued, with closed doors, as it were, by his followers. Never before had Bud's skill or efficiency been brought to criticism; but his glory was waning (and such is glory's fate) in the light of a newer star. The sentiment of the band was crystallizing into the opinion that Black Eagle could lead them with more lustre, profit and distinction.

This Black Eagle – sub-titled the 'Terror of the Border' – had been a member of the gang about three months.

One night while they were in camp on the San Miguel water-hole a solitary horseman on the regulation fiery steed dashed in among them. The new-comer was of a portentous and devastating aspect. A beak-like nose with a predatory curve projected above a mass of bristling, blue-black whiskers. His eye was cavernous and fierce. He was spurred, sombreroed, booted, garnished with revolvers, abundantly drunk, and very much unafraid. Few people in the country drained by the Rio Bravo would have cared thus to invade alone the camp of Bud King. But this fell bird swooped fearlessly upon them and demanded to be fed.

Hospitality in the prairie country is not limited. Even if your enemy pass your way you must feed him before you shoot him. You must empty your larder into him before you empty your lead. So the stranger of undeclared intentions was set down to a mighty feast.

A talkative bird he was, full of most marvellous loud tales and exploits, and speaking a language at times obscure but never colourless. He was a new sensation to Bud King's men, who rarely encountered new types. They hung, delighted, upon his vainglorious boasting, the spicy strangeness of his lingo, his contemptuous familiarity with life, the world, and remote places, and the extravagant frankness with which he conveyed his sentiments.

To their guest the band of outlaws seemed to be nothing more than a congregation of country bumpkins whom he was 'stringing for grub' just as he would have told his stories at the back door of a farmhouse to wheedle a meal. And, indeed, his ignorance was not without excuse, for the 'bad man' of the South-west does not run to extremes. Those brigands might justly have been taken for a little party of peaceable rustics assembled for a fish-fry or pecan gathering. Gentle of manner, slouching of gait, soft-voiced, unpicturesquely clothed; not one of them presented to the eye any witness of the desperate records they had earned.

For two days the glittering stranger within the camp was feasted. Then, by common consent, he was invited to become a member of the band. He consented, presenting for enrolment the prodigious name of 'Captain Montressor.' This name immediately overruled by the band, and 'Piggy' substituted as a compliment to the awful and insatiate appetite of its owner.

Thus did the Texas border receive the most spectacular brigand that ever rode its chaparral.

For the next three months Bud King conducted business as usual, escaping encounters with law officers and being content with reasonable profits. The band ran off some very good companies of horses from the ranges, and a few bunches of fine cattle which they got safely across the Rio Grande and disposed of to fair advantage. Often the band would ride into the little villages and Mexican settlements, terrorizing the inhabitants and plundering for the provisions and ammunition they needed. It was during these bloodless raids that Piggy's ferocious aspect and frightful voice gained him a renown more widespread and glorious than those other gentle-voiced and sad-faced desperadoes could have acquired in a lifetime.

The Mexicans, most apt in nomenclature, first called him The Black Eagle, and used to frighten the babes by threatening them with tales of the dreadful robber who carried off little children in his great beak. Soon the name extended, and Black Eagle, the Terror of the Border, became a recognized factor in exaggerated newspaper reports and ranch gossip.

The country from the Nueces to the Rio Grande was a wild but fertile stretch, given over to the sheep and cattle ranches. Range was free; the inhabitants were few; the law was mainly a letter, and the pirates met with little opposition until the flaunting and garish Piggy gave the band undue advertisement. Then McKinney's ranger company headed for those precincts, and Bud King knew that it meant grim and sudden war or else temporary retirement. Regarding the risk to be unnecessary, he drew off his band to an almost inaccessible spot on the bank of the Frio. Wherefore, as has been said, dissatisfaction arose among the members, and impeachment proceedings against Bud were premeditated with Black Eagle in high favour for the succession. Bud King was not unaware of the sentiment, and he called aside Cactus Taylor, his trusted lieutenant, to discuss it.

'If the boys,' said Bud, 'ain't satisfied with me, I'm willin' to step out. They're buckin' against my way of handlin' 'em. And 'specially because I concludes to hit the brush while Sam Kinney is ridin' the line. I saves 'em from bein' shot or sent up on a state contract, and they up and says I'm no good.'

'It ain't so much that,' explained Cactus, 'as it is they're plum locoed about Piggy. They want them whiskers and that nose of his to split the wind at the head of the column.'

'There's somethin' mighty seldom about Piggy,' declared Bud, musingly. 'I never yet see anything on the hoof that he exactly grades up with. He can shore holler a plenty, and he straddles a hoss from where you laid the chunk. But he ain't never been smoked yet. You know, Cactus, we ain't had a row since he's been with us. Piggy's all right for skearin' the greaser kids and layin' waste a crossroads store. I reckon he's the finest canned oyster buccaneer and cheese pirate that ever was, but how's his appetite for fightin'? I've knowed some citizens you'd think was starvin' for trouble get a bad case of dyspepsy the first dose of lead they had to take.'

'He talks all spraddled out,' said Cactus, ''bout the rookuses he's been in. He claims to have saw the elephant and hearn the owl.'

'I know,' replied Bud, using the cow-puncher's expressive phrase of scepticism, 'but it sounds to me!'

This conversation was held one night in camp while the other members of the band – eight in number – were sprawling around the fire, lingering over their supper. When Bud and Cactus ceased talking they heard Piggy's formidable voice holding forth to the others as usual while he was engaged in checking, though never satisfying, his ravening appetite.

'Wat's de use,' he was saying, 'of chasin' little red cowses and hosses 'round for t'ousands of miles? Dere ain't nuttin' in it. Gallopin' t'rough dese bushes and briers, and gettin' a t'irst dat a brewery couldn't put out, and missin' meals! Say! You know what I'd do if I was main finger of dis bunch? I'd stick up a train. I'd blow de express car and make hard dollars where you guys gets wind. Youse makes me tired. Dis sook-cow kind of cheap sport gives me a pain.'

Later on, a deputation waited on Bud. They stood on one leg, chewed mesquit twigs and circumlocuted, for they hated to hurt his feelings. Bud foresaw their business, and made it easy for them. Bigger risks and larger profits was what they wanted.

The suggestion of Piggy's about holding up a train had fired their imagination and increased their admiration for the dash and boldness of the instigator. They were such simple, artless, and custom-bound bushrangers that they had never before thought of extending their habits beyond the running off of live-stock and the shooting of such of their acquaintances as ventured to interfere.

Bud acted 'on the level,' agreeing to take a subordinate place in the gang until Black Eagle should have been given a trial as leader.

After a great deal of consultation, studying of time-tables, and discussion of the country's topography, the time and place for carrying out their new enterprise was decided upon. At that time there was a feedstuff famine in Mexico and a cattle famine in certain parts of the United States, and there was a brisk international trade. Much money was being shipped along the railroads that connected the two republics. It was agreed that the most promising place for the contemplated robbery was at Espina, a little station on the I. and G. N., about forty miles north of Laredo. The train stopped there one minute; the country around was wild and unsettled; the station consisted of but one house in which the agent lived.

Black Eagle's band set out, riding by night. Arriving in the vicinity of Espina, they rested their horses all day in a thicket a few miles distant.

The train was due at Espina at 10.30 p.m. They could rob the train and be well over the Mexican border with their booty by daylight the next morning.

To do Black Eagle justice, he exhibited no signs of flinching from the responsible honours that had been conferred upon him.

He assigned his men to their respective posts with discretion, and coached them carefully as to their duties. On each side of the track four of the band were to lie concealed in the chaparral. Gotch-Ear Rodgers was to stick up the station agent. Bronco Charlie was to remain with the horses, holding them in readiness. At a spot where it was calculated the engine would be when the train stopped, Bud King was to lie hidden on one side, Black Eagle himself on the other. The two would get the drop on the engineer and fireman, force them to descend and proceed to the rear. Then the express car would be looted, and the escape made. No one was to move until Black Eagle gave the signal by firing his revolver. The plan was perfect.

At ten minutes to train time every man was at his post, effectually concealed by the thick chaparral that grew almost to the rails. The night was dark and lowering, with a fine drizzle falling from the flying gulf clouds. Black Eagle crouched behind a bush within five yards of the track. Two six-shooters were belted around him. Occasionally he drew a large black bottle from his pocket and raised it to his mouth.

A star appeared far down the track which soon waxed into the headlight of the approaching train. It came on with an increasing roar; the engine bore down upon the ambushing desperadoes with a glare and a shriek like some avenging monster come to deliver them to justice. Black Eagle flattened himself upon the ground. The engine, contrary to their calculations, instead of stopping between him and Bud King's place of concealment, passed fully forty yards farther before it came to a stand.

The bandit leader rose to his feet and peered around the bush. His men all lay quiet, awaiting the signal. Immediately opposite Black Eagle was a thing that drew his attention. Instead of being a regular passenger train it was a mixed one. Before him stood a box car, the door of which, by some means, had been left slightly open. Black Eagle went up to it and pushed the door farther open. An odour came forth – a damp, rancid, familiar, musty, intoxicating, beloved odour stirring strongly at old memories of happy days and travels. Black Eagle sniffed at the witching smell as the returned wanderer smells of the rose that twines his boyhood's cottage home. Nostalgia seized him. He put his hand inside. Excelsior – dry, springy, curly, soft, enticing, covered the floor. Outside the drizzle had turned to a chilling rain.

The train bell clanged. The bandit chief unbuckled his belt and cast it, with its revolvers, upon the ground. His spurs followed quickly, and his broad sombrero. Black Eagle was moulting. The train started with a rattling jerk. The ex-Terror of the Border scrambled into the box car and closed the door. Stretched luxuriously upon the excelsior, with the black bottle clasped closely to his breast, his eyes closed, and a foolish, happy smile upon his terrible features, Chicken Ruggles started upon his return trip.

Undisturbed, with the band of desperate bandits lying motionless, awaiting the signal to attack, the train pulled out from Espina. As its speed increased and the black masses of chaparral went whizzing past on either side, the express messenger, lighting his pipe, looked through his window and remarked, feelingly:

'What a jim-dandy place for a hold-up!'

# SERGEANT HOUCK

## *Jack Schaefer*

SERGEANT HOUCK stopped his horse just below the top of the
ridge ahead. The upper part of his body was silhouetted against
the sky line as he rose in his stirrups to peer over the crest.
He urged the horse on up and the two of them, the man and the
horse, were sharp and distinct against the copper sky. After a
moment he turned and rode down to the small troop waiting. He
reined beside Lieutenant Imler.

'It's there, sir. Alongside a creek in the next hollow. Maybe a
third of a mile.'

Lieutenant Imler looked at him coldly. 'You took your time,
Sergeant. Smack on the top, too.'

'Couldn't see plain, sir. Sun was in my eyes.'

'Wanted them to spot you, eh, Sergeant?'

'No, sir. Sun was bothering me. I don't think—'

'Forget it, Sergeant. I don't like this either.'

Lieutenant Imler was in no hurry. He led the troop slowly up the
hill. The real fuss was fifty-some miles away. Captain McKay was
hogging the honours there. Here he was, tied to this sideline detail.
Twenty men. Ten would have been enough. Ten and an old hand
like Sergeant Houck.

With his drawn sabre pointing forward, Lieutenant Imler led the
charge up and over the crest and down the long slope to the Indian
village. There were some scattered shots from bushes by the creek,
ragged pops indicating poor powder and poorer weapons, probably
fired by the last of the old men left behind when the young braves
departed in war paint ten days before. The village was silent and
deserted.

Lieutenant Imler surveyed the ground they'd taken. 'Spectacular achievement,' he muttered to himself. He beckoned Sergeant Houck to him.

'Your redskin friend was right, Sergeant. This is it.'

'Knew he could be trusted, sir.'

'Our orders are to destroy the village. Send a squad out to round up any stock. There might be some horses around. We're to take them in.' Lieutenant Imler waved an arm at the thirty-odd skin-and-pole huts. 'Set the others to pulling those down. Burn what you can and smash everything else.'

'Right, sir.'

Lieutenant Imler rode into the slight shade of the cotton-woods along the creek. He wiped the dust from his face and set his campaign hat at a fresh angle to ease the crease the band had made on his forehead. Here he was, hot and tired and way out at the end of nowhere with another long ride ahead, while Captain McKay was having it out at last with Grey Otter and his renegade warriors somewhere between the Turkey Foot and the Washakie. He relaxed to wait in the saddle, beginning to frame his report in his mind.

'Pardon, sir.'

Lieutenant Imler looked around. Sergeant Houck was standing nearby with something in his arms, something that squirmed and seemed to have dozens of legs and arms.

'What the devil is that, Sergeant?'

'A baby, sir. Or rather, a boy. Two years old, sir.'

'How the devil do you know? By his teeth?'

'His mother told me, sir.'

'His mother?'

'Certainly, sir. She's right here.'

Lieutenant Imler saw her then, standing beside a neighbouring tree, shrinking into the shadow and staring at Sergeant Houck and the squirming child. He leaned to look closer. She wore a shapeless, sacklike covering with slits for her arms and head. She was sun-and-windburned, dark yet not as dark as he expected. And there was no mistaking the colour of her hair. It was light brown and long and coiled in a bun on her neck.

'Sergeant! It's a white woman!'

'Right, sir. Her name's Cora Sutliff. The wagon train she was with was wiped out by a raiding party. She and another woman were taken along. The other woman died. She didn't. The village bought her. She's been in Grey Otter's lodge.' Sergeant Houck smacked the squirming boy briskly and tucked him under one arm. He looked straight at Lieutenant Imler. 'That was three years ago, sir.'

'Three years? Then that boy—'

'That's right, sir.'

Captain McKay looked up from his desk to see Sergeant Houck stiff at attention before him. It always gave him a feeling of satisfaction to see this great, granite man. The replacements they were sending these days, raw and unseasoned, were enough to shake his faith in the service. But as long as there remained a sprinkling of these case-hardened old-time regulars, the Army would still be the Army.

'At ease, Sergeant.'

'Thank you, sir.'

Captain McKay drummed his fingers on the desk. This was a ridiculous situation and the solid, impassive bulk of Sergeant Houck made it seem even more so.

'That woman, Sergeant. She's married. The husband's alive – wasn't with the train when it was attacked. He's been located. Has a place about twenty miles out of Laramie. The name's right and everything checks. You're to take her there and turn her over with the troop's compliments.'

'Me, sir?'

'She asked for you. The big man who found her. Lieutenant Imler says that's you.'

Sergeant Houck considered this expressionlessly. 'And about the boy, sir?'

'He goes with her.' Captain McKay drummed on the desk again. 'Speaking frankly, Sergeant, I think she's making a mistake. I suggested she let us see that the boy got back to the tribe. Grey Otter's dead and after that affair two weeks ago there's not many of the men left. But they'll be on the reservation now and he'd be taken care of. She wouldn't hear of it; said if he had to go she would, too.' Captain McKay felt his former indignation rising again. 'I say she's playing the fool. You agree with me, of course.'

'No, sir. I don't.'

'And why the devil not?'

'He's her son, sir.'

'But he's – Well, that's neither here nor there, Sergeant. It's not our affair. We deliver her and there's an end to it. You'll draw expense money and start within the hour.'

'Right, sir.' The sergeant straightened and made for the door.

'Houck.'

'Yes, sir.'

'Take good care of her – and that damn' kid.'

'Right, sir.'

Captain McKay stood by the window and watched the small cavalcade go past toward the post gateway. Lucky that his wife had come with him to this god-forsaken station lost in the prairie wasteland. Without her they would have been in a fix with the woman. As it was, the woman looked like a woman now. And why shouldn't she, wearing his wife's third-best crinoline dress? It was a bit large, but it gave her a proper feminine appearance. His wife had enjoyed fitting her, from the skin out, everything except shoes. Those were too small. The woman seemed to prefer her worn moccasins anyway. And she was uncomfortable in the clothes. But she was decently grateful for them, insisting she would have them returned or would pay for them somehow. She was riding past the window, sidesaddle on his wife's horse, still with that strange shrinking air about her, not so much frightened as remote, as if she could not quite connect with what was happening to her, what was going on around her.

Behind her was Private Lakin, neat and spruce in his uniform, with the boy in front of him on the horse. The boy's legs stuck out on each side of the small, improvised pillow tied to the forward arch of the saddle to give him a better seat. He looked like a weird, dark-haired doll bobbing with the movements of the horse.

And there beside the woman, shadowing her in the mid-morning, was that extra incongruous touch, the great hulk of Sergeant Houck, straight in his saddle, taking this as he took everything, with no excitement and no show of any emotion, a job to be done.

They went past and Captain McKay watched them ride out through the gateway. It was not quite so incongruous after all. As he had discovered on many a tight occasion, there was something comforting in the presence of that big man. Nothing ever shook him. You might never know exactly what went on inside his close-cropped skull, but you could be certain that what needed to be done he would do.

They were scarcely out of sight of the post when the boy began squirming. Private Lakin clamped him to the pillow with a capable right hand. The squirming persisted. The boy seemed determined to escape from what he regarded as an alien captor. Silent, intent, he writhed on the pillow. Private Lakin's hand and arm grew weary. He tickled his horse forward with his heels until he was close behind the others.

'Beg pardon, sir.'

Sergeant Houck shifted in his saddle and looked around. 'Yes?'

'He's trying to get away, sir. It'd be easier if I tied him down. Could I use my belt, sir?'

Sergeant Houck held in his horse to drop back alongside Private Lakin. 'Kid's don't need tying,' he said. He reached out and plucked the boy from in front of Private Lakin and laid him, face down, across the withers of his own horse and smacked him sharply. Then he set him back on the pillow. The boy sat still, very still. Sergeant Houck pushed his left hand into his left side pocket and pulled out a fistful of small hard biscuits. He passed these to Private Lakin. 'Stick one of these in his mouth when he gets restless.'

Sergeant Houck urged his horse forward until he was beside the woman once more. She had turned her head to watch and she stared sidewise at him for a long moment, then looked straight forward again.

They came to the settlement in the same order: the woman and Sergeant Houck side by side in the lead, Private Lakin and the boy tagging behind at a respectful distance. Sergeant Houck dismounted and helped the woman down and handed the boy to her. He saw Private Lakin looking wistfully at the painted front of the settlement's one saloon and tapped him on one knee. 'Scat,' he said and watched Private Lakin turn his horse and ride off, leading the other two horses.

Then he led the woman into the squat frame building that served as general store and post office and stage stop. He settled the woman and her child on a preserved-goods box and went to the counter to arrange for their fares. When he came back to sit on another box near her, the entire permanent male population of the settlement was assembled just inside the door, all eleven of them staring at the woman.

'. . . that's the one. . . .'

'. . . an Indian had her. . . .'

'. . . shows in the kid. . . .'

Sergeant Houck looked at the woman. She was staring at the floor and the blood was leaving her face. He started to rise and felt her hand on his arm. She had leaned over quickly and clutched his sleeve.

'Please,' she said. 'Don't make trouble account of me.'

'Trouble?' said Sergeant Houck. 'No trouble.' He stood up and confronted the fidgeting men by the door. 'I've seen kids around this place. Some of them small. This one needs decent clothes and the store here doesn't stock them.'

The men stared at him, startled, and then at the wide-eyed boy in his clean but patched skimpy cloth covering. Five or six of them went out through the door and disappeared in various directions. The others scattered through the store. Sergeant Houck stood sentinel, relaxed and quiet by his box, and those who had gone out straggled back, several embarrassed and empty-handed, the rest proud with their offerings. Sergeant Houck took the boy from the woman's lap and stood him on his box. He measured the offerings against the small body and chose a small red checked shirt and a small pair of overalls. He set the one pair of small scuffed shoes aside. 'Kid's don't need shoes,' he said. 'Only in winter.'

When the coach rolled in, it was empty and they had it to themselves for the first hours. Dust drifted steadily through the windows and the silence inside was a persistent thing. The woman did not want to talk. She had lost all liking for it and would speak only when necessary. And Sergeant Houck used words with a natural economy, for the sole simple purpose of conveying or obtaining information that he regarded as pertinent to the business immediately in hand. Only once did he speak during these hours and then only to set a fact straight in his mind. He kept his eyes fixed on the scenery outside as he spoke.

'Did he treat you all right?'

The woman made no pretence of misunderstanding him. 'Yes,' she said.

The coach rolled on and the dust drifted. 'He beat me once,' she said and four full minutes passed before she finished the thought. 'Maybe it was right. I wouldn't work.'

They stopped for a quick meal at a lonely ranch house and ate in silence while the man there helped the driver change horses. It was two mail stops later, at the next change, that another passenger climbed in and plopped his battered suitcase and himself on the front seat opposite them. He was of medium height and plump. He wore city clothes and had quick eyes and features that seemed small in the plumpness of his face. He took out a handkerchief and wiped his face and took off his hat to wipe all the way up his forehead. He laid the hat on top of the suitcase and moved restlessly on the seat, trying to find a comfortable position.

'You three together?'

'Yes,' said Sergeant Houck.

'Your wife then?'

'No,' said Sergeant Houck. He looked out the window on his side and studied the far horizon.

The coach rolled on and the man's quick eyes examined the three of them and came to rest on the woman's feet.

'Begging your pardon, lady, but why do you wear these things? Moccasins, aren't they? They more comfortable?'

She shrank back further in the seat and the blood began to leave her face.

'No offence, lady,' said the man. 'I just wondered—' He stopped. Sergeant Houck was looking at him.

'Dust's bad,' said Sergeant Houck. 'And the flies this time of year. Best to keep your mouth closed.' He looked out the window again, and the only sounds were the running beat of the hoofs and the creakings of the old coach.

A front wheel struck a stone and the coach jolted up at an angle and lurched sideways and the boy gave a small whimper. The woman pulled him on to her lap.

'Say,' said the man. 'Where'd you ever pick up that kid? Looks like—' He stopped. Sergeant Houck was reaching up and rapping against the top of the coach. The driver's voice could be heard shouting at the horses and the coach stopped. One of the doors opened and the driver peered in. Instinctively he picked Sergeant Houck.

'What's the trouble, soldier?'

'No trouble,' said Sergeant Houck. 'Our friend here wants to ride up with you.' He looked at the plump man. 'Less dust up there. It's healthy and gives a good view.'

'Now, wait a minute,' said the man. 'Where'd you get the idea—'

'Healthy,' said Sergeant Houck.

The driver looked at the bleak, impassive hardness of Sergeant Houck and at the twitching softness of the plump man. 'Reckon it would be,' he said. 'Come along. I'll boost you up.'

The coach rolled along the false-fronted one street of a mushroom town and stopped before a frame building tagged Hotel. One of the coach doors opened and the plump man retrieved his hat and suitcase and scuttled into the building. The driver appeared at the coach door. 'Last meal here before the night run,' he said.

When they came out, the shadows were long and fresh horses had been harnessed. As they settled themselves again, a new driver, whip in hand, climbed up to the high seat and gathered the reins into his left hand. The whip cracked and the coach lurched forward and a young man ran out of the low building across the street carrying a saddle. He ran alongside and heaved the saddle up on the roof inside the guardrail. He pulled at the door and managed to scramble in as the coach picked up speed. He dropped on to the front seat, puffing deeply. 'Evening, ma'am,' he said between puffs. 'And you, general.' He leaned forward to slap the boy gently along the jaw. 'And you too, bub.'

Sergeant Houck looked at the lean young man, at the faded Levis tucked into high-heeled boots, the plaid shirt, the amiable competent young face. He grunted a greeting, unintelligible but a pleasant sound.

'A man's legs ain't made for running,' said the young man. 'Just to fork a horse. That last drink was near too long.'

'The Army'd put some starch in those legs,' said Sergeant Houck.

'Maybe. Maybe that's why I ain't in the Army.' The young man sat quietly, relaxed to the jolting of the coach. 'Is there some other topic of genteel conversation you folk'd want to worry some?'

'No,' said Sergeant Houck.

'Then maybe you'll pardon me,' said the young man. 'I hoofed it a lot of miles to-day.' He worked hard at his boots and at last got them off and tucked them out of the way on the floor. He hitched himself up and over on the seat until he was resting on one hip. He put an arm on the window sill and cradled his head on it. His head dropped down and he was asleep.

Sergeant Houck felt a small bump on his left side. The boy had toppled against him. Sergeant Houck set the small body across his lap with head nestled into the crook of his right arm. He leaned his head down and heard the soft little last sigh as drowsiness overcame the boy. He looked sidewise at the woman and dimly made out the outline of her head falling forward and jerking back up and he reached his left arm along the top of the seat until his hand touched her far shoulder. He felt her shoulder stiffen and then relax as she moved closer and leaned toward him. He slipped down lower in the seat so that her head could reach his shoulder and he felt the gentle touch of her brown hair on his neck above his shirt collar. He waited patiently and at last he could tell by her steady deep breathing that all fright had left her and all her thoughts were stilled.

The coach reached a rutted stretch and began to sway and the young man stirred and began to slide on the smooth leather of his seat. Sergeant Houck put up a foot and braced it against the seat edge and the young man's body rested against it. Sergeant Houck leaned his head back on the top of the seat. The stars came out in the clear sky and the running beat of the hoofs had the rhythm of a cavalry squad at a steady trot and gradually Sergeant Houck softened slightly into a sleep.

Sergeant Houck awoke, as always, all at once and aware. The coach had stopped. From the sounds outside, fresh horses were being buckled into the traces. The first light of dawn was creeping into the coach. He raised his head and he realized that he was stiff.

The young man was awake. He was inspecting the vast leather sole of Sergeant Houck's shoe. His eyes flicked up and met Sergeant Houck's eyes and he grinned.

'That's impressive footwear,' he whispered. 'You'd need starch in the legs with hoofs like that.' He sat up and stretched, long and reaching, like a lazy young animal. 'Hell,' he whispered again. 'You must be stiff as a branding iron.' He took hold of Sergeant Houck's leg at the knee and hoisted it slightly so that Sergeant Houck could bend it and ease the foot down to the floor without disturbing the sleeping woman leaning against him. He stretched out both hands and gently lifted the sleeping boy from Sergeant Houck's lap and sat back with the boy in his arms. The young man studied the boy's face. 'Can't be yours,' he whispered.

'No,' whispered Sergeant Houck.

'Must have some Indian strain.'

'Yes.'

The young man whispered down at the sleeping boy. 'You can't help that, can you, bub?'

'No,' said Sergeant Houck suddenly, out loud. 'He can't.'

The woman jerked upright and pulled over to the window on her side, rubbing at her eyes. The boy woke up, wide awake on the instant and saw the unfamiliar face above him and began to squirm violently. The young man clamped his arms tighter. 'Morning, ma'am,' he said. 'Looks like I ain't such a good nursemaid.'

Sergeant Houck reached out a hand and picked up the boy by a grip on the small overalls and deposited him in a sitting position on the seat beside the young man. The boy sat very still.

The sun climbed into plain view and now the coach was stirring the dust of a well-worn road. It stopped where another road crossed and the young man pulled on his boots. He bobbed his head in the direction of a group of low buildings up the side road. 'Think I'll try it there. They'll be peeling broncs about now and the foreman knows I can sit a saddle.' He opened a door and jumped to the ground and turned to poke his head in. 'Hope you make it right,' he said. 'Wherever you're heading.' The door closed and he could be heard scrambling up the back of the coach to get his saddle. There was a thump as he and the saddle hit the ground and then voices began outside, rising in tone.

Sergeant Houck pushed his head through the window beside him. The young man and the driver were facing each other over the saddle. The young man was pulling the pockets of his Levis inside out. 'Lookahere, Will,' he said. 'You know I'll kick in soon as I have some cash. Hell, I've hooked rides with you before.'

'Not now no more,' said the driver. 'The company's sore. They hear of this they'd have my job. I'll have to hold the saddle.'

'You touch that saddle and they'll pick you up in pieces from here to breakfast.'

Sergeant Houck fumbled for his inside jacket pocket. He whistled. The two men turned. He looked hard at the young man. 'There's something on the seat in here. Must have slipped out of your pocket.'

The young man leaned in and saw the two silver dollars on the hard seat and looked up at Sergeant Houck. 'You've been in spots yourself,' he said.

'Yes,' said Sergeant Houck.

The young man grinned. He picked up the coins in one hand and swung the other to slap Sergeant Houck's leg, sharp, stinging and grateful. 'Age ain't hurting you any, general,' he said.

The coach started up and the woman looked at Sergeant Houck. The minutes passed and still she looked at him.

'If I'd had brains enough to get married,' he said, 'might be I'd have had a son. Might have been one like that.'

The woman looked away, out of her window. She reached up to pat her hair and the firm line of her lips softened in the tiny imperceptible beginnings of a smile. The minutes passed and Sergeant Houck stirred again. 'It's the upbringing that counts,' he said and settled into silent immobility, watching the miles go by.

It was near noon when they stopped in Laramie and Sergeant Houck handed the woman out and tucked the boy under one arm and led the way to the waiting room. He settled the woman and the boy in two chairs and left them. He was back soon, driving a light buckboard wagon drawn by a pair of deep-barrelled chestnuts. The wagon bed was well padded with layers of empty burlap bags. He went into the waiting room and picked up the boy and beckoned to the woman to follow. He put the boy down on the burlap bags and helped the woman up on the driving seat.

'Straight out the road, they tell me,' he said. 'About fifteen miles. Then right along the creek. Can't miss it.'

He stood by the wagon, staring along the road. The woman leaned from the seat and clutched at his shoulder. Her voice was high and frightened. 'You're going with me?' Her fingers clung to his service jacket. 'Please! You've got to!'

Sergeant Houck put a hand over hers on his shoulder and released her fingers. 'Yes. I'm going.' He put the child in her lap and stepped to the seat and took the reins. The wagon moved forward.

'You're afraid,' he said.

'They haven't told him,' she said, 'about the boy.'

Sergeant Houck's hands tightened on the reins and the horses slowed to a walk. He clucked sharply to them and slapped the reins on their backs and they quickened again to a trot. The wagon topped a slight rise and the road sloped downward for a long stretch to where the green of trees and tall bushes showed in the distance. A jack rabbit started from the scrub growth by the roadside and leaped high and levelled out, a grey-brown streak. The horses shied and broke rhythm and quieted to a walk under the firm pressure of the reins. Sergeant Houck kept them at a walk, easing the heat out of their muscles, down the long slope to the trees. He let them step into the creek up to their knees and dip their muzzles in the clear running water. The front wheels of the wagon were in the creek and he reached behind him to find a tin dipper tucked among the burlap bags and leaned far out to dip up water for the woman, the boy and himself. He backed the team out of the creek and swung them into the ruts leading along the bank to the right.

The creek was on their left and the sun was behind them, warm on their backs, and the shadows of the horses pushed ahead. The shadows were longer, stretching farther ahead, when they rounded a bend along the creek and the buildings came in sight, the two-room cabin and the several lean-to sheds and the rickety pole corral. A man was standing by one of the sheds and when Sergeant Houck halted the team he came toward them and stopped about twenty feet away. He was not young, perhaps in his middle thirties, but with the young look of a man on whom the years have made no mark except that of the simple passing of time. He was tall, soft and loose-jointed in build, and indecisive in manner and movement. His eyes wavered as he looked at the woman, and the fingers of his hands hanging limp at his sides twitched as he waited for her to speak.

She climbed down her side of the wagon and faced him. She stood straight and the sun behind her shone on her hair. 'Well, Fred,' she said. 'I'm here.'

'Cora,' he said. 'It's been a long time, Cora. I didn't know you'd come so soon.'

'Why didn't you come get me? Why didn't you, Fred?'

'I didn't rightly know what to do, Cora. It was all so mixed up. Thinking you were dead. Then hearing about you. And I couldn't get away easy. I was going to try maybe next week.'

'I hoped you'd come. Right away you heard.'

His body twisted uneasily while his feet remained flat and motionless on the ground. 'Your hair's still pretty,' he said. 'The way it used to be.'

Something like a sob caught in her throat and she started toward him. Sergeant Houck stepped down on the other side of the wagon and walked off to the creek and kneeled to bend and wash the dust from his face. He stood drying his face with a handkerchief and watching the little eddies of the current around several stones in the creek. He heard the voices behind him.

'Wait, Fred. There's something you have to know.'

'That kid? What's it doing here with you?'

'It's mine, Fred.'

'Yours? Where'd you get it?'

'It's my child. Mine.'

There was silence and then the man's voice, bewildered, hurt. 'So it's really true what they said. About that Indian.'

'Yes. He bought me. By their rules I belonged to him. I wouldn't be alive and here now, any other way. I didn't have any say about it.'

There was silence again and then the man spoke, self-pity creeping into his tone. 'I didn't count on anything like this.'

Sergeant Houck walked back to the wagon. The woman seemed relieved at the interruption. 'This is Sergeant Houck,' she said. 'He brought me all the way.'

The man nodded his head and raised a hand to shove back the sandy hair that kept falling forward on his forehead. 'I suppose I ought to thank you, soldier. All that trouble.'

'No trouble,' said Sergeant Houck.

The man pushed at the ground in front of him with one shoe, poking the toe into the dirt and studying it. 'I suppose we ought to go inside. It's near suppertime. I guess you'll be taking a meal here, soldier, before you start back to town.'

'Right,' said Sergeant Houck. 'And I'm tired. I'll stay the night, too. Start in the morning. Sleep in one of those sheds.'

The man pushed at the ground more vigorously. The little pile

of dirt in front of his shoe seemed to interest him a great deal. 'All
right, soldier. Sorry there's no quarters inside.' He turned quickly
and started for the cabin.

The woman took the boy from the wagon and followed him.
Sergeant Houck unharnessed the horses and led them to the creek
for a drink and to the corral and let them through the gate. He
walked quietly to the cabin doorway and stopped just outside.

'For God's sake, Cora,' the man was saying, 'I don't see why you
had to bring that kid with you. You could have told me about it.
I didn't have to see him.'

'What do you mean?'

'Why, now we've got the problem of how to get rid of him.
Have to find a mission or some place that'll take him. Why didn't
you leave him where he came from?'

'No! He's mine!'

'Good God, Cora! Are you crazy? Think you can foist off a thing
like that on me?'

Sergeant Houck stepped through the doorway. 'Thought I heard
something about supper,' he said. He looked around the small room,
then let his eyes rest on the man. 'I see the makings on those shelves.
Come along, Mr Sutliff. A woman doesn't want men cluttering
about when she's getting a meal. Show me your place before it gets
dark.'

He stood, waiting, and the man scraped at the floor with one foot
and slowly stood up and went with him.

They were well beyond earshot of the cabin when Sergeant Houck
spoke again. 'How long were you married? Before it happened?'

'Six years,' said the man. 'No, seven. It was seven when we lost
the last place and headed this way with the train.'

'Seven years,' said Sergeant Houck. 'And no child.'

'It just didn't happen. I don't know why.' The man stopped and
looked sharply at Sergeant Houck. 'Oh. So that's the way you're
looking at it.'

'Yes,' said Sergeant Houck. 'Now you've got one. A son.'

'Not mine,' said the man. 'You can talk. It's not *your* wife. It's
bad enough thinking of taking an Indian's leavings.' He wiped his

lips on his sleeve and spat in disgust. 'I'll be damned if I'll take his kid.'

'Not his any more. He's dead.'

'Look, man. Look how it'd be. A damned little halfbreed. Around all the time to make me remember what she did. A reminder of things I'd want to forget.'

'Could be a reminder that she had some mighty hard going. And maybe come through the better for it.'

'*She* had hard going! What about me? Thinking she was dead. Getting used to that. Maybe thinking of another woman. Then she comes back and an Indian kid with her. What does that make me?'

'Could make you a man,' said Sergeant Houck. 'Think it over.' He turned away and went to the corral and leaned on the rail, watching the horses roll the sweat-itches out on the dry sod. The man went slowly down by the creek and stood on the bank, pushing at the dirt with one shoe and kicking small pebbles into the water. The sun, holding to the horizon rim, dropped suddenly out of sight and dusk came swiftly to blur the outlines of the buildings. The woman appeared in the doorway and called and they went in. There was simple food on the table and the woman stood beside it. 'I've already fed him,' she said and moved her head toward the door to the inner room.

Sergeant Houck ate steadily and reached to refill his plate. The man picked briefly at the food before him and stopped, and the woman ate nothing at all. The man put his hands on the table edge and pushed back and stood up. He went to a side shelf and took a bottle and two thick cups and set them by his plate. He filled the cups a third full from the bottle and shoved one along the table boards toward Sergeant Houck. He lifted the other. His voice was bitter. 'Happy home-coming,' he said. He waited and Sergeant Houck took the other cup and they drank. The man lifted the bottle and poured himself another drink.

The woman looked quickly at him and away.

'Please, Fred.'

The man paid no attention. He reached with the bottle toward the other cup.

'No,' said Sergeant Houck.

The man shrugged. 'You can think better on whisky. Sharpens the mind.' He set the bottle down and took his cup and drained it.

Sergeant Houck fumbled in his right side pocket and found a short straight straw there and pulled it out and put one end in his mouth and chewed slowly on it. The man and the woman sat still, opposite each other at the table, and seemed to forget his quiet presence. They stared everywhere except at each other. Yet their attention was plainly concentrated on each other. The man spoke first. His voice was restrained, carrying conscious patience.

'Look, Cora. You wouldn't want to do that to me. You can't mean what you said before.'

Her voice was determined. 'He's mine.'

'Now, Cora. You don't want to push it too far. A man can take just so much. I didn't know what to do after I heard about you. But I was all ready to forgive you. And now you—'

'Forgive me!' She knocked against her chair rising to her feet. Hurt and bewilderment made her voice ragged as she repeated the words. 'Forgive me?' She turned and ran into the inner room. The handleless door banged shut behind her.

The man stared after her and shook his head and reached again for the bottle.

'Enough's enough,' said Sergeant Houck.

The man shrugged in quick irritation. 'For you maybe,' he said and poured himself another drink. 'Is there any reason you should be noseying in on this?'

'My orders,' said Sergeant Houck, 'were to deliver them safely. Both of them.'

'You've done that,' said the man. He lifted the cup and drained it and set it down carefully. 'They're here.'

'Yes,' said Sergeant Houck. 'They're here.' He stood up and stepped to the outside door and looked into the night. He waited a moment until his eyes were accustomed to the darkness and could distinguish objects faintly in the starlight. He stepped out and went to the pile of straw behind one of the sheds and took an armload and carried it back by the cabin and dropped it at the foot of a tree by one corner. He sat on it, legs stretched out, his shoulders against the tree, and broke off a straw stem and chewed slowly on it. After a while his jaws stopped their slow slight movement and his head sank forward and his eyes closed.

Sergeant Houck woke up abruptly. He was on his feet in a moment, and listening. He heard the faint sound of voices in the cabin, indistinct but rising as the tension rose in them. He went toward the doorway and stopped just short of the rectangle of light from the lamp.

'You're not going to have anything to do with me!' The woman's voice was harsh with stubborn anger. 'Not until this has been settled right!'

'Aw, come on, Cora.' The man's voice was fuzzy, slow-paced. 'We'll talk about that in the morning.'

'No!'

'All right!' Sudden fury made the man's voice shake. 'You want it settled now. Well, it's settled! We're getting rid of that damn' kid first thing tomorrow!'

'No!'

'What gave you the idea you've got any say around here after what you did? I'm the one to say what's to be done. You don't be careful, maybe I won't take you back.'

'Maybe I don't want you to!'

'So damn' finicky all of a sudden! After being with that Indian and maybe a lot more!'

Sergeant Houck stepped through the doorway. The man's back was to him, and he spun him around and his right hand smacked against the side of the man's face and sent him staggering against the wall.

'Forgetting your manners won't help,' said Sergeant Houck. He looked around, and the woman had disappeared into the inner room. The man leaned against the wall, rubbing his cheek, and she came out, the boy in her arms, and ran toward the outer door.

'Cora!' the man shouted. 'Cora!'

She stopped, a brief hesitation in flight. 'I don't belong to you,' she said and was gone through the doorway. The man pushed out from the wall and started after her and the great bulk of Sergeant Houck blocked the way.

'You heard her,' said Sergeant Houck. 'She doesn't belong to anybody now. Nobody but that boy.'

The man stared at him and some of the fury went out of his eyes and he stumbled to his chair at the table and reached for the bottle. Sergeant Houck watched him a moment, then turned and quietly went outside. He walked toward the corral, and as he passed the second shed she came out of the darker shadows and her voice, low and intense, whispered at him: 'I've got to go. I can't stay here.'

Sergeant Houck nodded and went on to the corral. He harnessed the horses quickly and with a minimum of sound. He finished buckling the traces and stood straight and looked toward the cabin. He walked to the doorway and stepped inside. The man was leaning forward in his chair, his elbows on the table, staring at the empty bottle.

'It's finished,' said Sergeant Houck. 'She's leaving now.'

The man shook his head and pushed at the bottle with one forefinger. 'She can't do that.' He looked up at Sergeant Houck and sudden rage began to show in his eyes. 'She can't do that! She's my wife!'

'Not any more,' said Sergeant Houck. 'Best forget she ever came back.' He started toward the door and heard the sharp sound of the chair scraping on the floor behind him. The man's voice rose, shrilling up almost into a shriek.

'Stop!' The man rushed to the wall rack and grabbed the rifle there and held it low and aimed it at Sergeant Houck. 'Stop!' He was breathing deeply and he fought for control of his voice. 'You're not going to take her away!'

Sergeant Houck turned slowly. He stood still, a motionless granite shape in the lamplight.

'Threatening an Army man,' said Sergeant Houck. 'And with an empty gun.'

The man wavered and his eyes flicked down at the rifle. In the second of indecision Sergeant Houck plunged toward him and one hand grasped the gun barrel and pushed it aside and the shot thudded harmlessly into the cabin wall. He wrenched the gun from the man's grasp and his other hand took the man by the shirt front and pushed him down into the chair.

'No more of that,' said Sergeant Houck. 'Best sit quiet.' He looked around the room and found the box of cartridges on a shelf and he took this with the rifle and went to the door. 'Look around in the morning and you'll find these.' He went outside and tossed the gun up on the roof of one of the sheds and dropped the little box by the pile of straw and kicked some straw over it. He went to the wagon and stood by it and the woman came out of the darkness, carrying the boy.

The wagon wheels rolled silently. The small creakings of the wagon body and the thudding rhythm of the horses' hoofs were distinct, isolated sounds in the night. The creek was on their right and they followed the road back the way they had come. The woman moved on the seat, shifting the boy's weight from one arm to the other, until Sergeant Houck took him by the overalls and lifted him and reached behind to lay him on the burlap bags. 'A good boy,' he said. 'Has the Indian way of taking things without yapping. A good way.'

The thin new tracks in the dust unwound endlessly under the wheels and the waning moon climbed through the scattered bushes and the trees along the creek.

'I have relatives in Missouri,' said the woman. 'I could go there.'

Sergeant Houck fumbled in his side pocket and found a straw and put this in his mouth and chewed slowly on it. 'Is that what you want?'

'No.'

They came to the main-road crossing and swung left and the dust thickened under the horses' hoofs. The lean dark shape of a coyote slipped from the brush on one side and bounded along the road and disappeared on the other side.

'I'm forty-seven,' said Sergeant Houck. 'Nearly thirty of that in the Army. Makes a man rough.'

The woman looked straight ahead and a small smile showed in the corners of her mouth.

'Four months,' said Sergeant Houck, 'and this last hitch's done. I'm thinking of homesteading on out in the Territory.' He chewed on the straw and took it between a thumb and forefinger and flipped it away. 'You could get a room at the settlement.'

'I could,' said the woman. The horses slowed to a walk, breathing deeply, and he let them hold the steady, plodding pace. Far off a coyote howled and others caught the signal and the sounds echoed back and forth in the distance and died away into the night silence.'

'Four months,' said Sergeant Houck. 'That's not so long.'

'No,' said the woman. 'Not too long.'

A breeze stirred across the brush and she put out a hand and touched his shoulder. Her fingers moved down along his upper arm and curved over the big muscles there and the warmth of them sank through the cloth of his worn jacket. She dropped her hand in her lap again and looked ahead along the ribbon of the road. He clucked to the horses and urged them again into a trot and the small creakings of the wagon body and the dulled rhythm of the hoofs were gentle sounds in the night.

The late moon climbed and its pale light shone slantwise down on the moving wagon, on the sleeping boy and the woman looking straight ahead, and on the great solid figure of Sergeant Houck.

# THE TWO CARTRIDGES

## *Stewart Edward White*

THIS happened at the time Billy Knapp drove stage between Pierre and Deadwood. I think you can still see the stage in Buffalo Bill's show. Lest confusion arise and the reader be inclined to credit Billy with more years than are his due, it might be well also to mention that the period was some time after the summer he and Alfred and Jim Buckley had made their famous march with the only wagon-train that dared set out, and some time before Billy took to mining. Jim had already moved to Montana.

The journey from Pierre to Deadwood amounted to something. All day long the trail led up and down long grassy slopes, and across sweeping, intervening flats. While climbing the slopes, you could never get your experience to convince you that you were not, on topping the hill, about to overlook the entire country for miles around. This never happened; you saw no farther than the next roll of the prairie. While hurtling down the slopes, you saw the intervening flat as interminably broad and hot and breathless, or interminably broad and icy and full of arctic winds, according to the season of the year. Once in a dog's age you came to a straggling fringe of cottonwood-trees, indicating a creek bottom. The latter was either quite dry or in raging flood. Close under the hill huddled two buildings, half logs, half mud. There the horses were changed by strange men with steel glints in their eyes, like those you see under the brows of a north-country tug-boat captain. Passengers could there eat flap-jacks architecturally warranted to hold together against the most vigorous attack of the gastric juices, and drink green tea that tasted of tannin and really demanded for its proper accommodation porcelain-lined insides. It was not an inspiring trip.

Of course, Billy did not accompany the stage all of the way; only the last hundred miles; but the passengers did, and by the time they reached Billy they were usually heartily sick of their undertaking. Once a tenderfoot came through in the fall of the year, simply for the love of adventure. He got it.

'Driver,' said he to Billy, as the brakes set for another plunge, 'were you ever held up?'

Billy had been deluged with questions like this for the last two hours. Usually he looked straight in front of him, spat accurately between the tail of the wheel-horse and the whiffle-tree, and answered in monosyllables. The tenderfoot did not know that asking questions was not the way to induce Billy to talk.

'Held up?' replied Billy, with scorn. 'Young feller, I is held up thirty-seven times in th' last year.'

'Thunderation!' exclaimed the tenderfoot. 'What do you do? Do you have much trouble getting away? Have you had much fighting?'

'Fight nothin'. I ain't hired to fight. I'm hired to drive stage.'

'And you just let them go through you?' cried the tenderfoot.

Billy was stung by the contempt in the stranger's tone.

'Go through nothin',' he explained. 'They isn't touchin' *me* none whatever. Put her down fer argument that I'm damn fool enough to sprinkle lead 'round some, and that I gets away. What happens? Nex' time I drives stage some of there yere agents massacrees me from behind a bush. Whar do I come in? Nary bit!'

The tenderfoot, struck by the logic of this reasoning, fell silent. After an interval the sun set in a film of yellow light; then the afterglow followed; and finally the stars pricked out the true immensity of the prairies.

'*He's* the feller hired to fight,' observed the shadowy Billy, jerking his thumb backward.

The tenderfoot now understood the silent, grim man who, unapproachable and solitary, had alone occupied the seat on top of the stage. Looking with more curiosity, the tenderfoot observed a shotgun with abnormally short barrels, slung in two brass clips along the back of the seat in front of the messenger. The usual revolvers, too, were secured, instead of by the regulation holsters, in brass clips riveted to the belt, so that in case of necessity they could be snatched free with one forward sweep of the arm. The man met his gaze keenly.

'Them Hills ain't fur now,' vouchsafed Billy, as a cold breeze from the west lifted the limp brim of his hat, and a film of cloud drew with uncanny and silent rapidity across the stars.

The tenderfoot had turned again to look at the messenger, who interested him exceedingly, when the stage came to a stop so violent as almost to throw him from his seat. He recovered his balance with difficulty. Billy, his foot braced against the brake, was engaged in leisurely winding the reins around it.

'*Hands up, I say!*' cried a sharp voice from the darkness ahead.

'Meanin' you,' observed Billy to the tenderfoot, at the same time thrusting his own over his head and settling down comfortably on the small of his back. 'Time!' he called, facetiously, to the darkness.

As though at the signal the night split with the roar of buckshot, and splintered with the answering crackle of a six-shooter three times repeated. The screech of the brake had deceived the messenger as to the whereabouts of the voice. He had jumped to the ground on the wrong side of the stage, thus finding himself without protection against his opponent, who, firing at the flash of the shot-gun, had brought him to the ground.

The road-agent stepped confidently forward. 'Billy,' said he, pleasantly, 'jest pitch me that box.'

Billy climbed over the seat and dropped a heavy, iron-bound case to the ground. 'Danged if I thinks anybody *kin* git Buck, thar,' he remarked, in thoughtful reference to the messenger.

'Now, drive on,' commanded the road-agent.

Three hours later Billy and the sobered tenderfoot pulled into Deadwood. Ten minutes taught the camp what had occurred.

Now, it must be premised that Deadwood had recently chosen a sheriff. He did not look much like a sheriff, for he was small and weak and bald, and most childlike as to expression of countenance. But when I tell you that his name was Alfred, you will know that it was all right. To him the community looked for initiative. It expected him to organise a posse, which would, of course, consist of every man in the place not otherwise urgently employed, and to enter upon instant pursuit. He did not.

'How many is they?' he asked of Billy.

'One lonesome one,' replied the stage-driver.

'I plays her a lone hand,' announced Alfred.

You see, Alfred knew well enough his own defects. He never could make plans when anybody else was near, but always instinctively took the second place. Then, when the other's scheme had fallen into ruins, he would construct a most excellent expedient from the wreck of it. In the case under consideration he preferred to arrange his own campaign, and therefore to work alone.

By that time men knew Alfred. They made no objection.

'Snowin',' observed one of the chronic visitors of the saloon door. There are always two or three such in every Western gathering.

'One of you boys saddle my bronc,' suddenly requested Alfred, and began to examine his firearms by the light of the saloon lamp.

'Yo' ain't aimin' to set out to-night?' they asked, incredulously.

'I am. Th' snow will make a good trail, but she'll be covered come mornin'.'

So Alfred set out alone, at night, in a snowstorm, without the guidance of a solitary star, to find a single point in the vastness of the prairie.

He made the three hours of Billy and the tenderfoot in a little over an hour, because it was mostly down hill. So the agent had apparently four hours the start of him, which discrepancy was cut down, however, by the time consumed in breaking open the strong-box after Billy and the stage had surely departed beyond gunshot. The exact spot was easily marked by the body of Buck, the express messenger. Alfred convinced himself that the man was dead, but did not waste further time on him: the boys would take care of the remains next day. He remounted and struck out sharp for the east, though, according to Billy's statement, the agent had turned north.

'He is alone,' said Alfred to himself, 'so he ain't in that Black Hank outfit. Ain't nothin' to take him north, an' if he goes south he has to hit way down through the South Fork trail, which same takes him two weeks. Th' greenbacks in that plunder is numbered, and old Wells-Fargo has th' numbers. He sure has to pike in an' change them bills afore he is spotted. So he goes to Pierre.'

Alfred staked his all on this reasoning and rode blindly eastward. Fortunately the roll of the country was sufficiently definite to enable him to keep his general direction well enough until about three o'clock, when the snow ceased and the stars came out, together with the waning moon. Twenty minutes later he came to the bed of a stream.

'Up or down?' queried Alfred, thoughtfully. The state of the weather decided him. It had been blowing all night strongly from the north-west. Left without guidance a pony tends to edge more or less away from the wind, in order to turn tail to the weather. Alfred had diligently counteracted this tendency all night, but he doubted whether, in the hurry of flight, the fugitive had thought of it. Instead of keeping directly east toward Pierre, he had probably fallen away more or less toward the south. 'Down,' Alfred decided.

He dismounted from his horse and began to lead the animal parallel to the stream, but about two hundred yards from it, first taking care to ascertain that a little water flowed in the channel. On discovering that there did, he nodded his head in a satisfied manner.

'He doesn't leave no trail till she begins to snow,' he argued, 'an' he nat'rally doesn't expect no mud-turkles like me a followin' of him eastward. *Consequently* he feeds when he strikes water. This yere is water.'

All of which seemed satisfactory to Alfred. He walked on foot in order to discover the trail in the snow. He withdrew two hundred yards from the bank of the stream that his pony might not scent the other man's horse, and so give notice of approach by whinnying. After a time he came across the trail. So he left the pony and followed it to the creek-bottom on foot. At the top of the bluff he peered over cautiously.

'Well, you got nerve!' he remarked to himself. 'If I was runnin' this yere game, I'd sure scout with my blinders off.'

The fugitive evidently believed himself safe from pursuit, for he had made camp. His two ponies cropped browse and pawed for grass in the bottom land. He himself had prepared a warm niche and was sleeping in it with only one blanket over him, though by now the thermometer was well down toward zero. The affair had been simple. He had built a long, hot fire in the L of an upright ledge and the ground. When ready to sleep he had raked the fire three feet out from the angle, and had lain down on the heated ground between the fire and the ledge. His rifle and revolver lay where he could seize them at a moment's notice.

Alfred could stalk a deer, but he knew better than to attempt to stalk a man trained in the West. Instead, he worked himself into a protected position and carefully planted a Winchester bullet some six inches from the man's ear. The man woke up suddenly and made an instinctive grab toward his weapons.

'Drop it!' yelled Alfred.

So he dropped it, and lay like a rabbit in its form.

'Jest select that thar six-shooter by the end of the bar'l and hurl her from you some,' advised the sheriff. 'Now the Winchester. Now stand up an' let's look at you.' The man obeyed. 'Yo' don't really need that other gun, under th' circumstances,' pursued the little man. 'No, don't fetch her loose from the holster none; jest unbuckle th' whole outfit, belt and all. Good! Now, you freeze, and stay froze right whar you are.'

So Alfred arose and scrambled down to the bottom.

'Good-mornin',' he observed, pleasantly.

He cast about him and discovered the man's lariat, which he picked up and overran with one hand until he had loosened the noose.

'You-all are some sizable,' he remarked, in conversational tones, 'an' like enough you eats me up, if I gets clost enough to tie you. Hands up!'

With a deft twist and flip he tossed the open noose over his prisoner's upheld wrists and jerked it tight.

'Thar you be,' he observed, laying aside his rifle.

He loosened one of his revolvers suggestively and approached to tie the knot.

'Swing her down,' he commanded. He contemplated the result. 'Don't like that nohow – tied in front. Step through your hands a whole lot.' The man hesitated. 'Step, I say!' said Alfred, sharply, at the same time pricking the prisoner with his long knife.

The other contorted and twisted awkwardly, but finally managed to thrust first one foot, then the other, between his shackled wrists. Alfred bound together his elbows at the back.

'You'll do,' he approved, cheerfully. 'Now, we sees about grub.'

Two flat stones placed a few inches apart improvised a stove when fire thrust its tongue from the crevice, and a frying-pan and tin-cup laid across the opening cooked the outlaw's provisions. Alfred hospitably ladled some bacon and coffee into their former owner.

'Not that I needs to,' he observed, 'but I'm jest that tender-hearted.'

At the close of the meal, Alfred instituted a short and successful search for the plunder, which he found in the stranger's saddle-bag, open and unashamed.

'Yo're sure a tenderfoot at this game, stranger,' commented the sheriff. 'Thar is plenty abundance of spots to cache such plunder – like the linin' of yore saddle, or a holler horn. Has you any choice of cayuses for ridin'?' indicating the grazing ponies.

The man shook his head. He had maintained a lowering silence throughout all these cheerful proceedings.

Alfred and his prisoner finally mounted and rode northwest. As soon as they had scrambled up the precipitous side of the gully, the affair became a procession, with the stranger in front, and the stranger's second pony bringing up an obedient rear. Thus the robber was first to see a band of Sioux that topped a distant rise for a single instant. Of course the Sioux saw him, too. He communicated this discovery to Alfred.

'Well,' said Alfred, 'they ain't hostile.'

'These yere savages is plenty hostile,' contradicted the stranger, 'and don't you make no mistake thar. I jest nat'rally lifts that pinto offen them yisterday,' and he jerked his thumb toward the black-and-white pony in the rear.

'And you camps!' cried Alfred, in pure astonishment. 'You must be plumb locoed!'

'I ain't had no sleep in three nights,' explained the other, in apology.

Alfred's opinion of the man rose at once.

'Yo' has plumb nerve to tackle a hold-up under them circumstances,' he observed.

'I sets out to git that thar stage; and I gits her,' replied the agent, doggedly.

The savages appeared on the next rise, barely a half-mile away, and headed straight for the two men.

'I reckon yere's where you takes a hand,' remarked Alfred simply, and, riding alongside, he released the other man's arms by a single slash of his knife. The man slipped from his horse and stretched his arms wide apart and up over his head in order to loosen his muscles. Alfred likewise dismounted. The two, without further parley, tied their horses' noses close to their front fetlocks, and sat down back to back on the surface of the prairie. Each was armed with one of the new 44–40 Winchesters, just out, and with a brace of Colt's revolvers, chambering the same-sized cartridge as the rifle.

'How you heeled?' inquired Alfred.

The stranger took stock.

'Fifty-two,' he replied.

'Seventy for me,' vouchsafed Alfred. 'I goes plenty organised.'

Each man spread a little semicircle of shells in front of him. At the command of the two, without reloading, were forty-eight shots.

When the Indians had approached to within about four hundred yards of the white men they paused. Alfred rose and held his hand toward them, palm outward, in the peace sign. His response was a shot and a chorus of yells.

'I tells you,' commented the hold-up.

Alfred came back and sat down. The savages, one by one, broke away from the group and began to circle rapidly to the left in a constantly contracting spiral. They did a great deal of yelling. Occasionally they would shoot. To the latter feature the plainsmen lent an attentive ear, for to their trained senses each class of arm spoke with a different voice – the old muzzle-loader, the Remington, the long, heavy Sharp's 50, each proclaimed itself plainly. The mere bullets did not interest them in the least. Two men seated on the ground presented but a small mark to the Indians shooting uncleaned weapons from running horses at three or four hundred yards' range.

'That outfit is rank outsiders,' concluded Alfred. 'They ain't over a dozen britch-loaders in the layout.'

'Betcher anything you say I drops one,' offered the stranger, taking a knee-rest.

'Don't be so plumb fancy,' advised Alfred, 'but turn in and help.'

He was satisfied with the present state of affairs, and was hacking at the frozen ground with his knife. The light snow on the ridge-tops had been almost entirely drifted away. The stranger obeyed.

On seeing the men thus employed, the Indians turned their horses directly toward the group and charged in. At the range of perhaps two hundred yards the Winchesters began to speak. Alfred fired twice and the stranger three times. Then the circle broke and divided and passed by, leaving an oval of untrodden ground.

'How many did you get?' inquired Alfred, with professional interest.

'Two,' replied the man.

'Two here,' supplemented Alfred.

A commotion, a squeal, a thrashing-about near at hand caused both to turn suddenly. The pinto pony was down and kicking. Alfred walked over and struck him in the throat to save a cartridge.

'Move up, pardner,' said he.

The other moved up. Thus the men became possessed of protection from one side. The Indians had vented a yell of rage when the pony had dropped. Now as each warrior approached a certain point in the circle, he threw his horse back on its haunches, so that in a short time the entire band was once more gathered in a group. Alfred and the outlaw knew that this manœuvre portended a more serious charge than the impromptu affair they had broken with such comparative ease. An Indian is extremely gregarious when it comes to open fighting. He gets a lot of encouragement out of yells, the patter of many ponies' hoofs, and the flutter of an abundance of feathers. Running in from the circumference of a circle is a bit too individual to suit his taste.

Also, the savages had by now taken the measure of their white opponents. They knew they had to deal with experience. Suspicion of this must have been aroused by the practised manner in which the men had hobbled their horses and had assumed the easiest posture of defence. The idea would have gained strength from their superior marksmanship; but it would have become absolute certainty from the small detail that, in all this hurl and rush of excitement, they had fired but five shots, and those at close range. It is difficult to refrain from banging away for general results when so many marks so loudly present themselves. It is equally fatal to do so. A few misses are a great encouragement to a savage, and seem to breed their like in subsequent shooting. They destroy your own coolness and confidence, and they excite the enemy an inch nearer to that dead-line of the lust of fighting beyond which prudence gives place to the fury of killing. An Indian is the most cautious and wily of fighters before he goes mad: and the most terribly reckless after. In a few moments four of their numbers had passed to the happy hunting-grounds, and they were left, no nearer their prey, to contemplate the fact.

The tornado moved. It swept at the top jump of ponies used to the chase of the buffalo, as sudden and terrible and imminent as the loom of a black cloud on the wings of storm, and, like it, seeming to gather speed and awfulness as it rushed nearer. Each rider bent low over his pony's neck and shot – a hail of bullets, which, while most passed too high, nevertheless shrieked and spun through the volume of coarser sound. The ponies stretched their necks and opened their red mouths and made their little feet go with a rapidity that twinkled as bewilderingly as a picket-fence passing a train. And the light snow swirled and eddied behind them.

The two men behind the dead horse were not deceived by this excitement into rising to their knees. They realised that this was the critical point in their fight, and they shot hard and fast, concentrating all the energy of their souls into the steady glare of their eyes over the sights of the smoking rifles. In a moment the foremost warrior was trying to leap his pony at the barrier before him, but the little animal refused the strange jump and shied to the left, cannoning and plunging into the stream of braves rushing in on that side. Into the confusion Alfred emptied the last two shots of his Winchester, and was fortunate enough merely to cripple a pony with one of them. The kicking, screaming, little beast interposed a momentary but effective barrier between the sheriff and his foes. A rattling fire from one of his six-shooters into the brown of the hesitating charge broke it. The self-induced excitement ebbed, and the Indians swerved and swept on by.

On the other side, the outlaw had also managed to kill a pony within a few feet of the impromptu breastwork, and, direct riding-down being thus prevented in front, he was lying stretched on his side, coolly letting off first one revolver then the other in the face of imminent ruin. Alfred's attentions, however, and the defection of the right wing, drove these savages, too, into flight. Miraculously, neither man was more than scratched, though their clothes and the ground about them showed the marks of bullets. Strangely enough, too, the outlaw's other pony stood unhurt at a little distance whither the rush of the charge had sent him. Alfred arose and drove him back. Then both men made a triangular breastwork of the two dead horses and their saddles.

'Cyan't do that more'n once,' observed the outlaw, taking a long breath.

'They don't want her more'n once,' replied Alfred, sagely.

The men tried to take score. This was not easy. Out of the hundred and twelve cartridges with which they had started the fight, there remained sixty-eight. That meant they had expended thirty-nine in the last charge alone. As near as they could make out, they had accounted for eight of the enemy, four in the mêlée just finished. Besides, there were a number of ponies down. At first glance this might seem like poor shooting. It was not. A rapidly moving figure is a difficult rifle-mark with the best of conditions. In this case the conditions would have rendered an Easterner incapable of hitting a feather pillow at three yards.

And now began the most terrible part of this terrible day. A dozen of the warriors dismounted, made a short circle to the left, and disappeared in a thin growth of dried grasses, old mulliens, and stunted, scattered brush barely six inches high. There seemed hardly cover enough to hide a man, and yet the dozen were as completely swallowed up as though they had plunged beneath the waters of the sea. Only occasionally the top of a grass tuft or a greasewood shivered. It became the duty of Alfred and his companion to shoot suddenly and accurately at these motions. This was necessary in order to discourage the steady concealed advance of the dozen, who, when they had approached to within as few yards as their god of war would permit, purposed to rush in and finish their opponents out of hand. And that rush could never be stopped. The white men knew it perfectly well, so they set conscientiously to work with their handful of cartridges to convince the reds that it is not healthy to crawl along ridge-tops on an autumn day. Sundry outlying Indians, with ammunition to waste, took belly and knee rests and strengthened the thesis to the contrary.

The brisk fighting had warmed the contestants' blood. Now a cold wind penetrated through their woollens to the goose-flesh. It was impossible to judge of the effect of the shots, but both knew that the accuracy of their shooting was falling off. Clench his teeth as he would, hold his breath as steadfastly as he might, Alfred could not accomplish that steady, purposeful, unblinking pressure on the trigger so necessary to accuracy. In spite of himself, the rifle jerked ever so little to the right during the fall of the hammer. Soon he adopted the expedient of pulling it suddenly which is brilliant but uncertain. The ground was very cold. Before long both men would have felt inclined to risk everything for the sake of a little blood-stimulating tramp back and forth. The danger did not deter them. Only the plainsman's ingrained horror of throwing away a chance held them, shivering pitiably, to their places.

Still they managed to keep the dozen at a wary distance, and even, they suspected, to hit some. This was the Indians' game – to watch, to wait; to lie with infinite patience; to hitch nearer a yard, a foot, an inch even; and then to seize with the swiftness of the eagle's swoop an opportunity which the smallest imprudence, fruit of weariness, might offer. One by one the precious cartridges spit, and fell from the breech-blocks empty and useless. And still the tufts of grass wavered a little nearer.

'I wish t'hell, stranger, you-all hadn't edged off south,' chattered Alfred. 'We'd be nearer th' Pierre trail.'

'I'm puttin' in my spare wishin' on them Injins,' shivered the other; 'I sure hopes they aims to make a break pretty quick; I'm near froze.'

About two o'clock the sun came out and the wind died. Though its rays were feeble at that time of year, their contrast with the bleakness that had prevailed during the morning threw a perceptible warmth into the crouching men. Alfred succeeded, too, in wriggling a morsel of raw bacon from the pack, which the two men shared. But the cartridges were running very low.

'We establishes a dead-line,' suggested Alfred. 'S' long as they slinks beyond yonder greasewood, they lurks in safety. Plug 'em this side of her.'

'C'rrect,' agreed the stranger.

This brought them a season of comparative quiet. They even made out to smoke, and so were happy. Over near the hill the body of Indians had gone into camp and were taking it easy. The job of wiping out these troublesome whites had been sublet, and they wasted no further anxiety over the affair. This indifference irritated the outlaw exceedingly.

'Damn siwashes!' he grumbled.

'Look out!' warned Alfred.

The dead-line was overpassed. Swaying tufts of vegetation marked the rapid passage of eel-like bodies. The Indians had decided on an advance, being encouraged probably by the latter inaccuracy of the plainsmen's fire. Besides, the day was waning. It was no cat-and-mouse game now; but a rush, like the other except that all but the last twenty or thirty yards would be made under cover. The beseiged turned their attention to it. Over on the hill the bucks had arisen from their little fires of buffalo chips, and were watching. On the summit of the farther ridge rode silhouetted sentinels.

Alfred selected a tuft and fired just ahead of it. A *crack* at his side indicated that the stranger, too, had gone to work. It was a discouraging and nervous business. The shooter could never tell whether or not he had hit. The only thing he was sure of was that the line was wriggling nearer and nearer. He felt something as though he were shooting at a man with blank cartridges. This test of nerve was probably the most severe of the fight.

But it was successfully withstood. Alfred felt a degree of steadiness return to him with the excitement and the change of weather. The Winchester spat as carefully as before. Suddenly it could no longer be doubted that the line was beginning to hesitate. The outlaw saw it, too.

'Give it to 'em good!' he cried.

Both men shot, and then again.

The line wavered.

'Two more shots will stop 'em!' cried the road-agent, and pulled the trigger. The hammer clicked against an empty chamber.

'I'm done!' he cried, hopelessly. His cartridges were gone.

Alfred laid his own Winchester on the ground, turned over on his back, and puffed a cloud of smoke straight up toward the sky.

'Me, too,' said he.

The cessation of the shooting had put an end to the Indians' uncertainty. Another moment would bring them knowledge of the state of affairs.

'Don't get much outen my scalp, anyway,' said Alfred, uncovering his bald head.

The sentinel on the distant ridge was riding his pony in short-looped circles and waving a blanket in a peculiar way above his head. From the grass nine Indians arose, stooped, and scuttled off like a covey of running quail. Over by the fires warriors were leaping on their ponies, and some were leading other ponies in the direction of the nine. An air of furtive but urgent haste characterised all these movements. Alfred lent an attentive ear.

'Seem a whole lot like a rescue,' he remarked, quietly. 'I reckon th' boys been followin' of my trail.'

The stranger paused in the act of unhobbling the one remaining pony. In the distance, faintly, could be heard cheers and shots intended as encouragement.

'They's comin' on th' jump,' said Alfred.

By this time the stranger had unfastened the horse.

'I reckon we quits,' said he, mounting; 'I jest nat'rally takes this bronc, because I needs him more'n you do. So long. I may's well confide that I'm feelin' some glad jest now that them Injins comes along.'

And then his pony fell in a heap, and began to kick up dirt and to snort blood.

'I got another, so you just subside a lot,' commanded Alfred, recocking his six-shooter.

The stranger lay staring at him in astonishment.

'Thought you was busted on catridges!' he cried.

'You-all may as well know,' snapped Alfred, 'that's long as I'm an officer of this yere district, I'm a sheriff first and an Injin-fighter afterward.'

'What the hell!' wondered the road-agent, still in a daze.

'Them's th' two catridges that would have stopped 'em,' said Alfred.

# HAPPY-TEETH

## *Owen Wister*

SCIPIO LE MOYNE lay in bed, held together with bandages. His body had need for many bandages. A Bar-Circle-Zee three-year-old had done him violent mischief at the forks of Stinking Water.[1] But for the fence, Scipio might have swung clear of the wild, rearing animal. When they lifted his wrecked frame from the ground, one of them had said: —

'A spade's all he'll need now.'

Overhearing this with some still unconquered piece of his mind, Scipio made one last remark: 'I ain't going to die for years and years.'

Upon this his head had rolled over, and no further statements came from him for – I forget how long. Yet somehow, we all believed that last remark of his.

'Since I've known him,' said the Virginian, 'I have found him a truthful man.'

'Which don't mean,' Honey Wiggin put in, 'that he can't lie when he ought to.'

Judge Henry always sent his hurt cow-punchers to the nearest surgical aid, which in this case was the hospital on the reservation. Here then, one afternoon, Scipio lay, his body still bound tight at a number of places, but his brain needing no bandages whatever; he was able to see one friend for a little while each day. It was almost time for this day's visitor to go, and the visitor looked at his watch.

'Oh, don't do that!' pleaded the man in bed. 'I'm not sick any more.'

---

[1] Lately changed to Shoshone River by act of legislature. While we miss the old name, derived from certain sulphur springs, we agree that like the Indian and the cow-boy it belongs to the past.

'You will be sick some more if you keep talking,' replied the Virginian.

'Thinkin' is a heap more dangerous, if y'u can't let it out,' Scipio urged. 'I'm not half through tellin' y'u about Horacles.'

'Did his mother name him that?' inquired the Virginian.

'Naw! but his mother brought it on him. Didn't y'u know? Of course you don't often get so far north in the Basin as the Agency. His name is Horace Pericles Byram. Well, the Agent wasn't going to call his assistant store-clerk all that, y'u know, not even if he *has* got an uncle in the Senate of the United States, Couldn't spare the time. Days not long enough. Not even in June. So everybody calls him Horacles now. He's reconciled to it. But I ain't. It's too good for him. A heap too good. I've knowed him all my life, and I can't think of a name that's not less foolish than he is. Well, where was I? I was tellin' y'u how back in Gallipo*leece* he couldn't understand anything. Not dogs. Not horses. Not girls.'

'Do you understand girls?' the Virginian interrupted.

'Better'n Horacles. Well, now it seems he can't understand Indians. Here he is sellin' goods to 'em across the counter at the Agency store. I could sell twiced what he does, from what they tell me. I guess the Agent has begun to discover what a trick the Uncle played him when he unloaded Horacles on him. Now why did the Uncle do that?'

Scipio stopped in his rambling discourse, and his brows knitted as he began to think about the Uncle. The Virginian once again looked at his watch, but Scipio, deep in his thoughts, did not notice him. 'Uncle,' he resumed to himself, half aloud, 'Uncle was the damnedest scoundrel in Gallipo*leece*. – Say!' he exclaimed suddenly, and made an eager movement to sit up. 'Oh Lord!' he groaned, sinking back. 'I forgot. – What's your hurry?'

But the Virginian had seen the pain transfix his friend's face, and though that face had instantly smiled, it was white. He stood up. 'I'd ought to get kicked from here to the ranch,' he said, remorsefully. 'I'll get the doctor.'

Vainly the man in bed protested; his visitor was already at the door.

'I've not told y'u about his false teeth!' shrieked Scipio, hoping this would detain him. 'And he does tricks with a rabbit and a bowl of fish.'

But the guest was gone. In his place presently the Post surgeon came, and was not pleased. Indeed, this excellent army doctor swore. Still, it was not the first time that he had done so, nor did it prove the last; and Scipio, it soon appeared, had given himself no hurt. But in answer to a severe threat, he whined: —

'Oh, ain't y'u goin' to let me see him tomorro'?'

'You'll see nobody to'morrow except me.'

'Well, that'll be seein' nobody,' whined Scipio, more grievously.

The doctor grinned. 'In some ways you're incurable. Better go to sleep now.' And he left him.

Scipio did not go to sleep then, though by morning he had slept ten healthful hours, waking with the Uncle still at the centre of his thoughts. It made him again knit his brows.

'No, you can't see him to-day,' said the doctor, in reply to a request.

'But I hadn't finished sayin' something to him,' Scipio protested. 'And I'm well enough to see my dead grandmother.'

'That I'll not forbid,' answered the doctor. And he added that the Virginian had gone back to Sunk Creek with some horses.

'Oh, yes,' said Scipio. 'I'd forgot. Well, he'll be coming through on his way to Billings next week. You been up to the Agency lately? Yesterday? Well, there's going to be something new happen. Agent seem worried or anything?'

'Not that I noticed. Are the Indians going on the war-path?'

'Nothing like that. But why does a senator of the United States put his nephew in that store? Y'u needn't to tell me it's to provide for him, for it don't provide. I thought I had it figured out last night, but Horacles don't fit. I can't make him fit. He don't understand Injuns. That's my trouble. Now the Uncle must know Horacles don't understand. But if he didn't know?' pursued Scipio, and fell to thinking.

'Well,' said the doctor indulgently, as he rose, 'it's good you can invent these romances. Keeps you from fretting, shut up here alone.'

'There'd be no romances here,' retorted Scipio. 'Uncle is exclusively hard cash.' The doctor departed.

At his visit next morning, he was pleased with his patient's condition. 'Keep on,' said he, 'and I'll let you sit up Monday for ten minutes. Any more romances?'

'Been thinkin' of my past life,' said Scipio.

The doctor laughed long. 'Why, how old are you, anyhow?' he asked at length.

'Oh, there's some lovely years still to come before I'm thirty. But I've got a whole lot of past life, all the same.' Then he pointed a solemn, oracular finger at the doctor. 'What white man savvys the Injun? Not you. Not me. And I've drifted around some, too. The map of the United States has been my home. Been in Arizona and New Mexico and among the Siwashes – seen all kinds of Injun – but I don't savvy 'em. I know most any Injun's better'n most any white man till he meets the white man. Not smarter, y'u know, but better. And I do know this: You take an Injun and let him be a warrior and a chief and a grandfather who has killed heaps of white men in his day – but all that don't make him grown up. Not like we're grown up. He stays a child in some respects till he's dead. He'll believe things and be scared at things that ain't nothin' to you and me. You take Old High Bear right on this reservation. He's got hair like snow and eyes like an eagle's and he can sing a war-song about fights that happened when our fathers were kids. But if you want to deal with him, you got to remember he's a child of five.'

'I do know all this,' said the doctor, interested. 'I've not been twenty years on the frontier for nothing.'

'Horacles don't know it,' said Scipio. 'I've saw him in the store all season.'

'Well,' said the doctor, 'see you to-morrow. I've some new patients in the ward.'

'Soldiers?'

'Soldiers.'

'Guess I know why they're here.'

'Oh, yes,' sighed the doctor. 'You know. Few come here for any other reason.' The doctor held views about how a military post should be regulated, which popular sentiment will never share. 'Can I do anything for you?' he inquired.

'If I could have some newspapers?' said Scipio.

'Why didn't you tell me before?' said the doctor. After that he saw to it that Scipio had them liberally.

With newspapers the patient sat surrounded deep, when the Virginian, passing north on his way to Billings, looked in for a moment to give his friend the good word. That is what he came for, but what he said was:—

'So he has got false teeth?'

Scipio, hearing the voice at the door, looked over the top of his paper at the visitor.

'Yes,' he replied, precisely as if the visitor had never been out of the room.

'What d' y'u know?' inquired the Virginian.

'Nothing; what do you?'

'Nothing.'

After all, such brief greetings cover the ground.

'Better sit down,' suggested Scipio.

The Virginian sat, and took up a paper. Thus for a little while they both read in silence.

'Did y'u stop at the Agency as y'u came along?' asked Scipio, not looking up from his paper.

'No.'

There was silence again as they continued reading. The Virginian, just come from Sunk Creek, had seen no newspapers as recent as these. When two friends on meeting after absence can sit together for half an hour without a word passing between them, it is proof that they really enjoy each other's company. The gentle air came in the window, bringing the tonic odor of the sage-brush. Outside the window stretched a yellow world to distant golden hills. The talkative voice of a magpie somewhere near at hand was the only sound.

Nothing in the newspapers in particular,' said Scipio, finally.

'You expectin' something particular?' the Virginian asked.

'Yes.'

'Mind sayin' what it is?'

'Wish I knew what it is.'

'Always Horacles?'

'Always him – and Uncle. I'd like to spot Uncle.'

Mess call sounded from the parade ground. It recalled the flight of time to the Virginian.

'When you get back from Billings,' said Scipio, 'you're liable to find me up and around.'

'Hope so. Maybe you'll be well enough to go with me to the ranch.'

But when the Virginian returned, a great deal had happened all at once, as is the custom of events.

Scipio's vigorous convalescence brought him in the next few days to sitting about in the open air, and then enlarged his freedom to a crutch. He hobbled hither and yon, paying visits, many of them to the doctor. The doctor it was, and no newspaper, who gave to Scipio the first grain of that 'something particular' which he had been daily seeking and never found. He mentioned a new building that was being put up rather far away down in the corner of the reservation. The rumor in the air was that it had something to do with the Quartermaster's department. The odd thing was that the Quartermaster himself had heard nothing about it. The Agent up at the Agency store considered this extremely odd. But a profound absence of further explanations seemed to prevail. What possible need for a building was there at that inconvenient, isolated spot?

Scipio slapped his leg. 'I guess what y'u call my romance is about to start.'

'Well,' the doctor admitted, 'it may be. Curious things are done upon Indian reservations. Our management of them may be likened to putting the Lord's Prayer and the Ten Commandments into a bag and crushing them to powder. Let our statesmen at Washington get their hands on an Indian reservation, and not even honor among thieves remains.'

'Say, doc,' said Scipio, 'when d' y'u guess I can get off?'

'Don't be in too much of a hurry,' the doctor cautioned him. 'If you go to Sunk Creek—'

'Sunk Creek! I only want to go to the Agency.'

'Oh, well, you could do that to-day – but don't you want to see the entertainment? Conjuring tricks are promised.'

'I want to see Horacles.'

'But he is the entertainment. Supper comes after he's through.'

Scipio stayed. He was not repaid, he thought. 'A poor show,' was his comment as he went to bed. He came later to be very glad indeed that he had gone to that entertainment.

The next day found him seated in the Agency store, being warmly greeted by his friends the Indians. They knew him well; perhaps he understood them better than he had said. By Horacles he was not warmly greeted; perhaps Horacles did not wish to be understood – and then, Scipio, in his comings and goings through the reservation, had played with Horacles for the benefit of bystanders. There is no doubt whatever that Horacles did not understand Scipio. He was sorry to notice how the Agent, his employer, shook Scipio's hand and invited him to come and stop with him till he was fit to return to his work. And Scipio accepted this invitation. He sat him down in the store, and made himself at home. Legs stretched out on one chair, crutch within reach, hands comfortably clasped round the arms of the chair he sat in, head tilted back, eyes apparently studying the goods which hung from the beams overhead, he visibly sniffed the air.

'Smell anything you don't like?' inquired the clerk, tartly – and unwisely.

'Nothin' except you, Horacles,' was the perfectly amiable rejoinder. – 'It's good,' Scipio then confessed, 'to be smellin' buckskin and leather and groceries instead of ether and iodoform.'

'Guess you were pretty sick,' observed the clerk, with relish.

'Yes. Oh, yes. I was pretty sick. That's right. Yes.' Scipio had continued through these slowly drawled remarks to look at the ceiling. Then his glance dropped to the level of Horacles, and keenly fixed that unconscious youth's plump little form, pink little face, and mean little mustache. Behind one ear stuck a pen, behind the other a pencil, as the assistant clerk was arranging some tins of Arbuckle's Arioso coffee. Then Scipio took aim and fired: 'So you're going to quit your job?'

Horacles whirled round. 'Who says so?'

The chance shot – if there ever is such a thing, if such shots are not always the result of visions and perceptions which lie beyond our present knowledge – this chance shot had hit.

'First I've heard of it,' then said Horacles, sulkily. 'Guess you're delirious still.' He returned to his coffee, and life grew more interesting than ever to Scipio.

Instead of trickling back, health began to rush back into his long imprisoned body, and though he could not fully use it yet, and though if he hobbled a hundred yards he was compelled to rest it, his wiry mind knew no fatigue. How athletic his brains were was easily perceived by the Indian Agent. The convalescent would hobble over to the store after breakfast and hail the assistant clerk at once. 'Morning, Horacles,' he would begin; 'how's Uncle?' – Oh, when are you going to give us a new joke?' the worried Horacles would retort. – "Just as soon as you give us a new Uncle, Horacles. Or any other relation to make us feel proud we know you. What did his letter last night say?' The second or third time this had been asked still found Horacles with no better repartee than angry silence. 'Didn't he send me his love?' Scipio then said; and still the hapless Horacles said nothing. 'Well, y'u give him mine when you write him this afternoon.' – 'I ain't writing this afternoon,' snapped the clerk. – 'You're not! Why, I thought you wrote each other every day!' This was so near the truth that Horacles flared out: 'I'd be ashamed if I'd nothing better to do than spy on other people's mails.'

Thus by dinner-time generally an audience would be gathered round Scipio where he sat with his legs on the chair, and Horacles over his ledger would be furiously muttering that 'Some day they would all see.'

Horacles asked for a couple of days' holiday, and got it. He wished to hunt, he said. But the Agent happened to find that he had been to the railroad about some freight. This he mentioned to Scipio. 'I don't know what he's up to,' he said. He had found that worrying Horacles was merely one of the things that Scipio's brains were good for; Scipio had advised him prudently about a sale of beeves, and had introduced a simple contrivance for luring to the store the customers whom Horacles failed to attract. It was merely a free lunch counter – cheese and crackers every day, and deviled ham on pay-day – but it put up the daily receipts.

And next, one evening after the mail was in, Scipio, sitting alone in the front of the store, saw the Agent, sitting alone in the back of the store, spring suddenly from his chair, crush a newspaper into his pocket, and stride out to his house. At breakfast the Agent spoke thus to Scipio: —

'I must go to Washington. I shall be back before they let you and your leg run loose. Will you do something for me?'

'Name it. Just name it.'

'Run the store while I'm gone.'

'D' y'u think I can?'

'I know you can. There'll be no trouble under you. You understand Indians.'

'But suppose something turns up?'

'I don't think anything will before I'm back. I'd sooner leave you than Horacles in charge here. Will you do it and take two dollars a day?'

'Do it for nothing. Horacles'll be compensation enough.'

'No, he won't. – And see here, he can't help being himself.'

'Enough said. I'll strive to pity him. None of us was consulted about being born. And I'll keep remembering that we was both raised at Gallip*oleece*, Ohio, and that he inherited a bigger outrage of a name than I did. That's what comes of havin' a French ancestor. – Only, he used to steal my lunch at school.' And Scipio's bleached blue eye grew cold. Later injuries one may forgive, but school ones never.

'Didn't you whale him?' asked the Agent.

'Every time,' said Scipio, 'till he told Uncle. Uncle was mayor of Gallip*oleece* then. So I wasn't ready to get expelled, – I got ready later; nothin' is easier than gettin' expelled – but I locked up my lunch after that.'

'Uncle's pretty good to him,' muttered the Agent. 'Got him this position. – Well, nobody will expel you here. Look after things. I'll feel easy to think you're on hand.'

For that newspaper which the Agent had crushed into his pocket, Scipio searched cracks and corners, but searched in vain. A fear quite unreasoning possessed him for a while: could he but learn what was in the paper that had so stirred his patron, perhaps he could avert whatever the thing was that he felt in the air, threatening some sort of injury. He knew himself resourceful. Dislike of Horacles and Uncle had been enough to start his wish to thwart them – if there was anything to thwart; but now pride and gratitude fired him; he had been trusted; he cared more to be trusted than for anything on earth; he must rise equal to it now! The Agent had evidently taken the paper away with him – and so Scipio absurdly read all the papers. He collected old ones, and laid his hands upon the new they moment they were out of the mail-bag. It may be said that he lived daily in a wrapping of newspapers.

'Why, you have got Horacles laughing at you.'

This the observant Virginian pointed out to Scipio immediately on his arrival from Billings. Scipio turned a sickened look upon his friend. The look was accompanied by a cold wave in his stomach.

'Y'u cert'nly have,' the remorseless friend pursued. 'I reckon he must have had a plumb happy time watchin' y'u still-hunt them newspapers. Now who'd ever have foretold you would afford Horacles enjoyment?'

In a weak voice Scipio essayed to fight it off. 'Don't you try to hoodwink me with any of your frog lies.'

'No need,' said the Virginian. 'From the door as I came in I saw him at his desk lookin' at y'u easy-like. 'Twas a right quaint pictyeh – him smilin' at the desk, and your nose tight against the Omaha *Bee*. I thought first y'u didn't have a handkerchief.'

'I wonder if he has me beat?' muttered poor Scipio.

The Virginian now had a word of consolation. 'Don't y'u see,' he again pointed out, 'that no newspaper could have helped you? If it could why did he go away to Washington without tellin' you? He don't look for you to deal with troubles he don't mention to you.'

'I wonder if Horacles has me beat?' said Scipio once more.

The Virginian standing by the seated, brooding man clapped him twice on the shoulders, gently. It was enough. They were very fast friends.

'I know,' said Scipio in response. 'Thank y'u. But I'd hate for him to have me beat.'

It was the doctor who now furnished information that would have relieved any reasonable man from a sense of failure. The doctor was excited because his view of our faith in Indian matters was again justified by a further instance.

'Oh, yes!' he said. 'Just give those people at Washington time, and every step they've taken from the start will be in the mud puddle of a lie. Uncle's in the game all right. He's been meditating how to serve his country and increase his income. There's a railroad at the big end of his notion, but the entering wedge seems only to be a new store down in the corner of this reservation. You see, it has been long settled by the sacredest compacts that two stores shall be enough here – the Post-trader's and the Agent's – but the dear Indians need a third, Uncle says. He has told the Senate and the Interior Department and the White House that a lot of them have to travel too far for supplies. So now Washington is sure the Indians need a third store. The Post-trader and the Agent are stopping at the Post to-night. They got East too late to hold up the job. If Horacles opens that new store, the Agent might just as well shut up his own.'

'Ain't y'u going to look at my leg?' was all the reply that Scipio made.

The doctor laughed. It was to examine the leg that he had come, and he had forgotten all about it. 'You can forget all about it, too,' he told Scipio when he had finished. 'Go back to Sunk Creek when you like. Go back to full work next week, say. Your wicked body is sound again. A better man would unquestionably have died.'

But the cheery doctor could not cheer the unreasonable Scipio. In the morning the complacent Horacles made known to all the world his perfected arrangements. Directly the Agent had safely turned his back and gone to Washington, his disloyal clerk had become doubly busy. He had at once perceived that this was a comfortable time for him to hurry his new rival store into readiness and be securely established behind its counter before his betrayed employer should return. In this last he might not quite succeed; the Agent had come back a day or two sooner than Horacles had calculated, but it was a trifle; after all, he had carried through the small part of his uncle's scheme which he had been sent here to do. Inside that building in the far corner of the reservation, once rumored to be connected with the Quartermaster's department, he would now sell luxuries and necessities to the Indians at a price cheaper than his employer's, and his employer's store would henceforth be empty of customers. Perhaps the sweetest moment that Horacles had known for many weeks was when he said to Scipio:—

'I'm writing Uncle about it to-day.'

That this should have gone on under his nose while he sat searching the papers was to Scipio utterly unbearable. His mind was in a turmoil, feeling about helplessly but furiously for vengeance; and the Virginian's sane question – What could he have done to stop it if he had discovered it? – comforted him not at all. They were outside the store, sitting under a tree, waiting for the returning Agent to appear. But he did not come, and the suspense added to Scipio's wretchedness.

'He put me in charge,' he kept repeating.

'The driver ain't responsible when a stage is held up,' reasoned the Virginian.

Scipio hardly heard him. 'He put me in charge', he said. Then he worked round to Horacles again. 'He ain't got strength. He ain't got beauty. He ain't got riches. He ain't got brains. He's just got sense enough for parlor conjuring tricks – not good ones, either. And yet he has me beat.'

'He's got an uncle in the Senate',' said the Virginian.

The disconsolate Scipio took a pull at his cigar – he had taken one between every sentence. 'Damn his false teeth.'

The Virginian looked grave. 'Don't be hasty. Maybe the day will come when you and me'll need 'em to chew our tenderloin.'

'We'll be old. Horacles is twenty-five.'

'Twenty-five is certainly young to commence eatin' by machinery,' admitted the Virginian.

'And he's proud of 'em,' whined Scipio. 'Proud! Opens his bone box and sticks 'em out at y'u on the end of his tongue.'

'I hate an immodest man,' said the Virginian.

'Why, he hadn't any better sense than to do it over to the officers' club right before the ladies and everybody the other night. The K.O.'s wife said it gave her the creeps – and she don't look sensitive.'

'Well,' said the Virginian, 'if I weighed three hundred pound I'd be turrable sensitive.'

'She had to leave,' pursued Scipio. 'Had to take her little girl away from the show. Them teeth comin' out of Horacles's mouth the way they did sent the child into hysterics. Y'u could hear her screechin' half way down the line.'

The Virginian looked at his watch. 'I wonder if that Agent is coming here at all today?'

Scipio's worried face darkened again. 'What can I do? What *can* I?' he demanded. And he rose and limped up and down where the ponies were tied in front of the store. The fickle Indians would soon be tying these ponies in front of the rival store. 'I received this business in good shape,' continued Scipio, 'and I'll hand it back in bad.'

Horacles looked out of the door. He wore his hat tilted to make him look like the dare-devil that he was not; dare-devils seldom have soft pink hands, red eyelids, and a fluffy mustache. He smiled at Scipio, and Scipio smiled at him, sweetly and dangerously.

'Would you mind keeping store while I'm off?' inquired Horacles.

'Sure not!' cried Scipio, with heartiness. 'Goin' to have your grand opening this afternoon?'

'Well, I *was*,' Horacles replied, enjoying himself every moment. But Mr Forsythe' (this was the Agent) 'can't get over from the Post in time to be present this afternoon. It's very kind of him to want to be present when I start my new enterprise, and I appreciate it, boys, I can tell you. So I sent him word I wouldn't think of opening without him, and it's to be to-morrow morning.'

While Horacles was speaking thus, the Indians had gathered about to listen. It was plain that they understood that this was a white man's war; their great, grave, watching faces showed it. Young squaws, half-hooded in their shawls, looked on with bright eyes; a boy who had been sitting on the steps playing a pipe, stopped his music, and came in; the aged Pounded Meat, wrapped in scarlet and shrunk with years to the appearance of a dried apple, watched with eyes that still had in them the primal fear of life; tall in a corner stood the silver-haired High Bear, watching too. Did they understand the white man's war lying behind the complacent smile of Horacles and the dangerous smile of the lounging Scipio? The red man is grave when war is in question; all the Indians were perfectly still.

'Wish you boys could be there to give me a good send-off,' continued Horacles.

The pipe-playing Indian boy must have caught some flash of something beneath Scipio's smile, for his eye went to Scipio's pistol – but it returned to Scipio's face.

Horacles spoke on. 'Fine line of fresh Eastern goods, dry goods, candies, and – hee-hee! – free lunch. Mr Le Moyne, I want to thank you publicly for that idea.'

'Y'u're welcome to it. Guess I'll hardly be over to-morrow, though. With such a competitor as you, I expect I'll have to stay with my job and hustle.'

'Ah, well,' simpered Horacles, 'I couldn't have done it by myself. My Uncle – say, boys!' (Horacles in the elation of victory now melted to pure good-will) 'do come see me to-morrow. It's all business, this, you know. There's no hard feelings?'

The pipe boy couldn't help looking at the pistol again.

'Not a feeling!' cried Scipio. And he clapped Horacles between his little round shoulders. With head on one side, he looked down along his lengthy, jocular nose at Horacles for a moment. Then his eye shone upon the company like the edge of a knife – and they laughed at him because he was laughing so contagiously at them; a soft laugh, like the fall of moccasins. Often the Indian will join, like a child, in mirth which he does not comprehend. High Bear's smile shone from his corner at young Scipio, whom he fancied so much that he had offered him his fourteenth daughter to wed as soon as his leg should be well. But Scipio had sorrowfully explained to the father that he was already married – which was true, but which I fear would in former days have proved no impediment to him. Perhaps some day I may tell you of the early marriages of Scipio as Scipio in hospital narrated them to me.

'Hey!' said High Bear now, to Scipio. 'New store. Pretty good. Heap cheap.'

'Yes, High Bear. Heap cheap. You savvy why?'

With a long arm and an outstretched finger, Scipio suddenly pointed to Horacles. At this the Virginian's hitherto unchanging face wakened to curiosity and attention. Scipio was now impressively and mysteriously nodding at the silver-haired chief in his bright, green blanket, and his long, fringed, yellow, soft buckskins.

'No savvy,' said High Bear, after a pause, with a tinge of caution. He had followed Scipio's pointing finger to where Horacles was happily practising a trick with a glass and a silver dollar behind the counter.

'Heap cheap,' repeated Scipio, 'because' (here he leaned close to High Bear and whispered) 'because his uncle medicine-man. He big medicine-man, too.'

High Bear's eyes rested for a moment on Horacles. Then he shook his head. 'Ah, nah,' he grunted. 'He not medicine-man. He fall off horse. He no catch horse. My little girl catch him. Ah, nah!' High Bear laughed profusely at 'Sippo's' joke. 'Sippo' was the Indians' English name for their vivacious friend. In their own language they called him something complimentary in several syllables, but it was altogether too intimate and too plain-spoken for me to repeat aloud. Into his whisper Scipio now put more electricity. 'He's big medicine man,' he hissed again, and he drilled his bleached blue eye into the brown one of the savage. 'See him now!' He stretched out a vibrating finger.

It was a pack of cards that Horacles was lightly manipulating. He fluttered it open in the air and fluttered it shut again, drawing it out like a concertina and pushing it flat like an opera hat – nor did a card fall to the ground.

High Bear watched it hard; but soon High Bear laughed. 'He

pretty good,' he declared. 'All same tin-horn monte-man. I see one Miles City.'

'Maybe monte-man medicine-man too,' suggested Scipio.

'Ah, nah!' said High Bear. Yet nevertheless Scipio saw him shoot one or two more doubtful glances at Horacles as that happy clerk continued his activities.

Horacles had an audience (which he liked), and he held his audience – and who could help liking that? The bucks and squaws watched him, sometimes nudging one another, and they smiled and grunted their satisfaction at his news. Cheaper prices was something which their primitive minds could take in as well as any of us.

'Why you not sell cheap like him?' they asked their friend 'Sippo.'

'We stay then. Not go his store.' This was the burden of their chorus, soft, laughing, a little mocking, floating among them like a breeze, voice after voice: —

'We like buy everything you, we like buy everything cheap.'

'You make cheap, we buy heap shirts.'

'Buy heap tobacco.'

'Heap cartridge.'

'You not sell cheap, we go.'

'Ah!'

The chorus laughed like pleased children. Scipio looked at them solemnly. He explained how much he would like to sell cheap, if only he were a medicine-man like Horacles.

'You medicine-man?' they asked the assistant clerk.

'Yes,' said Horacles, pleased. 'I big medicine-man.'

'Ah, nah!' The soft, mocking words ran among them like the flight of a moth.

Soon with their hoods over their heads they began to go home on their ponies, blanketed, feathered, many-colored, moving and dispersing wide across the sage-brush to their far-scattered tepees.

High Bear lingered last. For a long while he had been standing silent and motionless. When the chorus spoke he had not; when the chorus laughed he had not. Now his head moved; he looked about him and saw that for a moment he was alone in a way. He saw the Virginian reading a newspaper, and his friend 'Sippo' bending down and attending to his leg. Horacles had gone into an inner room. Left on the counter lay the pack of cards. High Bear went quickly to the cards, touched them, lifted them, set them down, and looked about him again. But the Virginian was reading still, and Scipio was still bent down, having some trouble with his boot. High Bear looked at the cards, shook his head sceptically, laughed a little, grunted once, and went out where his pony was tied. As he was throwing his soft buckskin leg over the saddle, there was Scipio's head thrust out of the door and nodding strangely at him.

'Good night, High Bear. He big medicine-man.'

High Bear gave a quick slash to his pony, and galloped away into the dusk.

Then Scipio limped back into the store, sank into the first chair he came to, and doubled over. The Virginian looked up from his paper at this mirth, scowled, and turned back to his reading. If he was to be 'left out' of the joke, he would make it plain that he was not in the least interested in it.

Scipio now sat up straight, bursting to share what was in his mind; but he instantly perceived how it was with the Virginian. At this he redoubled his silent symptoms of delight. In a moment Horacles had come back from the inner room with his hair wet with ornamental brushing.

'Well, Horacles,' began Scipio in the voice of a purring cat, 'I expect y'u have me beat.'

The flattered clerk could only nod and show his bright, false teeth.

'Y'u have me beat,' repeated Scipio. 'Y'u have for a fact.'

'Not you, Mr Le Moyne. It's not you I'm making war on. I do hope there's no hard feelings—'

'Not a feelin', Horacles! How can y'u entertain such an idea?' Scipio shook him by the hand and smiled like an angel at him – a fallen angel. 'What's the use of me keepin' this store open to-morrow? Nobody'll be here to spend a cent. Guess I'll shut up, Horacles, and come watch the Injuns all shoppin' like Christmas over to your place.'

The Virginian sustained his indifference, and added to Scipio's pleasure. But during breakfast the Virginian broke down.

'Reckon you're ready to start to-day?' he said.

'Start? Where for?'

'Sunk Creek, y'u fool! Where else?'

'I'm beyond y'u! I'm sure beyond y'u for once!' screeched Scipio, beating his crutch on the floor.

'Oh, eat your grub, y'u fool.'

'I'd have told y'u last night,' said Scipio, remorselessly, 'only y'u were so awful anxious not to *be* told.'

As the Virginian drove him across the sagebrush, not to Sunk Creek, but to the new store, the suspense was once more too much for the Southerner's curiosity. He pulled up the horses as the inspiration struck him.

'You're going to tell the Indians you'll under-sell him!' he declared, over-hastily.

'Oh, drive on, y'u fool,' said Scipio.

The baffled Virginian grinned. 'I'll throw you out,' he said. 'and break all your laigs and bones and things fresh.'

'I wish Uncle was going to be there,' said Scipio.

Nearly everybody else was there: the Agent, bearing his ill fortune like a philosopher; some officers from the Post, and the doctor; some enlisted men, blue-legged with yellow stripes; civilians male and female, honorable and shady; and then the Indians. Wagons were drawn up, ponies stood about, the littered plain was populous. Horacles moved behind the counter, busy and happy; his little mustache was combed, his ornamental hair damp. He smiled and talked, and handled and displayed his abundance: the bright calicoes, the shining knives, the clean six-shooters and rifles, the bridles, the fishing-tackle, the gum-drops and chocolates – all his plenty and its cheapness.

Squaws and bucks young and old thronged his establishment, their soft footfalls and voices made a gentle continuous sound, while their green and yellow blankets bent and stood straight as they inspected and purchased. High Bear held an earthen crock with a luxury in it – a dozen of fresh eggs. 'Hey!' he said when he saw his friend 'Sippo' enter. 'Heap cheap.' And he showed the eggs to Scipio. He cherished the crock with one hand and arm while with the other hand he helped himself to the free lunch.

To Scipio Horacles 'extended' a special welcome; he made it ostentatious in order that all the world might know how perfectly absent 'hard feelings' were. And Scipio on his side wore openly the radiance of brotherhood and well-wishing. He went about admiring everything, exclaiming now and then over the excellence of the goods, or the cheapness of their price. His presence was soon no longer a cause of curiosity, and they forgot to watch him – all of them except the Virginian. The hours passed on, the little fires, where various noon meals were cooked, burnt out, satisfied individuals began to depart after an entertaining day, the Agent himself was sauntering toward his horse.

'What's your hurry?' said Scipio.

'Well, the show is over,' said the Agent.

'Oh, no, it ain't. Horacles is goin' to entertain us a whole lot.'

'Better stay,' said the Virginian.

The Agent looked from one to the other. Then he spoke anxiously. 'I don't want anything done to Horacles.'

'Nothing will be done,' stated Scipio.

The Agent stayed. The magnetic current of expectancy passed, none could say how, through the assembled people. No one departed after this, and the mere loitering of spectators turned to waiting. Particularly expectant was the Virginian, and this he betrayed by mechanically droning in his strongest accent a little song that bore no reference to the present occasion: —

> 'Of all my fatheh's familee
> I love myself the baist,
> And if Gawd will just look afteh me
> The devil may take the raist.'

The sun grew lower. The world outside was still full of light, but dimness had begun its subtle pervasion of the store. Horacles thanked the Indians and every one for their generous patronage on this his opening day, and intimated that it was time to close. Scipio rushed up and whispered to him: —

'My goodness, Horacles! You ain't going to send your friends home like that?'

Horacles was taken aback. 'Why,' he stammered, 'what's wrong?'

'Where's your vanishing handkerchief, Horacles? Get it out and entertain 'em some. Show you're grateful. Where's that trick dollar? Get 'em quick. – I tell you,' he declaimed aloud to the Indians, 'he big medicine-man. Make come. Make go. You no see. Nobody see. Make jack-rabbit in hat—'

'I couldn't to-night,' simpered Horacles. 'Needs preparation, you know.' And he winked at Scipio.

Scipio struggled upon the counter, and stood up above their heads to finish his speech. 'No jack-rabbit this time,' he said.

'Ah, nah!' laughed the Indians. 'No catch um.'

'Yes, catch um any time. Catch anything. Make anything. Make anything. Make all this store' – Scipio moved his arms about – 'that's how make heap cheap. See that!' He stopped dramatically, and clasped his hands together. Horacles tossed a handkerchief in the air, caught it, shut his hand upon it with a kneading motion, and opened the hand empty. 'His fingers swallow it, all same mouth!' shouted Scipio. 'He big medicine-man. You see. Now other hand spit out.' But Horacles varied the trick. Success and the staring crowd elated him; he was going to do his best. He opened both hands empty, felt about him in the air, clutched space suddenly, and drew two silver dollars from it. Then he threw them back into space, again felt about for them in the air, made a dive at High Bear's eggs, and brought handkerchief and dollars out of them.

'Ho!' went High Bear, catching his breath. He backed away from the reach of Horacles. He peered down into the crock among his eggs. Horacles whispered to Scipio: —

'Keep talking till I'm ready.'

'Oh, I'll talk. Go get ready quick – High Bear, what I tell you?' But High Bear's eye was now fixedly watching the door through which Horacles had withdrawn; he did not listen as Scipio proceeded. 'What I tell everybody? He do handkerchief. He do dollar. He do heap more. See me. I no can do like him. I not medicine-man. I throw handkerchief and dollar in the air, look! See! they tumble on floor no good – thank you, my kind noble friend from Virginia, you pick my fool dollar and my fool handkerchief up for me, *muy pronto*. Oh, thank you, black-haired, green-eyed son of Dixie, you have the manners of a queen, but I no medicine-man, I shall never turn a skunk into a watermelon, I innocent, I young, I helpless babe, I suck bottle when I can get it. Fire and water will not obey me. Old man Makes-the-Thunder does not know my name and address. He spit on me Wednesday night last, and there are no dollars in this man's hair.' (The Virginian winced beneath Scipio's vicious snatch at his scalp, and the Agent and the doctor retired to a dark corner and laid their heads in each other's waistcoats.) 'Ha! he comes! Big medicine-man comes. See him, High Bear! His father, his mother, his aunts all twins, he ninth dog-pup in three sets of triplets, and the great white Ram-of-the-Mountains fed him on punkin-seed. – Sick 'em, Horacles.'

The burning eye of High Bear now blazed with distended fascination, riveted upon Horacles, whom it never left. Darkness was gathering in the store.

'Hand all same foot,' shouted Scipio, with gestures, 'mouth all same hand. Can eat fire. Can throw ear mile off and listen you talk.' Here Horacles removed a dollar from the hair of High Bear's fourteenth daughter, threw it into one boot, and brought it out of the other. The daughter screamed and burrowed behind her sire. All the Indians had drawn close together, away from the counter, while Scipio on top of the counter talked high and low, and made gestures without ceasing. 'Hand all same mouth. Foot all same head. Take off head, throw it out window, it jump in door. See him, see big medicine-man!' And Scipio gave a great shriek.

A gasp went among the Indians; red fire was blowing from the jaws of Horacles. It ceased, and after it came slowly, horribly, a long red tongue, and riding on the tongue's end glittered a row of teeth. There was a crash upon the floor. It was High Bear's crock. The old chief was gone. Out of the door he flew, his blanket over his face, and up on his horse he sprang, wildly beating the animal. Squaws and bucks flapped after him like poultry, rushing over the ground, leaping on their ponies, melting away into the dusk. In a moment no sign of them was left but the broken eggs, oozing about on the deserted floor.

The white men there stood tearful, dazed, and weak with laughter.

' "Happy-Teeth" should be his name,' said the Virginian. 'It sounds Injun.' And Happy-Teeth it was. But Horacles did not remain long in the neighborhood after he realized what he had done; for never again did an Indian enter, or even come near, that den of flames and magic. They would not even ride past it; they circled it widely. The idle merchandise that filled it was at last bought by the Agent at a reduction.

'Well,' said Scipio bashfully to the Agent, 'I'd have sure hated to hand y'u back a ruined business. But he'll never understand Injuns.'

# THE GREAT SLAVE

## Zane Grey

A VOICE on the wind whispered to Siena the prophecy of his birth. 'A chief is born to save the vanishing tribe of Crows! A hunter to his starving people!' While he listened, at his feet swept swift waters, the rushing, green-white, thundering Athabasca, spirit-forsaken river; and it rumbled his name and murmured his fate. 'Siena! Siena! His bride will rise from a wind kiss on the flowers in the moonlight! A new land calls to the last of the Crows! Northward where the wild goose ends its flight Siena will father a great people!'

So Siena, a hunter of the leafy trails, dreamed his dreams; and at sixteen he was the hope of the remnant of a once powerful tribe, a stripling chief, beautiful as a bronzed autumn god, silent, proud, for ever listening to voices on the wind.

To Siena the lore of the woodland came as flight comes to the strong-winged wild fowl. The secrets of the forests were his, and of the rocks and rivers.

He knew how to find the nests of the plover, to call the loon, to net the heron, and spear the fish. He understood the language of the whispering pines. Where the deer came down to drink and the caribou browsed on moss and the white rabbit nibbled in the grass and the bear dug in the logs for grubs – all these he learned; and also when the black flies drove the moose into the water and when the honk of the geese meant the approach of the north wind.

He lived in the woods, with his bow, his net, and his spear. The trees were his brothers. The loon laughed for his happiness, the wolf mourned for his sadness. The bold crag above the river, Old Stoneface, heard his step when he climbed there in the twilight. He communed with the stern god of his ancestors and watched the flashing Northern Lights and listened.

From all four corners came his spirit guides with steps of destiny on his trail. On all the four winds breathed voices whispering of his future; loudest of all called the Athabasca, god-forsaken river, murmuring of the bride born of a wind kiss on the flowers in the moonlight.

It was autumn, with the flame of leaf fading, the haze rolling out of the hollows, the lull yielding to moan of coming wind. All the signs of a severe winter were in the hulls of the nuts, in the fur of the foxes, in the flight of water-fowl. Siena was spearing fish for winter store. None so keen of sight as Siena, so swift of arm; and as he was the hope, so he alone was the provider for the starving tribe. Siena stood to his knees in a brook where it flowed over its gravelly bed into the Athabasca. Poised high was his wooden spear. It glinted downward swift as a shaft of sunlight through the leaves. Then Siena lifted a quivering whitefish and tossed it upon the bank where his mother Ema, with other women of the tribe, sun-dried the fish upon a rock.

Again and again, many times, flashed the spear. The young chief seldom missed his aim. Early frosts on the uplands had driven the fish down to deeper water, and as they came darting over the bright pebbles Siena called them by name.

The oldest squaw could not remember such a run of fish. Ema sang the praises of her son; the other women ceased the hunger chant of the tribe.

Suddenly a hoarse shout pealed out over the waters.

Ema fell in a fright; her companions ran away; Siena leaped upon the bank, clutching his spear. A boat in which were men with white faces drifted down toward him.

'Hal-loa!' again sounded the hoarse cry.

Ema cowered in the grass. Siena saw a waving of white hands; his knees knocked together and he felt himself about to flee. But Siena of the Crows, the saviour of a vanishing tribe, must not fly from visible foes.

'Palefaces,' he whispered, trembling, yet stood his ground ready to fight for his mother. He remembered stories of an old Indian who had journeyed far to the south and had crossed the trails of the dreaded white men. There stirred in him vague memories of strange

Indian runners telling camp-fire tales of white hunters with weapons of lightning and thunder.

'Naza! Naza!' Siena cast one fleeting glance to the north and a prayer to his god of gods. He believed his spirit would soon be wandering in the shades of the other Indian world.

As the boat beached on the sand Siena saw men lying with pale faces upward to the sky, and voices in an unknown tongue greeted him. The tone was friendly, and he lowered his threatening spear. Then a man came up to the bank, his hungry eyes on the pile of fish, and he began to speak haltingly in mingled Cree and Chippewayan language:

'Boy – we're white friends – starving – let us buy fish – trade for fish – we're starving and we have many moons to travel.'

'Siena's tribe is poor,' replied the lad; 'sometimes they starve too. But Siena will divide his fish and wants no trade.'

His mother, seeing the white men intended no evil, came out of her fright and complained bitterly to Siena of his liberality. She spoke of the menacing winter, of the frozen streams, the snow-bound forest, the long night of hunger. Siena silenced her and waved the frightened braves and squaws back to their wigwams.

'Siena is young,' he said simply; 'but he is chief here. If we starve – we starve.'

Whereupon he portioned out a half of the fish. The white men built a fire and sat around it feasting like famished wolves around a fallen stag. When they had appeased their hunger they packed the remaining fish in the boat, whistling and singing the while. Then the leader made offer to pay, which Siena refused, though the covetous light in his mother's eyes hurt him sorely.

'Chief,' said the leader, 'the white man understands; now he offers presents as one chief to another.'

Thereupon he proffered bright beads and tinselled trinkets, yards of calico and strips of cloth. Siena accepted with a dignity in marked contrast to the way in which the greedy Ema pounced upon the glittering heap. Next the paleface presented a knife which, drawn from its scabbard, showed a blade that mirrored its brightness in Siena's eyes.

'Chief, your woman complains of a starving tribe,' went on the white man. 'Are there not many moose and reindeer?'

'Yes. But seldom can Siena creep within range of his arrow.'

'A-ha! Siena will starve no more,' replied the man, and from the boat he took a long iron tube with a wooden stock.

'What is that?' asked Siena.

'The wonderful shooting stick. Here, boy, watch! See the bark on the camp fire. Watch!'

He raised the stick to his shoulder. Then followed a streak of flame, a puff of smoke, a booming report; and the bark of the camp fire flew into bits.

The children dodged into the wigwams with loud cries, the women ran screaming, Ema dropped in the grass wailing that the end of the world had come, while Siena, unable to move hand or foot, breathed another prayer to Naza of the northland.

The white man laughed and, patting Siena's arm, he said: 'No fear.' Then he drew Siena away from the bank, and began to explain the meaning and use of the wonderful shooting stick. He reloaded it and fired again and yet again, until Siena understood and was all aflame at the possibilities of such a weapon.

Patiently the white man taught the Indian how to load it, sight, and shoot, and how to clean it with ramrod and buckskin. Next he placed at Siena's feet a keg of powder, a bag of lead bullets, and boxes full of caps. Then he bade Siena farewell, entered the boat with his men and drifted round a bend of the swift Athabasca.

Siena stood alone upon the bank, the wonderful shooting stick in his hands, and the wail of his frightened mother in his ears. He comforted her, telling her the white men were gone, that he was safe, and that the prophecy of his birth had at last begun its fulfilment. He carried the precious ammunition to a safe hiding-place in a hollow log near his wigwam and then he plunged into the forest.

Siena bent his course toward the runways of the moose. He walked in a kind of dream, for he both feared and believed. Soon the glimmer of water, splashes and widening ripples, caused him to crawl stealthily through the ferns and grasses to the border of a pond. The familiar hum of flies told him of the location of his quarry. The moose had taken to the water, driven by the swarms of black flies, and were standing neck deep, lifting their muzzles to feed on the drooping poplar branches. Their wide-spreading antlers, tipped back into the water, made the ripples.

Trembling as never before, Siena sank behind a log. He was

within fifty paces of the moose. How often in that very spot had he strung a feathered arrow and shot it vainly! But now he had the white man's weapon, charged with lightning and thunder. Just then the poplars parted above the shore, disclosing a bull in the act of stepping down. He tossed his antlered head at the cloud of humming flies, then stopped, lifting his nose to scent the wind.

'Naza!' whispered Siena in his swelling throat.

He rested the shooting stick on the log and tried to see over the brown barrel. But his eyes were dim. Again he whispered a prayer to Naza. His sight cleared, his shaking arms stilled, and with his soul waiting, hoping, doubting, he aimed and pulled the trigger.

Boom!

High the moose flung his ponderous head, to crash down upon his knees, to roll in the water and churn a bloody foam, and then lie still.

'Siena! Siena!'

Shrill the young chief's exultant yell pealed over the listening waters, piercing the still forest, to ring back in echo from Old Stoneface. It was Siena's triumphant call to his forefathers, watching him from the silence.

The herd of moose ploughed out of the pond and crashed into the woods, where, long after they had disappeared, their antlers could be heard cracking the saplings.

When Siena stood over the dead moose his doubts fled; he was indeed god-chosen. No longer chief of a starving tribe! Reverently and with immutable promise he raised the shooting stick to the north, toward Naza who had remembered him; and on the south, where dwelt the enemies of his tribe, his dark glance brooded wild and proud and savage.

Eight times the shooting stick boomed out in the stillness and eight moose lay dead in the wet grasses. In the twilight Siena wended his way home and placed eight moose tongues before the whimpering squaws.

'Siena is no longer a boy,' he said. 'Siena is a hunter. Let his women go bring in the meat.'

Then to the rejoicing and feasting and dancing of his tribe he turned a deaf ear, and in the night passed alone under the shadow of Old Stoneface, where he walked with the spirits of his ancestors and believed the voices on the wind.

Before the ice locked the ponds Siena killed a hundred moose and reindeer. Meat and fat and oil and robes changed the world for the Crow tribe.

Fires burned brightly all the long winter; the braves awoke from their stupor and chanted no more; the women sang of the Siena who had come, and prayed for summer wind and moonlight to bring his bride.

Spring went by, summer grew into blazing autumn, and Siena's fame and wonder of the shooting stick spread through the length and breadth of the land.

Another year passed, then another, and Siena was the great chief of the rejuvenated Crows. He had grown into a warrior's stature, his face had the beauty of the god-chosen, his eye the falcon flash of the Sienas of old. Long communion in the shadow of Old Stoneface had added wisdom to his other gifts; and now to his worshipping tribe all that was needed to complete the prophecy of his birth was the coming of an alien bride.

It was another autumn, with the wind whipping the tamaracks and moaning in the pines, and Siena stole along a brown, fern-lined trail. The dry smell of fallen leaves filled his nostrils; he tasted snow in the keen breezes. The flowers were dead, and still no dark-eyed bride sat in his wigwam. Siena sorrowed and strengthened his heart to wait. He saw her flitting in the shadows around him, a wraith with dusky eyes veiled by dusky wind-blown hair, and ever she hovered near him, whispering from every dark pine, from every waving tuft of grass.

To her whispers he replied: 'Siena waits.'

He wondered of what alien tribe she would come. He hoped not of the unfriendly Chippewayans or the far-distant Blackfeet; surely not of the hostile Crees, life enemies of his tribe, destroyers of its once puissant strength, jealous now of its resurging power.

Other shadows flitted through the forest, spirits that rose silently from the graves over which he trod, and warned him of double steps on his trail, of unseen foes watching him from the dark coverts. His braves had repeated gossip, filterings from stray Indian wanderers, hinting of plots against the risen Siena. To all these he gave no heed, for was not he Siena, god-chosen, and had he not the wonderful shooting stick?

It was the season that he loved, when dim forest and hazy fernland spoke most impellingly. The tamaracks talked to him, the poplars bowed as he passed, and the pines sang for him alone. The dying vines twined about his feet and clung to him, and the brown ferns, curling sadly, waved him a welcome that was a farewell. A bird twittered a plaintive note and a loon whistled a lonely call. Across the wide gray hollows and meadows of white moss moaned the north wind, bending all before it, blowing full into Siena's face with its bitter promise. The lichen-covered rocks and the rugged-barked trees and the creatures that moved among them – the whole world of earth and air heard Siena's step on the rustling leaves and a thousand voices hummed in the autumn stillness.

So he passed through the shadowy forest and over the gray muskeg flats to his hunting-place. With his birch-bark horn he blew the call of the moose. He alone of hunting Indians had the perfect moose call. There, hidden within a thicket, he waited, calling and listening till an angry reply bellowed from the depths of a hollow, and a bull moose, snorting fight, came cracking the saplings in his rush. When he sprang fierce and bristling into the glade, Siena killed him. Then, laying his shooting stick over a log, he drew his knife and approached the beast.

A snapping of twigs alarmed Siena and he whirled upon the defensive, but too late to save himself. A band of Indians pounced upon him and bore him to the ground. One wrestling heave Siena made, then he was overpowered and bound. Looking upward, he knew his captors, though he had never seen them before; they were the lifelong foes of his people, the fighting Crees.

A sturdy chief, bronze of face and sinister of eye, looked grimly down upon his captive. 'Baroma makes Siena a slave.'

Siena and his tribe were dragged far southward to the land of the Crees. The young chief was bound upon a block in the centre of the village where hundreds of Crees spat upon him, beat him, and outraged him in every way their cunning could devise. Siena's gaze was on the north and his face showed no sign that he felt the torments.

At last Baroma's old advisers stopped the spectacle, saying: 'This is a man!'

Siena and his people became slaves of the Crees. In Baroma's lodge, hung upon caribou antlers, was the wonderful shooting stick with Siena's powder horn and bullet pouch, objects of intense curiosity and fear.

None knew the mystery of this lightning-flashing, thunder-dealing thing; none dared touch it.

The heart of Siena was broken; not for his shattered dreams or the end of his freedom, but for his people. His fame had been their undoing. Slaves to the murderers of his forefathers! His spirit darkened, his soul sickened; no more did sweet voices sing to him on the wind, and his mind dwelt apart from his body among shadows and dim shapes.

Because of his strength he was worked like a dog at hauling packs and carrying wood; because of his frame he was set to cleaning fish and washing vessels with the squaws. Seldom did he get to speak a word to his mother or any of his people. Always he was driven.

One day, when he lagged almost fainting, a maiden brought him water to drink. Siena looked up, and all about him suddenly brightened, as when sunlight bursts from cloud.

'Who is kind to Siena?' he asked, drinking.

'Baroma's daughter,' replied the maiden.

'What is her name?'

Quickly the maiden bent her head, veiling dusky eyes with dusky hair. 'Emihiyah.'

'Siena has wandered on lonely trails and listened to voices not meant for other ears. He has heard the music of Emihiyah on the winds. Let the daughter of Siena's great foe not fear to tell of her name.'

'Emihiyah means a wind kiss on the flowers in the moonlight,' she whispered shyly and fled.

Love came to the last of the Sienas and it was like a glory. Death shuddered no more in Siena's soul. He saw into the future, and out of his gloom he rose again, god-chosen in his own sight, with such added beauty to his stern face and power to his piercing eye and strength to his lofty frame that the Crees quailed before him and marvelled. Once more sweet voices came to him, and ever on the soft winds were songs of the dewy moorlands to the northward, songs of the pines and the laugh of the loon and of the rushing, green-white, thundering Athabasca, god-forsaken river.

Siena's people saw him strong and patient, and they toiled on, unbroken, faithful. While he lived, the pride of Baroma was vaunting. 'Siena waits' were the simple words he said to his mother, and she repeated them as wisdom. But the flame in his eye was like the leaping Northern Lights, and it kept alive the fire deep down in their breasts.

In the winter when the Crees lolled in their wigwams, when less labour fell to Siena, he set traps in the snow trails for silver fox and marten. No Cree had ever been such a trapper as Siena. In the long months he captured many furs, with which he wrought a robe the like of which had not before been the delight of a maiden's eye. He kept it by him for seven nights, and always during this time his ear was turned to the wind. The seventh night was the night of the midwinter feast, and when the torches burned bright in front of Baroma's lodge Siena took the robe and, passing slowly and stately till he stood before Emihiyah, he laid it at her feet.

Emihiyah's dusky face paled, her eyes that shone like stars drooped behind her flying hair, and all her slender body trembled.

'Slave!' cried Baroma, leaping erect. 'Come closer that Baroma may see what kind of a dog approaches Emihiyah.'

Siena met Baroma's gaze, but spoke no word. His gift spoke for him. The hated slave had dared to ask in marriage the hand of the proud Baroma's daughter. Siena towered in the firelight with something in his presence that for a moment awed beholders. Then the passionate and untried braves broke the silence with a clamour of the wolf pack.

Tillimanqua, wild son of Baroma, strung an arrow to his bow and shot into Siena's hip, where it stuck, with feathered shaft quivering.

The spring of the panther was not swifter than Siena; he tossed Tillimanqua into the air and, flinging him down, trod on his neck and wrenched the bow away. Siena pealed out the long-drawn war whoop of his tribe that had not been heard for a hundred years, and the terrible cry stiffened the Crees in their tracks.

Then he plucked the arrow from his hip and, fitting it to the string, pointed the gory flint head at Tillimanqua's eyes and began to bend the bow. He bent the tough wood till the ends almost met, a feat of exceeding great strength, and thus he stood with brawny arms knotted and stretched.

A scream rent the suspense. Emihiyah fell upon her knees. 'Spare Emihiyah's brother!'

Siena cast one glance at the kneeling maiden, then, twanging the bowstring, he shot the arrow toward the sky.

'Baroma's slave is Siena,' he said, with scorn like the lash of a whip. 'Let the Cree learn wisdom.'

Then Siena strode away, with a stream of dark blood down his thigh, and went to his brush tepee, where he closed his wound.

In the still watches of the night, when the stars blinked through the leaves and the dew fell, when Siena burned and throbbed in pain, a shadow passed between his weary eyes and the pale light. And a voice that was not one of the spirit voices on the wind called softly over him, 'Siena! Emihiyah comes.'

The maiden bound the hot thigh with a soothing balm and bathed his fevered brow.

Then her hands found his in tender touch, her dark face bent low to his, her hair lay upon his cheek. 'Emihiyah keeps the robe,' she said.

'Siena loves Emihiyah,' he replied.

'Emihiyah loves Siena,' she whispered.

She kissed him and stole away.

On the morrow Siena's wound was as if it had never been; no eye saw his pain. Siena returned to his work and his trapping. The winter melted into spring, spring flowered into summer, summer withered into autumn.

Once in the melancholy days Siena visited Baroma in his wigwam. 'Baroma's hunters are slow. Siena sees a famine in the land.'

'Let Baroma's slave keep his place among the squaws,' was the reply.

That autumn the north wind came a moon before the Crees expected it; the reindeer took their annual march farther south; the moose herded warily in open groves; the whitefish did not run, and the seven-year pest depleted the rabbits.

When the first snow fell Baroma called a council and then sent his hunting braves far and wide.

One by one they straggled back to camp, footsore and hungry, and each with the same story. It was too late.

A few moose were in the forest, but they were wild and kept far out of range of the hunter's arrows, and there was no other game.

A blizzard clapped down upon the camp, and sleet and snow whitened the forest and filled the trails. Then winter froze everything in icy clutch. The old year drew to a close.

The Crees were on the brink of famine. All day and all night they kept up their chanting and incantations and beating of tom-toms to conjure the return of the reindeer. But no reindeer appeared.

It was then that the stubborn Baroma yielded to his advisers and consented to let Siena save them from starvation by means of his wonderful shooting stick. Accordingly Baroma sent word to Siena to appear at his wigwam.

Siena did not go, and said to the medicine men: 'Tell Baroma soon it will be for Siena to demand.'

Then the Cree chieftain stormed and stamped in his wigwam and swore away the life of his slave. Yet again the wise medicine men prevailed. Siena and the wonderful shooting stick would be the salvation of the Crees. Baroma, muttering deep in his throat like distant thunder, gave sentence to starve Siena until he volunteered to go forth and hunt, or let him be the first to die.

The last scraps of meat, except a little hoarded in Baroma's lodge, were devoured, and then began the boiling of bones and skins to make a soup to sustain life. The cold days passed and a silent gloom pervaded the camp. Sometimes a cry of a bereaved mother, mourning for a starved child, wailed through the darkness. Siena's people, long used to starvation, did not suffer or grow weak so soon as the Crees. They were of hardier frame, and they were upheld by faith in their chief. When he would sicken it would be time for them to despair. But Siena walked erect as in the days of his freedom, nor did he stagger under the loads of firewood, and there was a light on his face. The Crees, knowing of Baroma's order that Siena should be the first to perish of starvation, gazed at the slave first in awe, then in fear. The last of the Sienas was succoured by the spirits.

But god-chosen though Siena deemed himself, he knew it was not by the spirits that he was fed in this time of famine. At night in the dead stillness, when even no mourning of wolf came over the frozen wilderness, Siena lay in his brush tepee close and warm under his blanket. The wind was faint and low, yet still it brought the old familiar voices. And it bore another sound – the soft fall of a moccasin on the snow. A shadow passed between Siena's eyes and the pale light.

'Emihiyah comes,' whispered the shadow and knelt over him.

She tendered a slice of meat which she had stolen from Baroma's scanty hoard as he muttered and growled in uneasy slumber. Every night since her father's order to starve Siena, Emihiyah had made this perilous errand.

And now her hand sought his and her dusky hair swept his brow. 'Emihiyah is faithful,' she breathed low.

'Siena only waits,' he replied.

She kissed him and stole away.

Cruel days fell upon the Crees before Baroma's pride was broken. Many children died and some of the mothers were beyond help. Siena's people kept their strength, and he himself showed no effect of hunger. Long ago the Cree women had deemed him super-human, that the Great Spirit fed him from the happy hunting grounds.

At last Baroma went to Siena. 'Siena may save his people and the Crees.'

Siena regarded him long, then replied: 'Siena waits.'

'Let Baroma know. What does Siena wait for? While he waits we die.'

Siena smiled his slow, inscrutable smile and turned away.

Baroma sent for his daughter and ordered her to plead for her life.

Emihiyah came, fragile as a swaying reed, more beautiful than a rose choked in a tangled thicket, and she stood before Siena with doe eyes veiled. 'Emihiyah begs Siena to save her and the tribe of Crees.'

'Siena waits,' replied the slave.

Baroma roared his fury and bade his braves lash the slave. But the blows fell from feeble arms and Siena laughed at his captors.

Then, like a wild lion unleashed from long thrall, he turned upon them: 'Starve! Cree dogs! Starve! When the Crees all fall like leaves in autumn, then Siena and his people will go back to the north.'

Baroma's arrogance left him then, and on another day, when

Emihiyah lay weak and palid in his wigwam and the pangs of hunger gnawed at his own vitals, he again sought Siena. 'Let Siena tell for what he waits.'

Siena rose to his lofty height and the leaping flame of the Northern Light gathered in his eyes. 'Freedom!' One word he spoke and it rolled away on the wind.

'Baroma yields,' replied the Cree, and hung his head.

'Send the squaws who can walk and the braves who can crawl out upon Siena's trail.'

Then Siena went to Baroma's lodge and took up the wonderful shooting stick and, loading it, he set out upon snowshoes into the white forest. He knew where to find the moose yards in the sheltered corners. He heard the bulls pounding the hard-packed snow and cracking their antlers on the trees. The wary beasts would not have allowed him to steal close, as a warrior armed with a bow must have done, but Siena fired into the herd at long range. And when they dashed off, sending the snow up like a spray, a huge black bull lay dead. Siena followed them as they floundered through the drifts, and whenever he came within range he shot again. When five moose were killed he turned upon his trail to find almost the whole Cree tribe had followed him and were tearing the meat and crying out in a kind of crazy joy. That night the fires burned before the wigwams, the earthen pots steamed, and there was great rejoicing. Siena hunted the next day, and the next, and for ten days he went into the white forest with his wonderful shooting stick, and eighty moose fell to his unerring aim.

The famine was broken and the Crees were saved.

When the mad dances ended and the feasts were over, Siena appeared before Baroma's lodge. 'Siena will lead his people northward.'

Baroma, starving, was a different chief from Baroma well fed and in no pain. All his cunning had returned. 'Siena goes free. Baroma gave his word. But Siena's people remain slaves.'

'Siena demanded freedom for himself and people,' said the younger chief.

'Baroma heard no word of Siena's tribe. He would not have granted freedom for them. Siena's freedom was enough.'

'The Cree twists the truth. He knows Siena would not go without his people. Siena might have remembered Baroma's cunning. The Crees were ever liars.'

Baroma stalked before his fire with haughty presence. About him in the circle of light sat his medicine men, his braves and squaws. 'The Cree is kind. He gave his word. Siena is free. Let him take his wonderful shooting stick and go back to the north.'

Siena laid the shooting stick at Baroma's feet and likewise the powder horn and bullet pouch. Then he folded his arms, and his falcon eyes looked far beyond Baroma to the land of the changing lights and the old home on the green-white, rushing Athabasca, god-forsaken river. 'Siena stays.'

Baroma started in amaze and anger. 'Siena makes Baroma's word idle. Begone!'

'Siena stays!'

The look of Siena, the pealing reply, for a moment held the chief mute. Slowly Baroma stretched wide his arms and lifted them, while from his face flashed a sullen wonder. 'Great Slave!' he thundered.

So was respect forced from the soul of the Cree, and the name thus wrung from his jealous heart was one to live for ever in the lives and legends of Siena's people.

Baroma sought the silence of his lodge, and his medicine men and braves dispersed, leaving Siena standing in the circle, a magnificent statue facing the steely north.

From that day insult was never offered to Siena, nor word spoken to him by the Crees, nor work given. He was free to come and go where he willed, and he spent his time in lessening the tasks of his people.

The trails of the forest were always open to him, as were the streets of the Cree village. If a brave met him, it was to step aside; if a squaw met him, it was to bow her head; if a chief met him, it was to face him as warriors faced warriors.

One twilight Emihiyah crossed his path, and suddenly she stood as once before, like a frail reed about to break in the wind. But Siena passed on. The days went by and each one brought less labour to Siena's people, until that one came wherein there was no task save what they set themselves. Siena's tribe were slaves, yet not slaves.

The winter wore by and the spring and the autumn, and again

Siena's fame went abroad on the four winds. The Chippewayans journeyed from afar to see the Great Slave, and likewise the Blackfeet and the Yellow Knives. Honour would have been added to fame; councils called; overtures made to the sombre Baroma on behalf of the Great Slave, but Siena passed to and fro among his people, silent and cold to all others, true to the place which his great foe had given him. Captive to a lesser chief, they said; the Great Slave who would yet free his tribe and gather to him a new and powerful nation.

Once in the late autumn Siena sat brooding in the twilight by Ema's tepee. That night all who came near him were silent. Again Siena was listening to voices on the wind, voices that had been still for long, which he had tried to forget. It was the north wind, and it whipped the spruces and moaned through the pines. In its cold breath it bore a message to Siena, a hint of coming winter and a call from Naza, far north of the green-white, thundering Athabasca, river without a spirit.

In the darkness when the camp slumbered Siena faced the steely north. As he looked a golden shaft, arrow-shaped and arrow-swift, shot to the zenith.

'Naza!' he whispered to the winds. 'Siena watches.'

Then the gleaming, changing Northern Lights painted a picture of gold and silver bars, of flushes pink as shell, of opal fire and sunset red; and it was a picture of Siena's life from the moment the rushing Athabasca rumbled his name, to the far distant time when he would say farewell to his great nation and pass for ever to the retreat of the winds. God-chosen he was, and had power to read the story in the sky.

Seven nights Siena watched in the darkness; and on the seventh night, when the golden flare and silver shafts faded in the north, he passed from tepee to tepee, awakening his people. 'When Siena's people hear the sound of the shooting stick let them cry greatly: "Siena kills Baroma! Siena kills Baroma!" '

With noiseless stride Siena went among the wigwams and along the lanes until he reached Baroma's lodge. Entering the dark he groped with his hands upward to a moose's antlers and found the shooting stick. Outside he fired it into the air.

Like a lightning bolt the report ripped asunder the silence, and the echoes clapped and reclapped from the cliffs. Sharp on the dying echoes Siena bellowed his war whoop, and it was the second time in a hundred years for foes to hear that terrible, long-drawn cry.

Then followed the shrill yells of Siena's people: 'Siena kills Baroma . . . Siena kills Baroma . . . Siena kills Baroma!'

The slumber of the Crees awoke to a babel of many voices; it rose hoarsely on the night air, swelled hideously into a deafening roar that shook the earth.

In this din of confusion and terror when the Crees were lamenting the supposed death of Baroma and screaming in each other's ears, 'The Great Slave takes his freedom!' Siena ran to his people and, pointing to the north, drove them before him.

Single file, like a long line of flitting spectres, they passed out of the fields into the forest. Siena kept close on their trail, ever looking backward, and ready with the shooting stick.

The roar of the stricken Crees softened in his ears and at last died away.

Under the black canopy of whispering leaves, over the gray, mist-shrouded muskeg flats, around the glimmering reed-bordered ponds, Siena drove his people.

All night Siena hurried them northward and with every stride his heart beat higher. Only he was troubled by a sound like a voice that came to him on the wind.

But the wind was now blowing in his face, and the sound appeared to be at his back. It followed on his trail as had the step of destiny. When he strained his ears he could not hear it, yet when he had gone on swiftly, persuaded it was only fancy, then the voice that was not a voice came haunting him.

In the gray dawn Siena halted on the far side of a gray flat and peered through the mists on his back trail. Something moved out among the shadows, a gray shape that crept slowly, uttering a mournful cry.

'Siena is trailed by a wolf,' muttered the chief.

Yet he waited, and saw that the wolf was an Indian. He raised the fatal shooting stick.

As the Indian staggered forward, Siena recognized the robe of silver fox and marten, his gift to Emihiyah. He laughed in mockery. It was a Cree trick. Tillimanqua had led the pursuit disguised in his sister's robe. Baroma would find his son dead on the Great Slave's trail.

'Siena!' came the strange, low cry.

It was the cry that had haunted him like the voice on the wind. He leaped as a bounding deer.

Out of the gray fog burned dusky eyes half veiled by dusky hair, and little hands that he knew wavered as fluttering leaves. 'Emihiyah comes,' she said.

'Siena waits,' he replied.

Far to the northward he led his bride and his people, far beyond the old home on the green-white, thundering Athabasca, god-forsaken river; and there, on the lonely shores of an inland sea, he fathered the Great Slave Tribe.

# RANSON'S FOLLY

## Richard Harding Davis

### PART I

THE junior officers of Fort Crockett had organised a mess at the post-trader's. 'And a mess it certainly is,' said Lieutenant Ranson. The dining-table stood between hogsheads of molasses and a blazing log-fire, the counter of the store was their buffet, a pool-table with a cloth, blotted like a map of the Great Lakes, their sideboard, and Indian Pete acted as butler. But none of these things counted against the great fact that each evening Mary Cahill, the daughter of the post-trader, presided over the evening meal, and turned it into a banquet. From her high chair behind the counter, with the cash-register on her one side and the weighing-scales on the other, she gave her little Senate laws, and smiled upon each and all with the kind impartiality of a comrade.

At least, at one time she had been impartial. But of late she smiled upon all save Lieutenant Ranson. When he talked, she now looked at the blazing log-fire, and her cheeks glowed and her eyes seemed to reflect the lifting flame.

For five years, ever since her father brought her from the convent at St. Louis, Mary Cahill had watched officers come and officers go. Her knowledge concerning them, and their public and private affairs, was vast and miscellaneous. She was acquainted with the traditions of every regiment, with its war record, with its peacetime politics, its nicknames, its scandals, even with the earnings of each company-canteen. At Fort Crockett, which lay under her immediate observation, she knew more of what was going forward than did the regimental adjutant, more even than did the colonel's wife. If Trumpeter Tyler flatted on church call, if Mrs Stickney applied to the quartermaster for three feet of stovepipe, if Lieutenant Curtis were granted two days' leave for quail-shooting, Mary Cahill knew it; and if Mrs 'Captain' Stairs obtained the post-ambulance for a drive to Kiowa City, when Mrs 'Captain' Ross wanted it for a picnic, she knew what words passed between those ladies, and which of the two wept. She knew all of these things, for each evening they were retailed to her by her 'boarders.' Her boarders were very loyal to Mary Cahill. Her position was a difficult one, and had it not been that the boy-officers were so understanding, it would have been much more difficult. For the life of a regimental post is as circumscribed as the life on a ship-of-war, and it would no more be possible for the ship's barber to rub shoulders with the admiral's epaulets than that a post-trader's child should visit the ladies on the 'line,' or that the wives of the enlisted men should dine with the young girl from whom they 'took in' washing.

So, betwen the upper and the nether grind-stones, Mary Cahill was left without the society of her own sex, and was of necessity forced to content herself with the society of the officers. And the officers played fair. Loyalty to Mary Cahill was a tradition at Fort Crockett, which it was the duty of each succeeding regiment to sustain. Moreover, her father, a dark, sinister man, alive only to money-making, was known to handle a revolver with the alertness of a town-marshal.

Since the day she left the convent Mary Cahill had held but two affections: one for this grim taciturn parent, who brooded over her as jealously as a lover, and the other for the entire United States Army. The Army returned her affection without the jealousy of the father, and with much more than his effusiveness. But when Lieutenant Ranson arrived from the Philippines, the affections of Mary Cahill became less generously distributed, and her heart fluttered hourly between trouble and joy.

There were two rooms on the first floor of the post-trader's – this big one, which only officers and their women-folk might enter, and the other, the exchange of the enlisted men. The two were separated by a partition of logs and hung with shelves on which were displayed calicoes, tinned meats, and patent medicines. A door, cut in one end of the partition, with buffalo-robes for *portières*, permitted Cahill to pass from behind the counter of one store to behind the counter of the other. On one side Mary Cahill served the Colonel's wife with many yards of silk ribbons to be converted into german favours, on the other her father weighed out bears' claws (manufactured in Hartford, Conn. from turkey-bones) to make a necklace for Red Wing, the squaw of the Arrephao chieftain. He waited upon every one with gravity, and in obstinate silence. No one had ever seen Cahill smile. He himself occasionally joked with others in a grim and embarrassed manner. But no one had ever joked with him. It was reported that he came from New York, where, it was whispered, he had once kept bar on the Bowery for McTurk.

Sergeant Clancey, of G Troop, was the authority for this. But when, presuming on that supposition, he claimed acquaintanceship with Cahill, the post-trader spread out his hands on the counter and stared at the sergeant with cold and disconcerting eyes. 'I never kept bar nowhere,' he said. 'I never been on the Bowery, never been in New York, never been east of Denver in my life. What was it you ordered?'

'Well, mebbe I'm wrong,' growled the sergeant.

But a month later, when a coyote howled down near the Indian village, the sergeant said insinuatingly, 'Sounds just like the cry of the Whyos, don't it?' And Cahill, who was listening to the wolf, unthinkingly nodded his head.

The sergeant snorted in triumph. 'Yah, I told you so!' he cried, 'a man that's never been on the Bowery, and knows the call of the Whyo gang! The drinks are on you, Cahill.'

The post-trader did not raise his eyes, but drew a damp cloth up and down the counter, slowly and heavily, as a man sharpens a knife on a whetstone.

That night, as the sergeant went up the path to the post, a bullet passed through his hat. Clancey was a forceful man, and forceful men, unknown to themselves, makes enemies, so he was uncertain as to whether this came from a trooper he had borne upon too harshly, or whether, in the darkness, he had been picked off for some one else. The next night, as he passed in the full light of the post-trader's windows, a shot came from among the dark shadows of the corral, and when he immediately sought safety in numbers among the Indians, cowboys, and troopers in the exchange, he was in time to see Cahill enter it from the other store, wrapping up a bottle of pain-killer for Mrs Stickney's cook. But Clancey was not deceived. He observed with satisfaction that the soles and the heels of Cahill's boots were wet with the black mud of the corral.

The next morning, when the exchange was empty, the post-trader turned from arranging cans of condensed milk upon an upper shelf to face the sergeant's revolver.

He threw up his hands to the level of his ears as though expressing sharp unbelief, and waited in silence. The sergeant advanced until the gun rested on the counter, its muzzle pointing at the pit of Cahill's stomach. 'You or me has got to leave this post,' said the sergeant, 'and I can't desert, so I guess it's up to you.'

'What did you talk for?' asked Cahill. His attitude was still that of shocked disbelief, but his tone expressed a full acceptance of the situation and a desire to temporise.

'At first I thought it might be that new 'cruity' in F Troop,' explained the sergeant. 'You came near making me kill the wrong man. What harm did I do you by saying you kept bar for McTurk? What's there in that to get hot about?'

'You said I run with the Whyos.'

'What the h—l do I care what you've done!' roared the sergeant. 'I don't know nothing about you, but I don't mean you should shoot me in the back. I'm going to tell this to my bunky, an' if I get shot up, the Troop'll know who done it, and you'll hang for it. Now, what are you going to do?'

Cahill did not tell what he would do; for, from the other store, the low voice of Mary Cahill called, 'Father! Oh, Father!'

The two men dodged, and eyed each other guiltily. The sergeant gazed at the buffalo-robe *portières* with wide-opened eyes. Cahill's hands dropped from the region of his ears, and fell flat upon the counter.

When Miss Mary Cahill pushed aside the *portières* Sergeant Clancey, of G Troop, was showing her father the mechanism of the new regulation-revolver. He apparently was having some difficulty with the cylinder, for his face was red. Her father was eyeing the gun with the critical approval of an expert.

'Father,' said Miss Cahill petulantly, 'why didn't you answer? Where is the blue stationery – the sort Major Ogden always buys? He's waiting.'

The eyes of the post-trader did not wander from the gun before him. 'Next to the blank books, Mame,' he said. 'On the second shelf.'

Miss Cahill flashed a dazzling smile at the big sergeant, and whispered, so that the officer in the room behind her might not overhear, 'Is he trying to sell you Government property, dad? Don't touch it. Sergeant, I'm surprised at you tempting my poor father.' She pulled the two buffalo-robes close around her neck so that her face only showed between them. It was a sweet, lovely face, with frank, boyish eyes.

'When the major's gone, sergeant,' she whispered, 'bring your gun around my side of the store and I'll buy it from you.'

The sergeant nodded in violent assent, laughing noiselessly and slapping his knee in a perfect ecstasy of delight.

The curtains dropped and the face disappeared.

The sergeant fingered the gun and Cahill folded his arms defiantly.

'Well?' he said.

'Well?' asked the sergeant.

'I should think you could see how it is,' said Cahill, 'without my having to tell you.'

'You mean you don't want she should know?'

'My God, no! Not even that I kept a bar.'

'Well, I don't know nothing. I don't mean to tell nothing, any way, so if you'll promise to be good I'll call this off.'

For the first time in the history of Fort Crockett, Cahill was seen to smile. 'May I reach under the counter *now?*' he asked.

The sergeant grinned appreciatively, and shifted his gun. 'Yes, but I'll keep this out until I'm sure it's a bottle,' he said, and laughed boisterously.

For an instant, under the cover of the counter, Cahill's hand touched longingly upon the gun that lay there, and then passed on to the bottle beside it. He drew it forth, and there was the clink of glasses.

In the other room Mary Cahill winked at the major, but the officer pretended to be both deaf to the clink of the glasses and blind to the wink. And so the incident was closed. Had it not been for the folly of Lieutenant Ranson it would have remained closed.

A week before this happened a fire had started in the Willow Bottoms among the tepees of some Kiowas, and the prairie, as far as one could see, was bruised and black. From the post it looked as though the sky had been raining ink. At the time all of the regiment but G and H Troops was out on a practice-march, experimenting with a new-fangled tabloid-ration. As soon as it turned the buttes it saw from where the light in the heavens came and the practice-march became a race.

At the post the men had doubled out under Lieutenant Ranson with wet horse-blankets, and while he led G Troop to fight the flames, H Troop, under old Major Stickney, burned a space around the post, across which the men of G Troop retreated, stumbling, with their ears and shoulders wrapped in the smoking blankets. The sparks beat upon them and the flames followed so fast that, as they ran, the blazing grass burned their lacings, and they kicked their gaiters ahead of them.

When the regiment arrived it found everybody at Fort Crockett talking enthusiastically of Ranson's conduct and resentfully of the fact that he had regarded the fire as one which had been started for his especial amusement.

'I assure you,' said Mrs Bolland to the colonel, 'if it hadn't been for young Ranson we would have been burned in our beds; but he was most aggravating. He treated it as though it were Fourth of July fireworks. It is the only entertainment we have been able to offer him since he joined in which he has shown the slightest interest.' Nevertheless, it was generally admitted that Ranson had saved the post. He had been ubiquitous. He had been seen galloping into the advancing flames like a stampeded colt, he had reappeared like a wraith in columns of black, whirling smoke, at the same moment his voice issued orders from twenty places. One instant he was visible beating back the fire with a wet blanket, waving it above him jubilantly, like a substitute at the Army-Navy game when his side scores, and the next staggering from out of the furnace dragging an asphyxiated trooper by the collar, and shrieking, 'Hospital-steward, hospital-steward! here's a man on fire. Put him out, and send him back to me, quick!'

Those who met him in the whirlwind of smoke and billowing flame related that he chuckled continuously. 'Isn't this fun?' he yelled at them. 'Say, isn't this the best ever? I wouldn't have missed this for a trip to New York!'

When the colonel, having visited the hospital and spoken cheering words to those who were *sans* hair, *sans* eyebrows and with bandaged hands, complimented Lieutenant Ranson on the parade-ground before the assembled regiment, Ranson ran to his hut muttering strange and fearful oaths.

That night at mess he appealed to Mary Cahill for sympathy. 'Goodness, mighty me!' he cried, 'did you hear him? Wasn't it awful? If I'd thought he was going to hand me that I'd have deserted. What's the use of spoiling the only fun we've had that way? Why, if I'd known you could get that much excitement out of this rank prairie I'd have put a match to it myself three months ago. It's the only fun I've had, and he goes and preaches a funeral oration at me.'

Ranson came into the army at the time of the Spanish war because it promised a new form of excitement, and because everybody else he knew had gone into it too. As the son of his father he was made an adjutant-general of volunteers with the rank of captain, and unloaded on the staff of a Southern brigadier, who was slated never to leave Charleston. But Ranson suspected this, and, after telegraphing his father for three days, was attached to the Philippines contingent and sailed from San Francisco in time to carry messages through the surf when the volunteers moved upon Manila. More cabling at the cost of many Mexican dollars caused him to be removed from the staff, and given a second lieutenancy in a volunteer regiment, and for two years he pursued the little brown men over the paddy sluices, burned villages, looted churches, and collected bolos and altar-cloths with that irresponsibility and contempt for regulations which is found chiefly in the appointment from civil life. Incidentally, he enjoyed himself so much that he believed in the army he had found the one place where excitement is always in the air, and as excitement was the breath of his nostrils he applied for a commission in the regular army. On his record he was appointed a second lieutenant in the Twentieth Cavalry, and on the return of that regiment to the States – was buried alive at Fort Crockett.

After six months of this exile, one night at the mess-table Ranson broke forth in open rebellion. 'I tell you I can't stand it a day longer,' he cried. 'I'm going to resign!'

From behind the counter Mary Cahill heard him in horror. Second Lieutenants Crosby and Curtis shuddered. They were sons of officers of the regular army. Only six months before they themselves had been forwarded from West Point, done up in neat new uniforms. The traditions of the Academy of loyalty and discipline had been kneaded into their vertebræ. In Ranson they saw only the horrible result of giving commissions to civilians.

'Maybe the post will be gayer now that spring has come,' said Curtis hopefully, but with a doubtful look at the open fire.

'I wouldn't do anything rash,' urged Crosby.

Miss Cahill shook her head. 'Why, I like it at the post,' she said, 'and I've been here five years – ever since I left the convent – and I–'

Ranson interrupted, bowing gallantly. 'Yes, I know, Miss Cahill,' he said, 'but I didn't come here from a convent. I came here from the blood-stained fields of war. Now, out in the Philippines there's always something doing. They give you half a troop, and so long as you bring back enough Mausers and don't get your men cut up, you can fight all over the shop and no questions asked. But all I do here is take care of sick horses. Any vet in the States has seen as much fighting as I have in the last half-year. I might as well have had charge of horse-car stables.'

'There is some truth in that,' said Curtis cautiously. 'If you do resign, certainly no one can accuse you of resigning in the face of the enemy.'

'Enemy, ye gods,' roared Ranson. 'Why, if I were to see a Moro entering that door with a bolo in each fist I'd fall on his neck and kiss him. I'm not trained to this garrison business. You fellows are. They took all the sporting blood out of you at West Point; one bad mark for smoking a cigarette, two bad marks for failing to salute the instructor in botany, and all the excitement you ever knew were charades and a cadet-hop at Cullum Hall. But, you see, before I went to the Philippines with Merritt, I'd been there twice on a fellow's yacht, and we'd tucked the Spanish governor in his bed with his spurs on. Now, I have to sit around and hear old Bolland tell how he put down a car-strike in St. Louis, and Stickney's long-winded yarns of Table Mountain and the Bloody Angle. He doesn't know the Civil War's over. I tell you, if I can't get excitement on tap I've got to make it, and if I make it out here they'll court-martial me. So there's nothing for it but to resign.'

'You'd better wait till the end of the week,' said Crosby, grinning. 'It's going to be full of gaiety. Thursday, paymaster's coming out with our cash, and to-night that Miss Post from New York arrives

in the up stage. She's to visit the colonel, so everybody will have
to give her a good time.'

'Yes, I certainly must wait for that,' growled Ranson; 'there
probably will be progressive euchre parties all along the line, and
we'll sit up as late as ten o'clock and stick little gilt stars on ourselves.'

Crosby laughed tolerantly.

'I see your point of view,' he said. 'I remember when my father
took me to Monte Carlo I saw you at the tables with enough money
in front of you to start a bank. I remember my father asked the
croupiers why they allowed a child of your age to gamble. I was
just a kid then, and so were you, too. I remember I thought you
were the devil of a fellow.'

Ranson looked sheepishly at Miss Cahill and laughed. 'Well, so I
was – then,' he said. 'Anybody would be a devil of a fellow who'd
been brought up as I was, with a doting parent who owns a trust
and doesn't know the proper value of money. And yet you expect
me to be happy with a fifty-cent limit game, and twenty miles of
burned prairie. I tell you I've never been broken to it. I don't know
what not having your own way means. And discipline! Why, every
time I have to report one of my men to the colonel I send for him
afterward and give him a drink and apologise to him. I tell you the
army doesn't mean anything to me unless there's something doing,
and as there is no fighting out here I'm for the back room of the
Holland House and a rubber-tired automobile. Little old New York
is good enough for me!'

As he spoke these fateful words of mutiny Lieutenant Ranson
raised his black eyes and snatched a swift side-glance at the face of
Mary Cahill. It was almost as though it were from her he sought
his answer. He could not himself have told what it was he would
have her say. But ever since the idea of leaving the army had come
to him, Mary Cahill and the army had become interchangeable and
had grown to mean one and the same thing. He fought against this
condition of mind fiercely. He had determined that without active
service the army was intolerable; but that without Mary Cahill civil
life would also prove intolerable, he assured himself did not at all
follow. He had laughed at the idea. He had even argued it out
sensibly. Was it reasonable to suppose, he asked himself, that after
circling the great globe three times he should find the one girl on it

who alone could make him happy, sitting behind a post-trader's counter on the open prairie? His interest in Miss Cahill was the result of propinquity, that was all. It was due to the fact that there was no one else at hand, because he was sorry for her loneliness, because her absurd social ostracism had touched his sympathy. How long after he reached New York would he remember the little comrade with the brave, boyish eyes set in the delicate, feminine head, with its great waves of gorgeous hair? It would not be long, he guessed. He might remember the way she rode her pony, how she swung from her Mexican saddle and caught up a gauntlet from the ground. Yes, he certainly would remember that, and he would remember the day he had galloped after her and ridden with her through the Indian village, and again that day when they rode to the waterfall and the Lover's Leap. And he would remember her face at night as it bent over the books he borrowed for her, which she read while they were at mess, sitting in her high chair with her chin resting in her palms, staring down at the book before her. And the trick she had, whenever he spoke, of raising her head and looking into the fire, her eyes lighting and her lips smiling. They would be pleasant memories, he was sure. But once back again in the whirl and rush of the great world outside of Fort Crockett, even as memories they would pass away.

Mary Cahill made no outward answer to the rebellious utterance of Lieutenant Ranson. She only bent her eyes on her book and tried to think what the post would hold for her when he had carried out his threat and betaken himself into the world and out of her life for ever. Night after night she had sat enthroned behind her barrier and listened to his talk, wondering deeply. He had talked of a world she knew only in novels, in history, and in books of travel. His view of it was not an educational one: he was no philosopher, nor trained observer. He remembered London – to her the capital of the world – chiefly by its restaurants, Cairo on account of its execrable golf-links. He lived only to enjoy himself. His view was that of a boy, hearty and healthy and seeking only excitement and mischief. She had heard his tales of his brief career at Harvard, of the reunions at Henry's American bar, of the Futurity, the Suburban, the Grand Prix, of a yachting cruise which apparently had encountered every form of adventure, from the rescuing of a stranded opera company to the ramming of a slaver's dhow. The regret with which he spoke of these free days, which was the regret of an exile marooned upon a desert island, excited all her sympathy for an ill she had never known. His discourteous scorn of the social pleasures of the post, from which she herself was excluded, filled her with speculation. If he could forego these functions, how full and gay she argued his former life must have been. His attitude helped her to bear the deprivations more easily. And she, as a loyal child of the army, liked him also because he was no 'cracker-box' captain, but a fighter, who had fought with no morbid ideas as to the rights or wrongs of the cause, but for the fun of fighting.

And one night, after he had been telling the mess of a Filipino officer who alone had held back his men and himself, and who at last died in his arms cursing him, she went to sleep declaring to herself that Lieutenant Ranson was becoming too like the man she had pictured for her husband than was good for her peace of mind. He had told the story as his tribute to a brave man fighting for his independence and with such regret that such a one should have died so miserably, that, to the embarrassment of the mess, the tears rolled down his cheeks. But he wiped them away with his napkin as unconcernedly as though they were caused by the pepper-box, and said simply, 'He had sporting blood, he had. I've never felt so bad about anything as I did about that chap. Whenever I think of him standing up there with his back to the cathedral all shot to pieces, but giving us what for until he died, it makes me cry. So,' he added, blowing his nose vigorously, 'I won't think of it any more.'

Tears are properly a woman's weapon, and when a man makes use of them, even in spite of himself, he is taking an advantage over the other sex which is unfair and outrageous. Lieutenant Ranson never knew the mischief the sympathy he had shown for his enemy caused in the heart of Mary Cahill, nor that from that moment she loved him deeply.

The West Point graduates before they answered Ranson's ultimatum, smoked their cigarettes for some time in silence.

'Oh, there's been fighting even at Fort Crockett,' said Crosby. 'In the last two years the men have been ordered out seven times, haven't they, Miss Cahill? When the Indians got out of hand, and twice after cowboys, and twice after the Red Rider.'

'The Red Rider!' protested Ranson; 'I don't see anything exciting in rounding up one miserable horse thief.'

'Only they don't round him up,' returned Curtis crossly. 'That's why it's exciting. He's the best in his business. He's held up the stage six times now in a year. Whoever the fellow is, if he's one man or a gang of men, he's the nerviest road-agent since the days of Abe Case.'

Ranson in his then present mood was inclined toward pessimism. 'It doesn't take any nerve to hold up a coach,' he contradicted.

Curtis and Crosby snorted in chorus. 'That's what you say,' mocked Curtis.

'Well, it doesn't,' repeated Ranson. 'It's all a game of bluff. The etiquette is that the driver mustn't shoot the road-agent, and that the road-agent mustn't hurt the driver, and the passengers are too scared to move. The moment they see a man rise out of the night they throw up their hands. Why, even when a passenger does try to pull his gun the others won't let him. Each thinks sure that if there's any firing he will be the one to get hurt. And, besides, they don't know how many more men the road-agent may have behind him. I don't—'

A movement on the part of Miss Cahill caused him to pause abruptly. Miss Cahill had descended from her throne and was advancing to meet the post-trader, who came toward her from the exchange.

'Lightfoot's squaw,' he said. 'Her baby's worse. She's sent for you.'

Miss Cahill gave a gasp of sympathy, snatched up her hat from the counter, and the buffalo robes closed behind her.

Ranson stooped and reached for his sombrero. With the flight of Miss Cahill his interest in the courage of the Red Rider had departed also.

But Crosby appealed to the new-comer, 'Cahill, *you* know,' he said. ' We've been talking of the man they call the Red Rider, the chap that wears a red bandanna over his face. Ranson says he hasn't any nerve. That's not so, is it?'

'I said it didn't take any nerve to hold up a stage,' said Ranson; 'and it doesn't.'

The post-trader halted on his way back to the exchange and rubbed one hand meditatively over the other arm. With him speech was golden and difficult. After a pause he said: 'Oh, he takes his chances.'

'Of course he does,' cried Crosby, encouragingly. 'He takes the chance of being shot by the passengers, and of being caught by the posse and lynched, but this man's got away with it now six times in the last year. And I say that takes nerve.'

'Why, for fifty dollars—' laughed Ranson.

He checked himself, and glanced over his shoulder at the retreating figure of Cahill. The buffalo robes fell again, and the spurs of the post-trader could be heard jangling over the earth-floor of the exchange.

'For fifty dollars,' repeated Ranson, in brisk, business-like tones, 'I'll rob the up stage tonight – myself!'

Previous knowledge of his moods, the sudden look of mischief in his eyes and a certain vibration in his voice caused the two lieutenants to jump simultaneously to their feet. 'Ranson!' they shouted.

Ranson laughed mockingly. 'Oh, I'm bored to death,' he cried. 'What will you bet I don't?'

He had risen with them, but, without waiting for their answer, ran to where his horse stood at the open door. He sank on his knees and began tugging violently at the stirrup-straps. The two officers, their eyes filled with concern, pursued him across the room. With Cahill twenty feet away, they dared not raise their voices, but in pantomime they beckoned him vigorously to return. Ranson came at once, flushed and smiling, holding a hooded army-stirrup in each hand. 'Never do to have them see these!' he said. He threw the stirrups from him, behind the row of hogsheads. 'I'll ride in the stirrup straps!' He still spoke in the same low, brisk tone.

Crosby seized him savagely by the arm. 'No, you won't!' he hissed. 'Look here, Ranson. Listen to me; for Heaven's sake don't be an ass! They'll shoot you, you'll be killed—'

'And court-martialled,' panted Curtis.

'You'll go to Leavenworth for the rest of your life!'

Ranson threw off the detaining hand, and ran behind the counter. From a lower shelf he snatched a red bandanna kerchief. From another he dragged a rubber poncho, and buttoned it high about his throat. He picked up the steel shears which lay upon the counter, and snipping two holes in the red kerchief, stuck it under the brim of his sombrero. It fell before his face like a curtain. From his neck to his knees the poncho concealed his figure. All that was visible of him was his eyes, laughing through the holes in the red mask.

'Behold the Red Rider!' he groaned. 'Hold up your hands!'

He pulled the kerchief from his face and threw the poncho over his arm. 'Do you see these shears?' he whispered. 'I'm going to hold up the stage with 'em. No one ever fires at a road-agent. They just shout, "Don't shoot, colonel, and I'll come down." I'm going to bring 'em down with these shears.'

Crosby caught Curtis by the arm, laughing eagerly. 'Come to the stables, quick,' he cried. 'We'll get twenty troopers after him before he can go half a mile.' He turned on Ranson with a triumphant chuckle. 'You'll not be dismissed this regiment, if I can help it,' he cried.

Ranson gave an ugly laugh, like the snarl of a puppy over his bone. 'If you try to follow me, or interfere with me, Lieutenant Crosby,' he said, 'I'll shoot you and your troopers!'

'With a pair of shears?' jeered Crosby.

'No, with the gun I've got in my pocket. Now you listen to me. I'm not going to use that gun on any stage filled with women, driven by a man seventy years old, but – and I mean it – if you try to stop me, I'll use it on you. I'm going to show you how any one can bluff a stage full with a pair of tin shears and a red mask for a kicker. And I'll shoot the man that tries to stop me.'

Ranson sprang to his horse's side, and stuck his toe into the empty stirrup-strap; there was a scattering of pebbles, a scurry of hoofs, and the horse and rider became a grey blot in the moonlight.

The two lieutenants stood irresolute. Under his breath Crosby was swearing fiercely. Curtis stood staring out of the open door.

'Will he do it?' he asked.

'Of course he'll do it.'

Curtis crossed the room and dropped into a chair. 'And what – what had we better do?' he asked. For some time the other made no answer. His brows were knit, and he tramped the room, scowling at the floor. Then with an exclamation of alarm he stepped lightly to the door of the exchange and threw back the curtain. In the other room, Cahill stood at its furthest corner, scooping sugar from a hogshead.

Crosby's scowl relaxed, and, reseating himself at the table, he rolled a cigarette. 'Now, if he pulls it off,' he whispered, 'and gets back to quarters, then – it's a case of all's well. But, if he's shot, or caught, and it all comes out, then it's up to us to prove he meant it as a practical joke.'

'It isn't our duty to report it now, is it?' asked Curtis, nervously.

'Certainly not! If he chooses to make an ass of himself, that's none of our business. Unless he's found out, we have heard nothing and seen nothing. If he's caught, then we've got to stick by him, and testify that he did it on a bet. He'll probably win out all right. There is nobody expected on the stage but that Miss Post and her aunt. And the driver's an old hand. He knows better than to fight.'

'There may be some cowboys coming up.'

'That's Ranson's lookout. As Cahill says, the Red Rider takes his chances.'

'I wish there was something we could do now,' Curtis protested, petulantly. 'I suppose we've just got to sit still and wait for him?'

'That's all,' answered Crosby, and then leaped to his feet. 'What's that?' he asked. Out on the parade ground, a bugle-call broke suddenly on the soft spring air. It rang like an alarm. The noise of a man running swiftly sounded on the path, and before the officers reached the doorway Sergeant Clancy entered it, and halted at attention.

'The colonel's orders,' panted the sergeant, 'and the lieutenant's are to take twenty men from G and H Troops, and ride to Kiowa to escort the paymaster.'

'The paymaster!' Crosby cried. 'He's not coming till Thursday.'

'He's just telegraphed from Kiowa City, lieutenant. He's ahead of his schedule. He wants an escort for the money. He left Kiowa a few minutes ago in the up stage.'

The two lieutenants sprang forward, and shouted in chorus: 'The stage? He is in the stage!'

Sergeant Clancey stared dubiously from one officer to the other. He misunderstood their alarm, and with the privilege of long service attempted to allay it. 'The lieutenant knows nothing can happen to the stage till it reaches the buttes,' he said. 'There has never been a hold-up in the open, and the escort can reach the buttes long before the stage gets here.' He coughed consciously. 'Colonel's orders are to gallop, lieutenant.'

As the two officers rode knee to knee through the night, the pay escort pounding the trail behind them, Crosby leaned from his saddle. 'He has only ten minutes' start of us,' he whispered. 'We are certain to overtake him. We can't help but do it. We must do it. We *must!* If we don't, and he tries to stop Colonel Patten and the pay-roll, he'll die. Two women and a deaf driver, that – that's a joke. But an Indian fighter like old Patten, and Uncle Sam's money, that means a finish fight – and his death and disgrace.' He turned savagely in his saddle. 'Close up there!' he commanded. 'Stop that talking. You keep your breath till I want it – and ride hard.'

After the officers had galloped away from the mess-room, and Sergeant Clancey had hurried after them to the stables, the post-trader entered it from the exchange and barred the door, which they in their haste had left open. As he did this, the close observer, had one been present, might have noted that though his movements were now alert and eager, they no longer were betrayed by any sound, and that his spurs had ceased to jangle. Yet that he purposed to ride abroad was evident from the fact that from a far corner he dragged out a heavy saddle. He flung this upon the counter, and swiftly stripped it of its stirrups. These, with more than necessary care, he hid away upon the highest shelf of the shop, while from the lower shelves he snatched a rubber poncho and a red kerchief. For a moment, as he unbarred the door, the post-trader paused and cast a quick glance before and behind him, and then the door closed and there was silence. A minute later it was broken by the hoofs of a horse galloping swiftly along the trail to Kiowa City.

# PART II

That winter Miss Post had been going out a great deal more than was good for her, and when the spring came she broke down. The family doctor recommended Aiken, but an aunt of Miss Post's, Mrs Truesdall, had been at Farmington with Mrs 'Colonel' Bolland, and urged visiting her instead. The doctor agreed that the climatic conditions existing at Fort Crockett were quite as health-giving as those at Aiken, and of the two the invalid decided that the regimental post would be more of a novelty.

So she and her aunt and the maid changed cars twice after leaving St. Louis and then staged it to Kiowa City, where, while waiting for 'Pop' Henderson's coach to Fort Crockett, they dined with him on bacon, fried bread, and alkali water tinged with coffee.

It was at Kiowa City, a city of four hundred houses on blue-print paper and six on earth, that Miss Post first felt certain that she was going to enjoy her visit. It was there she first saw, at large on his native heath, a blanket Indian. He was a tall beautiful youth, with yellow ochre on his thin, brown arms and blue ochre on his cheek-bones, who sat on 'Pop's' steps, gazing impassively at the stars. Miss Post came out with her maid and fell over him. The maid screamed. Miss Post said: 'I beg your pardon'; and the brave expressed his contempt by guttural mutterings and by moving haughtily away. Miss Post was then glad that she had not gone to Aiken. For the twelve-mile drive through the moonlit buttes to Fort Crockett there was, besides the women, one other passenger. He was a travelling salesman of the Hancock Uniform Company, and was visiting Fort Crockett to measure the officers for their summer tunics. At dinner he passed Miss Post the condensed milk-can, and in other ways made himself agreeable. He informed her aunt that he was in the Military Equipment Department of the Army, but, much to that young woman's distress, addressed most of his remarks to the maid who, to his taste, was the most attractive of the three.

'I take it,' he said genially to Miss Post, 'that you and the young lady are sisters.'

'No,' said Miss Post, 'we are not related.'

It was eight o'clock, and the moon was full in the heavens when 'Pop' Henderson hoisted them into the stage and burdened his driver, Hunk Smith, with words of advice which were intended solely for the ears of the passengers.

'You want to be careful of the near wheeler, Hunk,' he said, 'or he'll upset you into a gully. An' in crossing the second ford, bear to the right; the water's running high, and it may carry youse all down stream. I don't want that these ladies should be drowned in any stage of mine. An' if the Red Rider jumps you don't put up no bluff, but sit still. The paymaster's due in a night or two, an' I've no doubt at all but that the Rider's laying for him. But if you tell him that there's no one inside but womenfolk and a tailor, mebbe he won't hurt youse. Now, ladies,' he added, putting his head under the leather flap, as though unconscious that all he had said had already reached them, 'without wishing to make you uneasy, I would advise your having your cash and jewellery ready in your hands. With road-agents it's mostly wisest to do what they say, an' to do it quick. Ef you give 'em all you've got, they sometimes go away without spilling blood, though, such being their habits, naturally disappointed.' He turned his face toward the shrinking figure of the military tailor. 'You, being an army man,' he said, 'will of course want to protect the ladies, but you mustn't do it. You must keep cool. Ef you pull your gun, like as not you'll all get killed. But I'm hoping for the best. Good-night all, an' a pleasant journey.'

The stage moved off with many creaks and many cracks of the whip, which in part smothered Hunk Smith's laughter. But after the first mile, he, being a man with feelings and a family, pulled the mules to a halt.

The voice of the drummer could instantly be heard calling loudly from the darkness of the stage: 'Don't open those flaps. If they see us, they'll fire!'

'I wanted you folks to know,' said Hunk Smith, leaning from the box-seat, 'that that talk of Pop's was all foolishness. You're as safe on this trail as in a Pullman palace-car. That was just his way. Pop will have his joke. You just go to sleep now, if you can, and trust to me. I'll get you there by eleven o'clock or break a trace. Breakin' a trace is all the danger there is, any way,' he added cheerfully, 'so don't fret.'

Miss Post could not resist saying to Mrs Truesdall: 'I told you he was joking.'

The stage had proceeded for two hours. Sometimes it dropped with locked wheels down sheer walls of clay, again it was dragged, careering drunkenly, out of fathomless pits. It pitched and tossed, slid and galloped, danced grotesquely from one wheel to another, from one stone to another, recoiled out of ruts, butted against rocks, and swept down and out of swollen streams that gurgled between the spokes.

'If ever I leave Fort Crockett,' gasped Mrs. Truesdall between jolts, 'I shall either wait until they build a railroad or walk.'

They had all but left the hills, and were approaching the level prairie. That they might see the better the flaps had been rolled up, and the soft dry air came freely through the open sides. The mules were straining over the last hill. On either side only a few of the buttes were still visible. They stood out in the moonlight as cleanly cut as the bows of great battleships. The trail at last was level. Mrs Truesdall's eyes closed. Her head fell forward. But Miss Post, weary as she was in body, could not sleep. To her the night-ride was full of strange and wonderful mysteries. Gratefully she drank in the dry scent of the prairie-grass, and, holding by the frame of the window, leaned far out over the wheel. As she did so, a man sprang into the trail from behind a wall of rock, and shouted hoarsely. He was covered to his knees with a black mantle. His face was hidden by a blood-red mask.

'Throw up your hands!' he commanded. There was a sharp creaking as the brakes locked, and from the driver's seat an amazed oath. The stage stopped with a violent jerk, and Mrs Truesdall pitched gently forward toward her niece.

'I really believe I was asleep, Helen,' she murmured. 'What are we waiting for?'

'I think we are held up,' said Miss Post.

The stage had halted beyond the wall of rock, and Miss Post looked behind it, but no other men were visible, only a horse with his bridle drawn around a stone. The man in the mask advanced upon the stage, holding a weapon at arm's-length. In the moonlight it flashed and glittered evilly. The man was but a few feet from Miss Post, and the light fell full upon her. Of him she could see only two black eyes that flashed as evilly as his weapon. For a period of suspense, which seemed cruelly prolonged, the man stood motionless, then he lowered his weapon. When he opened his lips the mask stuck to them, and his words came from behind it, broken and smothered. 'Sorry to trouble you, miss,' the mask said, 'but I want that man beside you to get out.'

Miss Post turned to the travelling salesman. 'He wants you to get out,' she said.

'Wants me!' exclaimed the drummer. 'I'm not armed, you know.' In a louder voice he protested, faintly: 'I say, I'm not armed.'

'Come out!' demanded the mask.

The drummer precipitated himself violently over the knees of the ladies into the road below, and held his hands high above him. 'I'm not armed,' he said; 'indeed I'm not.'

'Stand over there, with your back to that rock,' the mask ordered. For a moment the road-agent regarded him darkly, pointing his weapon meditatively at different parts of the salesman's person. He suggested a butcher designating certain choice cuts. The drummer's muscles jerked under the torture as though his anatomy were being prodded with an awl.

'I want your watch,' said the mask.

The drummer reached eagerly for his waistcoat.

'Hold up your hands!' roared the road-agent. 'By the eternal, if you play any rough-house tricks on me I'll—' He flourished his weapon until it flashed luminously.

An exclamation from Hunk Smith, opportunely uttered, saved the drummer from what was apparently instant annihilation. 'Say, Rider,' cried the driver, 'I can't hold my arms up no longer. I'm going to put 'em down. But you leave me alone, an' I'll leave you alone. Is that a bargain?'

The shrouded figure whirled his weapon upon the speaker. 'Have I ever stopped you before, Hunk?' he demanded.

Hunk, at this recognition of himself as a public character, softened instantly. 'I dunno whether 'twas you or one of your gang but—'

'Well, you've still got your health, haven't you?'

'Yes.'

'Then keep quiet,' snarled the mask.

In retort Hunk Smith muttered audible threatenings, but sank obediently into an inert heap. Only his eyes, under cover of his sombrero, roamed restlessly. They noted the McClennan saddle on the Red Rider's horse, the white patch on its near fore-foot, the empty stirrup-straps, and at a great distance, so great that the eyes only of a plainsman could have detected it, a cloud of dust, or smoke, or mist, that rode above the trail and seemed to be moving swiftly down upon them.

At the sight, Hunk shifted the tobacco in his cheek and nervously crossed his knees, while a grin of ineffable cunning passed across his face.

With his sombrero in his hand, the Red Rider stepped to the wheel of the stage. As he did so, Miss Post observed that above the line of his kerchief his hair was evenly and carefully parted in the middle.

'I'm afraid, ladies,' said the road-agent, 'that I have delayed you unnecessarily. It seems that I have called up the wrong number.' He emitted a reassuring chuckle, and, fanning himself with his sombrero, continued speaking in a tone of polite irony: 'The Wells, Fargo messenger is the party I am laying for. He's coming over this trail with a package of diamonds. That's what I'm after. At first I thought "Fighting Bob" over there by the rock might have it on him; but he doesn't act like any Wells, Fargo Express agent I have ever tackled before, and I guess the laugh's on me. I seem to have been weeping over the wrong grave.' He replaced his sombrero on his head at a rakish angle, and waved his hand. 'Ladies, you are at liberty to proceed.'

But instantly he stepped forward again, and brought his face so close to the window that they could see the whites of his eyes. 'Before we part,' he murmured, persuasively, 'you wouldn't mind leaving me something as a souvenir, would you?' He turned upon Miss Post.

Mrs Truesdall exclaimed, hysterically: 'Why, certainly not!' she cried. 'Here's everything I have, except what's sewn inside my waist, where I can't possibly get at it. I assure you I cannot. The proprietor of that hotel told us we'd probably – meet you, and so I have everything ready.' She thrust her two hands through the window. They held a roll of bills, a watch, and her rings.

Miss Post laughed in an ecstacy of merriment. 'Oh, no, aunt,' she protested, 'don't. No, not at all. The gentleman only wants a keepsake. Something to remember us by. Isn't that it?' she asked. She regarded the blood-red mask steadily with a brilliant smile.

The road-agent did not at once answer. At her words he had started back with such sharp suspicion that one might have thought he meditated instant flight. Through the holes in his mask he now glared searchingly at Miss Post, but still in silence.

'I think this will satisfy him,' said Miss Post.

Out of the collection in her aunt's hands she picked a silver coin and held it forward. 'Something to keep as a pocket-piece,' she said, mockingly, 'to remind you of your kindness to three lone females in distress.'

Still silent, the road-agent reached for the money, and then growled at her in a tone which had suddenly become gruff and overbearing. It suggested to Miss Post the voice of the head of the family playing Santa Claus for the children. 'And now you, miss,' he demanded.

Miss Post took another coin from the heap, studied its inscription, and passed it through the window. 'This one is from me,' she said. 'Mine is dated 1901. The moonlight,' she added, leaning far forward and smiling out at him, 'makes it quite easy to see the date; as easy,' she went on, picking her words, 'as it is to see your peculiar revolver and the coat-of-arms on your ring.' She drew her head back. 'Good-night,' she cooed, sweetly.

The Red Rider jumped from the door. An exclamation which might have been a laugh or an oath was smothered by his mask. He turned swiftly upon the salesman. 'Get back into the coach,' he commanded. 'And you, Hunk,' he called, 'if you send a posse after me, next night I ketch you out here alone you'll lose the top of your head.'

The salesman scrambled into the stage through the door opposite the one at which the Red Rider was standing, and the road-agent again raised his sombrero with a sweeping gesture worthy of D'Artagnan. 'Good-night, ladies,' he said.

'Good-night, sir,' Mrs Truesdall answered grimly, but exuding a relieved sigh. Then, her indignation giving her courage, she leaned from the window and hurled a Parthian arrow. 'I must say,' she protested, 'I think you might be in a better business.'

The road-agent waved his hand to the young lady. 'Good-bye,' he said.

'*Au revoir*,' said Miss Post, pleasantly.

'Good-bye, miss,' stammered the road-agent.

'I said "*Au revoir*",' repeated Miss Post.

The road-agent, apparently routed by these simple words, fled muttering toward his horse.

Hunk Smith was having trouble with his brake. He kicked at it and, stooping, pulled at it, but the wheels did not move.

Mrs Truesdall fell into a fresh panic. 'What is it now?' she called, miserably.

Before he answered, Hunk Smith threw a quick glance toward the column of moving dust. He was apparently reassured.

'The brake,' he grunted. 'The darned thing's stuck!'

The road-agent was tugging at the stone beneath which he had slipped his bridle. 'Can I help?' he asked, politely. But before he reached the stage, he suddenly stopped with an imperative sweep of his arm for silence. He stood motionless, his body bent to the ground, leaning forward and staring down the trail. Then he sprang upright. 'You old fox!' he roared, 'you're gaining time, are you?'

With a laugh he tore free his bridle and threw himself across his

horse. His legs locked under it, his hands clasped its mane, and with
a cowboy yell he dashed past the stage in the direction of Kiowa
City, his voice floating back in shouts of jeering laughter. From
behind him he heard Hunk Smith's voice answering his own in a
cry for 'Help!' and from a rapidly decreasing distance the throb of
many hoofs. For an instant he drew upon his rein, and then, with
a defiant chuckle, drove his spurs deep into his horse's side.

Mrs Truesdall also heard the pounding of many hoofs, as well as
Hunk Smith's howls for help, and feared a fresh attack. 'Oh, what
is it?' she begged.

'Soldiers from the fort,' Hunk called, excitedly, and again raised
his voice in a long dismal howl.

'Sounds cheery, doesn't it?' said the salesman; 'referring to the
soldiers,' he explained. It was his first coherent remark since the
Red Rider had appeared and disappeared.

'Oh, I hope they won't—' began Miss Post, anxiously.

The hoof-beats changed to thunder, and with the pounding on
the dry trail came the jangle of stirrups and sling-belts. Then a voice,
and the coach was surrounded by dust-covered troopers and horses
breathing heavily. Lieutenant Crosby pulled up beside the window
of the stage. 'Are you there, Colonel Patten?' he panted. He peered
forward into the stage, but no one answered him. 'Is the paymaster
in here?' he demanded.

The voice of Lieutenant Curtis shouted in turn at Hunk Smith.
'Is the paymaster in there, driver?'

'Paymaster? No!' Hunk roared. 'A drummer and three ladies.
We've been held up. The Red Rider – ' He rose and waved his whip
over the top of the coach. 'He went that way. You can catch him
easy.'

Sergeant Clancey and half a dozen troopers jerked at their bridles.
But Crosby, at the window, shouted 'Halt!'

'What's your name?' he demanded of the salesman.

'Myers,' stammered the drummer. 'I'm from the Hancock Uniform—'

Curtis had spurred his horse beside that of his brother officer. 'Is
Colonel Patten at Kiowa?' he interrupted.

'I can't give you any information as to that,' replied Mr Myers,
importantly; 'but these ladies and I have just been held up by the
Red Rider. If you'll hurry you'll—'

The two officers pulled back their horses from the stage and, leaning from their saddles, consulted in eager whispers. Their men fidgeted with their reins, and stared with amazed eyes at their officers. Lieutenant Crosby was openly smiling. 'He's got away with it,' he whispered. 'Patten missed the stage, thank God, and he's met nothing worse than these women.'

'We *must* make a bluff at following him,' whispered Curtis.

'Certainly not! Our orders are to report to Colonel Patten, and act as his escort.'

'But he's not at Kiowa; that fellow says so.'

'He telegraphed the Colonel from Kiowa,' returned Crosby. 'How could he do that if he wasn't there?' He turned upon Hunk Smith. 'When did you leave Henderson's?' he demanded.

'Seven o'clock,' answered Hunk Smith, sulkily. 'Say, if you young fellows want to catch—'

'And Patten telegraphed at eight,' cried Crosby. 'That's it. He reached Kiowa after the stage had gone. Sergeant Clancey!' he called.

The Sergeant pushed out from the mass of wondering troopers.

'When did the paymaster say he was leaving Kiowa?'

'Leaving at once, the telegram said,' answered Clancey.

' "Meet me with escort before I reach the buttes." That's the message I was told to give the lieutenant.'

Hunk Smith leaned from the box-seat. 'Mebbe Pop's driving him over himself in the buckboard,' he volunteered. 'Pop often takes 'em over that way if they miss the stage.'

'That's how it is, of course,' cried Crosby. 'He's on his way now in the buckboard.'

Hunk Smith surveyed the troopers dismally and shook his head. 'If he runs up against the Red Rider, it's "good-bye" your pay, boys,' he cried.

'Fall in there!' shouted Crosby. 'Corporal Tynan, fall out with two men and escort these ladies to the fort.' He touched his hat to Miss Post, and with Curtis at his side, sprang into the trail. 'Gallop! March!' he commanded.

'Do you think he'll tackle the buckboard, too,' whispered Curtis.

Crosby laughed joyously and drew a long breath of relief.

'No, he's all right now,' he answered. 'Don't you see, he doesn't know about Patten or the buckboard. He's probably well on his way to the post now. I delayed the game at the stage there on purpose to give him a good start. He's safe by now.'

'It was a close call,' laughed the other. 'He's got to give us a dinner for helping him out of this.'

'We'd have caught him red-handed,' said Crosby, 'if we'd been five minutes sooner. Lord!' he gasped. 'It makes me cold to think of it. The men would have shot him off his horse. But what a story for those women! I hope I'll be there when they tell it. If Ranson can keep his face straight, he's a wonder.' For some moments they raced silently neck by neck, and then Curtis again leaned from his saddle. 'I hope he *has* turned back to the post,' he said. 'Look at the men how they're keeping watch for him. They're scouts, all of them.'

'What if they are?' returned Crosby, easily. 'Ranson's in uniform – out for a moonlight canter. You can bet a million dollars he didn't wear his red mask long after he heard us coming.'

'I suppose he'll think we've followed to spoil his fun. You know you said we would.'

'Yes, he was going to shoot us,' laughed Crosby. 'I wonder why he packs a gun. It's a silly thing to do.'

The officers fell apart again, and there was silence over the prairie, save for the creaking of leather and the beat of the hoofs. And then, faint and far away, there came the quick crack of a revolver, another, and then a fusillade. 'My God!' gasped Crosby. He threw himself forward, digging his spurs into his horse, and rode as though he were trying to escape from his own men.

No one issued an order, no one looked a question; each, officer and enlisted man, bowed his head and raced to be the first.

The trail was barricaded by two struggling horses and an over-turned buckboard. The rigid figure of a man lay flat upon his back staring at the moon, another white-haired figure staggered forward from a rock. 'Who goes there?' it demanded.

'United States troops. Is that you, Colonel Patten?'

'Yes.'

Colonel Patten's right arm was swinging limply at his side. With his left hand he clasped his right shoulder. The blood, black in the moonlight, was oozing between his fingers.

'We were held up,' he said. 'He shot the driver and the horses. I fired at him, but he broke my arm. He shot the gun out of my hand. When he reached for the satchel I tried to beat him off with my left arm, but he threw me into the road. He went that way – toward Kiowa.'

Sergeant Clancey, who was kneeling by the figure in the trail, raised his hand in salute. 'Pop Henderson, lieutenant,' he said. 'He's shot through the heart. He's dead.'

'He took the money, ten thousand dollars,' cried Colonel Patten. 'He wore a red mask and a rubber poncho. And I saw that he had no stirrups in his stirrup-straps.'

Crosby dodged, as though some one had thrown a knife, and then raised his hand stiffly and heavily.

'Lieutenant Curtis, you will remain here with Colonel Patten,' he ordered. His voice was without emotion. It fell flat and dead. 'Deploy as skirmishers,' he commanded. 'G Troop to the right of the trail, H Troop to the left. Stop any one you see – any one. If he tries to escape, cry "Halt!" twice and then fire – to kill. Forward! Gallop! March! Toward the post.'

'No!' shouted Colonel Patten. 'He went toward Kiowa.'

Crosby replied in the same dead voice: 'He doubled after he left you, colonel. He has gone to the post.'

Colonel Patten struggled from the supporting arms that held him and leaned eagerly forward. 'You know him, then?' he demanded.

'Yes,' cried Crosby, 'God help him! Spread out there; you, in open order – and ride like hell!'

Just before the officers' club closed for the night Lieutenant Ranson came in and, seating himself at the piano; picked out 'The Queen of the Philippine Islands' with one finger. Major Stickney and others who were playing bridge were considerably annoyed. Ranson then demanded that every one present should drink his health in champagne for the reason that it was his birthday and that he was glad to be alive, and wished every one else to feel the same way about it. 'Or, for any other reason why,' he added, generously. This frontal attack upon the whist-players upset the game entirely, and Ranson, enthroned upon the piano-stool, addressed the room. He held up a buckskin tobacco-bag decorated with beads.

'I got this down at the Indian village tonight,' he said. 'That old squaw, Red Wing, makes 'em for two dollars. Crosby paid five dollars for his in New Mexico, and it isn't half as good. What do you think? I got lost coming back, and went all the way round by the buttes before I found the trail, and I've only been here six months. They certainly ought to make me chief of scouts.'

There was the polite laugh which is granted to any remark made by the one who is paying for the champagne.

'Oh, that's where you were, was it?' said the post-adjutant, genially. 'The colonel sent Clancey after you and Crosby. Clancey reported that he couldn't find you. So we sent Curtis. They went to act as escort for Colonel Patten and the pay. He's coming up to-night in the stage.' Ranson was gazing down into his glass. Before he raised his head he picked several pieces of ice out of it and then drained it.

'The paymaster, hey?' he said. 'He's in the stage to-night, is he?'

'Yes,' said the adjutant; and then as the bugle and stamp of hoofs sounded from the parade outside, 'and that's him now, I guess,' he added.

Ranson refilled his glass with infinite care, and then, in spite of a smile that twitched at the corners of his mouth, emptied it slowly.

There was the jingle of spurs and a measured tramp on the verandah of the club-house, and for the first time in its history four enlisted men, carrying their Krags, invaded its portals. They were led by Lieutenant Crosby; his face was white under the tan, and full of suffering. The officers in the room received the intrusion in amazed silence. Crosby strode among them, looking neither to the left nor right, and touched Lieutenant Ranson upon the shoulder.

'The colonel's orders, Lieutenant Ranson,' he said. 'You are under arrest.'

Ranson leaned back against the music-rack and placed his glass upon the keyboard. One leg was crossed over the other, and he did not remove it.

'Then you can't take a joke,' he said in a low tone. 'You had to run and tell.' He laughed and raised his voice so that all in the club might hear. 'What am I arrested for, Crosby?' he asked.

The lines in Crosby's face deepened, and only those who sat near could hear him. 'You are under arrest for attempting to kill a superior officer, for the robbery of the Government pay-train – and for murder.'

Ranson jumped to his feet. 'My God, Crosby!' he cried.

'Silence! Don't talk!' ordered Crosby. 'Come along with me.'

The four troopers fell in in rear of Lieutenant Crosby and their prisoner. He drew a quick, frightened breath, and then, throwing back his shoulders, fell into step, and the six men tramped from the club and out into the night.

## PART III

That night at the post there was little sleep for any one. The feet of hurrying orderlies beat upon the parade-ground, the windows of the Officers' Club blazed defiantly, and from the darkened quarters of the enlisted men came the sound of voices snarling in violent vituperation. At midnight, half of Ranson's troop, having attacked the rest of the regiment with cavalry-boots, were marched under arrest to the guard-house. As they passed Ranson's hut, where he still paced the verandah, a burning cigarette attesting his wakefulness, they cheered him riotously. At two o'clock it was announced from the hospital that both patients were out of danger; for it had developed that, in his hurried diagnosis, Sergeant Clancey had located Henderson's heart six inches from where it should have been.

When one of the men who guarded Ranson reported this good news the prisoner said, 'Still, I hope they'll hang whoever did it. They shouldn't hang a man for being a good shot and let him off because he's a bad one.'

At the time of the hold-up Mary Cahill had been a half-mile distant from the post at the camp of the Kiowas, where she had gone in answer to the cry of Lightfoot's squaw. When she returned she found Indian Peter in charge of the exchange. Her father, he told her, had ridden to the Indian village in search of her. As he spoke the post-trader appeared. 'I'm sorry I missed you,' his daughter called to him.

At the sound Cahill pulled his horse sharply toward the corral. 'I had a horse-deal on – with the chief,' he answered over his shoulder. 'When I got to Lightfoot's tent you had gone.'

After he had dismounted, and was coming toward her, she noted that his right hand was bound in a handkerchief, and exclaimed with apprehension.

'It is nothing,' Cahill protested. 'I was foolin' with one of the new regulation revolvers, with my hand over the muzzle. Ball went through the palm.'

Miss Cahill gave a tremulous cry and caught the injured hand to her lips.

Her father snatched it from her roughly.

'Let go!' he growled. 'It serves me right.'

A few minutes later Mary Cahill, bearing liniment for her father's hand, knocked at his bedroom, and found it empty. When she peered from the top of the stairs into the shop-window below she saw him busily engaged with his one hand buckling the stirrup-straps of his saddle.

When she called, he sprang upright with an oath. He had faced her so suddenly that it sounded as though he had sworn, not in surprise, but at her.

'You startled me,' he murmured. His eyes glanced suspiciously from her to the saddle. 'These stirrup-straps – they're too short,' he announced. 'Pete or somebody's been using my saddle.'

'I came to bring you this "first-aid" bandage for your hand,' said his daughter.

Cahill gave a shrug of impatience.

'My hand's all right,' he said; 'you go to bed. I've got to begin taking account of stock.'

'To-night?'

'There's no time by day. Go to bed.'

For nearly an hour Miss Cahill lay awake listening to her father moving about in the shop below. Never before had he spoken roughly to her, and she, knowing how much the thought that he had done so would distress him, was herself distressed.

In his lonely vigil on the verandah, Ranson looked from the post down the hill to where the light still shone from Mary Cahill's window. He wondered if she had heard the news, and if it were any thought of him that kept sleep from her.

'You ass! you idiot!' he muttered. 'You've worried and troubled her. She believes one of her precious army is a thief and a murderer.' He cursed himself picturesquely, but the thought that she might possibly be concerned on his account, did not, he found, distress him as greatly as it should. On the contrary, as he watched the light his heart glowed warmly. And long after the light went out he still looked toward the home of the post-trader, his brain filled with thoughts of his return to his former life outside the army, the old life to which he vowed he would not return alone.

The next morning Miss Cahill learned the news when the junior officers came to mess and explained why Ranson was not with them. Her only comment was to at once start for his quarters with his breakfast in a basket. She could have sent it by Pete, but, she argued, when one of her officers was in trouble that was not the time to turn him over to the mercies of a servant. No, she assured herself, it was not because the officer happened to be Ranson. She would have done as much, or as little, for any one of them. When Curtis and Haines were ill of the grippe, had she not carried them many good things of her own making?

But it was not an easy sacrifice. As she crossed the parade-ground she recognised that over night Ranson's hut, where he was a prisoner in his own quarters, had become to the post the storm-centre of interest, and to approach it was to invite the attention of the garrison. At headquarters a group of officers turned and looked her way, there was a flutter among the frocks on Mrs Bolland's porch, and the enlisted men, smoking their pipes on the rail of the barracks, whispered together. When she reached Ranson's hut over four hundred pairs of eyes were upon her, and her cheeks were flushing. Ranson came leaping to the gate, and lifted the basket from her arm as though he were removing an opera-cloak. He set it upon the gate-post, and nervously clasped the palings of the gate with both hands. He had not been to bed, but that fact alone could not explain the strangeness of his manner. Never before had she seen him disconcerted or abashed.

'You shouldn't have done it,' he stammered. 'Indeed, indeed, you are much too good. But you shouldn't have come.'

His voice shook slightly.

'Why not?' asked Mary Cahill. 'I couldn't let you go hungry.'

'You know it isn't that,' he said; 'it's your coming here at all. Why, only three of the fellows have been near me this morning. And they only came from a sense of duty. I know they did – I could feel it. You shouldn't have come here. I'm not a proper person; I'm an outlaw. You might think this was a pest-house, you might think I was a leper. Why, those Stickney girls have been watching me all the morning through a field-glass.' He clasped and unclasped his fingers around the palings. 'They believe I did it,' he protested, with the bewildered accents of a child. 'They all believe it.'

Miss Cahill laughed. The laugh was quieting and comforting. It brought him nearer to earth, and her next remark brought him still further.

'Have you had any breakfast?' she asked.

'Breakfast!' stammered Ranson. 'No. The guard brought some, but I couldn't eat it. This thing has taken the life out of me – to think sane, sensible people – my own people – could believe that I'd steal, that I'd kill a man for money.'

'Yes, I know,' said Miss Cahill soothingly; 'but you've not had any sleep, and you need your coffee.' She lifted the lid of the basket. 'It's getting cold,' she said. 'Don't you worry about what people think. You must remember you're a prisoner now under arrest. You can't expect the officers to run over here as freely as they used to. What do you want?' she laughed. 'Do you think the colonel should parade the band and give you a serenade?' For a moment Ranson stared at her dully, and then his sense of proportion returned to him. He threw back his head and laughed with her joyfully.

From verandahs, barracks, and headquarters, the four hundred pairs of eyes noted this evidence of heartlessness with varied emotions. But, unmindful of them, Ranson now leaned forward, the eager, searching look coming back into his black eyes. They were so close to Mary Cahill's that she drew away. He dropped his voice to a whisper and spoke swiftly.

'Miss Cahill, whatever happens to me I won't forget this. I won't forget your coming here and throwing heart into me. You were the only one who did. I haven't asked you if you believe that I—'

She raised her eyes reproachfully and smiled. 'You know you don't have to do that,' she said.

The prisoner seized the palings as though he meant to pull apart the barrier between them. He drew a long breath like one inhaling a draught of clean morning air.

'No,' he said, his voice ringing, 'I don't have to do that.'

He cast a swift glance to the left and right. The sentry's bayonet was just disappearing behind the corner of the hut. To the four hundred other eyes around the parade-ground Lieutenant Ranson's attitude suggested that he was explaining to Cahill's daughter what he wanted for his luncheon. His eyes held her as firmly as though the palings he clasped were her two hands.

'Mary,' he said, and the speaking of her name seemed to stop the beating of his heart. 'Mary,' he whispered, as softly as though he were beginning a prayer, 'you're the bravest, the sweetest, the dearest girl in all the world. And I've known it for months, and now you must know. And there'll never be any other girl in my life but you.'

Mary Cahill drew away from him in doubt and wonder.

'I didn't mean to tell you just yet,' he whispered, 'but now that I've seen you I can't help it. I knew it last night when I stood back here and watched your windows, and couldn't think of this trouble, nor of anything else, but just you. And you've got to promise me, if I get out of this all right – you must – must promise me—'

Mary Cahill's eyes, as she raised them to his, were moist and glowing. They promised him with a great love and tenderness. But at the sight Ranson protested wildly.

'No,' he whispered, 'you mustn't promise – anything. I shouldn't have asked it. After I'm out of this, after the court-martial, then you've got to promise that you'll never, never leave me.'

Miss Cahill knit her hands together and turned away her head. The happiness in her heart rose to her throat like a great melody and choked her. Before her, exposed in the thin spring sunshine, was the square of ugly brown cottages, the bare parade-ground, in its centre Trumpeter Tyler fingering his bugle, and beyond on every side an ocean of blackened prairie. But she saw nothing of this. She saw instead a beautiful world opening its arms to her, a world smiling with sunshine, glowing with colour, singing with love and content.

She turned to him with all that was in her heart showing in her face.

'Don't!' he begged, tremblingly, 'don't answer. I couldn't bear it – if you said "no" to me.' He jerked his head toward the men who guarded him. 'Wait until I'm tried, and not in disgrace.' He shook the gate between them savagely as though it actually held him a prisoner.

Mary Cahill raised her head proudly.

'You have no right. You've hurt me,' she whispered. 'You hurt me.'

'Hurt you!' he cried.

She pressed her hands together. It was impossible to tell him, it was impossible to speak of what she felt; of the pride, of the trust and love, to disclose this new and wonderful thing while the gate was between them, while the sentries paced on either side, while the curious eyes of the garrison were fastened upon her.

'Oh, can't you see?' she whispered. 'As though I cared for a court-martial! I *know* you. You are just the same. You are just what you have always been to me – what you always will be to me.'

She thrust her hand toward him and he seized it in both of his, and then released it instantly, and, as though afraid of his own self-control, backed hurriedly from her, and she turned and walked rapidly away.

Captain Carr, who had been Ranson's captain in the Philippines, and who was much his friend, had been appointed to act as his counsel. When later that morning he visited his client to lay out a line of defence he found Ranson inclined to treat the danger which threatened him with the most arrogant flippancy. He had never seen him in a more objectionable mood.

'You can call the charge "tommy-rot" if you like,' Carr protested, sharply. 'But, let me tell you that's not the view any one else takes of it, and if you expect the officers of the court-martial and the civil authorities to take that view of it you've got to get down to work and help me prove that it *is* "tommy-rot". That Miss Post, as soon as she got here, when she thought it was only a practical joke, told them that the road-agent threatened her with a pair of shears. Now, Crosby and Curtis will testify that you took a pair of shears from Cahill's, and from what Miss Post saw of your ring she can probably identify that, too; so—'

'Oh, we concede the shears,' declared Ranson, waving his hand grandly. 'We admit the first hold-up.'

'The devil we do!' returned Carr. 'Now, as your counsel, I advise nothing of the sort.'

'You advise me to lie?'

'Sir!' exclaimed Carr. 'A plea of not guilty is only a legal form. When you consider that the first hold-up in itself is enough to lose you your commission—'

'Well, it's *my* commission,' said Ranson. 'It was only a silly joke, any way. And the War Department must have some sense of humour or it wouldn't have given me a commission in the first place. Of course, we'll admit the first hold-up, but we won't stand

for the second one. I had no more to do with that than with the
Whitechapel murders.'

'How are we to prove that?' demanded Carr. 'Where's your alibi?
Where were you after the first hold-up?'

'I was making for home as fast as I could cut,' said Ranson. He
suddenly stopped in his walk up and down the room and confronted
his counsel sternly. 'Captain,' he demanded, 'I wish you to instruct
me on a point of law.'

Carr's brow relaxed. He was relieved to find that Ranson had
awakened to the seriousness of the charges against him.

'That's what I'm here for,' he said, encouragingly.

'Well, captain,' said Ranson, 'if an officer is under arrest as I am
and confined to his quarters, is he or is he not allowed to send to
the club for a bottle of champagne?'

'Really, Ranson!' cried the captain, angrily, 'you are impossible.'

'I only want to celebrate,' said Ranson, meekly. 'I'm a very happy
man; I'm the happiest man on earth. I want to ride across the prairie
shooting off both guns and yelling like a cowboy. Instead of which
I am locked up indoors and have to talk to you about a highway
robbery which does not amuse me, which does not concern me –
and of which I know nothing and care less. Now, *you* are detailed
to prove me innocent. That's your duty, and you ought to do your
duty. But don't drag me in. I've got much more important things
to think about.'

Bewilderment, rage, and despair were written upon the face of
the captain.

'Ranson!' he roared. 'Is this a pose, or are you mad? Can't you
understand that you came very near to being hanged for murder
and that you are in great danger of going to gaol for theft? Let me
put before you the extremely unpleasant position in which you have
been ass enough to place yourself. You don't quite seem to grasp
it. You tell two brother-officers that you are going to rob the stage.
To do so you disguise yourself in a poncho and a red handkerchief,
and you remove the army stirrups from your stirrup leathers. You
then do rob this coach, or at least hold it up, and you are recognised.
A few minutes later, in the same trail and in the same direction you
have taken, there is a second hold-up, this time of the paymaster.
The man who robs the paymaster wears a poncho and a red kerchief,
and he has no stirrups in his stirrup leathers. The two hold-ups take

place within a half-mile of each other, within five minutes of each other. Now, is it reasonable to believe that last night two men were hiding in the buttes intent upon robbery, each in an army poncho, each wearing a red bandanna handkerchief, and each riding without stirrups? Between believing in such a strange coincidence and that you did it, I'll be hanged if I don't believe you did it.'

'I don't blame you,' said Ranson. 'What can I do to set your mind at rest?'

'Well, tell me exactly what persons knew that you meant to hold up the stage.'

'Curtis and Crosby; no one else.'

'Not even Cahill?'

'No, Cahill came in just before I said I would stop the stage, but I remember particularly that before I spoke I waited for him to get back to the exchange.'

'And Crosby tells me,' continued Carr, 'that the instant you had gone he looked into the exchange and saw Cahill at the farthest corner from the door. He could have heard nothing.'

'If you ask me, I think you've begun at the wrong end,' said Ranson. 'If I were looking for the Red Rider I'd search for him in Kiowa City.'

'Why?'

'Because, at this end no one but a few officers knew that the paymaster was coming, while in Kiowa everybody in the town knew it, for they saw him start. It would be very easy for one of those cowboys to ride ahead and lie in wait for him in the buttes. There are several tough specimens in Kiowa. Any one of them would rob a man for twenty dollars – let alone ten thousand. 'There's "Abe" Fisher and Foster King, and the Chase boys, and I believe old "Pop" Henderson himself isn't above holding up one of his own stages.'

'He's above shooting himself in the lungs,' said Carr. 'Nonsense. No, I am convinced that some one followed you from this post, and perhaps Cahill can tell us who that was. I sent for him this morning, and he's waiting at my quarters now. Suppose I ask him to step over here, so that we can discuss it together.'

Before he answered, Ranson hesitated, with his eyes on the ground. He had no way of knowing whether Mary Cahill had told her father anything of what he had said to her that morning. But if she had done so, he did not want to meet Cahill in the presence of a third party for the first time since he had learned the news.

'I'll tell you what I wish you would do,' he said. 'I wish you'd let me see Cahill first, by myself. What I want to see him about has nothing to do with the hold-up,' he added. 'It concerns only us two, but I'd like to have it out of the way before we consult him as a witness.'

Carr rose doubtfully. 'Why, certainly,' he said; 'I'll send him over, and when you're ready for me step out on the porch and call. I'll be sitting on my verandah. I hope you've had no quarrel with Cahill – I mean, I hope this personal matter is nothing that will prejudice him against you.'

Ranson smiled. 'I hope not, too,' he said. 'No, we've not quarrelled – yet,' he added.

Carr still lingered. 'Cahill is like to be a very important witness for the other side—'

'I doubt it,' said Ranson easily. 'Cahill's a close-mouth chap, but when he does talk he talks to the point and he'll tell the truth. That can't hurt us.'

As Cahill crossed the parade-ground from Captain Carr's quarters on his way to Ranson's hut his brain was crowded swiftly with doubts, memories, and resolves. For him the interview held no alarms. He had no misgivings as to its outcome. For his daughter's sake he was determined that he himself must not be disgraced in her eyes and that to that end Ranson must be sacrificed. It was to make a lady of her, as he understood what a lady should be, that on six moonlit raids he had ventured forth in his red mask and robbed the Kiowa stage. That there were others who roamed abroad in the disguise of the Red Rider he was well aware. There were nights the stage was held up when he was innocently busy behind his counter in touch with the whole garrison. Of these nights he made much. They were alibis furnished by his rivals. They served to keep suspicion from himself, and he, working for the same object, was indefatigable in proclaiming that all the depredations of the Red Rider showed the handiwork of one and the same individual.

'He comes from Kiowa of course,' he would point out. 'Some feller who lives where the stage starts, and knows when the passengers carry money. You don't hear of him holding up a stage full of recruits or cow-punchers. It's always the drummers and the mine directors that the Red Rider lays for. How does he know they're in the stage if he don't see 'em start from Kiowa? Ask "Pop" Henderson. Ask "Abe" Fisher. Mebbe they know more than they'd care to tell.'

The money which at different times Cahill had taken from the Kiowa stage lay in a New York bank, and the law of limitation made it now possible for him to return to that city and claim it. Already his savings were sufficient in amount to support both his daughter and himself in one of those foreign cities, of which she had so often told him and for which he knew she hungered. And for the last five years he had had no other object in living than to feed her wants. Through some strange trick of the mind he remembered suddenly and vividly a long-forgotten scene in the back room of McTurk's, when he was McTurk's bouncer. The night before a girl had killed herself in this same back room; she made the third who had done so in the month. He recalled the faces of the reporters eyeing McTurk in cold distaste as that terror of the Bowery whimpered before them on his knees. 'But my daughters will read it,' he had begged. 'Suppose they believe I'm what you call me. Don't go and give me a bad name to them, gentlemen. It ain't my fault the girl's died here. You wouldn't have my daughters think I'm to blame for that? They're ladies, my daughters, they're just out of the convent, and they don't know that there is such women in the world as come to this place. And I can't have 'em turned against their old pop. For God's sake, gentlemen, don't let my girls know!'

Cahill remembered the contempt he had felt for his employer as he pulled him to his feet, but now McTurk's appeal seemed just and natural. His point of view was that of the loving and considerate parent. In Cahill's mind there was no moral question involved. If to make his girl rich and a lady, and to lift her out of the life of the exchange, was a sin the sin was his own and he was willing to 'stand for it'. And, like McTurk, he would see that the sin of the father was not visited upon the child. Ranson was rich, foolishly, selfishly rich; his father was a United States Senator with influence enough, and money enough, to fight the law – to buy his son out of gaol. Sooner than his daughter should know that her father was one of those who sometimes wore the mask of the Red Rider, Ranson, for all he cared, could go to gaol, or to hell. With this ultimatum in his mind, Cahill confronted his would-be son-in-law with a calm and assured countenance.

Ranson greeted him with respectful deference, and while Cahill seated himself, Ranson, chatting hospitably, placed cigars and glasses before him. He began upon the subject that touched him the most nearly.

'Miss Cahill was good enough to bring up my breakfast this morning,' he said. 'Has she told you of what I said to her?'

Cahill shook his head. 'No, I haven't seen her. We've been taking account of stock all morning.'

'Then – then you've heard nothing from her about me?' said Ranson.

The post-trader raised his head in surprise. 'No. Captain Carr spoke to me about your arrest, and then said you wanted to see me first about something private.' The post-trader fixed Ranson with his keen, unwavering eyes. 'What might that be?' he asked.

'Well, it doesn't matter now,' stammered Ranson; 'I'll wait until Miss Cahill tells you.'

'Any complaint about the food?' inquired the post-trader.

Ranson laughed nervously. 'No, it's not that,' he said. He rose, and, to protect what Miss Cahill evidently wished to remain a secret, changed the subject. 'You see you've lived in these parts so long, Mr Cahill,' he explained, 'and you know so many people, I thought maybe you could put me on the track or give me some hint as to which of that Kiowa gang really did rob the paymaster.' Ranson was pulling the cork from the whisky bottle, and when he asked the question Cahill pushed his glass from him and shook his head. Ranson looked up interrogatively and smiled. 'You mean you think I did it myself?' he asked.

'I didn't understand from Captain Carr,' the post-trader began in heavy tones, 'that it's my opinion you're after. He said I might be wanted to testify who was present last night in my store.'

'Certainly, that's all we want,' Ranson answered, genially. 'I only thought you might give me a friendly pointer or two on the outside. And, of course, if it's your opinion I did the deed we certainly don't want your opinion. But that needn't prevent your taking a drink with me, need it? Don't be afraid. I'm not trying to corrupt you. And I'm not trying to poison a witness for the other fellows, either. Help yourself.'

Cahill stretched out his left hand. His right remained hidden in the side pocket of his coat. 'What's the matter with your right hand?' Ranson asked. 'Are you holding a gun on me? Really, Mr Cahill, you're not taking any chances, are you?' Ranson gazed about the room as though seeking an appreciative audience. 'He's such an important witness,' he cried, delightedly, 'that first he's afraid I'll poison him and he won't drink with me, and now he covers me with a gun.'

Reluctantly, Cahill drew out his hand. 'I was putting the bridle on my pony last night,' he said. 'He bit me.'

Ranson exclaimed sympathetically, 'Oh, that's too bad,' he said. 'Well, you know you want to be careful. A horse's teeth really are poisonous.' He examined his own hands complacently. 'Now, if I had a bandage like that on my right hand they would hang me sure, no matter whether it was a bite, or a burn, or a bullet.'

Cahill raised the glass to his lips and sipped the whisky critically. 'Why?' he asked.

'Why? Why, didn't you know that the paymaster boasted last night to the surgeons that he hit this fellow in the hand? He says—'

Cahill snorted scornfully. 'How'd he know that? What makes him think so?'

'Well, never mind, let him think so,' Ranson answered, fervently. 'Don't discourage him. That's the only evidence I've got on my side. He says he fired to disarm the man, and that he saw him shift his gun to his left hand. It was the shot that the man fired when he held his gun in his left that broke the colonel's arm. Now, everybody knows I can't hit a barn with my left. And as for having any wounds concealed about my person' – Ranson turned his hands like a conjurer to show the front and back – 'they can search me. So, if the paymaster will only stick to that story – that he hit the man – it will help me a lot.' Ranson seated himself on the table and swung his leg. 'And of course it would be a big help, too, if you could remember who was in your exchange when I was planning to rob the coach. For some one certainly must have overheard me, some one must have copied my disguise, and that some one is the man we must find. Unless he came from Kiowa.'

Cahill shoved his glass from him across the table and, placing his hands on his knees, stared at his host coldly and defiantly. His would-be son-in-law observed the aggressiveness of his attitude, but, in his fuller knowledge of their prospective relations, smiled blandly.

'Mr Ranson,' began Cahill, 'I've no feelings against you personally. I've a friendly feeling for all of you young gentlemen at my mess. But you're not playing fair with me. I can see what you want, and I can tell you that you and Captain Carr are not helping your case by asking me up here to drink and smoke with you, when you know that I'm the most important witness they've got against you.'

Ranson stared at his father-in-law elect in genuine amazement, and then laughed lightly.

'Why, dear Mr Cahill,' he cried, 'I wouldn't think of bribing you with such a bad brand of whisky as this. And I didn't know you were such an important witness as all that. But, of course, I know whatever you say in this community goes, and if your testimony is against me, I'm sorry for it, very sorry. I suppose you will testify that there was no one in the exchange who could have heard my plan?'

Cahill nursed his bandaged hand with the other. 'That's the court's business,' he growled; 'I mean to tell the truth.'

'And the truth is?' asked Ranson.

'The truth is that last night there was no one in the exchange but you officers and me. If anybody'd come in on the store side you'd have seen him, wouldn't you? and if he'd come into the exchange I'd have seen him. But no one came in. I was there alone – certainly I didn't hear your plan, and I didn't rob the stage. When you fellows left I went down to the Indian village. Half the reservation can prove I was there all the evening – so of the four of us, that lets me out. Crosby and Curtis were in command of the pay escort – that's their alibi – and as far as I can see, lieutenant, that puts it up to you.'

Ranson laughed and shook his head. 'Yes, it certainly looks that way,' he said. 'Only I can't see why you need to be so damned pleased about it.' He grinned wickedly. 'If you weren't such a respectable member of Fort Crockett society I might say you listened at the door, and rode after me in one of your own ponchos. As for the Indian village, that's no alibi. A Kiowa will swear his skin's as white as yours if you give him a drink.'

'And is that why I get this one?' Cahill demanded. 'Am I a Kiowa?'

Ranson laughed and shoved the bottle toward his father-in-law-elect.

'Oh, can't you take a joke?' he said. 'Take another drink, then.'

The voice outside the hut was too low to reach the irate Cahill, but Ranson heard it and leaped to his feet.

'Wait,' he commanded. He ran to the door, and met Sergeant Clancey at the threshold.

'Miss Cahill, lieutenant,' said the sergeant, 'wants to see her father.'

Cahill had followed Ranson to the door. 'You want to see me, Mame?' he asked.

'Yes,' Miss Cahill cried: 'and Mr Ranson, too, if I may.' She caught her father eagerly by the arm, but her eyes were turned joyfully upon Ranson. They were laughing with excitement. Her voice was trembling and eager.

'It is something I have discovered,' she cried; 'I found it out just now, and I think – oh, I hope! – it is most important. I believe it will clear Mr Ranson!' she cried, happily. 'At least it will show that last night some one went out to rob the coach and went dressed as he was.'

Cahill gave a short laugh. 'What's his name?' he asked, mockingly. 'Have you seen him?'

'I didn't see him and I don't know his name, but—'

Cahill snorted, and picked up his sombrero from the table. 'Then it's not so very important after all,' he said. 'Is that all that brought you here?'

'The main thing is that she is here,' said Ranson; 'for which the poor prisoner is grateful – grateful to her and to the man she hasn't seen, in the mask and poncho, whose name she doesn't know. Mr Cahill, bad as it is, I insist on your finishing your whisky. Miss Cahill, please sit down.'

He moved a chair toward her and, as he did so, looked full into her face with such love and happiness that she turned her eyes away.

'Well?' asked Cahill.

'I must first explain to Lieutenant Ranson, father,' said his daughter, 'that to-day is the day we take account of stock.'

'Speaking of stock,' said Ranson, 'don't forget that I owe you for a red kerchief and a rubber poncho. You can have them back, if you like. I won't need a rain coat where I am going.'

'Don't,' said Miss Cahill. 'Please let me go on. After I brought you your breakfast here, I couldn't begin to work just at once. I was thinking about – something else. Everyone was talking of you – your arrest, and I couldn't settle down to take account of stock.' She threw a look at Ranson which asked for his sympathy. 'But when I did start I began with the ponchos and the red kerchiefs, and then I found out something.'

Cahill was regarding his daughter in strange distress, but Ranson appeared indifferent to her words, and intent only on the light and beauty in her face. But he asked, smiling, 'And that was?'

'You see,' continued Miss Cahill, eagerly, 'I always keep a dozen of each article, and as each one is sold I check it off in my day-book. Yesterday Mrs Bolland bought a poncho for the colonel. That left eleven ponchos. Then a few minutes later I gave Lightfoot a red kerchief for his squaw. That left eleven kerchiefs.'

'Stop!' cried Ranson. 'Miss Cahill,' he began, severely, 'I hope you do not mean to throw suspicion on the wife of my respected colonel, or on Mrs Lightfoot, "the Prairie Flower". Those ladies are my personal friends; I refuse to believe them guilty. And have you ever seen Mrs Bolland on horseback? You wrong her. It is impossible.'

'Please,' begged Miss Cahill, 'please let me explain. When you went to hold up the stage you took a poncho and a kerchief. That should have left ten of each. But when I counted them this morning there were nine red kerchiefs and nine ponchos.'

Ranson slapped his knee sharply. 'Good!' he said. 'That *is* interesting.'

'What does it prove?' demanded Cahill.

'It proves nothing, or it proves everything,' said Miss Cahill. 'To my mind it proves without any doubt that some one overheard Mr Ranson's plan, that he dressed like him to throw suspicion on him, and that this second person was the one who robbed the paymaster. Now, father, this is where you can help us. You were there then. Try to remember. It is so important. Who came into the store after the others had gone away?'

Cahill tossed his head like an angry bull.

'There are fifty places in this post,' he protested, roughly, 'where a man can get a poncho. Every trooper owns his slicker.'

'But, father, we don't know that theirs are missing,' cried Miss

Cahill, 'and we do know that those in our store are. Don't think I am foolish. It seemed such an important fact to me, and I had hoped it would help.'

'It does help – immensely!' cried Ranson. 'I think it's a splendid clue. But, unfortunately, I don't think we can prove anything by your father, for he's just been telling me that there was no one in the place but himself. No one came in, and he was quite alone—' Ranson had begun speaking eagerly, but either his own words or the intentness with which Cahill received them caused him to halt and hesitate – 'absolutely – alone.'

'You see,' said Cahill, thickly, 'as soon as they had gone I rode to the Indian village.'

'Why, no, father,' corrected Miss Cahill. 'Don't you remember, you told me last night that when you reached Lightfoot's tent I had just gone. That was quite two hours after the others left the store.' In her eagerness Miss Cahill had placed her hand upon her father's arm and clutched it eagerly. 'And you remember no one coming in before you left?' she asked. 'No one?'

Cahill had not replaced the bandaged hand in his pocket, but had shoved it inside the opening of his coat. As Mary Cahill caught his arm her fingers sank into the palm of the hand and he gave a slight grimace of pain.

'Oh, father,' Miss Cahill cried, 'your hand! I am so sorry. Did I hurt it? Please – let me see.'

Cahill drew back with sudden violence.

'No!' he cried. 'Leave it alone! Come, we must be going.' But Miss Cahill held the wounded hand in both her own. When she turned her eyes to Ranson they were filled with tender concern.

'I hurt him,' she said, reproachfully. 'He shot himself last night with one of those new cylinder revolvers.'

Her father snatched the hand from her. He tried to drown her voice by a sudden movement toward the door. 'Come!' he called. 'Do you hear me?'

But his daughter in her sympathy continued. 'He was holding it so,' she said, 'and it went off, and the bullet passed through here.' She laid the tip of a slim white finger on the palm of her right hand.

'The bullet!' cried Ranson. He repeated dully, 'The bullet!'

There was a sudden, tense silence. Outside they could hear the crunch of the sentry's heel in the gravel, and from the baseball field back of the barracks the soft spring air was rent with the jubilant crack of the bat as it drove the ball. Afterward Ranson remembered that while one half of his brain was terribly acute to the moment, the other was wondering whether the runner had made his base. It seemed an interminable time before Ranson raised his eyes from Miss Cahill's palm to her father's face. What he read in them caused Cahill to drop his hand swiftly to his hip.

Ranson saw the gesture and threw out both his hands. He gave a hysterical laugh, strangely boyish and immature, and ran to place himself between Cahill and the door. 'Drop it!' he whispered. 'My God, man!' he entreated, 'don't make a fool of yourself. Mr Cahill,' he cried aloud, 'you can't go till you know. Can he, Mary? Yes, Mary.' The tone in which he repeated the name was proprietary and commanding. He took her hand. 'Mr Cahill,' he said joyously, 'we've got something to tell you. I want you to understand that in spite of all *I've* done – I say in spite of all *I've* done – I mean getting into this trouble and disgrace, and all that – I've dared to ask your daughter to marry me.' He turned and led Miss Cahill swiftly toward the verandah. 'Oh, I knew he wouldn't like it,' he cried. 'You see. I told you so. You've got to let me talk to him alone. You go outside and wait. I can talk better when you are not here. I'll soon bring him around.'

'Father,' pleaded Miss Cahill, timidly. From behind her back Ranson shook his head at the post-trader in violent pantomime. 'She'd better go outside and wait, hadn't she, Mr Cahill?' he directed.

As he was bidden, the post-trader raised his head and nodded toward the door. The onslaught of sudden and new conditions overwhelmed and paralysed him.

'Father!' said Miss Cahill, 'it isn't just as you think. Mr Ranson did ask me to marry him – in a way – At least, I knew what he meant. But I did not say – in a way – that I would marry him. I mean it was not settled, or I would have told you. You mustn't think I would have left you out of this – of my happiness, you who have done everything to make me happy.'

She reproached her father with her eyes fastened on his face. His own were stern, fixed, and miserable. 'You will let it be, won't you, father?' she begged. 'It – it means so much. I – can't tell you—' She threw out her hand toward Ranson as though designating a superior being. 'Why, I can't tell *him*. But if you are harsh with him or with me it will break my heart. For as I love you, father, I love him – and it has got to be. It must be. For I love him so. I have always loved him. Father,' she whispered, 'I love him so.'

Ranson, humbly, gratefully, took the girl's hand and led her gently to the verandah and closed the door upon her. Then he came down the room and regarded his prospective father-in-law with an expression of amused exasperation. He thrust his hands deep into the pockets of his riding-breeches and nodded his head. 'Well,' he exclaimed, 'you've made a damned pretty mess of it, haven't you?'

Cahill had sunk heavily into a chair and was staring at Ranson with the stupid, wondering gaze of a dumb animal in pain. During the moments in which the two men eyed each other Ranson's smile disappeared. Cahill raised himself slowly as though with a great effort.

'I done it,' said Cahill, 'for her. I done it to make her happy.'

'That's all right,' said Ranson, briskly. 'She's going to be happy. We're all going to be happy.'

'An' all I did,' Cahill continued, as though unconscious of the interruption, 'was to disgrace her.' He rose suddenly to his feet. His mental sufferings were so keen that his huge body trembled. He recognised how truly he had 'made a mess of it'. He saw that all he had hoped to do for his daughter by crime would have been done for her by this marriage with Ranson, which would have made her a 'lady', made her rich, made her happy. Had it not been for his midnight raids she would have been honoured, loved, and envied, even by the wife of the colonel herself. But through him disgrace had come upon her, sorrow and trouble. She would not be known as the daughter of Senator Ranson, but of Cahill, an ex-member of the Whyo gang, a highway robber, as the daughter of a thief who was serving his time in State prison. At the thought Cahill stepped backward unsteadily as though he had been struck. He cried suddenly aloud. Then his hand whipped back to his revolver, but before he could use it Ranson had seized his wrist with both hands. The two struggled silently and fiercely. The fact of opposition brought back to Cahill all of his great strength.

'No, you don't!' Ranson muttered. 'Think of your daughter, man. Drop it!'

'I shall do it,' Cahill panted. 'I am thinking of my daughter. It's the only way out. Take your hands off me – I shall!'

With his knuckles Ranson bored cruelly into the wounded hand, and it opened and the gun dropped from it; but as it did so it went off with a report that rang through the building. There was an instant rush of feet upon the steps of the verandah, and at the sound the two men sprang apart, eyeing each other sheepishly like two discovered truants. When Sergeant Clancey and the guard pushed through the door Ranson stood facing it; spinning the revolver in cowboy fashion around his fourth finger. He addressed the sergeant in a tone of bitter irony.

'Oh, you've come at last,' he demanded. 'Are you deaf? Why didn't you come when I called?' His tone showed he considered he had just cause for annoyance.

'The gun brought me, I—' began Clancey.

'Yes, I hoped it might. That's why I fired it,' snapped Ranson. 'I want two whisky-and-sodas. Quick now!'

'Two—' gasped Clancey.

'Whisky-and-sodas. See how fast one of you can chase over to the club and get 'em. And next time I want a drink don't make me wake the entire garrison.'

As the soldiers retreated Ranson discovered Miss Cahill's white face beyond them. He ran and held the door open by a few inches.

'It's all right,' he whispered, reassuringly. 'He's nearly persuaded. Wait just a minute longer and he'll be giving us his blessing.'

'But the pistol-shot?' she asked.

'I was just calling the guard. The electric bell's broken, and your father wanted a drink. That's a good sign, isn't it? Shows he's friendly. What kind did you say you wanted, Mr Cahill – Scotch was it, or rye?' Ranson glanced back at the sombre, silent figure of Cahill, and then again opened the door sufficiently for him to stick out his head. 'Sergeant,' he called, 'make them both Scotch – long ones.'

He shut the door and turned upon the post-trader. 'Now, then, father-in-law,' he said, briskly, 'you've got to cut and run, and you've got to run quick. We'll tell 'em you're going to Fort Worth to buy the engagement ring, because I can't, being under arrest. But you go to Duncan City instead, and from there take the cars to—'

'Run away!' Cahill repeated, dazedly. 'But you'll be court-martialled.'

'There won't be any court-martial!'

Cahill glanced around the room quickly. 'I see,' he cried. In his eagerness he was almost smiling. 'I'm to leave a confession and give it to you.'

'Confession! What rot!' cried Ranson. 'They can't prove anything against me. Every one knows by now that there were two men on the trail, but they don't know who the other man was, and no one must ever know – especially Mary.'

Cahill struck the table with his fist. 'I won't stand for it!' he cried. 'I got you into this and I'm goin—'

'Yes, going to gaol,' retorted Ranson. 'You'll look nice behind the bars, won't you? Your daughter will be proud of you in a striped suit. Don't talk nonsense. You're going to run and hide in some place, somewhere, where Mary and I can come and pay you a visit. Say – Canada. No, not Canada. I'd rather visit you in gaol than in a Montreal hotel. Say Tangier, or Buenos Ayres, or Paris. Yes, Paris is safe enough – and so amusing.'

Cahill seated himself heavily. 'I trapped you into this fix, Mr Ranson,' he said, 'you know I did, and now I mean to get you out of it. I ain't going to leave the man my Mame wants to marry with a cloud on him. I ain't going to let her husband be gaoled.'

Ranson had run to his desk and from a drawer drew forth a roll of bills. He advanced with them in his hand.

'Yes, Paris is certainly the place,' he said. 'Here's three hundred dollars. I'll cable you the rest. You've never been to Paris, have you? It's full of beautiful sights – Henry's American Bar, for instance, and the courtyard of the Grand Hotel, and Maxim's. All good Americans go to Paris when they die and all the bad ones while they are alive. You'll find lots of both kinds, and you'll sit all day on the sidewalk and drink Bock and listen to Hungarian bands. And Mary and I will join you there and take you driving in the Bois. Now, you start at once. I'll tell her you've gone to New York to talk it over with father, and buy the ring. Then I'll say you've gone on to Paris to rent us apartments for the honeymoon. I'll explain it somehow. That's better than going to gaol, isn't it, and making us bow our heads in grief?'

Cahill, in his turn, approached the desk and, seating himself before it, began writing rapidly.

'What is it?' asked Ranson.

'A confession,' said Cahill, his pen scratching.

'I won't take it,' Ranson said, 'and I won't use it.'

'I ain't going to give it to you,' said Cahill, over his shoulder. 'I know better than that. But I don't go to Paris unless I leave a confession behind me. Call in the guard,' he commanded; 'I need two witnesses.'

'I'll see you hanged first,' said Ranson.

Cahill crossed the room to the door and, throwing it open, called, 'Corporal of the guard!'

As he spoke, Captain Carr and Mrs Bolland, accompanied by Miss Post and her aunt, were crossing the parade-ground. For a moment the post-trader surveyed them doubtfully, and then, stepping out upon the verandah, beckoned to them.

'Here's a paper I've signed, captain,' he said; 'I wish you'd witness my signature. It's my testimony for the court-martial.'

'Then some one else had better sign it,' said Carr. 'Might look prejudiced if I did.' He turned to the ladies. 'These ladies are coming in to see Ranson now. They'll witness it.'

Miss Cahill, from the other end of the verandah, and the visitors entered the room together.

'Mrs Truesdall!' cried Ranson. 'You are pouring coals of fire upon my head. And Miss Post! Indeed, this is too much honour. After the way I threatened and tried to frighten you last night I expected you to hang me, instead of which you have, I trust, come to tea.'

'Nothing of the sort,' said Mrs Bolland, sternly. 'These ladies insisted on my bringing them here to say how sorry they are that they talked so much and got you into this trouble. Understand, Mr Ranson,' the colonel's wife added, with dignity, 'that I am not here officially as Mrs Bolland, but as a friend of these ladies.'

'You are welcome in whatever form you take, Mrs Bolland,' cried Ranson, 'and, believe me, I am in no trouble – no trouble, I assure you. In fact, I am quite the most contented man in the world. Mrs Bolland, in spite of the cloud, the temporary cloud which rests upon my fair name, I take great pride in announcing to you that this young lady has done me the honour to consent to become my wife. Her father, a very old and dear friend, has given his consent. And

I take this occasion to tell you of my good fortune, both in your official capacity and as my friend.'

There was a chorus of exclamations and congratulations in which Mrs Bolland showed herself to be a true wife and a social diplomatist. In the post-trader's daughter she instantly recognised the heiress to the Ranson millions, and the daughter of a Senator who also was the chairman of the Senate Committee on Brevets and Promotions. She fell upon Miss Cahill's shoulder and kissed her on both cheeks. Turning eagerly upon Mrs Truesdall, she said, 'Alice, you can understand how I feel when I tell you that this child has always been to me like one of my own.'

Carr took Ranson's hand and wrung it. Sergeant Clancey grew purple with pleasure and stole back to the verandah, where he whispered joyfully to a sentry. In another moment a passing private was seen racing delightedly toward the baseball field.

At the same moment Lieutenants Crosby and Curtis and the regimental adjutant crossed the parade-ground from the colonel's quarters and ran up the steps of Ranson's hut. The expressions of goodwill, of smiling embarrassment and general satisfaction which Lieutenant Crosby observed on the countenances of those present seemed to give him a momentary check.

'Oh,' he exclaimed, disappointedly, 'some one has told you!'

Ranson laughed and took the hand which Crosby held doubtfully toward him. 'No one has told me,' he said. 'I've been telling them.'

'Then you haven't heard?' Crosby cried, delightedly. 'That's good. I begged to be the first to let you know, because I felt so badly at having doubted you. You must let me congratulate you. You are free.'

'Free?' smiled Ranson.

'Yes, relieved from arrest,' Crosby cried, joyfully. He turned and took Ranson's sword from the hands of the adjutant. 'And the colonel's let your troop have the band to give you a serenade.'

But Ranson's face showed no sign of satisfaction.

'Wait!' he cried. 'Why am I relieved from arrest?'

'Why? Because the other fellow has confessed.'

Ranson placed himself suddenly in front of Mary Cahill as though to shield her. His eyes stole stealthily towards Cahill's confession. Still unread and still unsigned, it lay unopened upon the table. Cahill was gazing upon Ranson in blank bewilderment.

Captain Carr gasped a sigh of relief that was far from complimentary to his client.

'Who confessed?' he cried.

' "Pop" Henderson,' said Crosby.

' "Pop" Henderson!' shouted Cahill. Unmindful of his wound, he struck the table savagely with his fist. For the first time in the knowledge of the post he exhibited emotion. ' "Pop" Henderson, by the eternal!' he cried. 'And I never guessed it!'

'Yes,' said Crosby, eagerly. 'Abe Fisher was in it. Henderson persuaded the paymaster to make the trip alone with him. Then he dressed up Fisher to represent the Red Rider and sent him on ahead to hold him up. They were to share the money afterward. But Fisher fired on "Pop" to kill, so as to have it all, and "Pop's" trying to get even. And what with wanting to hurt Fisher, and thinking he is going to die, and not wishing to see you hanged, he's told the truth. We wired Kiowa early this morning and arrested Fisher. They've found the money, and he has confessed, too.'

'But the poncho and the red kerchief?' protested Carr. 'And he had no stirrups!'

'Oh, Fisher had the make-up all right,' laughed Crosby; 'Henderson says Fisher's the "only, original" Red Rider. And as for the stirrups, I'm afraid that's my fault. I asked the colonel if the man wasn't riding without stirrups, and I guess the wish was father to the fact. He only imagined he hadn't seen any stirrups. The colonel was rattled. So, old man,' he added, turning to Ranson, 'here's your sword again, and God bless you.'

Already the post had learned the news from the band and the verandahs of the enlisted men overflowed with delighted troopers. From the stables and the ball field came the sound of hurrying feet, and a tumult of cheers and cowboy yells. Across the parade-ground the regimental band bore down upon Ranson's hut, proclaiming to the garrison that there would be a hot time in the old town that night. But Sergeant Clancey ran to meet the bandmaster, and shouted in his ear. 'He's going to marry Mary Cahill,' he cried. 'I heard him tell the colonel's wife. Play "Just Because She Made Them Goo-goo Eyes".'

'Like hell!' cried the bandmaster indignantly, breaking in on the tune with his baton. 'I know my business! Now, then, men, he commanded, ' "I'll Leave My Happy Home for You".'

As Mrs Bolland dragged Miss Cahill into view of the assembled troopers Ranson pulled his father-in-law into a far corner of the room. He shook the written confession in his face.

'Now, will you kindly tell me what that means?' he demanded. 'What sort of a gallery play were you trying to make?'

Cahill shifted his sombrero guiltily. 'I was trying to get you out of the hole,' he stammered. 'I – I thought you done it.'

'You thought I done it!'

'Sure. I never thought nothing else.'

'Then why do you say here that *you* did it?'

'Oh, because,' stammered Cahill, miserably, ''cause of Mary, 'cause she wanted to marry you – 'cause you were going to marry her.'

'Well – but – what good were you going to do by shooting yourself?'

'Oh, then?' Cahill jerked back his head as though casting out an unpleasant memory. 'I thought you'd caught me, you, too – between you!'

'Caught you! Then you did—?'

'No, but I tried to. I heard your plan, and I did follow you in the poncho and kerchief, meaning to hold up the stage first, and leave it to Crosby and Curtis to prove you did it. But when I reached the coach you were there ahead of me, and I rode away and put in my time at the Indian village. I never saw the paymaster's cart, never heard of it till this morning. But what with Mame missing the poncho out of our shop and the wound in my hand I guessed they'd all soon suspect me. I saw you did. So I thought I'd just confess to what I meant to do, even if I didn't do it.'

Ranson surveyed his father-in-law with a delighted grin. 'How did you get that bullet-hole in your hand?' he asked.

Cahill laughed shamefacedly. 'I hate to tell you that,' he said. 'I got it just as I said I did. My new gun went off while I was fooling with it, with my hand over the muzzle. And me the best shot in the territory! But when I heard the paymaster claimed he shot the Red Rider through the palm I knew no one would believe me if I told the truth. So I lied.'

Ranson glanced down at the written confession, and then tore it slowly into pieces. 'And you were sure I robbed the stage, and yet you believed that I'd use this? What sort of a son-in-law do you think you've got?'

'You thought *I* robbed the stage, didn't you?'

'Yes.'

'And you were going to stand for robbing it yourself, weren't you? Well, that's the sort of son-in-law I've got!'

The two men held out their hands at the same instant.

Mary Cahill, her face glowing with pride and besieged with blushes, came toward them from the verandah. She was laughing and radiant, but she turned her eyes on Ranson with a look of tender reproach.

'Why did you desert me?' she said. 'It was awful. They are calling you now. They are playing "The Conquering Hero".'

'Mr Cahill,' commanded Ranson, 'go out there and make a speech.' He turned to Mary Cahill and lifted one of her hands in both of his. 'Well, I *am* the conquering hero,' he said. 'I've won the only thing worth winning, dearest,' he whispered; 'we'll run away from them in a minute, and we'll ride to the waterfall and the Lover's Leap.' He looked down at her wistfully. 'Do you remember?'

Mary Cahill raised her head and smiled. He leaned toward her breathlessly.

'Why, did it mean that to you, too?' he asked.

She smiled up at him in assent.

'But I didn't say anything, did I?' whispered Ranson. 'I hardly knew you then. But I knew that day that I – that I would marry you or nobody else. And did you think that – that you—'

'Yes,' Mary Cahill whispered.

He bent his head and touched her hand with his lips.

'Then we'll go back this morning to the waterfall,' he said, 'and tell it that it's all come right. And now, we'll bow to those crazy people out there, those make-believe dream-people, who don't know that there is nothing real in this world but just you and me, and that we love each other.'

A dishevelled orderly bearing a tray with two glasses confronted Ranson at the door. 'Here's the Scotch and sodas, lieutenant,' he panted. 'I couldn't get 'em any sooner. The men wanted to take 'em off me – to drink Miss Cahill's health.'

'So they shall,' said Ranson. 'Tell them to drink the canteen dry and charge it to me. What's a little thing like the regulations between friends? They have taught me my manners. Mr Cahill,' he called.

The post-trader returned from the verandah.

Ranson solemnly handed him a glass and raised the other in the air. 'Here's hoping that the Red Rider rides on his raids no more,' he said; 'and to the future Mrs Ranson – to Mary Cahill, God bless her!'

He shattered the empty glass in the grate and took Cahill's hand.

'Father-in-law,' said Ranson, 'let's promise each other to lead a new and a better life.'